continued . . .

ALSO BY JO BEVERLEY

Devilish

Jo Beverley

A SIGNET BOOK

SIGNET
Published by New American Library, a division of
Penguin Group (USA) Inc., 375 Hudson Street,
New York, New York 10014, USA
Penguin Group (Canada), 90 Eglinton Avenue East, Suite 700, Toronto,
Ontario M4P 2Y3, Canada (a division of Pearson Penguin Canada Inc.)
Penguin Books Ltd., 80 Strand, London WC2R 0RL, England
Penguin Ireland, 25 St. Stephen's Green, Dublin 2,
Ireland (a division of Penguin Books Ltd.)
Penguin Group (Australia), 250 Camberwell Road, Camberwell, Victoria 3124,
Australia (a division of Pearson Australia Group Pty. Ltd.)
Penguin Books India Pvt. Ltd., 11 Community Centre, Panchsheel Park,
New Delhi - 110 017, India
Penguin Group (NZ), cnr Airborne and Rosedale Roads, Albany,
Auckland 1310, New Zealand (a division of Pearson New Zealand Ltd.)
Penguin Books (South Africa) (Pty.) Ltd., 24 Sturdee Avenue,
Rosebank, Johannesburg 2196, South Africa

Penguin Books Ltd., Registered Offices:
80 Strand, London WC2R 0RL, England

First published by Signet, an imprint of New American Library,
a division of Penguin Group (USA) Inc.

First Printing, April 2000
First Printing ($4.99 Edition), January 2006
10 9 8 7 6 5 4 3 2 1

This book has to be dedicated to the three important men in my life—Ken, Jonathan, and Philip. You've all made being an author possible and pleasurable. The gods are exceedingly kind.

ACKNOWLEDGMENTS

First, I want to acknowledge the years of support and wisdom of my agent, Alice Orr, who is moving into a more leisurely lifestyle. I wish her much joy.

Mixing with other authors is fruitful, and my critique group has been a great help in steering this tricky beast: Jane Wallace, Solveig McLaren, Karel Loganhume, Marjorie Daniels, and Anita Birt.

The Genie romance exchange is my on-line home and constant support, but one magical night in a realtime conference, my fellow authors there helped me find the true heart of this book.

Thanks also to Andrew Sigel of Genie, who managed to find what still exists of the libretto of Bach's opera *Orione* so I could be sure what it was actually about. (Not, of course, what I had first thought.) Also to Bibiana Behrendt, who knows *all* about port, and to the lemot@onelist.com group who checked my foreign languages.

And, of course, thanks to the Marquess of Rothgar, who strolled into an orgy eight years ago and uttered the prophetic words, "Your fate has arrived."

Chapter 1

T he doors of the Savoir Faire club opened, throwing a path of light into the midnight street, and causing a flurry among the idling servants. Linkboys ran forward, torches streaming, to offer the gentlemen light on their way home. A hovering footman blew a whistle, however, and a response shrilled back from one of the coaches lined up in the street. The coach's lamps sprang to light, and a groom could be seen removing nose bags from the two horses.

The liveried footman turned back to be sure the pesky linkboys didn't bother his master, the great Marquess of Rothgar, and his lordship's half-brother, Lord Bryght Malloren. With a few cheeky comments, the lads drifted back to an abandoned dice game in the shadows.

Despite precious lace gleaming pale at throat and wrist, and the flash of fire in jewels, the marquess and his brother didn't need protection. Both wore small swords, and gilded scabbards and ornamental ribbons did not make them any less lethal, especially in their hands.

They chatted as they waited for the coach to pull up in front of them. Then the doors of the fashionable club opened again, and a new group emerged laughing, one man singing badly out of tune.

Then the song changed:

> *"For chastity's a noble state,*
> *A pity it don't wear, eh?*
> *The lady doth protest too much*
> *For the gentleman was bare, eh!"*

Both brothers turned, swords hissing from their scabbards.

"I believe," the marquess said softly, "that song went out of fashion nearly two years back. You will, of course, apologize for being so out of style, sir?"

The song was one of the scurrilous ones which had flown about town when Lady Chastity Ware had been found in her bed with a naked man. The young lady had declared her innocence, but it had taken Malloren intervention to prove it, and have her restored to society. Chastity was now the wife of the marquess's youngest half-brother, Lord Cynric, now Lord Raymore.

The blond man who had been singing, disordered perhaps by drink, sneered at the swords. "Damned if I will. A man can sing a song."

"Not that one!" snapped Lord Bryght, blade point moving to touch the other man's throat. The singer didn't flinch, though his companions shrank back, pop-eyed.

The marquess used his blade tip to push his brother's away. "We'll have no street brawls, Bryght, or murders." He eyed the insolent singer. "Your name, sir?"

Most men in London would quail under the icy tone of the man many called the Dark Marquess, but this one only sneered more. "Curry, my lord. Sir Andrew Curry."

"Then, Sir Andrew, you will apologize for singing out of tune."

Nostrils flared, but the sneer stayed in place. "Don't tell me you're still trying to shovel blossoms over the dung heap, my lord marquess. Wealth and power can only do so much, and a stink will always linger."

"Especially in a corpse," the marquess remarked. "I fear we must meet, Sir Andrew. Your second?"

Instead of alarm, Curry smiled. "Giller?"

One of his hangers-on, overdressed and pug-faced, seemed to gulp, but said, "Of course, Curry. Your servant."

"Lord Bryght will act for me," said the marquess, "but we can settle the details I'm sure. Weapons?"

"Swords."

"Swords at nine, then, at the pond in St. James's Park. The

one so popular for suicide." He sheathed his sword, then entered his crested carriage.

Lord Bryght sheathed his own sword, made wary by Curry's good humor. "Giller? Step aside with me if you will."

"Why?" asked the pudgy man in alarm.

"Because you're my second, you numbskull," Curry said. "Lord Bryght is evidently meticulous about these things. Go and assure him that I won't apologize."

Giller teetered over on high heels, looking as if he feared to be skewered.

Bryght said, "It is our duty, Mr. Giller—"

"Sir Parkwood Giller, my lord."

"My apologies, Sir Parkwood. It is our duty to try to effect a reconciliation. Talk to Sir Andrew, and if he changes his mind, contact me at Malloren House, Marlborough Square."

"Changes his mind!" declared Giller. "Curry? I should think not. Try instead to convince the marquess not to commit suicide." He turned, nose in air, and teetered back to his friends.

So it was as he suspected. Curry was a professional duelist.

Bryght entered the carriage and it moved on, but behind them, singing started again. Bryght cursed but his brother put a hand on his arm. "It will be dealt with tomorrow in proper fashion, Bryght."

"Proper fashion? Why the devil are you fighting a man like that? You could have taken a whip to him for singing that song and no one would have objected."

"You think not? This is not autocratic France, and besides, he seemed intent on a duel."

"You aren't usually so obliging to those with intent," Bryght snapped, for it touched on an issue he'd come to London to raise. Now, however, was definitely not the time. If this went amiss, it would end the issue anyway.

Rothgar smiled slightly in the flickering light of the carriage lamp. "The duel would have been hard to avoid,

Bryght, and I found myself curious as to who wants me dead."

Bryght looked at his brother. "So, you do know the man's reputation?"

"A bully and probably a cheat who gets away with it because people are afraid of his skill with a sword. He needs a lesson."

"But why from you?" Rothgar was good, damn good, but there was always someone better. He'd drilled that into his younger half-brothers when preparing them for the world.

Rothgar didn't answer, and Bryght remembered what he'd said. "You think he's a hired killer? Devil take it, Bey, who would want you dead?"

Rothgar turned one of his deceptively mild looks on him. "You think me unworthy of hate and fear?"

Bryght laughed—Rothgar often had that effect on him— but said, "He'll not make a killing matter out of it. Deadly duels can land a man in prison these days."

"What else is the point? And he's just the sort of rootless rogue to flee to France without a care, especially with a large bag of blood money for comfort."

"Whose money?"

"That's the interesting question. I fail to see any enemies who would go to such extremes. Rather lowering, really. Surely the passion of one's enemies should mark the stature of one's triumphs."

"You probably have enemies you don't even know about." Rothgar's almost playful mood made Bryght snappish. "The trouble with being the 'Dark Marquess,' and the *éminence noire* of England is it makes it easy for anyone to blame their misfortunes on you."

Rothgar laughed. "Like a warty village crone? The sort simple people blame for every misshaped child or suddenly dead sheep?"

Bryght had to laugh, too, for a less likely image for his elegant, sophisticated brother was hard to imagine. As the coach halted in the front courtyard of Malloren House, however, humor faded. Did someone want his brother dead?

After a restless night, he was still asking that question the next morning when their coach arrived at the area of St. James's Park close to the gloomy pond. "Devil take it! Why are there so many people here? This is a duel, not a theatrical performance."

"Is there any difference?" Rothgar asked dryly as he climbed out of the carriage. Bryght could not know if his brother had slept well, but he seemed his normal, unruffled self.

Bryght climbed down, staring around at the crowd. Most of London Society seemed to be here—the male part at least. Behind the fashionable circle in lace and braid clustered the lower orders, bobbing up and down to try to see. Some, by Hades, carried children on their shoulders, and a number of men, women, and children were up in nearby trees. In the distance, people massed in the windows of overlooking houses. Flashes of reflected sunlight told him some had telescopes.

Anything his brother did was cause for public excitement, but this was damned improper for a meeting of honor. Who the devil had alerted the world? It almost turned the duel into a joke.

Then Bryght noticed Lord Selwyn at the front of the crowd. Selwyn had a morbid taste for public executions, and traveled Europe to watch the most gruesome. He wouldn't have risen early from his bed for a joke.

Selwyn, at least, expected to enjoy a death here today.

Bryght realized that he was staring around in far too revealing a manner. He forced himself to relax, pulled out a silver box, and took a pinch of snuff. Though he'd abandoned London's games for the country when he married, he still knew the rules. One did not show fear or even concern over personal safety. Rarely in private. Never in public.

Or, as in the animal world, they'd tear you apart.

He turned his attention to Rothgar's opponent. Curry was already down to shirt and breeches, showing a body that was whipcord thin and strong. Height and reach must be similar to his brother's.

Bryght wished to hell Cyn was here. Despite a lack of height Cyn had that extra something, that instinct and reflex that made a true swordsman. He was just possibly better than Rothgar. This was even Cyn's fight since the insult was to his wife.

Curry took his rapier from an attendant to begin some practice passes and lunges.

"Plague take it," Bryght muttered. "He's left-handed."

"A truly sinister advantage," Rothgar remarked as his valet eased him out of his coat. "I know."

It was like a rap on the knuckles. Of course Rothgar knew. His brother never moved into even a casual encounter without research. Between last night and now he'd doubtless discovered how many bugs Curry had in his bed.

"As I thought, he's good," Rothgar said as his valet relieved him of his long waistcoat. "He's fought three duels in England and won them all, leaving his opponents with nasty but nonlethal wounds. Rumor says he's killed two men in France."

Bryght drew on his training to act as unconcerned as his brother, but real worry churned. Rothgar practiced regularly with a master, and had insisted that all his brothers did the same as protection against just this sort of incident. A trumped-up excuse for a duel.

But was he good enough?

Fettler, his brother's valet, was calmly folding the discarded coat and waistcoat. The liveried footman who held his master's inlaid and gilded rapier case looked unalarmed. Clearly in the servants' eyes Rothgar was already cast in the role of victor. Bryght wished he had that ignorant security. No match between skilled swordsmen was ever certain.

Rothgar turned to him. "Go. Do your secondary duties."

"What are my primary ones?"

His brother twisted off his ruby signet and passed it over. "To take up my burden if things go awry." With a slight smile, he added, "Pray, my dear, for my success."

"Don't be damned stupid."

"You thirst after the marquisate?"

"You know I don't. I meant, of course I pray for your success."

"But I doubt either of us have voices heard by angels. Go, therefore, and make a last attempt at peace."

"Is there any basis upon which you would?"

Rothgar was tucking his lace ruffles into his cuff. "But of course! Am I an animal? If he crawls over here on his knees begging forgiveness, he may flee into exile unharmed."

Though his own terms would be exactly the same, Bryght felt like rolling his eyes as he walked partway between the two groups and waited. The chance of apology was nonexistent, but one must always go through the correct steps.

Sir Parkwood Giller minced forward to meet him, clearly enjoying his central role in this popular drama. He even produced a gaudy, lace-edged handkerchief to flourish as he bowed too low in a sickening cloud of cheap perfume. "My lord!"

Bryght cloaked his disgust and gave the slightest possible bow. "I come to ask if your principal has realized his error."

"Error!" The handkerchief wafted again. It could constitute a secret weapon. "Lud, no, my lord. But if the marquess realizes that his offense was misplaced—"

"You jest."

"Not at all. Everyone knows—"

"Giller, the days in which seconds engaged in combat are past, but I will oblige you if you insist."

Handkerchiefs at twenty paces. No, make it thirty.

White showed around Giller's eyes—or bloodshot pink to be precise. "No . . . not at all, my lord. I assure you!"

"How wise." Bryght then stated his brother's terms, at which Giller's snub nose pinched and he stiffened in affront. "Then the duel goes on, my lord!"

"It is your duty to put the terms to your principal, as I will put Curry's to mine." With a sharp bow, Bryght returned to his brother.

"Complete acceptance that Chastity is a trollop, of course."

Rothgar, warming and loosening his muscles, didn't respond. Bryght didn't say more, knowing his brother had a way of settling and focusing his mind before swordplay. It wasn't something he himself had ever been able to do well, which was doubtless why Rothgar and Cyn could always defeat him in the end.

Come to think of it, fire-eating Cyn didn't seem to do much mental settling before a contest either. With him it was pure lightning brilliance. Bryght wished again Cyn was here. He'd slice Curry to ribbons and enjoy every minute of it. Six years of soldiering had hardened him to death-dealing to a remarkable degree.

Everyone was waiting now for Rothgar to indicate he was ready. Bryght certainly didn't want to rush him, but he wished they'd get on with it, get it over with. Of course, it was quite likely this delay was designed to put Curry off balance. The man had already stopped his exercises and taken to marching back and forth in obvious impatience, playing to the crowd.

The crowd, though restive, showed no signs of siding with Curry in this. When death hovered, impatience was gauche.

As if judging his moment, Rothgar paused, straightened, gave Bryght one of his rare smiles, then walked into the center of the space.

Gad, but he was magnificent.

He always moved with a fluid grace, but before swordplay it changed slightly, as if the balance of his whole body shifted a lethal fraction. Of course, he'd taken off his heeled shoes, but he'd also dropped the studied grace of the courtier and released the beauty of the predator beneath.

Tall, broad-shouldered, lean, and muscled—the truth was no longer disguised by the elegance and artifice of the fashionable nobleman. A hush settled on the crowd, and Bryght knew it was more than anticipation of the duel. It was awe.

Everyone was familiar with the aristocrat who wielded great influence in England without taking political office. Few, however, had previously seen beneath the manners, wit, and silk.

Bryght wondered if Rothgar's reluctance to indulge in duels was not just that he had better things to do. Perhaps he disliked exposing this extra layer of power. It declared itself now in his strong body and lean features, still and focused on his deadly opponent.

Curry didn't seem to feel the change. With an audible huff, he stalked confidently to meet his opponent, only then settling into fencer's stance, and a rather rigid version.

Bryght relaxed slightly. Perhaps they were uneven after all.

Not enough. From the first click of the swords, Curry too changed, and it was clear he deserved his reputation. More of a fire-eater than a scientist, he was still strong, quick and skilled, and had that advantage of being left-handed. He even possessed some of the magic spark that took sword fighting beyond speed and mechanics, a separate sense that made him able to avoid the unavoidable, and take advantage of the slightest slip.

The light but lethal blades tapped and slithered, stockinged feet padded back and forth on the springy grass, agile bodies flexed and twisted, recovered, extended, retracted, lunged. . . .

Attacking blades were beaten back, but not always without contact. Soon, despite the cool morning air, both men poured sweat, and hair flew free of ribbons. Both shirts were gashed red. No more than scratches yet, but Bryght's heart was racing as his brother's must be. Plague take it but it was close. A slip could settle this, or it might come down to endurance.

The two men fought in silence to the music of the blades, all concentration in eye and hand, and on the sword—the flexible extension of the hand, arm, and body. Agile feet and strong legs moved them back and forth with lethal speed. Both must know it was even, for they pushed the risks now, hunting the falter.

Curry thrust high, forcing an awkward parry that still sent the point slicing across Rothgar's shoulder. Curry was ready with an echo thrust to the heart, but by some miracle Rothgar kept his balance and knocked the rapier wide.

Both men stepped back, panting and dripping, then lunged forward again. It could not go much longer. Then Rothgar parried another clever thrust and extended, extended almost beyond strength and balance so his rapier point penetrated Curry's chest just below the breastbone. Not deep enough to kill. Not even deep enough to seriously wound. But instinct staggered the man back, shocked, hand to the wound, and the crowd gasped.

Perhaps they thought him killed.

Perhaps he thought the same.

With a rapid flick, Rothgar pinked him in the thigh so blood ran free. Curry tried to collect himself, to get back his balance and control, but Rothgar's sword flickered past a confused defense of the heart to pierce deep into his left shoulder.

The maiming wound. Curry would live, but unless he was very lucky, he would not use a sword with his left arm again.

Bryght realized he'd stopped breathing, and sucked in air. All around, cheers and applause made this seem absurdly like a popular scene at the opera.

Curry, to give him credit, seized his fallen sword in his right hand and tried to go on, but Rothgar disarmed him in a few moves. His sword rested at the man's heaving chest, poised with intent over the false wound. Still sucking in breaths, he said, "I assume you are now . . . resolved to sing songs that are up to date and in tune?"

Rage flared in Curry's eyes, the rage of one who'd never been defeated, who had thought himself invulnerable, and in a way still did. "Singing be damned. Lady Chastity Ware was a whore, and still is—"

He died, his heart pierced, before more filth could spew forth.

Chapter 2

Rothgar pulled his sword free and the doctor came forward, in no great hurry, to confirm the end. None of Curry's stunned friends seemed inclined to gather around the corpse and mourn, and suddenly, like a flock of birds released from cages, chatter rose all around.

Rothgar looked around at his audience. "Gentlemen," he said, instantly gaining silence and attention, "as you heard, Sir Andrew Curry tried to bring a lady's name into this, thereby offending not just my family's honor, but that of our gracious monarch and his wife. The king and queen have accepted Lady Raymore at Court as a woman of virtue. Their wisdom and judgment is not to be questioned."

After a startled moment, mutters of support swelled, scattered with calls of "Aye!" "God save the king!" and "Devil take him who thought it!" Curry's cronies shared panicked glances and slipped hastily away.

As men gathered around Rothgar to congratulate, and to relive the fight, Bryght saw that no one remained to arrange for removal of the body. He took the Malloren footman over to the doctor and put matters in hand. With luck Dr. Gibson or one of his colleagues needed a cadaver to mangle. By the time he'd dealt with that, Fettler was assisting his brother back into his coat.

"Were you as pressed there as you looked?" Bryght asked.

Rothgar took a deep swallow from a flask. It was doubtless the pure water he had brought in daily from a spring on the chalk downs. "He was good. But he never dug beneath the surface."

They climbed into the coach, the valet sitting opposite, and it moved off to take them back to Malloren House.

"Are any of the wounds serious?"

"Mere scratches."

"I don't suppose he thought to poison his sword."

Rothgar's lips twitched. "Don't be theatrical."

"It's just the sort of thing scum like that would do—"

But his brother had leaned his head back and closed his eyes, so Bryght cut off more words. Even Rothgar must feel some effect of peril, exertion, and dealing out death. Bryght considered his own nervous reaction and knew he had lost all taste for this sort of thing. He wondered if his brother was feeling the same way.

When they arrived at Malloren House, he couldn't stop himself following Rothgar up and into his handsome suite of rooms. He knew common sense and a host of excellent servants would take care of him, but he had to follow. Rothgar raised his brows, but didn't throw him out as he stripped off his ruined shirt. There were, in truth, only small cuts and scratches. The worst was the slash across the shoulder, and that wasn't deep.

Bryght began to get his brain back. "So," he said, "do you think that was one rash man, or a plot?"

Stripped down to drawers, his brother was washing. "If it was a plot, I assume they will try again. It will be informative to see how."

"Again? Plague take it, you can't just wait for the next attack."

"How do you suggest I prevent it? Nor would I wish to. I prefer to have any murderous enemy flushed out of cover and dealt with." Rothgar toweled dry and issued crisp commands about bandages and clothes. "You take an interest in mathematics. One point tells us nothing. Three should pin down the source."

"Next time it might be poison, or a pistol in the dark."

His brother sat so his barber could dress the wound on his shoulder. "I do my best to guard against such things."

"Even so—"

"Heaven save me from newly hatched family men!" Rothgar turned sharply toward him. "It can be the only explanation for all this fussing. Nothing is particularly changed, Bryght. Except you."

The barber patiently shifted to work from the new angle.

To hell with it, Bryght thought. He'd have the discussion he'd been seeking. "My circumstances *have* changed," he said, passing the ruby signet back to his brother. "Having found domestic comfort, I quake at the prospect of having to take up your responsibilities."

"I will do my best to spare you that fate until you are far too old to care."

"Can you spare Francis, too?"

He was referring to his son. For a telling pause, Rothgar concentrated on sliding the ring back onto his right hand, then on flexing his bandaged shoulder and nodding his approval. At a murmur from the barber, he turned again and the man began to shave him.

Bryght's jaw tensed. The issue here was marriage—Rothgar's marriage and siring of a son and heir—and his brother was warning him off. Because Rothgar's mother had gone mad, he had resolved not to continue that tainted blood in the line. It had always been understood that Bryght or one of his brothers, sons of a different mother, would produce future generations of Mallorens.

The subject was forbidden, but Bryght couldn't take the warning this time. As soon as the barber put down the razor and began to wipe away traces of soap, he demanded, "Well?"

Rothgar rose to put on the shirt and breeches offered by junior valets. "Perhaps one day high rank and power will be your son's delight."

"And if it isn't?"

"He will, I assume, be trained to do his duty anyway." The exquisitely embroidered gray silk waistcoat came next, and a valet set to fastening the long line of chased silver buttons.

Bryght was sweating as if he was in fact engaged in a duel.

He had long accepted his place as Rothgar's heir. Growing up the son of a marquess, he had willy-nilly learned a great deal about the business, and Rothgar had insisted that he learn more. Though unwilling, he was capable of taking up the burden if necessary.

When he had married last year, he'd accepted that his eldest son would one day inherit the marquisate. Now, however, that theoretical heir was a nine-month-old child with copper curls and a beloved smile. Francis, whom Bryght and Portia wanted to grow up free to explore the whole of this exciting modern world. How was Francis to shape a life of his own, yet be ready to take on awesome responsibilities tomorrow, or next year, or forty years from now?

Or never.

Intolerable.

But how to argue the case . . . ?

He realized that he'd let Rothgar have his way. He'd let the matter drop. Perhaps his nerve had failed him, for he knew his brother would fight any pressure to marry as fiercely, as ruthlessly, as he had fought Curry.

The coiffeur carried in a gray wig, back hair hidden in a gray silk bag gathered by a black ribbon. The grandeur of his brother's preparations finally caught Bryght's attention. "Where the devil are you going?"

"You have forgotten that it's Friday?"

He had. Every Wednesday and Friday the king held a levee. Attendance was not precisely compulsory, but any man of importance at court or in government was expected to attend if he was in London. If he did not, the king could assume that he was siding with one of the factions opposed to his policies.

"You still intend to go?" Bryght queried. "The king must know you just fought a duel."

"He will wish to be assured of my good health."

"There'll be a dozen men there able to—"

His brother's raised left hand, glittering now with two fine jewels, silenced him. "Country living is corroding your instincts, Bryght. The king will wish to see me, and it is necessary that the world see that I am completely unharmed and unshaken. Besides which," he added, glancing at a tray of cravat pins presented for his selection, "the Uftons are in town and I am promised to present them."

"Who the devil are the Uftons?"

"A small estate near Crowthorne." He touched a black, baroque pearl. "Solid people. Sir George is showing his son and heir the wicked wonders of London, doubtless in the same way he has shown him hoof rot, mange, and sour land. Carruthers has them in hand."

Bryght abandoned his protests. Rothgar might, if so inclined, disappoint the king. He would not disappoint the Uftons.

He would not disappoint anyone today. He was preparing for a grand entrance. The scarce-noticed barbering had doubtless been the second of the day, removing any trace of dark bristle in preparation for the powder and paint. Essential, of course, to give an impression of noble delicacy. Though normal for court, the extreme care now was doubtless intended to restore the veil after the earlier exhibition of lethal strength.

Bryght thought of Shakespeare. "All the world's a stage . . ." First the violence of the duel, then the studied artifice of the court. Perhaps later the wit of a salon, the seductive magic of a ball, or the danger of the gaming tables. He himself had played on these stages before his marriage and enjoyed them, but he had always lacked his brother's consummate art.

"Have you thought that the king might disapprove of Curry's death?" he asked.

"If he wishes to rebuke me, he must be given the opportunity."

"What if he wishes to throw you in the Tower? Make you stand your trial?"

"That too. It was a properly run affair, however, in front of many witnesses."

"Your killing blow could be seen as unorthodox."

Rothgar turned to Bryght. "You wish me to skulk here until I know the king's mind? Or perhaps you think I should flee to Holland, or even take ship to the New World?"

Put like that, attending the levee was the only course, and
in full magnificence. He should have known. When did
Rothgar ever misplay a hand in this game?

His brother was fascinating and admirable, but at times he
seemed scarcely human. His attention to detail, even the detail of his costume for this appearance, the fact that he was
almost always on stage and in complex roles, had to take a
toll. It was not a lifestyle to wish on a laughing cherub.
Rothgar, after all, had been shaped by terrible losses and demands.

Perhaps the dark steel had always been there, but four
tragic deaths had formed him into the man he was today—a
man who had been plunged into his powers and responsibilities at nineteen. A man who had created and now controlled
a small empire, who perhaps needed that empire, and control of it, as guard against fears of loss.

Or guard against fears of madness.

His mother had gone mad and murdered her newborn
child. Rothgar, a young child himself, had been a powerless
witness. Sometimes Bryght thought that his brother's need
to control was a kind of madness in itself. He tried to make
the world a theater stage, with himself as director. Or perhaps one of the complex automatons he liked so well. A machine controlled by him; his, and his alone, to keep in
working order; a world where he truly could keep disaster at
bay.

It was an awe-inspiring performance, and Rothgar did remarkable things for his family and for England, but Bryght
wished no crucible of pain to form his son into his brother's
like. Yet he had let the subject slip away.

Before he could gather courage to try again, Rothgar
eased into his precisely cut jacket. The dull steel-gray silk fit
without a ripple, and was lavishly embroidered with black
and silver six inches deep all down the front. Fettler
smoothed the silk across his shoulders and down the back,
chasing nonexistent flaws. Though Rothgar wore an ornate
small sword, Bryght knew he could never fight in such a re-
strictive garment. However, he looked, doubtless by design,
like an ornamental steel blade himself.

His breeches were of the same gray, as were his stockings. He stepped into black shoes with silver heels and buckles and chose a snowy silk handkerchief edged by the most subtle band of silk lace. Lastly, Fettler pinned the silver star of the Order of the Bath to his left breast, the gold cross in the middle being the only color about him.

Then he turned, and flourishing the handkerchief in fashionable style, bowed with perfect grace.

Beauty and threat, precisely blended.

Bryght clapped, and his brother's lips twitched. Though Rothgar could play his role on this stage to the hilt, unlike many he did not get lost in the artifice. As he'd frequently pointed out to his family, their world was a costume ball, but a ball at which momentous matters were decided.

They left the room and a subtle perfume traveled with them. Rothgar had put a touch of it on his handkerchief, and the contrast with that popinjay's cheap drenching stuff was almost worthy of tears.

As was the fact that Bryght had let a golden opportunity slip away. "About Francis," he said, knowing it wasn't a good moment.

"Yes?"

The single word was cold as steel, but Bryght persisted. "You'll get to know him better, during the journey to Brand's wedding."

"I tremble in delight." But Rothgar glanced over and smiled. "He is a charming child, Bryght. Do you think Brand's plans of living in the north will work?"

"Probably. He's never had a taste for fashionable life." Bryght was aware, however, of being deflected. More gently this time, but just as firmly.

"He won't be able to avoid it entirely," Rothgar said as they entered the landing at the top of the sweeping main stairs. "His bride's cousin holds a grand estate there. Her home rivals Rothgar Abbey."

"The Countess of Arradale? Bey—"

"A formidable northern warrior maid, with weapons of curls, bright eyes, silk, and pistols. And skillful with all of them."

"Bey—"

"Did Brand tell you she nearly killed him? And, of course, she ran me and my men off with her own small army."

Idle chat as a defensive weapon, wielded like a rapier so Bryght couldn't quite see how to say what he needed to say.

"A countess in her own right," his brother was saying as they began to descend the stairs to the spacious hall. "She holds considerable power, and intends to keep it."

Aha! "Not everyone likes power," Bryght interjected firmly. "Bey, I don't want Francis burdened with being your heir."

It was as if an icy mist lowered around them. "Then assure him, when he is old enough, that I will do my best to outlive him."

"I wish you would marry, Bey."

"Even for you, Bryght, no."

"There's no other insanity in your mother's family. Perhaps it was a disease, a freak!"

"Everything has to start somewhere. I prefer not to take the risk."

"Do my concerns carry no weight at all?"

They'd reached the base of the stairs and Rothgar turned to him. "I embrace all my family's concerns. One solution would be to give me the child to raise as my heir." Bryght had not found words to respond to that when Rothgar carried on, "The other is for me to die soon. Then you would be marquess and Francis could grow up secure in his future role. Shall I let the assassins do their work?"

Plague take him for a heartless devil. Beneath love and friendship this always lingered—a rivalry and opposition that came from their roles, their natures, and their history.

Though Bryght feared it was pointless, he persisted. "You could marry. Take the risk."

Rothgar's brows rose. "Risk-tainted generations merely to spare you some concern, and your son some uncertainty? I think not. Raise Francis to accept whatever burdens fall on his shoulders. It is the only way. For coddle him as you will, those burdens will fall. That, at least, I have learned."

He turned and accepted cloak and hat from a hovering footman then walked out of the tall double doors to enter his painted and gilded sedan chair for the short journey to St. James's Palace. For once, he ignored the petitioners hovering in hope of a moment of the great marquess's time, for a scrap of his power and influence directed to their cause.

The liveried chairmen picked up the poles and set off, armed footmen walking at either side.

The Marquess of Rothgar was once more on stage.

Bryght turned away, shaken by anger and sheer nervous tension. There were times when he'd like to skewer his brother himself if only he were able.

Harrogate, Yorkshire

"Blast your eyes!" The Countess of Arradale stepped back from the tip of the foil that would have threatened her heart if the point hadn't been buttoned, and she hadn't been wearing a padded chest protector.

Her fencing master pulled the shield from his craggy face. "You don't practice enough, my lady."

Diana pulled off her own face mask, passing it to her hovering maid. "How can I, Carr, when you won't come to Arradale to practice with me?" Clara hung up the mask and hurried back to untie the laces holding the chest guard in place.

William Carr shrugged out of his own protective equipment. "You know I adore you, my lady, but I will not let you eat me whole."

Diana cast a look at the handsome Irishman, with his dark curly hair and twinkling blue eyes. She had thought once or twice of letting him flirt with her, but she knew by instinct that he was too dangerous to be a plaything. He, like most men, would love to possess her, her power and wealth, to turn her into a mere wife.

"At least you won't find my shooting inferior," she said as she went to a mirror and tidied her chestnut hair.

"It won't bring such a fine blush to your cheek either, alas."

"Will it not? It will make my heart beat faster."

"That's power, my lady," he said with a lazy smile. "It's a devil you are for power, and yes, it makes you a beautiful woman. But dangerous. Very dangerous."

She cast him a quelling look, though he always knew the right thing to say. Dangerous. She liked the thought of being dangerous.

The glass told her he spoke the truth about her looks; exertion flushed her cheeks and made her eyes sparkle. A shame it was all for nothing. Yes, she was the sort of woman who could attract men, even without rank, wealth, and power. It was her tragedy that rank, wealth, and power barred her from encouraging them.

She turned back. "Come, let me show you just how dangerous I have become. With a pistol, I don't need a partner, so I do practice. Daily."

"I believe you," he said, opening the door for her into a sunlit courtyard. "You like to win."

"Yes."

"And you're still furious with yourself for missing that shot last year, even though you were firing at a man you wouldn't want dead."

"Of course I'm glad I didn't kill Lord Brand, Carr, but I shouldn't have fired wildly. It was a weakness." She turned to face him. "You must teach me how to avoid that. How to make a steady shot in an emergency."

They'd arrived at the door to his pistol gallery, and he paused. "Sure, and how would such an emergency happen to a grand lady like you?"

"It happened once," she retorted. "If it happens again, I must be ready. If circumstances had been the way I thought, I could have lost my life, and so could Rosa! Why else do I work so hard at this?"

"For the pure, devilish challenge of it, Lady Arradale."

At that dry comment, she laughed aloud. "True. You know me too well, Carr. But it's also because I *will* be ready to defend me and mine if the time ever comes. Teach me. Teach me as if I were a man."

He unlocked the door, but said, "Who threatens you, my lady? I'd be honored to kill him for you."

"No one," she said, walking into the long room, where lingering smells of gunpowder and smoke sang to her senses. It was true that she loved the power of the pistol.

It was also true that she was not threatened—physically, at least. Her life flowed calm and smooth, except for the awareness of a certain marquess.

She took her custom-made weapons out of their case to prepare them, something she always did for herself. As she poured powder down the barrel of the first, she acknowledged that it was the marquess who had brought her here today. She hadn't visited Carr for months, but the news that Dark Marquess would soon come north had driven her here to hone her skills.

As she wrapped the ball in cloth and rammed it down the barrel, she remembered their last encounter. It had been at pistol point. She'd defeated him, and he wasn't a man to forget a defeat.

She put that pistol aside and began the other one. That violent encounter wasn't the only cause of the warning prickle of her nerves.

Oh no—she rammed the next ball down—it was memory of him, of the effect he had on her, that lurked. Last year, when he'd been in the north and visited her home, they'd challenged constantly, mostly with words. Verbal fencing, however, had drifted into a contest of flirtation.

She opened the pan to put in the fine powder, but halted, thinking.

One unforgettable night he had offered seduction. He hadn't really meant it—it had been part of their ongoing battle, and he'd been testing her—but the moment had nibbled away at common sense and reason ever since.

After her refusal, he'd said, *"If you ever change your mind, Lady Arradale. . . ."*

Those were the words that lingered by day, and haunted by night, and there had been many lunatic times when she'd wished she'd accepted that cynical offer.

She shook her head and carefully poured the powder into

the priming pan. The marquess wasn't a physical threat, no, but even so, over the past year, she'd practiced her pistol shooting harder than ever before.

Now she practiced daily, and had taken time from her busy schedule to come here especially to see Carr. For the marquess was coming north again, returning to disturb her land, and her peace of mind.

She closed the pan cover, then filled the pan of the other. Then she set the lock of the first pistol to full-cock, ready to fire. "If anyone threatens me, Carr, I can deal with them myself."

But as she took her stance in front of the targets—rough silhouettes with a red heart pinned to each—she knew that a pistol ball, even to the heart, was no defense against the threat she faced.

Chapter 3

Noon approached and people streamed through the gate-house off Pall Mall into the warren of old buildings known as St. James's Palace. Ministers of the Crown were present, along with military officers, jaded courtiers, and country gentlemen wishing a once-in-a-lifetime audience with the king. All wore full court dress—elegant clothes, small sword, and powdered hair—for otherwise they would not be admitted.

Those accustomed to going through this two or three times a week wandered across the courtyard chatting, or with minds clearly on other things. The gentlemen up from the country, on the other hand, looked around wide-eyed, shining with expectation. To see the king so close. To be ac-knowledged. To speak a word or two with him!

The marquess's chairmen carried him through the gate-house and into the Great Court, where he emerged adjusting the frothing lace at his wrists. He acknowledged various greetings, assessing the mood. Curiosity, and some excited anticipation of him ending up in the Tower. It might happen. The young king was unpredictable, and burdened by a strong sense of his position as moral leader of his realm.

He spotted his secretary, and strolled over to join him and two of the wide-eyed countrymen. Before Carruthers could introduce them, the older man, tall and hearty, though clearly ill-at-ease in his grand clothes, stepped forward to bow. "My lord marquess! We are infinitely obliged."

Rothgar bowed in turn. "Not at all, Sir George. I am de-lighted to see you in London. This must be your son . . ." As he spoke, his eyes flickered to his secretary who mouthed "George." Suppressing a smile, he added, "George."

The handsome, dazed youth, also bowed, hand sensibly on his small sword. They were notoriously tricky to handle and had tripped up many, and even poked ladies in unfortunate places on occasion. Young George looked likely to grow up to be as sound a man as his father.

The marquess indicated that they should proceed into the building. "I hope my people have made your visit to London everything you could wish, Sir George."

"Indeed they have, my lord!" Sir George declared, and related all the wonders as they progressed toward the presence chamber. As they approached the chamber, however, he began to falter with nervousness and excitement. "Upon my soul, my lord, I don't know what I should say."

"Follow His Majesty's lead, Sir George, but do talk to him. His greatest complaint of these events is that people stare and say, 'Yes, sire,' 'No, sire.'"

"Indeed, my lord!" Sir George looked as if he was swallowing hard. "Well, by Gemini, I will do my best then. But you, Georgie," he said to his son, trailing behind and staring at the array of weapons on the paneled walls, "you'd best keep to yes sire and no sire. You hear?"

"Yes, Father!"

Rothgar hid a smile. Levees were a boring obligation, so he quite enjoyed presenting his country neighbors. Seen through their eyes, this took on some freshness and flavor, and reminded him that it was central to English government that good men have access to the monarch. He regretted not putting off the duel a day. He'd make sure the Uftons weren't caught in any unpleasantness, but if the king decided to make as issue of dueling and death, it would mar their enjoyment.

They entered the presence chamber, magnificent with tapestries and paintings, but bare of furniture, and took a place in the circle forming against the wall. Rothgar chose a spot near some other country people and soon the Uftons were chatting comfortably to their own kind. Meanwhile, a number of men came over to talk to him. None of these men disapproved of the duel, but a number were clearly unsure of the outcome. He also noted those who seemed to be suddenly blind to his existence.

When the king finally entered, there was no way to tell his mood. Only twenty-five, George III was tall and of pleasing appearance, with a fresh complexion and large blue eyes. Because he took his duties seriously, he moved slowly around the room, pausing to speak to each man. Even if his mind was on Rothgar, he would not let his attention wander. As he progressed down the room, however, the attention of everyone else shifted.

The king spoke briefly to the Earl of Marlbury beside Rothgar, and then his eyes moved on, sober and thoughtful. Rothgar could feel the room hold its breath, wondering if they were to witness an event worthy of recording for their descendants.

Then the king inclined his head. "My lord marquess, we are pleased to see you here, and in good health. Very pleased."

As a stir ruffled the air, Rothgar bowed. "Your Majesty is gracious as always. May I present Sir George Ufton, of Ufton Green, Berkshire, and his son George."

From there, all went smoothly. Sir George spoke briefly and sensibly of conditions near his home. The king then inquired of young George as to whether he was enjoying his visit to London and received a nervous, "Yes, sire," in reply.

Then he moved on.

Sir George *wooshed* out a big breath. Rothgar restrained himself from any similar sign of relief. He allowed no sign of victory to show as he returned the bows of the passing Ministers of the Crown, even though some of them persisted in viewing him as a rival.

Though it was perfectly permissible to leave when the king had passed by, Rothgar gave the Uftons a moment to recover from their experience before guiding them out into the fresh air. Carruthers awaited to pass them on to a liveried footman who would take them on to yet more delights, but he stepped aside to tell Rothgar that the king commanded him to a private audience.

"Ah, so I have not escaped entirely," Rothgar murmured, summoning a wry look even from his discreet secretary.

He made his way to the King's Bedchamber, now used only for audiences, knowing that in fact he would not be scolded, but fussed over, then put to work advising the king on the many complex matters on hand.

At times he tired of the role. At times he even wished to be like Sir George, responsible only for a small estate and his family. He was born to his duties, however, and God had given him talents of use to his country. He could not, in honor, hold back.

Upon his return to Malloren House, Rothgar stripped out of his stiff court dress with relief, and put in hand a number of matters arising out of his time with the king.

Though the peace treaty with France had been signed, there were still those in Paris who longed to return to war, to wipe out defeat. It was necessary to know what they planned, and to watch for their spies in England. He could often discover things that more official investigators could not, especially as he maintained a spy network of his own.

Next, he attended to a pile of documents requiring his seal and signature, then he turned to idle matters—to letters and catalogs from people hoping for his custom or his patronage. He flipped through them, in no mood for such matters, but he paused at a package sent by a publisher.

It contained a variety of poems, and he glanced through them, putting a few aside as of interest. Then he came upon some sheets entitled, *Diana, a cantata*. It was attributed to Monsieur Rousseau, but translated into English. A light piece, but intriguing because another Diana came immediately to mind.

> *The sun was now descended to the main,*
> *When chaste Diana and her virgin train. . . .*

Lady Arradale. Straight of spine, clear of eye, and a body made for love. She was, however, almost certainly a chaste virgin, and somewhat irked by the fact.

A copy of this could make an amusing gift.

He understood her choice not to marry, but that decision carried costs, especially for a woman. There would be no easy way for her to satisfy her sexual nature, and to many people, an unmarried woman was an affront against heaven, destined in fact to lead apes in hell.

Today, for some reason, the king had asked about her, and he was clearly one of the ones affronted. George was even more affronted by the notion of a young single woman in the peculiar position of being a peer of the realm.

Rothgar had given bland responses hoping that the conventional monarch forgot her existence entirely. The kings of England were constrained by many rules, but they still had teeth.

He read quickly through the cantata. It described an attack by the goddess Diana on Cupid, and thus on love. The countess, he thought, would appreciate that. Would it also serve as a warning? In the end, one dart is missed, and Diana succumbs to love.

Perhaps, he thought, as he put the sheets with those of interest, he should keep a copy close to hand himself.

He was aware—he was always aware of such things—that Lady Arradale could be a lurking arrow. She was pretty and lively, but those were the least of her charms. From her unusual rank, she had become an exceptional woman, clever, bold, and brave.

She was also willful, impulsive, and perhaps even spoiled. Normally such qualities would wipe away any interest he had, but in her case, they stirred his instinct to protect. As cousin to Brand's bride, she was almost within his sacred limits, his family.

A wise man avoided danger. Sliding his signet ring up and down his finger, he considered not going to Brand's Yorkshire wedding after all. That would keep him well out of arrow range.

The rest of the family planned to attend, however, and he wanted to be there, to see the happy end to Brand's adventure.

He checked that there were no papers left untended, and

rose from the desk. It should be safe enough. The complications following the end of the war with France were reason to return quickly to London. He'd also arrange for Carruthers to send papers to him by swift courier to make the situation clear.

A defensive maneuver, but wise. Survival was best achieved by avoidance of peril. He'd arrive the day before the wedding, and stay one day after it. Three days. He could easily avoid entanglement with the countess for three busy days.

As he left to prepare for his evening engagements, however, he was aware of many historical dramas, even tragedies, proving that to be nonsense.

Three days was time enough for complete disaster.

Three days, Diana told herself as she waited for the her gatekeeper's horn to announce the arrival of the Malloren carriages. He would be here for only three days. She could navigate those three days without crashing into any kind of disaster.

Despite reason, however, when the distant horn blasted, every nerve jumped. In days gone by, that horn had belonged to the castle lookout and had warned of enemies. Perhaps some memory of that ran in her blood, causing her heart to race, her mouth to dry.

She struggled for common sense. This was not an invasion. It was a house party and a wedding. She would be the perfect lady, the marquess would be the perfect gentleman, and in three days they would part again.

With luck, this time forever.

"Diana?"

She swung to face her mother. The dowager countess was complicating everything by hearing not one set of wedding bells, but two. She'd decided Diana's nervousness was due to a fondness for the marquess.

"That, I assume, is the Mallorens," her mother said blandly. "Are you not going down to greet them?"

"Yes, of course, Mother."

Her mother's lips curled up in an almost mischievous

smile. "You've turned Arradale inside out to get it ready, dear, and you've been pacing this room for the past hour, yet now you dither. What is the matter with you?"

Not maidenly flutters, Mother.

"Nothing," said Diana, forcing a smile and hurrying away from that knowing look.

Diana's mother had never been able to understand her motives for remaining unmarried. She saw the responsibilities of the earldom as a terrible burden, not an exciting challenge. She was stubbornly convinced that her daughter was just seeking the right man, and hopeful that in the marquess, she had found him.

The last man in the world to be suitable.

Swishing down the wide stairs into the paneled front hall, Diana hoped the next few days wouldn't push her mother to embarrassing lengths. She clung to one comfort. The marquess was as determined to avoid marriage as she was.

The carriages would still be making their way up the drive, so Diana paused to assess herself in the great, gilded mirror. She had chosen her appearance with great care.

When she and the marquess had last met he'd been trying to kidnap her cousin Rosa. With her own pistol and a small army of men from the estate, she had stopped him. She didn't regret it. It was possibly the most glorious moment of her life. However, today she had dressed to remind him that she was above all a lady.

Her gown was pale yellow sprigged with cream blossoms, and she wore simple pearls in her ears, and on a cream ribbon around her throat. Her hair curled from under a cap of muslin and ribbons frivolous enough to be silly, and she even wore one of the fashionable, purely ornamental aprons of silk gauze and lace. Her glowing complexion was slightly deadened by powder.

She raised her hands, palms toward her face, so her eight rings flashed in the mirror. No matter how soft and sweet she wanted to appear, she could not bear to be without them, even though they'd betrayed her once to the marquess. In fact, she was wearing exactly the same betraying

baubles that she'd worn last time she'd welcomed him to
Arradale.

He had a reputation for uncanny observation and omniscience, so he should remember every one. He would recognize the challenge. She was a lady, but she was also the
Countess of Arradale.

And he was on her land.

Judging the moment, she walked toward the great doors.
Her footmen swung them open, letting sunshine flood in,
and she saw four grand traveling carriages coming to a halt
in front of the double sweep of steps. Three others, doubtless containing baggage and servants, had turned off to go
around to the back of the house.

Seven! And outriders, she saw. She traveled in state herself, but this was excessive, even for a whole family. They
were also bringing children, which had required an overhaul
of the long-unused nurseries. Only the Mallorens would do
something so extravagantly absurd.

Just three days, she told herself as she walked unhurriedly
through the open doors, concealing a rapid heartbeat. Gracious smile in place, she raised her wide skirts a little and
walked down the steps to greet the people climbing out of
the carriages. Silently, she rehearsed cool, courteous words
of welcome, but then she saw a lady being handed down
from the second coach and forgot decorum.

"Rosa!" she cried, and ran forward to meet her cousin and
dearest friend in a crushing hug. They'd not met for nine
months.

It was some moments before she realized she'd abandoned her hostess duties entirely. Blushing, she dragged her
attention away from her happy and healthy friend to apologize. As she wiped some tears from her eyes, she found herself face to face with an amused Lord Brand Malloren.

With russet hair tied simply back, and his tanned face
shaped by smiles, he was perfect for Rosa. He had even forgiven Diana for trying to shoot him.

While speaking to Lord Brand, however, Diana found
herself hardly able to think or speak coherently. *He* was
nearby. She couldn't see him, yet she knew. Ridiculous, but

she felt him behind her as a sudden hot prickle down her spine.

Somehow she made a sensible end of one conversation and turned, hoping she was mistaken, that he was elsewhere and it had been only imagination, or the sun.

Chapter 4

The marquess stood there, however, only feet away and patiently awaiting. Had he always had that kind of effect on her, or was this some new torment?

"Lord Rothgar!" she declared, praying that her racing heart wasn't obvious, and desperately following her script. "How fortunate we are to have you here in Arradale once more."

He kissed her hand. It was the very lightest, proper brush in the air above her knuckles, and yet his fingers on hers were another shocking sensation.

Perdition. This was what came of thinking so much of a man for a year!

"The good fortune is all ours, Lady Arradale. Especially as you are willing to house a massing of Mallorens."

No sign that *he* was affected. She slipped her hand free. "For Rosa's wedding?" she said lightly. "For that, I would welcome a massing of *monsters*, my lord."

"Then you should manage to survive us. Permit me to introduce you."

With a light touch on her elbow he directed her to a family emerging from a coach beyond, but even that formal touch seemed to cause sparks. Seeking help, she cast a look toward Rosa, but her cousin was smiling up at Lord Brand, blind to the world.

"Indeed," the marquess murmured as if she'd spoken. "They behave like that all the time. How fortunate are we who have renounced such weakening folly."

If he'd planned to help steady her mind, he could not have

found better words. She gathered every scrap of calm dignity as she approached the family.

It consisted of husband, wife, and four children ranging in age from toddler to about eight.

"Lord and Lady Steen," he said, "the lady being my sister Hilda. The infantry are endlessly confusing, so I will let them do the honors."

Despite this, the smallest child, topped with rod-straight brown hair, trotted over with a big smile and open arms, announcing something that sounded like, "Unkabay! Unkabay!"

The marquess astonished Diana by picking him up, though with an audible sigh. "This is Arthur Groves, Lady Arradale, a lad of no discrimination, as you can see. He'd make friendly overtures to a tiger." Certainly the boy, arm confidently around his uncle's neck, didn't seem to be wary of teeth.

Diana almost felt bitten herself. She had prepared to meet the Dark Marquess, but what was she to do with this man? The Dark Marquess did *not* carry infants around!

"My brother is at his wit's end."

Diana turned dazedly to Lady Steen. She was what Diana was beginning to think of as a "red Malloren" though her hair was a soft brown just highlighted with warmer tones. Her easy smile was very like Lord Brand's, however.

"It's hard to be the *éminence noire* of England," the lady continued, "with a grubby infant following you everywhere you go."

A glance showed Diana that far from being at his wit's end, the *éminence noire* appeared completely at his ease, and was engaged in a conversation of some sort with the child about the horses. On little Arthur's side it involved a great deal of babbling and pointing, but anyone would think it was wisdom by the marquess's attention and rational responses.

She mustn't notice, she decided, many seconds too late. She mustn't look, listen, or pay any kind of attention to things like that. He was the Dark Marquess, and she would ignore him as much as possible over the next three days.

Lady Steen drew forward two girls who seemed to be trying to hide behind her skirts. "May I present my daughters,
Lady Arradale. Sarah and Eleanor." The two girls shyly
dropped neat curtsies. "And this," she added, stretching a
hand to an on-best-behavior boy, standing by his father, "is
Charles, Lord Harber." A correct bow and steady, intelligent
eyes.

"I can't promise perfect order from them all," Lady Steen
remarked, giving one daughter a look when she giggled,
"but I hope they won't upset your household too much. We
brought them because we are all continuing on from here
into Scotland."

As they exchanged commonplaces about traveling, Diana
found herself relaxing. Astonishing that the Mallorens included this pleasant, easy natured woman and her amiable,
devoted husband.

A moment later she realized it was dangerous. It could un-
dermine her caution. She was pleased enough to move on to
the next coach's passengers.

The marquess, still uncomplainingly burdened with the
chattering child, presented her to a man as dark and dramatic
as himself. As Diana greeted Lord Bryght Malloren, she
thought that *this* was what she had expected from them all.

He was possibly the handsomest man she'd ever seen.
Dark and lean, with very fine eyes and a slightly cynical
manner, he was designed to turn any woman to jelly on the
spot. This, she was armored to resist.

His wife was the shock, being short, slight, and almost
plain, with red hair and an embarrassment of freckles. To
make it worse, as she welcomed them, the two shared a
flashing moment of eye contact that might as well have
screamed love, passion, and abiding understanding.

"Yes," murmured the marquess as they moved on. "More
of the besotted. I warn you, it appears to be contagious. It's
roared through my family in short order. I am immune, of
course, but you must take your chances."

"I am immune, too, my lord, I assure you."

"You cannot imagine my relief, since I am the only unattached male present. We can sit together of an evening in an enclave of disinfection."

She laughed, but wondered if any of her panic rang through it. He was right. He and she were the odd couple in this company! They couldn't be thrown together by that. They couldn't. A few minutes in his company was assuring her that she hadn't imagined the effect he could have on her.

And then—dear heaven!—there were the sleeping arrangements.

Even in a house as grand as Arradale, this number of guests required all the good bedrooms. She slept in the earl's suite, but her mother had long since vacated the countess's rooms for different ones elsewhere. Someone had had to be allocated the "Countess's Chambers," and so she had decided the marquess could sleep there—not without a touch of malice. They were decorated in an extremely feminine style.

She had not thought that they were truly adjoining, nor how it might appear to others.

Lud! Was there any way to change things at this late date?

Young Arthur suddenly demanded to be put down, and he ran to join a red-haired lad who was only just steady on his feet, clinging to a maidservant's hand.

"Our son, Francis," said Lord Bryght, strolling over to give his own hand to the child, then swinging him into his arms, to a crow of delight. "We don't expect you to remember which is which or whose is whose, Lady Arradale," continuing to play a swinging game that had the child fizzing with delight. "There's always hope that they'll stay out of sight and hearing."

His wife snorted with laughter. Diana just tried not to gape. Dark, dramatic, rakish men were not supposed to be adoring fathers!

Lord Rothgar steered her toward the last coach. "I fear Portia is right, though at least your house is much larger than the inns, some of which may wish never to see us again."

Humor and tolerance, now. Diana was perilously adrift. She no longer knew what might come next, or how she should behave, or how to protect herself.

Or even, exactly what she needed to protect herself from.

"I believe you have met my sister Elf," the marquess said, snapping her out of bewilderment and indicating another couple. Indeed, in one of her two trips to London, Diana had met and liked Lady Elfled Malloren.

"May I present Lord Walgrave, her husband."

Lady Elf was another red Malloren—lighter colored and lighter hearted. Her husband was brown and handsome, but not in the dramatic way of Lord Bryght. More solid. In this company, almost ordinary.

Almost a kindred spirit! Perhaps she could spend time with Lord Walgrave talking about Mallorens instead of with Lord Rothgar being noticeably a couple. After all, it wasn't the thing for married couples to seek each other's company in public.

She was beginning to recognize, however, that the Mallorens were careless enough of fashionable standards to do exactly as they pleased. How was she to deal with that?

At least there were no children here, and the Walgraves were the last of them. There was another brother, she knew. Lord Cynric. He and his wife were in Canada, thank heavens. Enough was enough.

Three days, she repeated silently in her head like a protective incantation as she turned and led the Walgraves toward the house.

"You can't imagine how relieved I am to have this journey done," said Lady Elf. "I'm increasing, and it is proving tedious beyond belief."

Diana should have known it. Besotted and fertile, the lot of them. Perhaps it was their plan to dominate England by force of numbers!

Except the marquess, who had made it clear that he didn't intend to marry or sire children. That ensured her safety from the worst kind of folly, but for some reason it did not completely reassure . . .

She pushed all thought of him from her mind. "Nausea?" she asked.

"At unpredictable times. If I sometimes flee the company, just be grateful I escaped in time."

"Then it's good of you to make the effort to be at the wedding."

"Oh, we couldn't possibly miss a family wedding, could we?" she asked, flashing a smile at her husband

"Of course not," he said, though Diana had the feeling he didn't entirely agree. Being a Malloren spouse was doubtless a demanding role.

"We've been enjoying such a spurt of them," Lady Elf said, and Diana remembered that she was a chatterer. "Weddings, I mean. And at least this one has been planned in a leisurely manner and is free of royalty."

Diana resisted the urge to ask. She'd learn the family gossip from Rosa. She couldn't help wondering, however, whether Lady Elf had had to rush to the altar because of her increasing state.

"And I'm delighted to visit the north," Lady Elf added. No. Diana must remember that she was Lady Walgrave now. "It's so lovely up here. All the wildflowers in the meadows. The hills. The vistas! If I could paint, I'd try to capture it. As it is, I plan to explore some industry while we're here."

"Industry?" Diana feared that her mind had wandered and she'd lost the meaning.

"Woolen mills. Cotton manufactures. That sort of thing."

Diana blinked at her. A tour of Scotland was not unusual, but a tour of manufactures?

"It's an interest of mine," said Lady Elf, with what seemed to be a mischievous smile. "We'll be traveling on with Bryght and Portia, for they want to see the Duke of Bridgewater's aqueduct. And we all have an interest in the port at Liverpool."

Diana made some vague response, but she was beginning to wonder if this was all a dream. She'd had some nightmares about this meeting.

It was not surprising that visitors from the south wished to see the famous aqueduct—she'd been present at its opening four years earlier herself—but the port at Liverpool? And manufactures?

She'd planned a house party for bored southerners looking down their long noses at the less luxurious north. Now she didn't know what to expect. The marquess wanting to go down a lead mine, perhaps, or proposing a trip to dig in the peat bogs?

She looked around. This was real, however, and she felt ready to run away to hide in the bogs herself for the next three days. Instead, she drew on a lifetime's training, and concealed her uneasiness as she handed the massing of Mallorens over to her servants. It offered some respite, at least.

She reviewed plans for the rest of the day.

They'd all spend time now in their rooms recovering from the journey. Dinner next, but she'd already arranged the seating with herself and the marquess at opposite ends of the table. Afterward, music and cards, which should keep everyone occupied and allow her to stay out of his way.

Tomorrow was the wedding. It was going to be all right—

A sudden shriek filled the air. It bounced off the high ceiling, then ricocheted off marble walls and pillars to join new screams.

Little Arthur was throwing a tantrum, the sort of uncontrollable, overtired tantrum that could not be silenced.

Baby Francis, in his father's arms, had decided to scream in red-faced sympathy. As Lord Bryght hastily dumped his son on one maid, and another scooped up the wriggling tantrum and hurried away, Diana resisted the urge to clap her hands over her ears.

The maids had disappeared with remarkable speed. Anxious and perhaps embarrassed parents hastened after. Echoes died and peace returned. With wry looks, the Walgraves headed up the stairs.

True to his prediction, only the marquess and she remained.

Diana turned to say something light before escaping, but paused when she saw his expression. "Are you all right, my lord?"

The look of strain vanished, though he still seemed pale. "A slight headache, that is all," he said, adding with a rueful smile, "The acoustics of this hall, however, are astonishing."

Diana found herself returning that smile, a smile which

conveyed the notion that they were the only sane people in an insane world.

Oh, but this was dangerous. She hastily made her escape, heading for the estate office, where no guest could pursue.

It didn't seem to help. That smile had seemed to spin a dangerous, silken thread between them, a thread that did not break even when she was safe, the door closed firmly behind her.

Chapter 5

They sat fourteen at table that night—the Malloren adults, Rosa, Diana, her mother, and some members of the household—and the marquess was where Diana had planned for him to be—at the opposite end of the table, at her mother's right hand.

All the same, that silken thread still held.

She reminded herself not to even look at him, and concentrated on the men to either side of her—Lord Steen, and Lord Brand.

The Mallorens were good company, and seemed to be on friendly terms with each other. Their spouses could hold their own. Conversation was often lively, and bounced across the table and even up and down it, rather than politely to neighbors only.

The marquess was perhaps the quietest, though his occasional comments were witty. Diana, despite her intentions, found herself stealing glances at him even as she maintained her share of the light chatter around her.

He was part of this family and yet not completely part. As the night wore on, she had the strange thought that he was more like a father than a brother to them, though he could not be many years older than Lord Bryght.

She knew that the marquess's mother had died when he was a child—the infamous mad one who'd murdered her newborn baby. And that his father had married again. She hadn't known until Rosa told her before dinner, that father and stepmother had died within days of each other of sickness when the marquess was only nineteen. Or that the marquess held himself responsible for bringing the fever back to his home.

Rosa said Brand believed his brother had some memory of the murder of his baby sister, for he'd been there at the time, and carried guilt over that, too. Even without that, nineteen was a difficult age to assume such huge responsibilities. Her own father had died suddenly when she was twenty-two, which had seemed young enough, and she'd had neither guilt nor siblings to worry about.

Loving family and friends had tried to relieve Lord Rothgar of responsibility for the five youngsters. He'd stood firm, however, and kept them all under one roof. That was doubtless when he'd taken on the role of father. How else to manage?

No wonder there was a challenging edge to Lord Bryght's comments now and then. He must have been about sixteen—just the right age to be difficult in his grief.

No wonder Lord Rothgar had been so protective of Lord Brand last year. She contemplated her sliver of artichoke pie, appetite fading. She and Rosa had drugged Lord Brand and abandoned him in a barn, even though they'd known he'd be violently ill afterward. It had mostly been her fault, too, for Rosa would have stayed to help him if she'd not been unwell herself from sharing the drugged drink.

Lord Brand had forgiven them both, but had Lord Rothgar? She did not want his attentions, but she did not want his enmity, either.

"Are you all right, Lady Arradale?" asked Lord Steen.

Diana produced a smile and cut through the pastry. "Yes, of course, my lord. I was merely tracing an errant memory." She ventured a question. "You must find being part of the Malloren family interesting."

His lips twitched. "Interesting enough to enjoy life in a secluded part of Devon."

She chuckled and moved on to other subjects, but she couldn't stop both eyes and mind darting back to the marquess, drawn by the enigmatic puzzle he presented.

He was elegant, effortlessly courteous, and, she thought, much loved. Yet something jarred.

Eventually, she realized what it was.

He was apart.

By the time the ladies left the gentlemen to their relaxed drinking, she had the disconcerting feeling that the Marquess of Rothgar might be in many ways as isolated and alone as she. Perhaps that was the thread that ran between them, that both tugged and threatened at the same time.

Over tea, Diana chatted to Elf and Rosa, and after a half hour of spicy, humorous gossip about London, Elf asked to be on first-name terms. Diana was beginning to feel that perhaps she had a new friend, and regretted that this visit would only last three days. She would have been happy if the men had lingered over brandy and snuff, but they joined the ladies quite quickly. She arranged card tables, and Lady Steen played the harp.

After a while, Rosa took up music duty at the harpsichord, and Lord Brand joined her to play a duet. He did not have equal skill, but listening to the melded notes, seeing the bodies side by side, the occasional glances, Diana felt a deep quiver of envy.

She had never realized how exact the phrase "speaking glances" truly was. She swallowed and looked away.

Did her guests have everything they needed?

Was the marquess still apart?

Was he eyeing her darkly and plotting revenge?

Of course he wasn't. He was playing whist with Lord Bryght, Elf, and Lord Walgrave. Interestingly, Lord Walgrave was playing as the marquess's partner, not his wife's.

Diana wandered over to watch, and being skilled at cards, soon saw that Lord Bryght and the marquess were players of extraordinary skill. No doubt their family knew never to let them partner each other.

When the hand finished, the marquess looked up. "Do you wish to play, Lady Arradale?"

As he began to rise and she demurred, Lord Walgrave rose. "Please, dear lady, rescue me. It's like eating a chicken between three tigers."

His wife chuckled and turned to Diana. "Truly, it would be a kindness. He doesn't have the lethal instinct."

Since Lord Walgrave had already moved away to speak to Lord Steen, it would be awkward to object. Diana took his seat across from the marquess.

Another freak connection, or was there a conspiracy here? She shook off that thought. The adjoining rooms were her own doing, and nothing had contrived their solitary single status, or this partnering over cards.

"I didn't know whist could be so dangerous," she remarked lightly as Elf dealt.

"You haven't asked what stakes we play for," the marquess pointed out, eyes resting on her almost speculatively.

Her shoulders twitched, and to counteract it, she sat up straighter. It occurred to her that this was the most intimate situation they had ever been in, sitting close and unavoidably face to face.

"And what stakes *do* we play for, my lord?" she asked, fanning her hand and assessing her cards.

"Love."

She looked up sharply.

"Points," Elf said simultaneously and in quite a different tone. "My brother doesn't permit gambling within the family."

Diana looked only at him, the thread stretched taut. "Isn't it dangerous to gamble with love, my lord—in a family?"

"Or the safest place to do it. Appropriate, then," he said, laying down a card, "that I play the ace of hearts."

Diana watched the cards instead of him, as everyone discarded low. "Not King of Hearts?" she asked lightly as she gathered their trick.

"Perhaps that, too," he said, playing the card.

As she placed those cards in front of her, she looked straight at him. "Oh, do say you have the *knave* as well, my lord."

His lips twitched. "Whatever I have, I play low."

The play came toward her. There was no way he could know she held the queen, but when she played it—her only remaining heart—she felt as if he had forced the move. She was also aware during the rest of the hand of speculative interest from his brother and sister on either side.

Plague take the man, he was flirting with her! Why? Whatever his reasons, plague take her own absurd reaction. She took the last trick and smiled calmly at him. "Our hand, love or not."

He gathered the cards and shuffled, long fingers deft within the froth of lace, one large ruby flashing in candlelight. Aware of staring at their beauty, of sudden curiosity about how they would feel in contact with her skin, she looked down at her own hands, glittering ring on every finger.

He began to deal. "I do not insist on my rules in your house, Lady Arradale. If you would prefer to play for stakes . . ."

She met his eyes, smiling calmly. "Not at all, my lord. The pleasure of the game is in the skill of it."

"My thought entirely, my lady," he said as he picked up his hand. "And you play very skillfully indeed."

Heart suddenly pounding, Diana swallowed and fixed her attention firmly on her cards. Skillful or not, she was too sensible to play flirtatious games with him.

Three days, though.

Despite her new friendship with Elf, Diana wished the three days over.

She and the marquess won decisively. They had the luck of the cards, but there was also a fine meshing of skills, almost an ability to read each other's mind. She'd seen Elf and her brother exchanging more looks, and had wanted to protest, *This is nothing. This is just good card play.*

She wasn't sure that was true, however, so by the time she went up to bed, her nervousness about his bedchamber had reached the snapping point. It was just a room, and someone had to sleep in it, but still, as her maid stood waiting to undress her, she looked at the adjoining door, wishing she could see through it.

On this side the door was gleaming mahogany inlaid with decorative woods. On the other side, she knew, it was sparkling white paint with flower decorations on the panels, and details picked out in gold.

Beyond the door lay a lady's bedchamber of the most

flowery type. The colors were all white, pink, and gold, with
shell-pink draperies swagged up by plaster cupids. It had
been created for her mother and kept unchanged through the
years, perhaps in memory of magical times.

What was his reaction?

Curiosity warred with caution, and curiosity won.

After all, the marquess had been coming upstairs not far
behind her. He could hardly have undressed already.

She turned the key and knocked.

After a moment, the door opened, and he stood there coat-
less. His cravat was still tied, his waistcoat still buttoned,
and yet with the full sleeves of his shirt exposed, he seemed
shockingly underdressed.

And mildly, but forcefully, astonished.

Diana swallowed and put on a hostess's smile. "I hesitate
to disturb you, my lord, but I did want to be sure you had
everything you required."

His eyes rested on her a moment, then moved behind,
where she knew he could see her bed, dark, solid, and masculine. He, on the other hand, was framed by white, pink,
and gold. In dark gray waistcoat and breeches, and with that
other essential darkness which surrounded him, he was truly
midnight in lace.

"The hospitality of Arradale is perfect as always, my
lady."

Oh, perdition. This had been folly and was now embarrassing, but to rush away and slam the door would make it
more so. "We had to use every room, my lord. I hope you
are not uncomfortable in such a feminine setting."

A brow rose. "I believe I have slept in such surroundings
before."

Hades! Diana colored, and hurried into speech. "Your
room was my mother's, of course, before my father's death.
Doubtless I should have it redecorated in a more neutral
style."

"Why not wait, and let your husband choose his setting?"

Diana raised her chin. "You know I have as little intention
as you of marrying."

"Ah, yes." His eyes rested on hers. "In that case, you should certainly change the room, and your own as well."

"My own?" She turned and looked, as if something might suddenly be wrong with it.

"Take possession of it for yourself. You are not your father. Stay there."

She turned back to see him order his valet to move the long cheval mirror in front of her. Suddenly Diana saw herself, standing in the ornate white doorway. It hadn't occurred to her before, but she—trying yet again to be supremely feminine—was dressed in creamy white embroidered in pink, and wore gold and pearls. She matched his room, and contrasted as sharply with her own behind her as he did with his.

"I don't want a bedroom in pink and white," she said to herself.

"You have wealth and power. Your choices are infinite." A simple gesture of his beautiful hand seemed to open doors all around her.

She was still standing there, looking at herself in her inappropriate setting—lace against midnight—when he said, "Are your hostess's instincts satisfied, Lady Arradale? I fear we will all be expected to rise early tomorrow to engage in prenuptial festivities."

She snapped her wits together. "Yes, of course. Good night, my lord."

He bowed. She was accustomed to bows, but she had the unnerving feeling that the Marquess of Rothgar had perfected every degree of bow. "Good night, Lady Arradale. Though your setting is dark, may your dreams be light."

He closed the door.

She turned the key.

And may yours be dark, damn you! Even so, she was not angry except because he might have had the last word. Instead, a place deep inside suggested that she leave the door unlocked.

Folly. Utter folly! Had she not decided to keep her distance?

As Clara began to undress her, however, Diana had to accept that when she'd opened that door a part of her had hoped he would continue the earlier flirtation.

How appallingly weak. She'd charted her course and must stick to it!

Yet, as her gown came off, then her stays, Diana couldn't help playing with wicked ideas.

An unlocked door.

Lord Rothgar invading her chamber in the night.

Invading her bed, touching her with those long, skillful hands.

He would be cool in his mastery. He would never embarrass her with fervor or false passion, and that image of cool mastery sent a shiver through her, a shiver of pure longing.

Perhaps with him she could coolly surrender. Surrender to seduction, and finally experience all the physical mysteries she so longed to know, without losing her dignity or control.

She shivered, and pulled the wrap Clara gave her close around. She must not think things like this. They were wicked, and more dangerously, they could lead her into folly.

And yet, the wicked thoughts would not stop, stirred, she knew, by the peculiarity of having a man there—and such a man—where a spouse should be.

If she hadn't turned the key, would he have taken that as an invitation? She had no idea how these things were done. She shook her head. He had no interest in her. She could have left the door wide open and slept undisturbed. And, she told herself, she had no interest in him other than the fact that he was a very attractive man, and she was weary of virginal ignorance.

If she could experience the joining of man and woman once, perhaps it would stop buzzing in her mind and she could concentrate on other matters. Important matters to do with the earldom, and business, and the welfare of her people.

He was right about her room, however. She'd never thought before that it wasn't truly hers. It was still as her father had left it. She had moved into it, and left it untouched, to help her become what he had been—the earl.

Looking around the sober room, tears stung her eyes, and she could curse the man who had opened her eyes to this. The moment, however, could not be reversed.

She saw that she was trying to be two people—the earl, and the woman. Somehow, for sanity, she had to blend the two, to become a womanly earl. That was the role she had chosen for the rest of her life, and she must embrace it wholeheartedly.

A womanly, virginal earl.

Ridiculous to feel tears spill at the thought.

Chapter 6

The wedding went off perfectly, even the reception afterward at Rosa's parents' home. Diana had been nervous about this, for Coniston Hall was a farmhouse. It was a large farmhouse belonging to a prosperous gentleman farmer, but still, it lacked spacious rooms intended for entertaining, especially rooms intended for entertaining the nobility.

She'd offered Arradale, of course, but everyone had refused. The general opinion, in typical northern fashion, was that the grand Malloren family must take them as they were.

And the grand Malloren family had. The wedding finery had been nicely judged for the occasion, and they mixed comfortably with all. They were even joining in the country dancing in the cleared and decorated barn, cheerfully welcoming any and all partners. She herself had partnered the vicar, Squire Hobwick, Rosa's brother-in-law Harold Davenport, and her own estate manager, all the while itched by a wish that the marquess would appear and ask for a dance.

She still felt him as a dark threat, but also as a teasing, tantalizing promise.

"If you ever change your mind, my lady . . ."

For a mercy, he did not appear, and when she returned to the bustling house seeking refreshment, she saw him sitting with some local gentlemen in the paneled parlor. She felt an absurd urge to rescue him, to drag him out to the more youthful amusements. He was not a staid older man.

She pushed the notion away—she must stop thinking of him all the time!—and joined the ladies on the other side of the parlor where a maid was serving gingered lemon water.

Held in ice from the Arradale icehouse, the drink was deliciously cool. Diana sipped and tried to fix herself on the talk around her, but it was mostly of husbands and children, and her mind and eyes kept drifting toward Lord Rothgar.

He was making no attempt to be one of the locals. Of course. He would never attempt anything so foolish any more than she would. Apart from that distancing aura which always surrounded him, everyone here knew his rank and powers. He was not trumpeting his rank either, however.

He'd chosen clothing of a lighter shade—a suit of buff-colored cloth which nicely suggested country pursuits while the cut and elegant braiding rang of fashionable London. The ruffles at throat and wrist were moderate and of fine linen rather than lace, but that in itself set him apart. The local men, dressed in their best, were more ostentatious but not at all more fine.

Most of the men wore powdered wigs, but then most of them kept to the old fashion of shaven head and wig all the time. It was eas r than wearing their own hair long, and hid the thinning hair of passing years. Lord Rothgar, in fact all the Malloren men, kept their own hair, and for this occasion they had all chosen to do without a wig or powder.

A pleasantly informal touch, and yet again it set them apart. Of course, they were fortunate to all have excellent heads of hair.

Strong, she thought, considering the marquess's dark hair, waving back from his high brow to be tied neatly with a black bow at his nape. Loose it might spring beneath the fingers . . .

She turned back to demand another glass of the icy cold drink, and even pressed it for a moment against her cheek trying to block him from her mind. After a moment or two, however, she couldn't help but glance back. The honest truth was that assessing the eminent marquess as to his points was far too much fun to forgo.

Strong lines to his face, too, though with an elegance of bone that took any heaviness from it. Long straight nose and a fine arch over the eye emphasized by dark, well-shaped brows.

Eyes set a little deep, which perhaps gave them that sense of power. Dark lashes, too, of course, which also drew attention to the eyes. A mouth that could look cold, but bracketed by creases that deepened with his occasional restrained but strangely alluring smiles.

The conversation among the men suddenly settled to an argument between two others and he glanced around. Hastily, Diana looked back at the ladies, feeling her face heat. Had she been quick enough, or did he know she'd been staring at him? Someone did. Rosa, who'd joined the group without her being aware of it, gave her a thoughtful look.

Plague take the man. And plague take her for sliding into such folly. It was the wedding. Weddings were not good for the nerves of a woman resolved on lifelong chastity.

Rosa strolled over, beaded glass in hand. "If you keep looking at the man like that," she said quietly, "you'll stir rumors."

"Don't be silly."

Rosa drew her away a little from the other women. "Elf has already asked me a couple of oblique questions."

"About me and the marquess? How peculiar."

This was Rosa, however, who knew her far too well to be deceived. Diana led the way out of the door and down the corridor toward open air.

"He's a fascinating man," Rosa said when they were outside. "And handsome—if one admires a finely-made blade."

Diana stopped to face her. "That's not fair. There's more to him than a weapon." When her cousin's brows rose, she cursed her impulsive tongue. "Perdition, Rosa, I just feel sorry for him."

"*Sorry* . . ." Rosa echoed. "For the Marquess of Rothgar?"

"You're as bad as the rest! I thought you said he was the one who sorted out your problems and made this all happen. You should be grateful."

"I am, but—"

"Yes he's brilliant, elegant, and carries England in the cup of his hand, but . . ." Knowing she was going to regret her words Diana still couldn't stop. "He's alone, Rosa. Don't you see that? He's created a loving family, but he's not part of it—"

"Of course he is."

"Well, yes. But not as a *brother*. Not quite. And his mother's madness means he won't create a family of his own. You must see how that resonates with me. I have no siblings, and I will never have a family."

"There's nothing to stop—"

Diana waved that aside. "His gifts, his powers, must set him apart from other men. How many men in England feel truly at ease with him? And how many can he allow himself to be at ease with?"

Rosa was studying her with a frown. "But the marquess knows everyone, and is known everywhere. He can't go down the street in London without being recognized."

Diana knew the "delights" of that. Doubtless he, like she, even had his face on inn-signs. True, the picture of her hanging outside the Countess of Arradale Inn in Ripon wasn't an excellent likeness, but it was close enough. She could not go anywhere in the north in private.

Unless she adopted a disguise, she thought, remembering the time last year when she'd played the part of Rosa's spotty maid. When she met the Marquess of Rothgar for the first time—

She snapped herself out of that. "What of his more intimate friends?"

And what of mine? echoed inside, as she made herself move, strolling back to the barn and the dancing.

Yes, she too had a wide acquaintance, and was recognized all over these parts, but who could she count as a true friend? Only Rosa, who today was taking up a new life that must surely absorb her interest.

"He does have a magnificent mistress."

Diana's heart missed a beat, but she instantly recovered. "He doesn't worry about passing on his madness through her?"

"Rumor says she is barren."

"Convenient." Diana realized that yet again she was

wrapped up in the marquess and his affairs. It seemed like a thorny thicket, snagging her whichever way she turned.

"She's very striking, too," Rosa was saying. "In a foreign style."

Something suddenly struck Diana. "Are you saying the Mallorens introduced you to her? To a member of the demi-monde?"

"Of course not. I really shouldn't have called her his mistress. It's only hinted at. She's a scholar and poet who holds select salons. I went to one with Brand."

A scholar and poet. Though well-educated, Diana was neither of those things. A painful little knot formed inside her, and she had the dreadful feeling that it might be jealousy.

Obsessive curiosity was bad enough. Jealousy would be the final ridiculous straw!

"A formidable mind?" she asked, only because she had to say something. "So that is what draws the marquess to a woman."

They had reached the big open doors to the barn, where merry dance music greeted them. "They certainly seem to have a great deal in common," Rosa said. "Elegance. Intellect. They both seem as self-sufficient as silky, aristocratic cats."

"Cats?" Diana queried in surprise. "Hard to imagine Lord Rothgar sprawled bonelessly on someone's lap purring."

Rosa smothered a hoot of laughter. "Oh, I don't know. He must be human once in a while."

Diana forced a grin, but she knew she was blushing. Comments like that made her sharply aware of how little she really knew of the business of intimacy.

Men sprawled on laps? Purring?

Lord Rothgar?

She couldn't help trying to imagine it, but despite having read books of the most explicit kind, she failed. All the same, as an imaginary notion, it swirled in her brain . . .

Flute, fiddle, and drum rang around her, and within the barn happy couples skipped up and down lines. Other people sat around chatting, and she glimpsed quite a few young

couples in quiet corners stealing a moment for courting conversation or even kisses. One swain rubbed his head against
his companion's in a movement that was strangely catlike—

"Curiosity satisfied?" Rosa asked.

"I'm not curious," Diana instinctively protested, but then
pulled a face. There was no hiding it. Seeing a group of
young children, she allowed herself one more indulgence. "I
saw him with his little nephew."

"Remarkable, isn't it? Even shocking in a way. Like seeing an infant with a tiger. But he seems genuinely fond of
them all."

Lord Steen's daughters—flushed and bright-eyed—were
being included in the adult dances, but Diana saw young
Arthur stamping and swaying to the music with the other
small children.

Lord Bryght's copper-haired infant sprawled asleep in his
mother's arms where she sat with two local matrons as if she
were just another gentleman's wife.

One of the other ladies, Mrs. Knowlsworth, broke off
what she was saying to pay attention to a young girl who had
run up with a complaint of some sort.

A dancing child—her cousin Sukey's second, she
thought—tumbled and was picked up and soothed . . .

Another world.

The world of mothers and children.

Not for her.

Never for her, for she had rank and privileges granted to
few women.

"You're right," she said crisply. "The marquess should
marry. I'm surprised someone hasn't persuaded him."

"That his mother wasn't mad?"

"That it's worth the risk."

"Apparently Lord Bryght tried not long ago. I gather it
was not a pretty scene."

Diana might have weakened and probed for details on
that if Lord Brand hadn't come into the barn then. The look
in his eyes, when he spotted his bride almost stopped her
breath.

"I think your husband is growing impatient, Rosa."

Rosa turned, lovely color flushing her smiling face. She laughed in the way of a person suddenly bubbling with delight and extended both hands to her smiling husband. "After nearly a year? We've perfected patience, haven't we, my lord?"

Diana knew that after their brief flare of illicit passion they had agreed to wait until they could marry.

Turning soberly intent, Lord Brand carried both hands to his lips. "After nearly a year, my lady, my patience is in short supply."

Both stilled for a moment like statues. A framed moment of deep desire. Wasn't it worth the loss of everything to have a man look at her like that?

Just once.

"It is time," Rosa said, now a deep pink and sliding against her husband, within his arms, while hardly seeming aware of it. She held out one hand to Diana. "Thank you for all you did last year. And"—she pulled free and hugged Diana—"be *happy,* Diana! Whatever you do, be happy. See. It is real. It can be grasped. I want for you what I have found for myself."

Diana returned the fierce hug, blinking back tears. "Of course I'll be happy!" she declared. "I *am* happy. You know our tastes often differ. I enjoy politics, and administration, and grand entertainments. I even enjoy accounts and legal matters." She pulled back and summoned a brilliant smile. "I'll be wonderfully happy being the Grande Seigneuress of the North, and driving the stodgy world of men distracted."

It looked as if Rosa would protest, but she just shook her head and kissed Diana's cheek, then let her impatient husband lead her back to the house. Doubtless their horses were already waiting at the front. It was some distance to their new home at Wenscote, with little that could be called a road in between.

Diana called for the music to stop, and for the guests to send the couple off with grain and flowers. She picked up her pale skirts and ran to the house to seize one of the prepared baskets of flowers herself. Then she wove through the gathering crowd so that people could take a handful.

She would see her cousin into her new life with smiles and flowers.

When she came up to the marquess, she offered the basket teasingly, but to her surprise, he gathered a mass of blossoms in both hands. Then, strolling over to where Brand and Rosa were saying farewell to her parents, he poured them over his brother's head.

Brand turned, laughing, complaining, and trying to brush multicolored petals from his hair. After a still, smiling moment, he embraced his brother without restraint. Shockingly, at least to Diana, the marquess embraced him back, even lowering his head a moment to rest against the other.

A large part of this happy outcome had been Lord Rothgar's work, but she had thought it came from pride, duty, and a love of efficiency. She saw now that she'd been wrong. Nor was it all fueled by guilt. He loved. Though generally he sheathed it in steel and velvet like the dangerous blade it was, he loved his brothers and sisters to a remarkable degree.

Swallowing, she moved on quickly, offering her flowers, eyes a little blurred. What did it matter? It was nothing to do with her.

She kept the last handful of flowers and threw them at Rosa as the happy couple rode off. She stamped on the thought that she was waving goodbye to her closest friend, to someone who had been as close as a sister, as a twin even—

"Is marriage such undiluted tragedy, Lady Arradale?"

Diana started, and found the marquess by her side. "Not at all, my lord."

"Ah, tears of happiness, I gather."

He didn't think that for a moment. "I am not crying," she stated, and indeed, she was not, though they clogged her throat.

"Tears are not always visible."

Diana faced him, eyes deliberately wide, and dry. "You wax metaphysical, my lord."

"Perhaps everything of importance is metaphysical, my lady."

"Faith, but if everything of importance is beyond our senses, we are like feathers on the wind."

"Have you never felt exactly like that?"

She caught her breath, for it did describe her state today. "Have you?"

It burst out of raw curiosity. Though she might have glimpsed some of his vulnerabilities, she'd never imagined the marquess blown on the wind. Not even on a hurricane.

"The coaches await," he said, taking her basket and turning her toward the road with the slightest touch on her arm. "I do my best to tether to rock, my lady, though even rocks prove untrustworthy at times. You will miss your cousin, I think."

As an instinctive defensive move, she retorted, "You will miss your brother."

A sharp look told her she'd scored. "Your last brother," she continued with sudden realization. "All your family save you are now married, are they not, my lord?"

If there had been a hit, he'd recovered. "A Herculean task, but accomplished, yes."

"So what will you do with your matchmaking instincts now?"

"Turn all my tender care to my country, dear lady."

"Matchmaking Britannia with whom?"

"Why, with peace, of course. Does a long period of peace not seem desirable to you?" He passed the basket to a servant, but picked something out of it. She saw that one scarlet poppy had caught there. Poppy, which could aid peaceful sleep, or become a perilous addiction.

"Peace is excellent," she said.

"You don't regret the lost opportunity to seize all of France's holdings?"

"Do you?"

"I thought the cost too great."

With the slightest of smiles he tucked the stem down her bodice, down behind her busk so it tickled between her breasts. In the end, only the vibrant blossom rested against the frill of white lace there.

And she let him.

She looked up into his dark, disturbing eyes, seeing that they were not dark brown, but a steely dark gray. "What do you want with me, my lord?"

He murmured something in Greek.

She said: "Aristotle."

Those heavy-lidded eyes widened, and with considerable satisfaction, she knew she had startled him. "Easier to study others than ourselves," she translated. "More comfortable to judge their actions than our own."

After a moment, he said, "Of course. Having only a daughter, and one who would inherit, your father gave you a man's education."

"And a devilish bore it was at times. Though," she added mischievously, "it has occasional reward."

A true smile touched his lips. "Indeed. You are very good for me, Lady Arradale. A constant reminder not to underestimate women."

They moved on toward the coaches. "I would have thought the poet Sappho acted as reminder of that." Instantly, she regretted it.

He didn't seem disturbed. "Nothing Sappho does surprises anyone. Perhaps I should have said 'apparently conventional' women."

She turned to look up at him, deliberately astonished. "You find me conventional?"

His smile was even more pronounced this time, warming his eyes. "A mistake. I apologize profusely. So, Lady Arradale, what sort of woman are you?"

"My lord Rothgar, turn your microscope on yourself."

She found the strength to walk away then. As she let a footman hand her up into a waiting coach, she gave thanks that the men were traveling on horseback. She'd rather be riding, too, for the road was not really smooth enough for carriages, but she had accepted the need to act the lady for today and now was grateful.

Conventional? she thought, squeezing in beside her Aunt Mary. He had mostly seen her trying to act her part, but surely he couldn't ignore their adventures last year, especially the one where she had held him at pistol point.

Oh, plague take the man. She must stop this!

It would be easier to stop thinking about him, however, if she didn't have the unnerving sense that he was reacting to her just as she was to him. She looked down at the red poppy, particularly startling against her outfit of pale yellow and cream, and touched a frilly petal.

A bold move. One that had to mean something.

What?

He was a man who did nothing without intent.

Lord Rothgar was catlike, yes. But not a domestic cat. Not a domestic cat at all. And big, predatory cats did not sprawl in anyone's lap, purring.

They devoured.

Rothgar very carefully didn't watch the coach begin its swaying journey down to Arradale. Really, it had been infernally stupid to play that little game with the flower. Weddings seemed to have a softening effect on the brain, particularly joyful country weddings such as this one.

He looked around for a moment, at smiling, uncomplicated faces, at old friends, close families, and familiar neighbors. This was a different world to the one he moved in, and not for him since birth.

Not for her, either, and yet she had a foot here through her mother who had grown up in this pleasant house.

He shrugged and went over to where the horses were being prepared, but a shrug could not cast off a new awareness of the Countess of Arradale. A pretty, quick-witted woman and, it would seem, an educated one. It had been clear from talk among the men that she played a full part in local affairs. Though some of the men were uncomfortable with it, none had suggested that she ran her affairs badly.

And she had knocked on his door last night.

As he swung on his horse, he acknowledged that Lady Arradale was even more dangerous than he'd thought, but that the real danger came from his own reaction to the woman.

Chapter 7

Back at Arradale, Diana watched everyone disperse to their rooms to change and rest before a late dinner. Once she was sure all was in order, she retreated to her own quarters.

In her father's somber bedchamber she reviewed the wedding, going over her conversation with Lord Rothgar, and deciding strategy for the next couple of days.

The problem was, she was no longer sure of her purpose. Oh, she knew what it *should* be, but as if softened by the summer sun, it was reforming into other, dangerous things.

Dinner tonight would be followed by more music and cards. Tomorrow she had a number of outdoor activities arranged. Angling on the river, boating on the lake, and a trip to the local falls for those interested. The day after, they—he—would leave.

Given that he would leave, could she not allow herself to indulge in this fascinating study? Could she not flirt, and perhaps even steal a kiss? What a waste to wave Lord Rothgar off the day after tomorrow without even experiencing a kiss.

Feeling hot and dusty, Diana let her maid take off everything and washed from head to toe before slipping into a loose silk gown for an hour or two's relaxation.

Just a kiss . . .

She pushed the idea away. Every grain of sense and intelligence told her she would be playing with wildfire.

On the other hand, he'd soon be leaving. It was an unrepeatable opportunity—

Oh, enough of this! She needed rational occupation, and marched into her boudoir where a pile of papers awaited her attention. She sat at her desk and made herself concentrate on them, and only them.

She went through them, scribbling her required action on most, but putting a few aside to be dealt with when she had more time. The work soothed her until she came to a personal letter from a second cousin informing her, as head of the family, of engagement to marry. Lud, was the whole world hell bent on matrimony, while she languished hardly kissed?

She let the letter drop.

Just a kiss . . . ?

When younger she'd permitted the bolder local lads a kiss now and then. Sometimes at a masquerade she allowed some gallant carefully controlled liberties. It had been safe enough.

The Marquess of Rothgar would not be safe, of that she was sure, and that in truth was part of his appeal. Wiser to avoid, of course, and yet . . . from her chilly eminence, he was a most tempting blaze. And, remarkably, a safe one.

Chin on hand, she allowed herself to consider it.

Despite heat and flame he was safe because he, even more than she, did not intend to wed. A safe blaze, like one confined in a solid hearth.

Could she?

She tidied the piles of papers, then strolled, twirling the wilting poppy, back to her bedroom to relax on her chaise longue by an open window. Amid birdsong and summer breeze, she let her mind return to that minuet a year ago.

"What would have happened, my lord, if I had not objected to . . ."

"To my kissing your palm? Why, we would have indulged in dalliance, my lady."

"Dalliance?"

"One step beyond flirtation, but one step below seduction."

"I know nothing of dalliance then."

"Would you care to learn?"

Heart beating just a little faster at the memory, she brushed the soft petals of the poppy across her lips.

"If you ever change your mind, my lady . . ."

If you ever change your mind.

"Clara," she said to the maid, who was busily laying out her clothes for the evening.

"Yes, milady?"

"Tell Ecclesby that we will offer dancing tonight after dinner."

Rothgar, down to breeches and open-necked shirt, was in the frilly boudoir that was part of his suite, attending to correspondence sent on by Carruthers. Disguised among routine business lay a coded report on affairs in Paris, and the actions of the acting French ambassador in London. He frowned over the fact that D'Eon was insinuating himself into the queen's good graces all too well. He needed to get back and deal with that.

He next opened a well-sealed letter and found it was a handwritten one from the king. He quickly assessed that it contained nothing urgent—then he came to a passage about Lady Arradale. After a while, he leaned back, looking out of the window over the lady's beautifully landscaped grounds.

King George should be paying more attention to his queen and less to the countess, but for some reason he was obsessed with her. This development was going to be somewhat difficult—

Someone tapped on the door.

He folded the letter. "Come."

He half expected the impetuous countess, but his sister Elf slipped in with a smile that didn't quite hide uneasiness.

"A lovely wedding, wasn't it?" she chattered, but then paused to look around the pink and white room. "Oh my."

"The Countess's Chambers," he said blandly. "Pink lightens and brightens my thoughts. If you have come to tell me you've plunged us all into poverty with an excess purchase of serge, I will merely smile."

That made her laugh. "I suppose there was a shortage of

grand chambers, but . . ." She looked around again. "Bey, please may I peep into the bedroom?"

He rose and opened the door for her. She stood in rapt study of the swathed bed, the pink and cream silk hangings held up by plaster cherubs, the pristine white posts carved with flowers, the coverlet of heavy white lace.

"Could we swap?" she said at last. "I'm overcome by a need to be taken with violent passion upon that virginal bed."

He laughed. "Perhaps that is the purpose. I have to say, however, that it hasn't had the same effect on me." All the same, a sudden erotic vision to do with the countess assailed him.

"It would be very strange if it had," Elf said, sitting in a spindle-legged white chair.

"Or perhaps I am kept sane by cool liquids," he replied, pouring himself some from a silver pitcher set in a ceramic bowl of ice. "Lemon barley water?" he asked her.

"Oh, lovely!" She sipped the delicious cold drink. "How did you obtain this?"

"I ordered it. After all, I did bring a gross of lemons north with me."

"Not expecting the countess to be well supplied?"

"Imagining hot days and my fondness for lemons. So, Elf, what brings you to my feminine bower?"

Elf took time to sip, feeling strangely nervous. Her brother didn't intimidate her, but then, she'd never tried to meddle in his intimate affairs before. "I have become quite fond of Lady Arradale," she said at last. "I saw you tuck that flower down her bodice, Bey. You're not flirting with her, are you?"

His eyes were steady on hers. "And if I were?"

"I'd object."

"Your objections must always carry weight, of course, but why? You can hardly think I'll ruin her, and I doubt she would permit herself to be ruined."

"There are many sorts of ruin."

"And which do you fear?"

She was feeling more foolish by the moment, and yet more concerned as well. "You could break her heart."

"I have no doubt she recognizes flirtation, Elf."

"But why are you flirting with her? I heard about events last summer. She bested you at least once . . ."

His brows rose. "You think me intent on dark revenge?"

She considered him. "Not dark. And perhaps not revenge. But . . . retribution, perhaps."

"By making the poor lady fall in love with me and then leaving with a cruel laugh. Elf, really!"

She smiled, feeling her cheeks heat. "Then why? We leave the day after tomorrow."

He shrugged. "Perhaps because we leave the day after tomorrow. A wedding creates a spirit of flirtation, and Lady Arradale and I are the only two unattached people here apart from the dowager."

"Then spend more time with the dowager."

"But she, alas, wishes me to marry her daughter."

Elf slumped slightly. "Nothing could be more ridiculous."

"Ridiculous?"

She frowned at him. "Never tell me you are finally looking for a bride, and in that direction."

"No, I never will. I was merely curious as to why you think it ridiculous."

She made a dismissive gesture. "If Diana marries, and she swears she will not, she will need a man who can devote himself to her properties and responsibilities up here. You will need a woman who will be a hostess for you in the south."

"So, you need not fear a match between us. I have nothing but benign intentions toward the lady."

It should have reassured, but Elf couldn't banish a gnawing unease. "Then don't pay her particular attentions, Bey. She's chosen a hard path, and might be vulnerable to temptation. From the comments of nearly every lady I know, you are temptation incarnate."

He laughed, shaking his head.

She rose. "Sometimes I wonder if you know your own powers."

He rose courteously to open the door for her. "I thought I had made them my lifetime's study."

"Not all of them if you don't know how devastating you can be to a woman's good sense."

"I will bear that most carefully in mind," he said, and closed the door between them.

Elf paused in the corridor contemplating a large Grecian urn without really seeing it. Everything Bey had said was reassuring, but still her instincts warned. She walked on to knock on a door a little farther down.

A square-faced plump maid opened it. "Yes, milady?"

"I would like to speak to the countess if she is available."

"Elf?" Diana's voice. "Come in, do."

The maid opened the door wide, and Elf saw Diana rise from a chaise dressed in a loose robe of clear light green.

"I'm sorry, you were resting."

"The sort of rest that goes best with conversation," Diana assured her, indicating the cushioned window seat. "Would you like some lemonade?"

Elf looked at an identical silver jug set in an identical ceramic iceholder. "How delightful."

The maid poured the drink and then Diana said, "You may go, Clara, until it is time for me to dress."

Elf sipped. "Lemon is so refreshing on a hot summer day, is it not?"

"Wonderfully so. Your brother was kind enough to bring extra supplies north or we would doubtless have run out by now."

"Bey has a certain ability for planning."

Diana chuckled. "An understatement. He's a remarkable man." It was said casually, but Elf was not fooled.

Diana was her own age—twenty-six—but if anything, she seemed somewhat more mature because of her training and responsibilities. She had avoided suitable and unsuitable suitors for years, and should be in no danger, even from Bey. And yet, though the square chin and steady eyes spoke of strength, the soft lips and the occasional sadness in those eyes told Elf otherwise.

She understood, indeed she did. She knew only too well

how frustration, impatience, and wild desire could sweep even a sensible woman out of her wits entirely.

Diana cocked her head. "Penny for your thoughts."

"Last year," Elf said, abandoning a search for subtlety and throwing out a blunt warning, "I set out to lose my virginity."

Diana gasped.

"I was so very tired of guarding it! And so tired of being good. It was surprisingly difficult. With Fort, I mean."

"He wanted to wait until marriage?"

Elf snorted with laughter. "Fort? No. He . . . Oh, it's complicated. He hated all things Malloren. I was mad to choose him of all men."

Diana's look suggested that she saw where this was heading. "And yet you ended up married. A happy outcome, surely?"

"We married four months later after many trials and tribulations," Elf said bluntly. "It could well have worked another way, and I was very lucky not to end up inconveniently with child."

Diana's cheeks had turned a little pink at this. "Then your brother would have made him marry you, and you would be in the same happy state."

"I wouldn't have married him for that, and Bey—all my brothers, even Cyn—were lined up to prevent me forcing Fort to the altar."

Diana stared. "Lord Rothgar *knew* what you had done? What did he do?"

"Gave me a short, sharp lecture on using people." Elf pulled out a handkerchief and blew her nose. "The point is, I feared what he'd do to Fort, but I never feared for myself. I always knew he wouldn't reject me or punish me." 'Struth, this wasn't the right message, either!

Diana looked down, running a beringed hand over the green silk. "Have I just received a warning against maidenly restlessness?" She looked up. "Your wickedness led to a happy outcome."

"But could well not have." Elf leaned forward to take her new friend's restless hand. "I worry, Diana. I'm sorry if that seems intrusive on such short acquaintance, but I truly understand how you feel, and I know the dangers. I recommend the conventional route. I can vouch for the delights of the wedded state."

Diana slid her hand free. "I'm sure it can be delightful," she said coolly. "The price, however, will always be too high for me."

Lud! Elf thought. Diana could warn a person off as icily as Bey. Despite that, she persisted. "You would still be the countess if married."

"But not the *lord*. Believe me, Elf, as soon as any man became my husband he would be earl in the eyes of the world. Apart from that, he would have all the legal rights of a husband. Most women have no power to lose, but I do, and I will not toss it away. I will not marry, no matter what the delights."

Elf stared. She'd seen the social face of the Countess of Arradale, but now she saw a steely will and determination worthy of an earl. She shouldn't be surprised, but she was.

And worried. If marriage was impossible, then illicit love would beckon. She knew that. It wasn't long since she had felt the same hungry yearning—for knowledge and excitement, but also for someone to replace the void left when her twin married.

Diana had just lost Rosa.

It was as if she stood on a hill watching a horse and rider head toward a hidden ditch. Nothing she could say seemed likely to prevent the fall, yet she must shout a warning.

Rising, she said, "If that is the case, you must be careful. I have one thing that might help. I will send a maid with it."

She paused, knowing it would be wiser to leave the subject, yet impelled. "The trouble is," she said, "that we women find it hard to be intimate without caring for the men involved, particularly when it is our first time. And that, my dear, is a slippery slope."

Diana rose, too. "Rosa said the same. She thought she could do it with Brand and be emotionally untouched . . ."

"Brand would touch the emotions of a stone statue. My brothers are all rather dangerous in that respect." Since there was only one brother left unwed, Elf didn't belabor the point, but took her leave.

Back in her bedroom, she found a copy of the leaflet she and Sappho published anonymously and distributed as widely as they could. It was a short treatise on things a woman could do to reduce the chances of getting with child. She wrapped it in plain paper and sent it to Diana.

Of course Bey knew all these things. He'd been intent on not getting a woman with child since the beginning. But, even if Diana wished it, Bey would not be the man to introduce her to womanly pleasures. That could not come about in a day and a half.

Elf couldn't help thinking it a shame. She had no doubt he was a skillful and generous lover, and from nature and intent, he was the last man to try to seduce Diana to the altar.

But in Diana's mind it wouldn't stop at curious exploration.

In the mind, it never did.

Diana retired to her bedroom that night in a state of considerable annoyance and frustration. She hadn't exactly expected the marquess to repeat his seductive invitation of last year, or to continue the flirtation after the wedding, but she had expected *something*. Something she could tentatively build on to reach, at least, an interesting kiss.

Instead, she could have been one of his sisters. In fact, though he'd been scrupulously polite, he'd been somewhat warmer with his sisters!

The dancing party had consisted of four ladies and four gentlemen—a comfortable number, allowing for lines and circles. The ladies had changed partners with every dance, but in such a small group, she and the marquess had met, turned, and passed again and again.

The result?

Not even a *look* to match the moment when he'd slid that poppy stem down her bodice.

She'd managed to once sit by him between dances—and they'd talked about the weather! She'd learned more than she cared to know about the causes of climatic variations around England, and its influence on national prosperity. She had the lowering thought that the marquess had been deliberately trying to bore her.

As Clara stripped her out of her most becoming gown—deep blue satin trimmed with blonde, and very low in the bodice—Diana accepted that he'd flirted with her earlier in the playful spirit of a country wedding. That was all. She'd read too much into it. The Marquess of Rothgar thought nothing of her. Why should he? They were mere acquaintances.

She slipped into her silk nightgown and sat to let Clara brush her hair. As always, it soothed her and restored her sense of balance and humor.

It couldn't wipe away embarrassment, however. Elf had guessed some of her feelings. Pray heaven no one else had, especially the marquess. She pushed aside the knowledge that the man had a reputation of being devilishly perceptive. Thank heavens he'd be gone soon.

She couldn't entirely crush disappointment, however.

When she dismissed Clara, she drank a glass of water while looking out over her dark domain by the light of a swelling three-quarter moon. Mistress of all she surveyed, yet mistress of no man. She laid the cool glass against her cheek, trying to chill the gnawing dissatisfaction stirred by the wedding, and by a year that had brought great changes. The day after tomorrow the Mallorens would be on their way and she would be left to peace and routine.

It seemed as bleak a future as life on the chilly moon. Didn't they say that all treasures lost or neglected on earth were stored there? Abandoned dreams, lost hopes, wasted opportunities, and tragic loves. And the full moon was her symbol, symbol of the goddess Diana. Perhaps she had been destined for this from birth.

Oh, nonsense. The world doubtless contained a great many happily married Dianas.

She turned toward the bed, but saw the paper that Elf had sent earlier. She'd put it aside when called upon to deal with a question about wine. She broke the seal and unfolded the thin leaflet within. A tract? A sermon on self-control and chastity?

Then she read the simple, direct text which was even accompanied by a few drawings to aid those who might struggle to read it. Shocked, she put the leaflet down. But then she picked it up again and read it through.

Fascinating.

As she read, however, she smiled wryly. One thing was sure: Elf did not expect her to lose her remaining ignorance with Lord Rothgar. He must surely know all these interesting techniques.

Chapter 8

It seemed in keeping with the snarled state of Diana's life that she woke the next morning to the splatter of rain on her window. A glance showed the sort of sullen gray sky that offered no hope for her carefully planned outdoor pursuits. Now, when she wanted to be rid of the Mallorens, she'd have them underfoot all day.

With a sigh, she rang for Clara and considered indoor occupations. The billiard table might amuse the gentlemen, and perhaps some of the ladies played. Would the ladies be content all day with chat, music, and cards? What would the children do? Though she'd had the nursery floor freshened and prepared for them, she had not expected to provide entertainments. Wondering what had happened to her childhood toys, she sent for her housekeeper.

Darkling thoughts of the uninterested marquess caused her to choose a simple dress of buff and green and to fill in the low neckline with a demure fichu. There. If he held any suspicions about her desires last night, this outfit should allay them.

She ate breakfast while dealing with papers and household matters then, equipped with one of the housekeeper's keys, she ventured up to the nursery floor.

The two infants seemed happily engaged in making mess with their breakfasts. The Steen's three older children, however—Eleanor, Sarah, and Lord Harber—were looking disconsolately out at the dismal weather. She heard the older girl say, "I hate Yorkshire," before they became aware of her and gave flustered curtsies and a bow.

She smiled. "Bad weather is a horrible burden, isn't it? And I foolishly didn't make provision. However, I once had toys and I have hopes that some are still in the storerooms at the end of this floor. Would you care to come and explore with me?"

With gleeful smiles, the three ran to the door and Diana followed, her own smile doubtless as bright. She'd not thought of her toys for years, but there had been some splendid ones. She led the way toward a door at the end of the corridor, unlocked it, and pushed it open. She had to admit to some disappointment. Though she'd known the place would be kept clean, a part of her had hoped for mystery.

"Alas," she remarked, "no gloomy corners or moldering corpses."

Rewarded with giggles, she led the children to one large armoire and opened a drawer. "Clothes. You could play dress-up."

They smiled politely, but it was clear this was not their idea of prime adventure. She turned to the boxes stacked nearby, each neatly labeled. "Gloves?" she asked.

The three shook their heads.

She peered at the next. "Artificial flowers?"

Three more shakes, but a glimmer of excitement starting. They had realized she was teasing.

She moved to a larger box. "Winter stockings . . ."

"Lady Arradale!" Eleanor complained, laughing.

"Oh, you think there might be toys here somewhere. Very well, come with me." She opened a door to reveal another well-lit room, many more boxes, and a number of large, shrouded objects.

"I give you permission to uncover one each," she said. "But be gentle. They might be breakable."

The three moved forward, clearly deliberating as to which was most likely to be exciting.

Sarah declared that as eldest, she should choose first, and lifted off one heavy cloth. "A rocking horse!" she exclaimed. "A splendid one!"

The other two turned to gather around Bella, and Diana stroked the real white mane on the dappled horse she'd en-

joyed so much as a child. The scarlet leather saddle and
reins were still in excellent condition, still hung with silver
bells that tinkled as Sarah made it rock a little.

"May I ride it, my lady?"

Diana made sure the rockers were free of other objects,
then said, "Certainly. You may all have a turn."

Sarah mounted neatly, arranging her full skirts, and set
the horse into jingling motion.

"What *is* it?" Charlie asked.

She turned to see that he and his sister were unwrapping
his choice. Sarah slid off her horse and came over to look at
the wooden cabinet on legs.

"It's a magical picture box." Diana went forward and
opened the doors to show the tube. "You look down this."

Charlie put his eyes somewhat tentatively to it, but said,
"I don't see anything."

"You need both light and something to see." She opened
a drawer, took out one of the disks, and slid it into place.
Then she wheeled the box next to the window. "It's best
with a candle, but if you look through the glass and turn the
handle, you will see pictures of people moving."

The boy put his face to the view piece again and began to
turn the handle. "It *is!* It *does!*" He stepped back. "Try it,
Nell."

His sister, teeth sunk in lower lip, eagerly pressed her face
to the viewer and turned the handle. "Those people look as
if they're moving!"

After a while, the lad said, "If you don't give me another
chance, Nell, I'm going to make your choice for you."

The girl leaped back. "Don't you dare!" She hurried over
to her shape—and began to pull at the covering cloth.

"Gently, Eleanor," Diana reminded her.

The girl obeyed, and worked the sheet off more carefully.
"It's a doll," she said. "A large doll." A life-size boy of about
five stood against a rock, a drum around his neck, sticks in
his raised hands. "His hair's real, Charlie," Eleanor said,
touching the blond curls gently. "And his clothes." She
turned to Diana. "What is he?"

The girl sounded a little uneasy, and Diana felt the same

way. She'd assumed this item had been disposed of decades ago, for her mother had never liked it. When the novelty had worn off for Diana, it had disappeared.

She smiled for the children. "There's a handle at the back of the rock. If you turn it carefully just twenty times, you will see."

"I know what it is," Charlie declared, reaching the handle first. "It's an automaton like the ones Uncle Bey has!"

The marquess had a number of automata? She wouldn't have thought him a man for toys, and the devices were expensive and rare. At least the children would be unlikely to be alarmed at the figure's lifelike behavior. She remembered being frightened when first seeing this one in action on her sixth birthday.

When they reached twenty she told them to stand clear and then pushed down the lever that started it.

The wheeze of the machinery was audible, but it still startled when the child turned his curly head to look at them, blink, and bow in greeting.

One child whispered, "Oh."

He turned then, eyes first then head, toward a bird sitting on the rock behind him. The bird came to life, spreading its wings for a moment, then raising its head to start a trilling song. The boy turned forward again and began to beat time on his drum, toe tapping, body moving a little in time with the music. Sometimes his eyes moved from drum to audience as if gauging their appreciation.

Then, with a *twang* one hand went limp while the other tapped on.

"Oh!" It was all three children at once.

Diana leaped to switch it off. Silence settled with the figure caught eerily looking at her as if in reproach. "Oh dear," she said.

"Oh dear, indeed," said a voice behind and she turned to see the marquess in the doorway. "Unwise to play such an instrument without carefully checking it over, Lady Arradale."

He came over and touched the curly hair. "*Pauvre enfant.*" He traced the arm that had stopped, running fingers down the blue suit of clothes, then raising the jacket. "If you will permit, *mon brave*."

One of the children giggled, but they all pressed close to look at the complicated rods and wheels that disappeared into the rock where the principal mechanism lay.

One rod hung loose.

"Not too serious a problem," he said, looking up—at the children, not at her. "But it shouldn't be played again until it has been thoroughly checked."

He rose smoothly and spoke to Diana. "A very fine object, my lady. Made by Vaucanson, perhaps?"

"I don't know. My father gave it to me for my sixth birthday. I didn't know it was still here." She turned to Eleanor. "I think you should pick another toy to unwrap, dear."

In moments, Eleanor had uncovered a small theater complete with puppets and the three children were engaged in devising a play. Diana turned back to the marquess, regretting—though only for a moment—her sober dress. Begone, folly! "You wished to speak to me, my lord?"

"I came up to visit the children."

Diana gave thanks for her unenticing dress.

He turned back to the automaton. "I am curious about this. You must know how precious it is. Why is it up here, neglected?"

"I have no idea. I enjoyed it, but something about it made me uncomfortable, so when it disappeared, I suppose I didn't ask. Looking back," she added, "I think my mother did not like it."

"I see why."

She stepped up beside him to share his view of the figure, but saw nothing unusual. "Why?"

He looked down at her. "It is a boy child."

Diana stared at the innocent thing. "My father would never have meant that," she said, but she could see how it might have seemed to her mother. She'd been wife—and a rather unworthy one, too, being merely the daughter of a local gentleman—to a man of great title and long heritage. In ten years of marriage, she had produced only one child, and that a girl.

Had her father meant this subtle reproach? Diana had always been aware, despite loving parents, of the fierce hope for a son. It had only been when she was about twelve that her education for future responsibilities had begun. That had marked the point of abandoned hope.

The marquess gently raised the drummer boy's chin. Because of the mechanisms, she supposed, it moved hesitantly, rather as a shy child's head might. The wide blue eyes ending up looking into his. "A pretty infant," he said, "with a marked resemblance to the portrait of you as a child that hangs in the countess's bedchamber."

With a breath, Diana went closer. Indeed, with shorter hair it did. "He had it made from the picture . . . ?" How much worse that was. It must have looked to her mother exactly like the son she had not produced.

"He likely thought it only a pleasant whim," the marquess said.

"With part of his mind."

Those dark eyes looked down at her, understanding a great deal too much. "Yes, we do sometimes act from more secret places, do we not?" He studied the child again. "A pretty infant," he repeated, "with spirit and willfulness already established, but showing warmth and great charm. I have thought so of the portrait, too."

Oh no, don't do this now. I'm too shaken by the automaton to know what to do, what to say.

He carefully let the chin lower and turned to her. "If you don't know anyone able to mend and tend it, I can take it to London and give it into the hands of a Mr. Merlin. It is an interest of mine."

"So I gather," Diana said, striving for a cool tone. "I confess to being surprised. Toys, my lord?"

"Machines, Lady Arradale. Ones that, when well made, do complex things precisely to order. A pleasing notion, is it not?"

"With a touch of magic? Merlin?"

"It really is his name. And the Duke of Bridgewater builds canals and aqueducts that go over rivers."

"And Byrd wrote choral music to rival birdsong?"

The corners of his lips deepened with humor. "It makes one wonder, does it not, about the power of names."

"Arradale carries no particular meaning other than the dale of the Arra. Rothgar, however, does suggest wrath, my lord. And Bey, which I gather your family call you, an eastern potentate."

"And Diana is the huntress. What, I wonder, do you hunt?" Before she could think of a clever reply, he said, "I understand that you have a shooting gallery here. I confess to being curious about your skill with a pistol."

Uncomfortably reminded of the events of last year, Diana seized on the children as an excuse and turned to them. "Come. You must return to the nursery. I will have these objects and some of the boxes taken there for you." She shepherded them out and made the arrangements, then turned to find the marquess behind her, still politely waiting.

"Are you suggesting a shooting contest, my lord?"

"Why not? The men will doubtless enjoy it, and Elf is quite skilled. And I wish to see you shoot."

As hostess, she could hardly refuse, but as she led the way downstairs, she said, "Why this interest in my abilities, my lord? Last year I had a pistol pressed to your back. I could hardly have missed."

"You missed Brand."

"I was flustered and he was moving too fast."

"You would rather have hit him?"

"Of course not, but it irritates to have made that mistake. What if he'd been a villain about to shoot me?"

"You would, I fear, be dead."

She cast him a quick look. "Quite. I do not intend to be flustered the next time."

Rothgar watched with amusement as the countess organized the shooting contest. She set herself high standards, and was used to meeting them. Most interesting. Unfortunately, everything about the Countess of Arradale was interesting, and much of it was dangerous.

He had no doubt that in the past year she had been working not just on aim but on the mind. However, he did not believe any skill stayed within bounds. There was a reason to train a boy in weapons and Greek, and in this world, reason not to so train a girl. Perhaps if he'd not let Cyn and Elf grow up together, Elf would not have thrown herself into such wild adventures. It had turned out well, but could have been a tragedy.

The countess carried the same fizz of frustration and boldness. In some ways, she would make an excellent man, but she was not one. Nor was she the type of woman able to drive out her femininity and live in manly ways. This made her a dangerous, disturbing woman—to him, to others, and to herself. And now he had the king's commands regarding her.

Lady Arradale had apparently petitioned the king to be allowed to take her earldom's seat in the House of Lords. It was, of course, out of the question. Parliament was for men only. Rothgar could see why she would want the tradition changed, but he was sure the king could not. George was very conventional about such things.

George was so conventional that he'd flown into a rage at the thought. It didn't help that he'd suddenly become aware that a young, unmarried woman wielded a great deal of power in his realm. That was intolerable, too. The letter commanded Rothgar to study this unnatural creature and report back to him about what could be done to restrain her.

On second thoughts, this shooting match had perhaps not been a wise suggestion. The last thing needed was for the king to learn she was skilled in such a manly sport. He followed the countess's straight back down a corridor, disturbed to have been so thoughtless, and aware that it might be symptom of worse.

He'd have to warn the others not to speak of it.

By the time they arrived at the long chamber lit by high windows, servants already had four pairs of pistols out and loaded. The targets, he noted, were of human figures, two men and two women with heart shaped "bulls" pinned to their chests.

" 'Pon my soul," Steen said. "We're to shoot at women?"

"Women," Rothgar pointed out, "are not always harmless."

"We most certainly are not," the countess agreed without a trace of womanly modesty or gentility. "If a woman was firing at you, Lord Steen, it would be folly to hesitate to fire back."

"Firing at me?" echoed Steen, clearly at a loss.

"Portia fired at me," said Bryght.

"Elf just threw a knife at me," said Fort.

"I did not," Elf objected. "I aimed at the paper you were holding, and hit exactly where I aimed!"

"A foolish trick, all the same," said Rothgar. He turned to the countess. "How will this be arranged?"

"Closest to the center of the heart wins."

Rothgar looked at the pistols. "Are those yours, Lady Arradale?" he asked, indicating a slightly smaller pair.

"Yes. Elf can use them, too, if she wishes."

"But in that case, the gentlemen should use their own, don't you think?"

"You have dueling pistols with you?" she asked, clearly startled at the thought. It was oddly pleasant to shock her.

"One never knows . . ." he murmured. But then he admitted, "No, but I have my own custom-made traveling pistols."

He looked at the other men, and Bryght, as he'd expected, admitted to having his own, too. His brothers were well trained. With a shrug, Elf confessed to having her own pair with her, making Fort roll his eyes, but humorously. That match was turning out surprisingly well without Elf having to try to hide what she was. A Malloren, through and through.

Servants were sent to bring the familiar weapons, and as they waited, Rothgar asked, "And the prize, Countess?"

She turned to him, suddenly guarded. "What would you suggest, my lord? I think none of us here would care about a purse of money."

"For love, then," he said deliberately to disconcert her. "We are family, after all."

"I am not."

"By connection. Do we draw for who shoots first?"

Her color blossomed interestingly before she turned to pick up a dice box. "We roll for it."

He gestured and she rolled the dice, getting eight. He rolled ones so when his pistols arrived and he had loaded them, he went first. He made no attempt not to put a pistol ball in the dead center of two hearts, one male, one female. If it came to a contest, he wanted her to know what she faced.

Among congratulations, he looked at her and saw the spark of true competitiveness in her eyes. *Ah, my lady, it is not wise to care so much about mere games.*

Elf, Fort, and Bryght were next in order. Elf took unashamed pleasure in doing a little better than her husband, and Bryght, like Rothgar, made two bulls. Then Lady Arradale stepped up to the mark, back straight, chin set. She might as well have declared her intention to win. Each ball went straight to the center and she turned to meet his eyes as if it were a personal challenge.

He was not surprised, but was perhaps a little shocked by that degree of skill. Even, in the most subtle sense, aroused. He delighted in excellence.

Steen was no great shot and amiably waived his turn.

"What now?" Rothgar asked. "We fire again to settle it?"

"Into the same targets," she said, "with white paper behind. We try to make exactly the same hole."

"Good lord," said Steen, and even Bryght looked startled.

Rothgar, however, picked up his first pistol. "A most intriguing test, Lady Arradale, though such accuracy can serve no purpose in a real situation. A pistol ball in the heart will do the job. In fact, a pistol ball anywhere in the torso is usually effective."

"But this is perfection for perfection's sake, is it not, my lord? As with machines?"

"Ah. Then by all means let us see who is the most perfect machine."

When the white paper had been pinned behind the red heart, he sighted. An interesting challenge, which appealed to his sense of absolutes, of precision. His first shot went very slightly off, he thought, though it was hard to tell at a distance. The second, too. When the papers were brought to him, everyone gathered to study them.

"The exact mark!" Steen exclaimed. Rothgar was fond of Steen but the man did not think in terms of absolute perfection.

"No, a trace of white shows," he said. "Bryght, your turn."

Bryght shook his head. "I see no point in this. What good does it do?"

"You disappoint me. Think of it in mathematical terms. There is right and there is not right."

"With figures I grant you, but not with this. I bow out."

"Elf?"

Elf shook her head, too. "I know I cannot do it."

Rothgar turned to the countess. "I trust you will not disappoint me, my lady."

She already had her first pistol in hand. "Of course not. It was my suggestion."

She again took that purposeful stance. He wondered who her weapons master was, for the man was good. At the same time, he couldn't help wishing he had the training of her. She needed to go a little further into the mind, into the soul, to achieve the level she sought.

But then again, perhaps not. He watched as both pistol balls hit the dead spot. Among cheers the papers were retrieved and studied.

"A touch of white too," she said with annoyance.

"But less, I think," Bryght said. "Let's take these back to the house and find some way to measure them. *That* appeals to my mathematical mind. By gad, Bey, I think she's bested you!"

"Which clearly brings solace to your bitter heart. Lady Arradale, do you fence?"

"Bey—" Bryght protested, but the countess merely smiled.

"Yes, but not as well as I shoot. I lack a daily training partner."

He only just caught himself from offering a bout anyway.

His height, reach, and skill would make it no contest at all, but even without that, it would not be wise. All the same, he'd like to test her mettle with a blade, too. He was sure she was devilishly good.

Chapter 9

Diana led the way back to the house, outpacing the others deliberately to avoid conversation. Simple matters immediately became complex with the Marquess of Rothgar. She sensed a mix of approval and disapproval in him, and berated herself for caring.

She did care, however. She cared what he thought of her, and she wanted to win.

An hour later, after many cups of tea, and the use of measuring sticks and a magnifying glass, the contest was declared to be a draw.

"Did you notice," Lord Bryght asked his brother, and Diana thought she saw a glint of amused speculation in his eyes, "that you were both off a fraction to the northeast?" He picked up the four hearts and laid them one over the other.

Diana took them and riffled through. Not identical, no. That would be beyond reason. But he was right. The error in all four was in the same direction. She took the two that belonged to the marquess and offered them. "A keepsake?"

"A treasure," he said, putting them into a pocket with a slight smile. "This time at least I managed to contrive a draw."

Elf leaped up. "Diana, I'm told you are skilled at that wretched game of billiards. I am determined to learn, but the men *cannot* teach me. They have no idea . . ."

Diana allowed herself to be swept away on a tide of chatter, and by a very firm grip on her hand. She resisted an urge to look back. There was nothing intimate in his manner.

Nothing. It was all her imagination, and she should be grateful to Elf for rescuing her.

She helped Elf to learn the game then escaped another challenge. She could probably beat most of the men at billiards, too, but she was beginning to feel all the awkwardness of her unusual skills. Worse, there was always the chance that the marquess would be her equal and create that strange connection she was fighting to ignore.

Intolerable if he defeated her.

She took refuge again in work. Two peaceful hours with her secretary and paperwork were exactly what she needed. They steadied her, but that seemed to open the way to clearer thoughts. When Turcott left to send the correspondence on its way, she stayed in the sober, masculine study to be businesslike about her personal affairs.

Fact one. The Marquess of Rothgar was a fascinating man. To deny that would be foolish. If she understood matters, half the world was fascinated by him.

Fact two. There was something between them that went beyond the ordinary. She had met other attractive men, after all. Brand Malloren had the appeal of a warm fire. Bryght Malloren was more like a glittering jewel. Both attracted, but in different ways, but neither made her skin quiver, her heart speed, her stomach clench, as Lord Rothgar did.

Was that something he created wherever he went? She didn't think so. It had to be more particular than that.

She remembered Rosa last year trying to deny herself one last night with Brand, mind and soul clearly intent on that one thing. Of course, Rosa had been falling in love with Brand, but Diana didn't think that had been the force just then. It had been lust, but a very specific lust.

Like a key and a lock.

A special key for each lock.

Even though she winced at the sexual imagery of that, she pondered the fact that Rosa and Brand were ideally suited, and yet might never have met. Did everyone have just one special person, and did they not always meet? Or did the fates arrange at least one chance for every couple?

How many such opportunities were lost, stored on the chilly moon?

Could the marquess be that special person for her? With a restless shrug she decided she'd much rather think of him as a master key, suited to a great many locks.

She leaned back in her leather chair trying to assess the feelings that ran between them. Did they run both ways? She'd seen enough cases of unrequited love to know it was not always so. She remembered one young man who had felt so strongly for a woman that he could not believe the object of his devotion felt nothing. He'd thrown himself off Hardraw Force and taken poor Maddy Stawkes with him.

She would rather die than reveal that kind of unreciprocated need. And she didn't feel it. When the marquess left tomorrow, she would hardly think of him thereafter. For the moment, however, a certain heat glowed inside.

Fact three. Lord Rothgar was a possible lover. She often considered men as potential lovers. In fact, it was getting to the point where she considered every man between twenty and forty as a potential lover! But none had seemed so clearly a possible lover as the marquess.

She was aware of his body in a way she'd never experienced before. Certainly she'd admired men—the width of their shoulders, the muscles of their legs, their elegance, strength, or agility. With the marquess, however, it was as if she could see *through* his clothes. She was constantly aware of skin, muscles, and shapes that were not actually visible.

It was an embarrassing nuisance, but it made the vision of him naked in a bed, leaning over her, shockingly easy to create.

Fact four. Ridiculous as it seemed, he was the safest potential lover in England for her. He did not intend to marry. Even if she lost all sense and willpower and begged him to marry her, he'd refuse.

Fact five. She need never see him again. He was leaving tomorrow.

Fact six. He was leaving tomorrow. Which meant that if anything were to happen, it would have to be tonight.

She rose to restlessly wander the room, hand trailing over desk, along shelf, around globe . . .

Tonight.

She gave a little laugh. No, really. It was impossible.

Halfway to the door she paused again. Was that wisdom or cowardice? What chance would ever again present itself so perfectly to her? Her perfect, possible lover in the adjoining bedroom.

Perfect except . . .

What would *his* reaction be?

Diana worked hard through the rest of the day to appear normal, but she wasn't sure what normal was anymore. At least the marquess was little in evidence. More correspondence from London had arrived.

"Is your brother always pursued so relentlessly by business?" she asked Elf when they assembled before dinner.

"Not always, no. I gather there's a great deal going on at the moment to do with France and the recent peace."

"But the marquess is not in the government."

"No."

"Or, not exactly?"

Elf's lips quirked. "Quite. Bey has a remarkable information-gathering machine, and a trick of noticing everything and holding it all in his mind for analysis. The king finds that useful."

"I understand the relationship goes a little further than that."

"The king has an admiration for him, yes, and seeks his advice on many matters." But Elf then turned the conversation to other matters, and Diana understood that there was a limit to what she would reveal about her brother. It was as well, for the marquess came into the room soon after, and she would have hated to have been caught talking about him.

After dinner, the little theater was brought down and the children performed a short play to warm applause. When they spoke of the other toys, the magical picture box and the broken automaton were brought to the drawing room, too.

The picture box gave great amusement, but the automaton could only be looked at.

Diana glanced at her mother. The dowager was smiling politely, but she thought she saw a hint of strain in her eyes. She would have gone to offer comfort, but she had no idea what to say. It was probably one of these matters best left in silence.

She did, however, go over to the marquess. "If you are still willing, my lord, I would like you to take the automaton to London to be repaired. In fact," she added on impulse, "I would like to make a gift of it to you."

It was an extravagant gift, but he did not protest. "You are most generous, my lady. I will see it carefully tended."

The evening passed in cards with Diana's own musicians providing musical entertainment. Diana made sure she did not sit at the same table as Lord Rothgar, but all the same her mind buzzed around and around her wicked dilemma like a bee trapped in a glass jar. The circling did no good, and yet she was powerless to stop it.

This was the last night.

Should she, shouldn't she?

Would he, wouldn't he?

She found herself admiring the line of the marquess's body as he turned to speak to Lord Bryght. A twinkle in his eye as he teased Lady Steen. His deft, long-fingered hands on the cards.

She could almost feel those fingers on her skin in the night . . .

Oh lud! Missed opportunities, stored on the moon.

When the party finally broke up and she could seek the sanctuary of her room she felt mentally exhausted.

But not physically.

No, her body seethed with restless and demanding energy.

Once she was ready for bed, dressed in just her loose silk nightgown, she dismissed Clara and stood facing the adjoining door. She hadn't noticed noises from the other room, but surely the marquess was there by now.

She paced for a moment or two then grabbed the wrap

that went over her gown. The gown was light, but the wrap was ivory damask and covered her as well as a day gown.

Still, it was nightwear, and no one could deny that.

Even so, she walked over to the door and knocked.

After a moment it opened—to reveal the marquess's middle-aged manservant. "My lady?"

A flicker of the eyes showed no one visible in the room behind him. Perdition! She wanted to instantly slam the door and hide under the covers, but she had to rescue some trace of her dignity. "I had a question about the plans for Lord Rothgar's journey. Tomorrow."

The man was studiously impassive. "Shall I give him a message when he comes up, my lady?"

Nerve crumbling to dust, Diana said, "No, no. It will wait."

She closed the door, then staggered to fling herself on the bed. Why, oh why, had she given in to that lunatic impulse? It gave her away!

Could she hope the man would not mention her visit at all? She prayed for it, cursing her hungry body which had pitched her into such an embarrassing situation.

She rolled to lie spreadeagled on the bed, looking up at the gray silk underside of her bed's canopy. Dark gray, like his eyes . . . She'd always feared this—that her fiery obsession would lead to embarrassment.

She should conquer her wicked urges. She should resign herself to true, eternal chastity. Like a nun.

Through the window, she could see the growing moon.

What a terrible, terrible waste it was, though.

A knock had her suddenly upright. She stared at the adjoining door as if it had become the portal to hell. She'd imagined it. She must have—

Another sharp rap.

She slid off the bed and walked forward, heart pounding. If *he* was coming to *her* with lascivious intent, what should she do? Why did everything suddenly seem different?

Swallowing, she opened the door.

He was still completely dressed, which made her clutch her wrap around her. "Yes, my lord?"

"I apologize for the intrusion, Lady Arradale, especially at this late hour. But I request a few moments of your time."

Diana swallowed again, this time swallowing disappointment. No, he hadn't come with lascivious intent, and he hardly seemed aware that she was dressed for bed.

She stepped back and gestured him in, countess to marquess. "Of course, my lord. Some matter I can assist you with? I have port here if you would care for some."

He declined, which meant she couldn't seek courage in a bottle either. After a moment she indicated the two chairs that bracketed the empty fireplace, and they sat.

Like husband and wife.

Stop it, Diana—

"I am commanded to take you to London, Lady Arradale."

Snapped out of foolish fancies, Diana sat upright. "What? By whom?"

"The king, of course. By way of the queen." He handed her a folded, sealed letter.

She opened it and read an invitation from Queen Charlotte to spend a short time as a lady-in-waiting.

"Why?" she demanded, then added, "I will not go, of course."

"It would not be wise to defy the king."

"He has no right—" She stopped, forcing her tangled and startled wits into order. This was far from any expectation she had had of this night.

"Why?" she asked again, a germ of real fear stirring inside. Some of her ancestors—northern rebels—had been commanded to London, never to return. The powers of the kings of England had been restricted since then, but they still could be turned on enemies and rebels.

"You brought yourself to his attention, Lady Arradale." Perhaps her confusion showed, for he added, "You petitioned him to allow you to take the earldom's seat in Parliament."

"And why not?" she demanded, though she felt some embarrassment. She'd always known it was hopeless, but it had irritated her so much that she'd had to try. "My lands are un-

fairly unrepresented. The earldom has a right to a seat in the
House of Lords, and I have the right to demand it."

"Children think in terms of rights and demands."

"Are you calling me a child, my lord?"

"In this, yes. Or perhaps undereducated."

Anger began to burn. "I have had an extensive and thorough education."

"You have stayed too much in the north."

"I like it in the north."

"Because here you can play childish games without consequences."

She glared at him, but beneath anger fear lurked, fueled
by his obvious seriousness. "What does the king intend?"
She forced out the terrifying words. "The Tower?"

"I do hope not. I would have to invoke *habeas corpus* on
your behalf."

"Would he respect that?"

"He has just been forced to do so in the case of Mr.
Wilkes. Here, unlike in France, a person may not be confined at the king's will, but must be brought to trial. However, the troubles of Mr. Wilkes serve to remind us that the
king has sharp teeth and can bite."

Wilkes had written a piece for the *North Briton* critical of
the king. He had ended up in the Tower for it, and was still
only protected by his position as a member of Parliament.

Diana steadied her nerves. Ironhand, she chanted to herself. Her great ancestor would not be cowed by a monarch
even younger than herself. "There is no similarity, my lord.
I have not written articles criticizing the king. In fact, I have
done nothing illegal or offensive at all."

"Precisely my point, if you will recall. However, you are
in some danger."

"Why? Merely for requesting consideration of a plea to
take my earldom's seat? Is it not everyone's right—"

With a flash of ruby, he waved that aside. "We have disposed of rights. Your petition disturbed the king, as it would
disturb most men. I believe he wrote words such as *unnatural* and *rebellious*. More dangerously, it drew his attention
to your existence and influence up here—you, a young, un-

married woman in a part of the country which still seems inclined to unrest. A part of the country close to Scotland, which still poses a threat."

"I'm not a *rebel*," she protested. "I'm as loyal and true as anyone. And he cannot dispose of me. The peers, the nation, would never stand for it!"

"Nor—more to the point—would I."

She wanted to laugh, but she had an unwelcome feeling that the marquess's support might well carry the most weight. "Then what danger do I face, my lord? This danger which presumably you cannot guard against."

Relaxed, long fingers lightly laced, he said, "First, pressure to marry." Before she could erupt over that, he added, "And second that you be declared insane. I will be most disappointed if I cannot guard you from these dangers as well."

"No more disappointed than I," she muttered, throat suddenly tight, and a chill rippling through her.

Consigning etiquette to the devil, she rose and poured herself a glass of ruby port. As the second warming mouthful went down and eased her, she turned back to him. "He cannot do it, can he? Declare me insane?"

He had not moved, or even unlaced those relaxed hands. "Not alone. However, definition of insanity is an interesting matter. Have you followed the recent report of the parliamentary committee?"

She nodded. "Many of the 'insane' in private madhouses are merely inconvenient. People locked away as long as their enemies can pay. A scandalous number are women locked away by fathers or husbands. I have taken measures to make sure that cannot happen here. That sort of trumped up insanity could not happen to me."

"True. However, the committee did not address the problem of people confined on a doctor's orders. It's not difficult to find a doctor who thinks that extravagance, excessive gaming, or frequent attendance at the theater are forms of madness in a wife. Or that a son or daughter's desire to marry unwisely shows derangement of the mind."

"Or a woman's desire to speak in Parliament?" She was proud of her calm tone. "Her intention not to marry at all?"

"Precisely."

She leaned back against the table and sipped her wine. She would not show fear in front of him. "I still don't think the king—even with doctors—could have a peeress locked away for that."

"That is why you need to go south. You have visited London how often?"

"Twice. Once, six years ago to spend some time with an aunt. And again for the coronation."

Where I saw you, she thought, *in the distance. Assured, powerful, subject of whispered, mysterious warnings. I was intrigued, but I never suspected that one day you would be such a presence in my life.*

"You need to show yourself in society, and be seen to be loyal and sane. You will also benefit from some time at court. You must understand that world and learn how it works, or I truly fear it will harm you."

"And yet that world is where the danger lies."

"The time is past when northern barons could ignore the south. Mere days separate you now, and with toll roads and improvements in carriages, within our lifetimes that will shorten."

She topped up her glass and returned to the chair facing him. "Why should I trust your advice?"

"I speak of what I know. Why would you think I'd misguide you?"

"The ways of the *éminence noire* could be beyond human understanding."

His lips twitched. "I do hope so. In this case, however, I am at my most benign. Rosa will be upset if any harm comes to you, and that will distress Brand. You must know that I try to guard my family from all harm. Also, I think it undesirable for the king to treat a peer of the realm as a woman. Even if she is a woman."

"But you would think it reasonable for a woman to be forced to choose between marriage or the madhouse, if she was not a peer?"

"Would an ordinary woman not be mad to refuse a good marriage?"

"No, and this is no time for humor, my lord. I ask you directly, do you think it right for a woman to be forced into marriage by father, or brother, or guardian, or king?"

"No. I was a firm supporter of the Hardwicke Act, and I have a hand in other legal matters designed to protect women from abuse. However, in practical terms we must deal with the world we have now. If the king chooses a suitable man for your husband, you will be hard pressed to refuse without giving offense, and without danger of being thought mad. However, we can guard against it, if you are willing to be wise."

Diana eyed him suspiciously. It went against her nature to even pretend to accept this. "Wise?"

"You have shown your ability to act the part of a servant, Lady Arradale, and you act the proper lady very well too."

"I *am* a proper lady, Lord Rothgar."

"A quibble over terms. If you come to London and act wisely, you will allay the king's fears. It might be as simple as that."

"And if he presents me with a husband?"

"Then you can, still the proper lady, plead a wish to make your own choice. The king loves his queen and is a supporter of the ideal of marital fondness. It might well sway him."

"And if it does not?"

"Your time in London will be limited, as the letter says. The queen expects to be confined in August, and at that time both king and queen will lose interest in other matters. They are doting parents. If you have lulled them, you will doubtless be allowed to return here then."

"Ah." She sipped some more of the comforting port though it was his calm practicality and expertise that was soothing her best. "I will be a perfect lullaby, then."

"I see you understand."

Bitterness rose. "I will be allowed to come home, but wings well clipped, never to stir questions again."

"If you don't challenge the king's sense of propriety, you should be able to live your life here as usual."

"A caged bird knows it is surrounded by bars."

"Lady Arradale, I am offering a return to what you have now."

"But not a return to what I had an hour ago."

He studied her, then nodded. "True. But an hour ago, you thought like a child. You thought you could live without restriction."

The galling thing was that he was right. He was even right, she supposed, that she needed this imprisonment in the south in order to fully understand the world in which she wanted to play a part.

She drained her glass. "What happens," she asked, "if it does not go as you expect? What if the king insists on a marriage—to one of his favorites, no doubt? What if he tries to paint me mad for refusing."

"Then," he said, "you will marry me."

Alarm flaring, she almost snapped something rude, but she made herself think. "Clever," she eventually acknowledged.

He inclined his head. "I'm pleased you can leap beyond instinct to reason."

"The ultimate security," she said, trying to hide how unbalanced the notion made her. "It saves me from threat of forced marriage, and of confinement for insanity, because a husband would have the last word there."

"And of course, if it should come to that, it would be a marriage in name only. You would remain in complete control of your property, your person, and your life."

She rested her chin on her hand, eyeing him. "In that case, my lord—"

He rose. "No. To save you from dire fates, Lady Arradale, but not for your convenience."

She rose too, smiling, and it was a true smile because he was offering a sacrifice. "I do thank you, my lord."

"If you are wise and clever, it will not be necessary."

"I fear I may be tempted to be unwise, you know, just to cause a thousand ladies to tear out their hair."

A hint of humor echoed hers. "Don't. I promise I will beat you every day."

"You won't. I'd tell Elf."

He actually laughed. " 'A monstrous regiment of women.' Lady Arradale, remember, at court, you are to act the perfect dull lady."

"Or . . . ?"

"Or I will leave you to your fate."

He turned to leave, but she put a hand on his arm, perhaps startling him as much as she startled herself. "We could seal this pact with a kiss, my lord."

His eyes rested on hers for a moment, but then he removed her hand. "I think not, Lady Arradale. Can you be ready to leave tomorrow? I can delay for a few days, if necessary."

The rejection stung a little, but his expression made her think it might have been self-protection rather than rejection. He had flirted with her, and there was a connection between them. She could even think that he was right. If she was to travel with him to London it would be dangerous to move their relationship into more intimate areas.

She considered his offer and shook her head. "Like a trip to the dentist, this is best done swiftly. If we start a little later than you planned, I can cancel my engagements, speak to my officers, and be ready."

"Very well. I do regret this development, Lady Arradale, but it will have many benefits."

"Exactly like a trip to the dentist. Unpleasant, but beneficial in the end."

"You have it. There only remain the details of the journey. Will you want your own coach?"

That pushed her directly into some startling thoughts. Days beside him in a closed carriage? And yet, how ridiculous to roll down the Great North Road in separate vehicles. "I would be delighted to travel with you, my lord. My maid, of course, would share the coach."

"And my valet." A neat parry. Almost as if he might fear assault by her.

"And I would require my own servants and baggage, so at least one more coach and a baggage cart."

"But of course."

She nodded. "Then we should be able to leave by noon."

He looked at her, and truly those dark eyes were capable of expressing an elusive but comforting warmth. He took her hand and raised it to his lips. "I will stand your friend, Lady Arradale, my word on it. And send you home again safe, still free to fly."

She let her hand linger in his for a moment, relishing the warmth and truly regretting the kiss he would not allow. "I resent needing your protection, you know."

His lips twitched. "An almost universal emotion," he remarked, and releasing her hand, he returned to his own room.

Diana stood for a moment, gazing at the door, but stroking the hand he had kissed with the other. So, this wasn't the last night after all, and soon they would be together as never before, for days. She wasn't sure what would come of that, or what she wanted.

With a sigh, she took off her robe, extinguished her candles, and climbed into the big bed, where a sudden fit of shivering overtook her. To be declared insane! She lived in a modern age, and in a nation where the power of kings was supposed to be curtailed by his lords and commons, and yet she was at risk. If not for the Marquess of Rothgar she could be at very serious risk.

She thanked heaven for him, for the events that had tangled his family with hers, but at the same time, as she had said, she resented it. It was so unfair that her sex created such problems. Perhaps she resented and feared most the fact that when she'd asked for the kiss, it had not been lust, or even curiosity. It had been something deeper, a sense of common cause and understanding. That silken thread, grown strong and warm.

She was fascinated by the Marquess of Rothgar, and he saw her as nothing but another dependent needing his protection.

One thing was sure. Despite her teasing, she would do nothing to risk him having to make the ultimate sacrifice and marry her. Returning home a virgin countess, free to rule again in the north was one thing. Returning home Lord

Rothgar's virgin bride was surely more than her over-wrought and frustrated senses could bear.

Rothgar had sent Fettler off to his bed before visiting the countess. His valet was extremely discreet, but there was no reason to test the poor man beyond bearing.

He undressed without assistance. Absurd to have servants to do such things for him except that it was expected and provided worthwhile employment. All was image. Sometimes he felt an urge to rebel, but he'd put that sort of rebellion behind him long ago.

At his father's graveside, in fact.

As he untied his cravat and the ribbon tying back his hair, his eyes came to rest on the small portrait of a child that hung above the white marble fireplace, and he strolled over. Reluctantly. He'd spent too much time looking at the picture as it was.

Though there was no indication of the artist, it was excellently done. It captured a young child in a natural pose, sitting on a grassy bank, holding two restless kittens in plump arms. The dark blond curls were doubtless silky, because the blue ribbon that was supposed to hold them back had slipped to one side. Her simple white dress was rucked up, showing a stockinged leg from the knee down. The stocking had sagged into rumples around her ankle.

Unconscious or uncaring of disarray, she looked up at the world, rosy with laughter and joy, soft lips parted, blue eyes twinkling. The sort of child anyone would want to pick up and hug.

He became aware for the first time that he was barred from going closer by a cloth-shrouded shape. He'd forgotten—alarming in itself. After the display of the automaton earlier, he'd had it brought here so he could supervise its packing in the morning.

He gently removed the cloth and considered both children.

Identical, though the boy was more solemn. There was even a detail he hadn't noticed before. At the girl's shoulder, a bluebird sat on a branch.

The son who would never be. The daughter who, though perfect in herself, would never be the son so desperately wanted.

Would the countess have been happier if the boy had been real? Very likely. People were usually happier in conventional situations. With luck she would have married a man who appreciated her spirit and intelligence, and be an adored wife and mother by now. Mother perhaps to another happy little girl, and a solemn, impish little boy.

Children who would never exist, because of the hard choices she had made.

Understandable choices.

Marriage presented tremendous dangers to her. Few men could accept subordinate status to their wife, and if they wished to, society would not permit it. If she married, the men around here would breathe a sigh of relief and deal with the husband, who would legally be her representative as soon as the vows were said. After all, any decisions or administrative actions he objected to would instantly become null.

"A husband and wife are one person," the law said, "and that person is the husband."

The men would ignore her, and the women would expect her to surrender manly interests and become one of themselves.

Though marriage settlements could be drawn up so that her property was secure, her husband would have many rights of access to it. If she protested and he beat her, she would have no recourse unless she could prove excessive cruelty.

These matters did not stop most women from marrying. They had less to lose, and their income and dower property could be well protected by sound marriage settlements. They were an immense barrier to a woman in the countess's unusual position.

If she could magically produce a brother now and no longer be the troubled Countess of Arradale, would she?

Unlikely. It went against nature to retreat from hard-won

achievements, even if they were a burden. To do so made nonsense of the pain along the way.

He touched the lad's hair, allowing himself to think for a moment of the children he would never have. He had not recognized the sacrifice it was until recently, with tiny Mallorens springing up around him. He was not unsympathetic to Bryght's position, either. In his situation he'd feel the same protectiveness toward his child, and the same anger if others would not bend.

He, no more than the countess, could change course, however. His decision was logical, and any wavering was only because of the spate of weddings and births. This, thank heavens, was the last of the weddings.

Perhaps, he admitted, he also wavered because of the Countess of Arradale. Unique could well describe her, and her unique nature drew him. Bold, clever, direct, daring. And hauntingly vulnerable.

He remembered what Fettler had said—about her knocking on the door earlier. He thought he knew what she'd had in mind, and it suggested that a marriage in name only would not be easy for either of them.

So. He flung the cloth back over the automaton and stripped quickly out of the rest of his clothes. Such a marriage must be avoided at all costs. He must see her safe home from London without it.

Chapter 10

It was no hardship for Diana to rise early because she'd hardly slept for thoughts of madhouses, the marquess, unfinished tasks, the marquess, kisses, the marquess, coach journeys, the marquess . . .

Before the clock struck two she knew she should have decided to travel in her own coach, but it was too late now. At least in part because she didn't want to. The thought of days by his side sent shivers through her, good and bad.

And nights at inns. At least two nights at inns. They'd dine together, just the two of them. They'd talk, intimately across a table as in the card game. Surely she'd learn more of him. Perhaps she'd be able to satisfy some of her itching curiosity about his nature, his mind, his view of the world.

At three she rose to light her candles and write out lists of the instructions bubbling through her mind. She managed to fall asleep then, but woke at first light and gave up. She summoned Clara and put into action the extensive and complicated plans for departure and absence.

She sent a note up to Wenscote, summoning Rosa and Brand. She hated to bother them so soon after the wedding, but she knew Rosa would never forgive her if she left without a proper farewell.

With her rooms already a swirl of packing, and Mr. Turcott supervising instructions and plans for a month or so, she sent to ask if her mother was awake yet. When the maid returned to say yes, she hurried off to inform the dowager of her journey to London, wondering how to explain it without worrying her.

Her mother, however, propped up in bed eating breakfast while Mrs. Turcott read to her from a memoir of some sort, seemed to think a trip to court delightful.

"How kind of the queen. And how kind of the marquess to escort you. So unpleasant to travel without a gentleman." Her eyes twinkled with other meanings and hopes.

"I usually travel without difficulty, Mother. And I expect court to be a dead bore."

"Of course," her mother agreed, startling her. "But there will be opportunity for livelier entertainments, and enjoyment of London."

"London will be emptying for the summer."

That did daunt her mother a little, but then she smiled. "I'm sure you'll find some excitement, dear. You always do. And I'm sure the marquess will want to keep an eye on you. After all, you're almost family to him now, aren't you?"

That was too close to the point. In the night Diana had realized that no matter what happened, there would always be a connection through Rosa. She'd never be able to put the marquess completely out of her life.

She gave up trying to explain things, and hurried on her way. A footman brought the news that Rosa was here, so after a pause in the estate office to deal with a few more matters of business, she went to the drawing room, finding all her guests there.

Aware of looks both curious and speculative, she joined Brand and Rosa, taking Rosa's hands. "You look radiant."

"Well of course." Rosa smiled at Brand by her side, but then turned back to Diana. "What is all this about London? I thought you never wanted to go there again."

"I'm given little choice. The queen—"

"Diana!" She was swept into Elf's arms. "Oh, you poor thing!"

What had the marquess said? Diana didn't want to tell anyone about the threat of the madhouse.

"Court!" Elf exclaimed. "You'll *expire* of tedium! Especially now the queen is so near her time."

"At least that means it will only be for a few weeks," Diana said.

"That will seem like an eon, I promise you. I told Bey we'd return to London with him, but he thinks not."

Diana glanced over to where he was chatting to Lord Bryght and Lord Steen, wondering if there was some dark motive in that. But to Elf she said, "Of course not. You have things you want to do up here."

"But we will return speedily. Fort agrees." With a grin, she added, "Cutting short an exploration of cloth manufacturies is no great hardship to him."

Diana felt a tension ease. "I confess, having you nearby would be a relief."

Elf smiled, but her eyes flickered to the marquess. "Will you mind traveling south with my brother?"

"No more than he will mind traveling south with me," Diana replied, striving for a note of boredom. "I plan to take a number of books I have been wishing to read."

"His coach is very comfortable, at least. Just remember, don't play cards with him for anything but love!" Then she seemed to rethink her words and flush, but the Steens broke the moment by declaring that they were ready to leave.

Their children were already restless, eager to get on with the journey, so Diana went over to say farewell. Lady Steen smiled. "I don't envy you your weeks at court, Lady Arradale, but my brother will take care of you."

Lord Steen kissed her hand and thanked her for her hospitality. "If Rothgar tries to order you about, Lady Arradale, tell him to go to the devil."

Everyone went out to wave them on their way. Soon Lord and Lady Bryght with offspring, and Elf and her husband, were climbing into one carriage for the journey into Lancashire. Only a few days ago Diana had felt invaded, but now she felt bereft, as if this were her own family departing.

Now just Rosa, Brand, and the marquess were left, and in the stable courtyard her chosen belongings were being loaded into carriages and carts for the journey south.

"I don't want to go," she said, but then shook her head. "That's folly."

"Of course you don't," Rosa said. "Neither did I. But as with me, it's just for a little while. You'll be home before the leaves turn color. Come, let me help you with the final packing."

Rothgar watched the two women hurry away, arms around each other, and turned to his brother, prepared for questions.

"Is this truly necessary, Bey?" Brand asked as they strolled back inside the house.

"The king's command?"

"You can usually get the king to do as you wish."

"You overestimate my powers. You know of Lady Arradale's obsession with the earldom's seat in the House of Lords?"

Brand grimaced. "Rosa mentioned it. For a clever woman, she can be foolish—the countess, I mean."

"If even you cannot see any justice in it—"

Brand glanced over. "Are you saying you support her cause?"

"I support the essential logic of it."

"As well say an eldest daughter should inherit a title when there are sons."

"Why not?" Rothgar couldn't resist asking. Levelheaded Brand could rarely be stirred like this.

" 'Struth! But then the whole thing would go through her husband to another family."

"The property would continue in *her* family. Rather more reliably than through a man."

Brand frowned at him. "You're not serious, are you?"

"Consider a world in which inheritance is by age, and if the inheritor is a female, her husband takes her name. Why not?"

Brand shook his head. "Bey, if you go around preaching that idea, you'll end up in Bedlam."

Rothgar laughed. "That, my dear, is precisely my point. However, it has nothing to say about the justice of the countess's cause. Now," he said, as they sat in the drawing room to wait for the countess to be ready to leave, "I want you to keep alert in this region for the unruly French."

"Here?" Brand asked.

"Anywhere in the north. I know you plan to live quietly,

but news travels, especially of foreigners. With peace, some French are visiting England, and some, alas, are spies. Invasion through Ireland is still a threat, and you might hear of matters on the Lancashire coast. If you hear anything suspicious, send word."

"Does it never stop? I suppose Bryght and Elf have orders, too, on their trip to Liverpool."

"Of course, though I have my own people there. King Louis has a burning desire to be avenged for defeat in the past war."

Brand sat up straight. "The devil you say. He'd be mad to restart hostilities."

"Not if he waits for the right moment. One of his acting ambassador's duties is to find, perhaps create, that moment. The Chevalier D'Eon is not to be underestimated."

"A notable swordsman too, according to Bryght. A man who doubtless knows others of that type. Did he have anything to do with that duel with Curry?"

Rothgar didn't want to get into these matters, especially with Brand, who should be enjoying a carefree marriage. A mistake to have asked his help. Too many mistakes these days. Anyone might think that he was distracted.

"The chevalier and I are on extremely cordial terms," he said.

Brand frowned, undeceived. "Be careful, Bey. From what I hear, that duel was a close-run thing."

Noises in the hall indicated that it was time to depart. Rothgar rose. "All the interesting adventures in life are." He embraced Brand. "Ignore French spies. Grow turnips and babies, and be happy."

"I wish I could give you the same command. But I have one. Don't harm the countess. She's more vulnerable than she appears."

"She'd shoot you for saying it. I intend her no harm, Brand. Only good."

Brand looked at him. "That's what I worry about."

Rothgar laughed and left to set out on a challenging journey south.

*   *   *

By the time they stopped for the night at the Swan in the bustling coaching town of Ferry Bridge, Diana was exhausted. They were expected, a whole floor already claimed and prepared for them, but rather than comforting her, this strained her even more. She was accustomed to traveling in state, but not in quite such grand state as this.

It was the long day's journey which had worn her down, however—that and the marquess's complete lack of interest in her. As planned, she'd provided herself with a number of interesting books, but she'd also hoped to talk to him. The presence of the servants would make it completely safe, and she longed to learn more of his mind.

He, however, had spent the whole time working through what appeared to be important documents. These had even been increased in the mid-afternoon by a courier who had intercepted them and delivered a thick sealed package.

During each break to change horses, he had courteously strolled with her, making effortless small talk about the countryside, or the lighter aspects of national affairs. Even when they stopped to eat it had been the same.

She'd recognized that these were skillfully woven barriers and felt mortified. Clearly Fettler had told him of her visit to his rooms and he'd guessed the reason.

Damn him!

Two more days of this, she thought with a sigh as Clara tidied her for a supper that would doubtless involve more of that deflective small talk. She was tempted to eat in her room, but she'd go down and somehow make it clear to him that she had no designs on his body!

When she entered their private dining room, however, she was surprised to find two strangers with the marquess.

He turned to her. "Ah, Lady Arradale, may I present to you Monsieur de Couriac and his lady?"

The young couple bowed and curtsied, and Diana inclined her head, concealing astonishment. French? Here? But then she remembered that they were now at peace. Officially, at least.

Then her cheeks heated. He was not depending on small talk. He'd gathered distraction and chaperons! Diana smiled

brightly at the wretched people, and declared herself delighted.

Madame de Couriac was not so much pretty as intriguing,
with pointed chin and bright dark eyes. "Lady Arradale,"
she declared with a marked accent, "we are enjoying your so
beautiful country!"

Her tall, square-jawed husband, added, "It has been a sadness not to be able to visit England for so many years."

His English was very good, but he didn't sound as if he
meant what he said. Diana wasn't surprised. The French
rarely pined for English food and landscapes.

She switched to her excellent French. "War is always a
sadness, is it not? You are to dine with us, madame, monsieur? How delightful. You must tell me the latest news from
Paris."

The soup was brought in and they took their places, but
Monsieur de Couriac said, "Alas, my lady, we live quietly in
Normandy and have not recently been to Paris."

Soup passed in talk of travels, but when the fish was
served, Diana caught an intent glance the Frenchman cast
his wife. Diana had been talking almost exclusively to de
Couriac, but now she followed the look. Madame de
Couriac had placed her hand on the marquess's arm and was
leaning toward him as if fascinated.

That raised an even more unwelcome reason for the
French couple being at dinner. Was Lord Rothgar attempting
seduction of the pretty young wife? Despite a pang of hurt,
Diana turned brightly to the husband and asked his opinion
of London.

Lud, but the marquess must be mad. They were in danger
of having a duel on their hands!

Could such a clever man really be so foolish? She contrived to observe him while trying to hold the husband's
attention. Soon she knew she wasn't imagining it.

She'd never seen anyone eat a meal with the blatant sen-
suality that Madame de Couriac displayed. The woman ate
little, but that was because she made such a performance of
it. She bit slowly into food, and chewed slowly, often lick-

ing her red lips. Once or twice, she even licked her fingers, gazing into the marquess's eyes.

Right under her husband's nose!

Despite Diana's efforts, de Couriac was clearly aware, so why was he doing nothing about it? Perhaps he thought a Frenchman here was powerless against an Englishman, especially a marquess. The French aristocracy had far more sweeping powers than the English.

Whatever the reason, he must surely take action sooner or later. Having failed to distract him, Diana turned her attention to Madame de Couriac and engaged her in conversation about fashion.

The woman was clearly not pleased, but had to oblige. For the rest of the meal, Diana relentlessly held her attention with talk of hairstyles, slippers, lotions for the complexion, and means of polishing the nails. She had never talked so long about such matters before in her life.

By the time the meal ended, Madame de Couriac had— despite efforts—managed only the occasional aside to Lord Rothgar. Diana couldn't tell how the marquess felt about it. If anything, he seemed amused. She resisted with difficulty an urge to glower at the man. Couldn't he sense the fiery tension coming from Monsieur de Couriac?

Thoroughly disgusted, she did finally flash a dark look at him and found him at his most enigmatic. He did not, however, look at all put out. Of course not. All her efforts had only delayed the inevitable. A tendency to burst into tears about it was her own problem entirely. Even though he was a reckless philanderer, she'd still do her best to protect him from himself.

She rose from the table, smiling at the French couple. "I'm sure you will want to retire early, so as to make a good start on your journey tomorrow."

"On the contrary," said Madame de Couriac with a smug smile. "We are spending some days here."

"Well *we* must continue on tomorrow," Diana said.

"And thus *we* must retire, dear lady?" the marquess asked, making it sound wicked.

She glared at him, but had to abandon the struggle. If he

was determined on folly, there was nothing she could do. "*I* must," she said frostily, and inclined her head to them all. "Good night."

They all rose, but as she left she was sure they would immediately sit again, though she couldn't imagine why Monsieur de Couriac wouldn't take the excuse to drag his wife away. Perhaps, she suddenly thought, they planned one of those *ménage à trois* events she had read about. Bizarre, but what did she really know of such matters?

Closing the door of her room with a sharp snap, she acknowledged that a good part of her ill-feeling was jealousy. She was jealous of Madame de Couriac for the pleasures of the coming night, but also of her freedom to seduce a man who took her fancy.

Oh, what folly, she thought, unpinning her cap and pulling out the pins that confined her curls. The lady had a husband, and therefore should not be free at all.

Thoroughly disgruntled, she went to the window to look down on the street. It was quiet now that the sun was setting, except for the occasional rattle of a late coach seeking a change before pushing on to York or Doncaster. She was tempted to go out to enjoy some fresh air and exercise, but she would only be an object of curiosity. Everyone here must know that the Countess of Arradale was resting at the Swan, and with the great Marquess of Rothgar, no less!

She remembered her few hours of freedom last year when she'd played the part of Rosa's spotty serving maid. There had been heady pleasure in being ignored and unremarkable. That maid could be out there now, chatting to other servants, eating a bun with sticky fingers, perhaps even flirting a bit . . .

She eyed Clara, who was much of a size, but then put the idea aside. It wouldn't do. Without the face paint, servant's clothes were pointless.

The marquess could go out, of course. He'd be recognized, but he wouldn't care. She couldn't put her finger on why it was different for a lady but she knew it was.

There was the simple danger of abduction. The new laws made abduction into marriage less likely, but the laws that gave a husband control over his wife's property meant it was always a risk. Of course, any man who tried that with her would regret it, but how to *show* that so a fortune hunter would never even consider it?

She was a woman, and therefore—the world assumed—weak and vulnerable. With a wry smile she contemplated walking around with a pistol strapped to her waist. And a knife or two . . .

She might even have done it except that now she couldn't afford extra notoriety. She had to be a perfect, vulnerable lady or risk being clapped into a madhouse.

Oh God. She rested her face in her hands. During her recent inquiries she'd visited the asylum in York. It was a well-run place, but hell on earth, with screams and cries, inmates with blank faces or manic laughter, and others who appeared normal until they started to speak.

What if the woman who'd earnestly whispered that she was a foreign princess—

No, no. Of course she wasn't. She spoke broad Yorkshire. All the same, Diana could imagine herself, bedraggled by merely being there, trying to convince a stranger that she was a grand lady, unfairly imprisoned.

She straightened, fighting back from panic. One thing she knew. The marquess would never permit that. She'd spoken truly when she said that she resented needing his protection, but she was grateful for it, too. Grateful especially for his promise to marry her as ultimate security.

Then her eyes narrowed as she imagined having to be a complaisant wife as he sought the beds of women like Madame de Couriac. And the exotic Sappho. Perdition, that was certainly another reason to avoid that extreme. She'd end up shooting someone!

She leaned at the open window, elbows on the sill, wondering if he and the damnable Frenchwoman were already tangled in his sheets. Then she heard a patter of rapid French below.

Well, she thought, spirits lifting, at least they weren't tangled yet. Madame de Couriac and her husband were below in the street, talking rapidly and quietly.

Arguing? Perhaps he'd finally put his foot down.

"I have tried!" the woman exclaimed.

"Not hard enough. I saw his interest."

"What do you want me to do? Go to his room naked?"

"If it serves the king, yes."

The woman made a hissing noise. "He is not that sort of man, Jean-Louis. He must do the asking."

"Then make him ask."

A sudden menace in the man's voice made Diana lean out far enough to see. He had his wife's arm in what looked like a cruel grasp and she was staring up at him, angry but afraid. "I don't know—" She broke off a cry. He must have tightened that grip. "I'll try!"

He let her go, casting a quick look around. He didn't look up, but Diana ducked back anyway.

What were they up to? Why would the man be so desperate to have his wife become Lord Rothgar's mistress? For money? A threat to tell the world if not paid? She shook her head. She couldn't imagine the marquess caring about that.

But then she sucked in a breath. For blood? If Monsieur de Couriac came upon his wife in the marquess's bed, he could force a duel over it. She knew Lord Rothgar was a formidable swordsman, but there must be better in the world. Elf had mentioned some concern that the previous duel had been an attempt to kill her brother.

Was this another?

With a more skillful swordsman?

Heart pounding, she peered out again, but the French couple had gone.

Chapter 11

"Clara," Diana said. "Go to Lord Rothgar's room and say that I wish to speak with him."

As she waited, she tried to think how to phrase her delicate warning, but in moments Clara returned. "He's not in at the moment, milady."

Already at an assignation? No, there hadn't been time. How inconsiderate of him, however, to leave the inn. "Go back and say that I must speak to him as soon as he returns."

Clara hurried out and Diana went over that conversation again. Had de Couriac said something about serving the king? Perdition. She couldn't quite remember. She thought so.

Perhaps it wasn't attempted assassination, but espionage. All those documents. Some were doubtless sensitive, perhaps even secret. Perhaps Madame de Couriac was meant to steal them.

A less dangerous plan than murder, but still the marquess should be warned. And he, plague take him, was out.

This fine and comfortable room in the best inn was beginning to feel like a prison. When Clara returned, Diana demanded a light cloak and the attendance of her footman, and escaped to enjoy the evening. People did notice her, but it wasn't unbearable.

She was alert for sight of the French couple or the marquess, and it was the latter she saw first, taking farewell of a man who looked like a country lawyer. She hurried over, but conscious of the windows of the inn above their heads, she said, "I request a moment of your time, my lord."

"I lay a hundred, a thousand at your command, dear lady."

Rolling her eyes at this courtly manner, she turned to stroll down the street, until they were far enough from the inn. "I overheard the de Couriacs speaking, my lord."

"And?"

She glanced up, embarrassed by the implication of what she was about to say. "He seemed to be urging her to . . . to make advances to you."

"The lady did seem a little bold."

"And perhaps dangerous?" she pointed out, wanting to poke him. Were all men so oblivious when a pretty woman made sheep's eyes at them?

"All women are dangerous, Lady Arradale, as we have already established."

"*I* am not likely to get you killed."

"I wish I could be sure of that. But," he continued, "why do you think Madame de Couriac's charms fatal?"

Her fears began to seem overblown. "For no reason except their urgency. I think he mentioned something about service to the king. Could they be spies? Have an eye to your papers? Or am I foolish to think them up to no good?"

"Not foolish, no." He turned them back toward the inn. "Thank you for the warning. I will take care of it."

Despite that, he was disregarding the more serious danger. "What if the plan is to force a duel, my lord? To murder you."

His eyes met hers. "I am hard to kill."

"But not impossible! I heard of the duel you fought in London. If anyone plans such mischief, they have a measure of your skill now."

"You think Monsieur de Couriac is sent to be my executioner?"

"I think a wise man would give him no cause for a challenge."

His eyes twinkled. "Ah, but she is charming, is she not—?"

Before Diana could argue further, Madame de Couriac dashed out of the door of the Swan. "Ah, Lord Rothgar. Thank heavens you are here!" she declared in rapid French. "Jean-Louis is suffering the most dreadful pains. We have sent for the doctor, but our English is not so good and at times like these, not even so good as that. It is a dreadful imposition, but pleas . . ."

Hands on his arm, she looked up piteously.

"Perhaps I could help, madame," Diana said sweetly. "My French is tolerable."

The Frenchwoman turned with a false, rather frantic smile. "Alas, Lady Arradale, my poor husband, he is half undressed—"

"I see. I do hope it is nothing serious, Madame. Please call on me if you should need anything. Womanly comfort, perhaps."

Diana resisted the urge to flash the marquess a warning glance as she left them. Surely it wasn't necessary. He was reputed to be devilishly clever. He must be able to see through a stratagem such as this.

Rothgar went with Madame de Couriac, on guard but also curious to know exactly what she and her husband were up to. The countess could be right in thinking they were after his documents, but equally correct in thinking they were after his life.

If the latter, it would be another mathematical point. He suspected D'Eon of involvement in the duel with Curry. If the de Couriacs were up to mischief, it was all likely linked to the French.

He smiled over Lady Arradale's sharp wits and swift action. Admirable, but not particularly welcome when she must play the part of the perfect lady—the sort who would be blind to plots and politics. A lady who would scream at a mouse, faint at a shock, and react to danger by throwing herself into the arms of the nearest male.

Not by trying to rescue him.

The next weeks were likely to be even more difficult than he'd anticipated.

But interesting.

Monsieur de Couriac was lying on top of the bedclothes, groaning. The extent of his undress was an undone waistband and a loosened shirt.

"You have sent for the doctor, you said?" Rothgar asked.

"Yes." Madame de Couriac put her hand to her head. "At least, I think so . . . I am so frightened . . ." She moved close, and he obliged by putting his arm around her. She turned to press her face into his chest. A knock at the door didn't even make her twitch.

So.

He put her aside and opened it.

"Doctor Ribble," the young man there said. Slim and serious, he at least seemed likely to play his part properly.

"Come in, Doctor. You see your patient. I am Lord Rothgar, serving as translator if needed."

The doctor's sharp look said he recognized the name, but pleasantly, his demeanor did not change. He went over to the bed and asked questions, which Rothgar translated, then examined the patient.

In the end the doctor said, "I can see no reason for the pain, monsieur, though there is some tenderness. All I can suggest is rest. Often these things pass of themselves and medicines can make them worse."

Rothgar approved, but Madame de Couriac stiffened. "And you think we *pay* for that!" she snapped in her imperfect English. "You must do something!"

"Madame, there is nothing—"

"You are a . . . a *charlatan!*" She turned to Rothgar. "How do you say?"

"Exactly that, madame. Charlatan. However, the good doctor is probably correct. It is doubtless something your husband ate."

"But you, but I, we ate the same! I insist on treatment, or me, I will not pay."

Tight-lipped, Doctor Ribble opened his bag and took out a bottle, pouring some dark liquid into a glass. "There, madame. If you give him a teaspoonful of that in water every hour it might soothe him, and it will do no harm."

"So," the lady declared, magnificent dark eyes flashing, "first there is nothing. Now there is something. Me, I think you hate the French! You want us all to die!"

"Not at all, madame. That will be five shillings for the

visit, and a further two for the medicine. If you need more, you can send a servant to my house for it. However, do not hesitate to summon me if your husband's condition worsens."

Madame de Couriac extracted a silk purse from her pocket and passed it to Rothgar with a faltering hand. "Please, my lord. I am too distressed . . . Please find the coins for him."

As she staggered back to hover over the bed, Rothgar obliged, resisting the urge to share a smile with the doctor. He would remember Doctor Ribble if he ever had need of a physician in this locality. He was sure the medicine was a harmless syrup with some herbs to make it taste unpleasant. Who, after all, would believe in a pleasant medicine? Perhaps even a touch of opium to send the patient to sleep.

When the doctor had left, he turned to find Madame de Couriac tenderly feeding some of the medicine to a resistant husband. The man saw Rothgar watching and said in French, "It tastes foul, my lord."

"Such things usually do, monsieur. I advise you to take it, however. The doctor seemed to know what he was about."

De Couriac drained the glass then shuddered.

"Now," cooed his wife, "get under the covers, my darling, and rest. Soon, I am sure, you will be completely well again."

Though he had no reason to stay, Rothgar did, intrigued to see what happened next. His journey had been no secret. His night here had been arranged in advance. He'd be flattered to think Madame de Couriac was taking extreme measures to get into his bed, but it was more likely to be another attempt on his life.

The interesting question was, why? Why were the French so desperate to dispose of him? He had influence with the king, and was known to advise the king to stand firm against them. He was urging limits on exports of anything that would help them rebuild their fleet, and the speedy destruction of the fortifications at Dunkirk.

None of it seemed justification for murder. There was always the chance that Madame de Couriac could shed some light on matters.

When the woman had her husband settled to her liking she turned to Rothgar, a picture of grateful womanhood, and ran forward to seize his hands. "How can I thank you, my lord? You have been so kind, so gracious . . ." Then she swayed. "Oh, I feel . . . Oh."

He caught her against his body as he was clearly expected to. So tempting at such moments to step aside, leaving the lady to tumble to the floor. He'd done it a time or two.

This time, however, he tenderly supported. "Madame, please. Come to my dining room for a little cognac. We must let your husband sleep."

"You are too kind," she whispered, limp against him. His role now was to sweep her into his arms, but he merely supported her toward the door and down the stairs. On the lower floor he glanced at Lady Arradale's door, expecting to see her peering out. He was sure she would be if she'd known just when he'd return.

He sympathized with her curiosity, but hoped she'd not interfere before he discovered exactly what was going on.

He guided the Frenchwoman into the dining parlor, and to the chaise, slipping off her shoes and raising her feet so she was reclining. Having made it impossible for him to sit beside her, he poured cognac—his own reserve, carried with him—for both of them.

She sipped, sighed, and said, "You are extraordinarily kind, my lord. I am so grateful. I find many of your countrymen are not so sympathetic."

"Our nations were so recently at war, madame."

"Alas. But you?" Eyes on him, she drank from her glass with an exaggerated pursing of the lips, pressing her lower lip down with the glass as she slowly drew it away. A whore's trick. "Do you," she purred, "still feel enmity toward the people of France?"

"I try not to let my feelings for a nation affect my feelings for individuals, madame."

"So," she said with another enticing sip and a sliding look

from under her long, darkened lashes, "you do not feel enmity for *me*?"

"Assuredly not."

"I am so glad," she murmured, holding out a hand. When he took it, she curled her legs and predictably drew him down to sit on the chaise beside her feet. "I feel no enmity toward you, Lord Rothgar. None at all . . ."

"Why should you, indeed?"

That seemed to disconcert her for a moment, but she put aside her glass and pressed her stockinged feet against his thigh, flexing her toes there. "Quite the reverse, in fact . . ." She held out both hands, swaying closer. "Oh, my lord, this is a madness . . . But . . . I cannot resist you. All evening I have wanted you!"

Agile as a cat, she was on him, her arms snaked around his neck. "Take me!"

He obliged, and at least took her hungry, perfumed mouth, though he was not at all fond of patchouli. Her hands began to work frantically at the buttons of his waistcoat.

He seized them. "Slowly, madame, slowly. I am a man who likes to drink pleasure's cup one sip at a time . . ."

Sitting bolt upright on a chair in her bedroom, Diana seethed with restlessness. What was going on? What should she do?

She'd set her own servants to watching, and knew the doctor had visited, found nothing particularly wrong, and left. She also knew that the marquess had taken the Frenchwoman, swooning, to his private dining room.

Why? She could guess. In his place, she too would want to find out exactly what the de Couriacs were up to. A little part of her, however, still worried that he'd been sucked into the viperous woman's coils. The urge to rush to interrupt was almost uncontrollable, but she did control it.

She had a man watching de Couriac's room who would tell her if the Frenchman began to stir.

It was surely folly to think that the marquess was putting himself in danger, especially after her warning, but she couldn't just ignore it and go to bed.

She was *not*, she told herself, upset at the thought of what might be going on in the dining room next door. Not at all. She didn't deny curiosity—she'd give a great deal for a hole in the wall—but that's all it was.

Not jealousy. She could never be jealous of a creature like Madame de Couriac.

At that moment her footman knocked and came in. "There's some noises from the Frenchie's room, milady. He's likely dressing."

At last! She leaped up. "Go back to the bottom of the stairs. Here." She thrust a heavy book into his hands. "If he starts to come downstairs, drop it. Go!"

She left the door open and stood there, ears straining for the thump though she knew it would be loud enough to hear through the closed door.

Perhaps the Frenchman had just been finding the chamberpot. If not, he was either preparing to search through the marquess's papers, or more likely, to burst in and issue a lethal challenge.

Come on. Come on.

If Monsieur de Couriac did not come downstairs she'd have no excuse to interrupt the marquess and the Frenchwoman. That would be a shame both for her curiosity and her jealousy.

No. She would *not* be jealous or she'd go mad. Doubtless London was full of the man's lovers, including the mysterious scholarly poet—

Thump.

Diana jumped, then with a deep breath, followed her plan. She walked briskly along the corridor and into the dining room without knocking, ready with her exclamation of shock.

"Oh," she said, finding the marquess sitting on the chaise with one of Madame de Couriac's slender stockinged feet in his hands. He appeared to be massaging it, and the lady had been lounging back languorously.

Madame had given a little scream, however, and sat up. Now she was staring at Diana in befuddlement. Clearly not whom she had expected. She pulled her foot free even so, and swiveled to sit straight and put on her shoes. "So sooth-ing, my lord."

"Indeed." He rose, expression unreadable. "You require something, my lady?"

You could rub my feet, she thought, but said, "Cognac."

"The servants are not available? I must speak to them about it."

Was he annoyed? Impossible to tell. However, he poured some cognac into a glass, and turned to pass it to her. The door burst open and a disheveled Monsieur de Couriac stag-gered in.

And stopped.

"Monsieur," said Lord Rothgar at his most benign, "you are recovered. How wonderful. Cognac?"

After a frozen moment, Madame de Couriac leaped to her feet and ran over to her husband. "Jean-Louis, *cheri*. I am so happy! But come back to bed and rest. You cannot be com-pletely well."

After a furious, frustrated glare, Monsieur de Couriac al-lowed himself to be led out.

The marquess walked over and shut the door, leaving Diana alone with him. Her nerves twitched. He was angry? How could he be angry? She might have just saved his life!

He put the glass of brandy into her hands. "Perhaps we have some confusion, Lady Arradale, as to who is guarding whom."

He *was* angry. How typical of a man. Warming the cognac between her palms, she said, "Are you saying you wanted to be caught, my lord?"

"Massaging the lady's feet? Unusual, but hardly more than that. Especially when she was so very distressed about her poor husband's illness."

"*I* couldn't know you would be doing that."

He sipped and made no comment.

Diana tasted the cognac, then warmed it some more. "So, you were deliberately avoiding anything more scandalous?"

"It seemed wise."

Should she apologize? Damned if she would. Damned,

too, if she'd be dismissed without knowing what was happening.

"Very well," she said, sitting on the chaise still warm from Madame de Couriac's body, and even carrying a ghost of her suggestive perfume. "What are they up to?"

He came and sat at the other end, as he'd sat with the other woman except that three feet of blue damask stretched between them, uninvaded. "Perhaps it is as it appears, Lady Arradale. She is wanton, he is ill."

"Perhaps."

"You doubt it?" He put his glass aside. "Put your foot in my lap."

Diana stared at him. "Why?"

"I am in the mood for rubbing feet."

He was in a strange and possibly dangerous mood, but she longed to know what it felt like. She slipped her left foot out of her shoe and shifted so she could place it on his thigh. That alone required a mouthful of fortifying spirits. He put both hands around her foot and began to rub her instep with his thumbs.

She suppressed a moan of pleasure. "She may be wanton," she said as steadily as she could, "but he is not ill."

"He likely is somewhat after the potion the doctor left. But no, you are fundamentally correct."

"So, what are they up to?"

His thumbs were working now along the base of her toes. She could not help but relax back and feared she must look as limp and languorous as the Frenchwoman had.

"They could have been after my documents," he said, thumbs working magic, but eyes on hers, "but then de Couriac would have gone to my bedchamber, not here. Therefore . . ."

"Therefore," she supplied, "he was hoping to force a duel. Are you further ahead for knowing that?"

"A little."

"He could have demanded a duel anyway. You were alone with his wife."

"Who had asked for my help and been seen in distress. No, he could not have insisted on a duel."

She had to believe he understood these arcane male ways. "What now, then?"

His hands stilled. "Now, Lady Arradale, I should kiss your foot." One hand, one nail, trailed along her instep around her heel and up to the bone of her ankle. "But that requires the removal of your stocking. Which is an interlude of its own . . ."

As his fingers slipped up from her ankle toward her calf, she stared into his dark eyes, dizzied.

"Do you wish the game to continue?" he asked.

Her rising heart rate steadied. This, she saw, was like his invitation to seduction at the ball. Not so much an amorous petition as a dare. Even, perhaps, a minor punishment for meddling in his affairs.

With aching regret, she pulled her foot out of his lax hands and sat up straight. "I don't think so."

"I didn't think so, either."

She drained her brandy and stood, but had to ask, "Why did you do that?"

He, against etiquette, remained seated. "Your curiosity was palpable."

Yes, punishment of a sort. She refused to show embarrassment.

Perhaps she should have called his bluff, but she knew he'd have gone through with it, even to sex. Which was an interesting thought in itself. He might think of it as punishment, but she could see it in a completely different light.

"I *am* curious," she said, ignoring the heat in her cheeks. "About a great many things."

"Curiosity, however, is one of the scourges of the soul, and enlightenment can lead to the darkest paths."

"How tedious to always move in the light." Could she? Here? With him?

"But safer."

"Do we want to be safe?"

He did rise then. "Some perils are far too serious for games. And you, my dear, are playing games." He raised her hand to kiss it with no greater warmth than courtesy required. "Good night, Lady Arradale. We leave early in the morning."

Dismissed, Diana could do nothing but leave, though she couldn't resist one glance back. Had he really meant what she thought he'd meant—that their interlude had been perilous for *him*?

In her room, she stood limp as Clara undressed her and prepared her for bed, trying to grasp what had just happened.

His hands on her feet.

A simple thing, and not particularly wicked. She could have Clara do that for her if she wished.

It would not be the same.

The slide of his fingers up from her ankle to her calf.

Still, nothing shocking except the suggestion that she let him remove her stocking. When she'd thought longingly of lust and sin, the removal of her stocking had not been a significant part of it.

Nor had massage of her feet. What a lot there was to learn!

Curiosity, however, did not explain this devastation in her mind. She was overcome, dazzled, by the suggestion that despite his cool manner, the Marquess of Rothgar might be experiencing the same perilous pull to dangerous interaction that she was.

In bed in the dark, with Clara sleeping beside her, Diana lay awake, mind fluttering around ideas like a moth around a glass lamp. And that, of course, was the problem.

A clear barrier stood between her and the tantalizing flame. Beat against it as she might, the fire was not for her. She could not afford to marry, and now she knew that he could not be a casual lover.

As he had implied, the very heat between them made it far too dangerous to approach.

Chapter 12

Diana descended to breakfast the next morning warily, but if the marquess had slid out of control for even one moment the night before, he had corrected the flaw. Over eggs and excellent sausages, he treated her precisely as an aristocratic lady he was escorting to London. The effortless flow of small talk was again a carefully woven iron grille between them.

Diana could only be relieved when his manservant, Fettler, knocked and entered.

"Yes?" the marquess asked.

"About the French couple, my lord. They left in the night."

Lord Rothgar's brows rose. "Without paying their shot? How reprehensible."

Diana came to the alert. The marquess did not, in fact, sound surprised. For the first time she wondered if he had ruthlessly disposed of his potential assassins.

"As to that, milord," the valet said, "they left adequate coins. And traces of blood on the floor."

Diana stared. Her speculations had been idle, but now she had to take them seriously.

"What is more," the valet said, "a servant nearby heard a scream and then a cry."

"A feminine scream, and then a masculine cry?" Diana demanded. First one murder, then the other. She was beginning to be shocked after all.

The middle-aged man turned to her. "Precisely, milady."

"Then," she asked, "did anyone actually see them leave?"

"Oh yes, milady. They roused a groom to saddle their horses. It was with him they left the money. He would not have let them depart otherwise."

"Wounded?" she asked, both deflated and relieved, and casting a quick glance at the marquess. Amused by her again.

"The groom could not be sure, milady, but he thought Monsieur de Couriac favored his arm, and the lady might have had a mark on her face."

"Anything else, Fettler?" the marquess asked. When the valet said no, he dismissed him, then turned to her, easing the plate of sausages toward her side of the table. "Do have more of these, Lady Arradale, as you speculate."

Diana speared one with her sharp fork. "Don't patronize me, my lord." It also galled that he had noticed that she'd enjoyed two of the sausages already.

"I do beg your pardon. I certainly have no desire to be fatherly. What do you make of the little saga?"

Ignoring a twitch at the thought of what relationship he might desire, Diana said, "That he hit her for failing to compromise you, and she did something—perhaps with a knife—in response." She cut into the meat. "I certainly would have done."

"I will bear that in mind." He served himself more coffee. "So why leave, especially if he was wounded?"

Diana chewed, thinking. "Out of fear of you? Or," she added, "out of fear of their master." She halted in the process of raising another piece of sausage to her mouth. "To prepare some other trap?"

He did not pale in apprehension, of course, but he did say, "How fortunate that we travel with armed outriders."

Diana put her food down. "Lord Rothgar, why would the French be so determined to murder you? As one caught in the middle, I think I have a right to know."

"What reasons does anyone have for wishing the death of another?"

"A tendency to ask too many questions?" she responded tartly. "You are not Socrates, my lord, and I am not your pupil."

A smile tugged at his lips. "Then I will play Socrates to myself. What reasons does anyone have for murder?" He counted on his long fingers. "One: revenge. Extreme, and I don't think I have hurt France to that extent. Two: gain. The only person to gain materially from my death would be Bryght, and he isn't working for the French."

"Three," offered Diana, "fear of what you might reveal."

"I have no secrets." Over her snort of disbelief, he said, "Four: fear of what the victim might do."

"If you have no secrets, milord, you delight in being falsely mysterious." But she sat in thought, meeting his eyes. "The French fear what you might do? You are a one-man Armada?"

"I would like to think so."

"Need I remind you that the Armada failed and sank?"

"Alas," he said, eyes crinkling with what looked like true hilarity. "We can only hope that my armed fleet would manage somewhat better."

"Which presents another problem, my lord," she said, trying to be stern. "The Armada was our enemy. I take as model Great Queen Bess, who stirred the opposition to the Spanish fleet."

"And think foul scorn that any prince of Europe should dare to invade the borders of your realm?" he said, giving a version of the queen's famous speech at Tilbury, when she dispatched her navy to face the mighty foe.

"Precisely, my lord. As I showed last year."

The smile tugged at his lips again, but he said, "Oh dear. Must I remind you of the plan for you to act the *conventional* lady?"

"Perdition." Her cheeks warmed with guilt. "I will do it when necessary."

"So says the drunkard ordered to give up brandy."

"This is my problem, my lord, and I will deal with it."

"Yet I have yoked myself to you in this."

"Not of my choosing!"

"No, but we are bound by fate."

She stared at him. "Until this is over."

He took another sip of coffee. "And when will it be over?"

"When I return north." She was unsure now what they were speaking about.

"This engagement will be over then, but as with the French, the problem will linger. Constant vigilance will be required. This connection, my lady, ends with death. Or with your marriage."

They were not speaking of her behavior.

"Or yours," she suggested breathlessly.

"I will not marry. But even so, it would not end your need of my protection. Outside of marriage, your situation makes you vulnerable."

Now she didn't know what they were talking about.

"I cannot ignore your situation," he said. "I will not intrude, but if problems arise in the future, I will be at your service."

She was not so foolish as to deny the benefits of that, but swallowed bitter disappointment. Protection again. Was that all? "We were talking, I think, of your problems, my lord, not mine. If the French wish to be rid of you, what will you do?"

"There is little defense against a resolute assassin. In this case, however, it seems they wish to make it look like an act of passion rather than one of cold blood."

"Resist passion, then, my lord, and we are both safe."

His tranquil gaze came to rest on hers. "My thought entirely, dear lady."

So, they had not only been speaking of the French. After a frozen moment, Diana looked down at her half-eaten sausage, and found her appetite completely gone.

Safe.

She'd always thought safety promised a damn dull life.

Scarce noticed at the time, she had just enjoyed a heady exchange of wits and barbs of a rare and precious kind. There'd also been something close to friendship, which she certainly had never expected of this man. Not the cozy friendship she had with Rosa, but friendship all the same.

Or perhaps something more.

Safe, indeed.

She put her knife and fork down, pushing the plate aside, and picked up her cup. One sip told her the coffee was cold. She put it down and looked up to find him still watching her, as if he expected some kind of answer.

She took a breath and gave it—the same response she'd given last night. "And if I don't want to be safe?"

"I am pledged to keep you so. From everything. Even despite yourself." He rose and indicated the door. "We should be on our way, Lady Arradale, if we are to make Stamford tonight."

Diana took another deep breath, and released it with care. That was a clear enough warning and statement of intent, and he was doubtless wise. But like the drunkard with a taste for brandy, she didn't want to be wise just yet.

Especially as she felt that she had just started to savor the full riches of the potent spirit.

By the time they rattled over the bridge in Stamford that evening, Diana had a headache and a fierce desire to be unwise, danger or not. Never, never had she imagined that merely sitting by a man for eight hours could cause such wreckage!

It was the fact that he had returned to distant courtesy that had made it all so unendurable.

He had continued to deal with papers, though occasionally—perhaps as light relief—he had read what looked like a dense tome. Out of curiosity, Diana had tried to glimpse the title, but as she was more determined not to be caught looking at him, she had failed.

After all, she'd told herself mile after mile, he was right. If some kind of attraction had sparked between them, it promised disaster not delight. Neither of them wanted to let it develop.

Or rather, it would be highly unwise for either of them to want that.

Aware of him at every moment, she had gone through the motions of reading her books. Even witty Pope had not held her attention.

Her only true distraction had come from studying the roadside and passing riders, alert for sight of the de Couriacs or other potential assassins. By midday, however, she'd decided that fear was a phantasm. The French couple had doubtless realized that they'd made an enemy of an important man and fled.

For the midday meal she and the marquess had shared a table and conversation. She'd not expected anything like that brief spurt of untrammeled conversation at breakfast, of course, but she had hoped for a little of the same warmth.

He had himself completely under control, however. They could have been strangers.

Sometimes she thought they were.

In fact, they were strangers, she told herself as the coach rattled down a narrow Stamford street. They knew little of each other's lives or inner thoughts. Logic fizzled, however, when desire burned, and Diana had to accept that she had fallen into an embarrassing desire for the Marquess of Rothgar.

Throughout the day she had been aware of his body taking up space beside her in the coach. Only inches away, he had even stirred her clothes occasionally when he moved. With any other man she wouldn't have noticed, but with this man every movement sent sparkles down her skin, and each breath was like her own.

Pretending to sleep at one point, she had watched him from under lowered lids. Watched his hands. Feasted on them.

She glanced at them again now. So very beautiful. Long in palm and fingers, but strong in the elegant bones, tendons, and muscles as they moved flexibly, putting away papers and books. That one large ruby set in gold occasionally caught the sunset flame to glow with crimson fire. The delicate beauty of his lace cuffs only emphasized the power of his hands.

Midnight in lace, she remembered. But his hands were not dark or threatening. Not threatening at all. She could imagine them strong around the hilt of a sword, but also re-member them clever against her ankle . . .

Steely power amid silken fragility.

Male and female.

His masculine strength and her silken fragility. Oh yes, she thought as the coach shuddered to a halt in the inn yard of the George, against reason, she would love to be all silken fragility beneath the attention of those very mascu-line hands.

In dazed moments she was in her bedchamber, which was of course perfect and completely prepared for her, in-cluding her own feather pillow. Free of his presence, she recognized that she had teetered on the edge of disaster.

And still did.

After a struggle, she found the strength to resist and sent a message to say she had a headache and would dine in her room. She might long for fragments of the marquess's heady company and attention, but she was sensible enough, she hoped, to avoid fruitless suffering.

And if another set of French spies awaited here, plotting the marquess's demise, he could damn well handle it him-self!

After an hour's rest and a light meal, however, Diana's common sense and equilibrium returned. She could even laugh a little at her overwrought reactions, and wish Rosa were here to share the silliness. She even sent her footman to find out if there were any French guests at the George, especially the de Couriacs. The marquess did not need her protection, did not want her protection, but it was in her nature as much as his to provide it.

After all, she thought, he was having a truly debilitating effect on her, and had implied that he was suffering some-thing similar. Perhaps he wasn't thinking clearly.

Her footman returned to say that there were no French guests.

"And the marquess?" she asked the servant. "Do we know where he is?"

"In his dining room, milady. With a guest."

Images of the de Couriacs immediately popped up. "What sort of guest?"

"A lady, milady, traveling to Nottinghamshire."

Again? Was he mad? "Who?"

"Well, milady, the strange thing is that she goes by just one name, and an unusual one at that." Before he said it, Diana knew. "Sappho."

Breath caught. A planned meeting after so many days apart? Even if it was chance, clearly it provided an opportunity for the marquess to distract himself from any minor effect she, Diana, might be having on him.

Damn him. Damn them both.

What she should do was dress in her finest, go downstairs, and find someone to flirt with. Instead, a sick hollow feeling pinned her in her chair. One thing was sure. She would not barge into the dining room tonight, and she did not wish for a hole in the wall.

She didn't want to know.

She made Clara play cards with her, and lost. So she drank a couple of glasses of the inn's adequate port, and went early to bed.

Rothgar poured port for Sappho. "I'm sorry Lady Arradale didn't come to dinner. You would like her."

"You like her?" Sappho asked.

"Very much." It was a shame Sappho was heading north. He suspected he was going to need a friend he could talk to. He hadn't been aware until he'd seen her arrive here how tense he'd been all day.

"Why?" she asked.

Ah, the trouble with old friends. They saw too much. "Why do I like her? For the usual things. Courage, honor, spirit, intelligence."

"For most men it would be breasts, hips, lips, and generosity."

He smiled. "I am not most men. She has the requisite parts in pleasing form, but those are not the things that matter."

She leaned back in her chair, sipping her wine, the can-

dlelight playing on her unusual, beautiful face. Her skin
had the soft duskiness of well-creamed coffee. Her cheekbones were high and her eyes the large, dark almonds of
Byzantine art. She had all the other usual parts and in magnificent form, but it wasn't what had made a relationship
which had lasted over ten years.

It might be useful to let her probe. She knew him as well
as anyone, and as a surgeon of the soul she had some skill.

"It is an attraction of the spirit?" she asked.

"I didn't say that."

She studied him. "Does your resolve crumble at last,
Bey?"

"Not at all."

"Pity."

They had spoken of it before, of course, and with her, he
did not react with sharpness. "Self-indulgence is a virtue
now?"

"Flexibility is. Sometimes, even, to retreat is wise."

"Only in order to fight another day."

"Sometimes peace is made."

"After a retreat? A peace with great concessions and
losses."

She drained her glass. "Who is your enemy?"

"In this, madness."

"You fight a phantom."

"No."

She looked at him steadily. Though they came together
physically when it suited them, their deepest connection
was of the mind. For her, because few men loved her sen-
suality and her intelligence equally. For him, because with
her he did not need to accommodate, pretend, or compete.
And of course, she could be assumed to be barren after
twenty sexual years without conception.

She placed her hands, loosely linked, on the table.
"Many years ago, you decided that the enemy was dire and
the battles minor. Now, that balance has changed."

He felt the scalpel's sting, and an instinct to flinch away.
But he said, "Why do you think anything has changed?"

"Not because of this Lady Arradale, Bey. Over the past few years things have changed around you."

"A plague of marriages and births? She noted the same thing."

Her eyes sharpened. "Ah, then I do wish I had met her. What happened today to cause her headache?"

"Travel," he said, but then realized that he'd looked down. He picked up his neglected glass and drank from it to cover the act, but knew she would not be deceived.

"You have been cruel to her?" she asked.

"Only to be kind."

She made a *tsk* of disapproval.

"Yes, there is something," he said sharply. "But my resolve has not weakened, so it were better it died now."

"Died young. Like your sister."

He hissed in a breath. "That was crude."

"Sometimes crudeness is necessary. As in amputation."

"What bit of me should I lose?"

"Your iron-clad will."

"Never."

"Then, Bey, I fear you will die."

"We all die in the end."

"And yet life doesn't have to be a tragedy."

He stood then, moved away from the table and from her. "My life is not a tragedy."

"Not yet."

He turned. "Enough, Sappho." He meant it to be a warning, but could hear for himself that it sounded like a plea.

Like a good surgeon, she ignored both threat and plea. "You are a wonderful man, Bey, but you are incomplete. If you die incomplete, it will be tragedy."

"There are worse things than tragedy. One is weakness. Another is stupidity. A third is self-indulgence. A fourth," he said, feeling his temper snap, "is friends who don't know when to stop."

She rose, perhaps in response to the challenge. "I don't want you to die."

"You said that before. You are not God. Even I am not God."

"Bey, I fear that one day, in the not too distant future, you will kill yourself."

He stared at her, anger washed away by blank surprise. "That's absurd. What sign have I ever given of self-destructiveness?"

"You fought Curry."

"That was for other reasons entirely. I wasn't looking for death." When she continued to look at him, he said, "I give you my word, Sappho. I will never put a pistol to my head."

"Of course you won't," she said with what looked like a frown of impatience. "It would leave a mess for someone else to tidy up."

"I won't put an end to myself in any way. I promise."

She walked around the table toward him, moving with that special grace which was neither studied fashion nor erotic sway. He loved the way she moved. For the first time he wondered if she would want to make love tonight, and was surprised by an unwillingness that had nothing to do with this battle they engaged in now.

If she asked, however, he would oblige. It was part of the nature of their friendship.

Instead, she put a hand to his cheek. "I worry, Bey. I worry that one day you will, like a machine, just stop."

"I am not a machine."

He put an arm around her waist and drew her close. Perhaps sex wasn't a bad idea after all. It would put an end to this and might shake him free of uncomfortable reactions to Lady Arradale.

"No, but you share some of the properties of a machine." She neither encouraged nor resisted his hold. "You require to be wound up before you can function."

A laugh escaped him at that. "Then thank God you're good at it."

She smiled, but continued. "Now your family is all settled, who will wind the spring so the machine can go through its paces day after day?"

He put her aside. "Family problems won't end. They never do."

"But they all have someone else to take care of them now."

"I am not exactly short of occupation."

She approached again, and he found he'd let himself be backed into a corner. Short of obvious flight, he could not escape.

"You need passion, Bey," Sappho said. "Do you not know you are a man who cannot live without passion? No," she said as he drew her against him again, hoping to shut her up. "Not sex. Passion. Your family has been your passion since you were nineteen years old. Everything you have done since then has been directly or indirectly because of them."

"Even you?" He used it as an attack.

"Of course, even me. I am safe. I have a full life and other lovers. I am happily undemanding. What we have physically is delightful, but most of what we have is of the mind. I have been necessary to you, because even without your concerns over your mother's blood, you could not have married until now. You could not have weakened the completeness of your dedication to your brothers and sisters."

With hands on her arms, he pushed her away. "What book does all this nonsense come from?"

She smiled. Pityingly?

"Take comfort then," he said, stepping sideways and away. "For at least a few weeks I will have the Countess of Arradale to fret over."

"With passion?" she queried, still calm.

"Not if I can help it."

He heard the desperate edge in his own voice, and saw her smile widen. Devil take her.

She held out a hand. "Come, kiss me, Bey."

For the first time ever, he refused. "The mood is awry."

"Just a kiss." She came to him, and took his hands between hers. "I think it might be the last."

With a shake of his head, he carried her hands to his lips. "I do not intend to marry, Sappho. Nothing has changed.

And Lady Arradale has equally excellent reasons to stay single."

"I know," she said, but without losing her smile.

"So this will not be the last time unless you choose it to be so."

She stepped close, and with one hand, drew his head down to hers. "I will not refuse you if you come to me for love, Bey. Ever." Then she put her lips to his and asked for their familiar kiss. She was mistress of the art and he was her equal. It was long, and as satisfying as a favorite meal.

When it ended, however, she drew back. "However, if you come to me again for love, I will be very disappointed. Good night, my dear."

He stared at the door as it closed behind her, very tempted to pick up his glass and hurl it against a wall.

Chapter 13

The next morning, Diana ventured warily to the private dining room for breakfast, but was still shocked to find a tall, handsome woman in the room. The stranger was dressed in a conventional plain traveling gown of rust-colored cloth, hair hidden by a cap and hat, but no one would think her conventional.

Her smooth skin had a dusky tone, and high cheekbones and dark eyes suggested the East.

"Lady Arradale," the marquess said, not apparently discomposed by being found with his mistress. "May I present the poet, Sappho?"

Diana would be within her rights to refuse to acknowledge such an unusual creature, but that might send the wrong message. How, she wondered, did one address a stranger with only one name? "Good morning, madam. You are traveling to London?"

"From London, Lady Arradale." The woman seemed happy. Contented? Satisfied? Damn them both! "I am to join a literary house party in Nottinghamshire, and I must be on my way. If you are still in London when I return, I do hope you will honor one of my salons with your presence."

Diana made polite noises—though inside she was muttering, "When the moon fails from the sky, madam."

Sappho took leave of Lord Rothgar without any intimate gestures at all. Despite their conventional behavior, however, a connection flowed between and around them, and as a parting shot, she said to him, "Very disappointed."

Diana stared at the door. She had to ask. "You have disappointed Mistress Sappho in some way?"

He came to hold out her chair. "Not yet. She was talking
of future matters."

His future with the poet. Perhaps *they* would marry. If the
woman was barren, why not? Knowing she was likely to say
something spiteful and revealing, Diana put a large piece of
ham into her mouth and forced herself to eat it with an appearance of relish.

When she'd swallowed ham and ill-temper, she asked,
"Will we reach London today?"

"If the day goes smoothly. That will give you a soothing
night's rest before the Queen's Drawing Room tomorrow."

Tomorrow. Tomorrow her trial began. That did give her
more important matters to think about. She ate quickly then
rose. "We had best be off."

Heading for the coach yard she gave thanks that this would
be the end of this difficult journey. Much more and she would
embarrass herself. Then she paused in surprise to see Clara
climbing into the second coach.

"Clara, what's happening?"

The maid turned. "Me and Mr. Fettler are to travel in the
baggage coach today, milady. The marquess's orders."

Diana thought she could see a speculative light in her
maid's eyes, and speculations were buzzing inside her as
well. She turned to the main coach with little bubbles of excitement starting to fizz.

Not, of course, that she had any intention of allowing him
to seduce her—especially straight from another woman's
arms!—but still . . .

Perhaps he wanted to talk more of this feeling that burned
between them.

Perhaps he would rub her feet again.

Perhaps . . .

Only as she entered the luxurious coach did she notice
that the opposite seats had disappeared. It took only a little
investigation to see that they folded up into the front wall of
the carriage. An ingenious design, especially for an owner
with long legs.

Had he sent the servants to the other coach merely to be able to stretch his legs? He climbed in and did stretch his legs out. "A more comfortable arrangement, my lady. Don't you agree?"

She just might scream. "I was not particularly cramped, my lord, though it is a useful feature for a coach."

"My own design. What is more, those seats can be re-arranged to make the entire carriage a bed."

She glanced at him sharply, but managed to resist any further reaction. "So," she said as the coach rolled out of the inn yard, "is that your sole reason for the change, my lord? To stretch your legs?"

"Not at all. We must rehearse you for your role in London."

Thank heavens she'd said or done nothing to reveal the way her mind had run! She gathered her composure. "I do believe I know how to act the lady without practice, my lord."

"But can you maintain it under fire? What do you do, for example, when the king tells you that women are put on this earth to serve men and bear their children, and nothing more?"

Diana felt her jaw tense, but she inclined her head. "Sire, I think women blessed who achieve such a happy situation."

"So," he said, his voice changing a little to a sharper, higher pitch, presumably in imitation of King George, "you wish to marry, Lady Arradale?"

She fluttered her lashes. "What woman would not wish to marry, sire, if she could find a man worthy of her true regard?"

"And in what direction does your inclination lie, my lady? What? What?"

She stared at him. "What? What?"

His lips twitched. "A mannerism of his. What would you answer?"

Diana thought. "Sire," she said, lowering her head again, "my inclination lies toward a man of courage, honor, and strength."

"A soldier, then, what?"

"Not only soldiers are brave, sire. A man of intelligence, with an understanding of the world. Someone able to advise me on my many responsibilities, but also kind and gentle, and considerate of all. One who will love me to the exclusion of all others. Especially that," she said, looking up at him. "I require a husband who will be as *absolutely faithful* to me as I will be to him."

In his own voice, the marquess asked, "You think you are setting an impossible standard? Brand will be that kind of husband to Rosa."

"I had not finished, my lord."

"Ah, continue."

"I require a husband, sire, who will not need me to act a docile part, not protest at my determination, or try to restrict my actions."

His brows rose. "And that, of course, is why we are going to spend today in rehearsal."

She realized with annoyance that indeed she had fallen out of her role. "I would not say that to the king."

"And a drunkard will give up brandy tomorrow."

"I am *not* addicted to independence and power."

"Are you not?"

"No more than you!"

"But for me, Lady Arradale, it is permitted."

She resisted the urge to protest the unfairness of it. As he'd said before, that would be childish.

"So," he continued, "when the king inquires about the state of your estates and affairs, what will you say?"

"I am able to explain them, I assure you."

He shook his head. "No, Lady Arradale, you profess ignorance and confusion."

"But then he will feel justified in imposing a man on me to manage them!"

"He will feel justified in that anyway. Any sign of manly expertise will only alarm him further."

She turned to face forward again. "You're right. I can't do this."

His fingers touched her cheek, turned her to face him

again. "I believe that is where we started. Now, let's try
again . . ."

By evening, as they left Ware for the last stage to London,
Diana was worn out. She was ready to hate her taskmaster,
even though she saw that he had at times lightened the
lessons and practices with humor. The stressful day had
been even longer than expected, because of a loose wheel
pin which had required a stop at a village wheelwright.

Beneath irritation and exhaustion, however, ran fear. If
the marquess had planned to teach her that she faced a grueling time, that she could fail and plunge into disaster, he
had succeeded.

In the ruddy light of the setting sun, she put a hand to her
weary head. "My lord, I think you wish quite desperately to
marry me."

He was lounging back, but she thought perhaps he looked
as tired as she. "Why would you think that, Lady Arradale?"

"You are close to convincing me that I cannot do this. If
that's true, I might as well abandon the effort now, and
throw myself on your mercy."

"You have more fighting spirit than that."

She turned to look out of the window at the intense pink
of the sky. "But you have succeeded in teaching me that I
must not fight."

"There are many kinds of battles, and different strategies.
And weapons beyond the imagining of ordinary souls."

She rolled her head back. "You think me extraordinary?"

"Don't beg for compliments." But his tired eyes were
warm.

"I need some."

She realized then that they had reached a different place
during this grueling day. Not friendship exactly. Perhaps ca-
maraderie? Certainly all barriers of formality had gone.

That could be dangerous, but she was too exhausted to
care.

"You are without doubt extraordinary," he said. "That,
after all, is our problem."

She laughed. "Could you not, for a moment, allow me to be extraordinary in a *desirable* way?"

"That was my precise meaning."

She stared at him, throat constricting.

He reached out and drew the knuckle of one finger down the line of her jaw. "It does no good to ignore it. Better a battle faced. Yes, I desire you—strength, honor, courage, and all. However"—he took his hand away—"I am well skilled at resisting temptation."

She captured that hand. "So am I, which is why we don't have to resist everything. Kiss me."

His hand lay lax in her grasp. "You know that would be most unwise."

"Do I? Explain it to me."

"Have you never experienced a kiss that demands more, much more?"

She shivered. "Perhaps . . ."

"I think not."

"Why?"

"If you had, you would not risk it now."

"You have?"

"You think me made of ice?"

Of course he had, and doubtless surrendered, too. It would be permitted, for a man. "I cannot endure this . . . incompletion," she whispered.

"The ordeal is nearly over. After tomorrow we will see each other only occasionally. There will be distractions. Others."

Sappho, she thought with a poisonous burst of spite. Had the woman really been on her way north?

"Where do I sleep tonight?"

"At Malloren House. But not," he added, "in adjoining rooms."

There was a tease in it, and a warning. "Then there is little danger, is there? In a kiss now?"

"My dear Lady Arradale, we are alone in a closed carriage. It would be perilous."

"My control must be greater than yours, then. It does not seem so perilous to me." She shifted, his hand still in hers, and leaned lightly against him raising her head. "I promise on my honor not to let you ravish me, my lord."

Hands still joined, his finger traced her lips. "You are frighteningly naive."

Dalliance. One step above flirtation. One step below seduction.

"Then educate me," she said.

His eyes seemed surprisingly dark. Perhaps it was the shadowing effect of the setting sun, but she didn't think so. "You do need to recognize the fire with which you so foolishly play . . ." He freed his fingers and lightly cupped her head, lowering his lips.

She had been kissed in many ways—with mashing passion, and tentative sucking; with intent to impress, and with frantic hope of passing muster. She suddenly felt, however, that she had never experienced a true kiss. A simple kiss, as direct, as honest as a joining of loving hands.

Breath stealing, mind dazzling, soul shaking in its simplicity, power, and connection.

Her lids fluttered open and she stared at him. "What was that?"

A stupid question.

The answer was: a kiss.

But he did not say *a* kiss. He said, "That was our kiss. Do you understand now?"

She understood that she might be sick with the force of the changes shuddering inside her. "I understand that I want more."

"My point, I believe." He put her gently from him, back into her corner of the carriage.

She opened her mouth to protest, but then closed it. She couldn't sort through all this now, but yes, at last she understood the forces with which they contended. "How long have you known?" she asked.

"Since I rubbed your feet."

"We could be lovers." It burst through all her attempts to contain it.

He shook his head. "This is a fire that can never burn

tamely. It will consume. We must each guard our flame, and never let them join."

She covered her face with her hands. Two flames in separate glass lamps. For eternity.

She would not protest. Not now. Perhaps if she thought about it, she could find a way. Or find a way back to the safer shore she had so tempestuously abandoned. A place to live for the rest of her life in some sort of peace without him.

Without him.

She lowered her hands to speak, to protest, and found he was looking away. Out of the coach.

That the coach had halted.

For a moment she thought it an illusion of her disordered mind. Then that he'd stopped the coach to get out. To leave her.

But she heard one of the outriders saying, "There's something wrong with the horses, my lord."

Chapter 14

The marquess opened the door and stepped down. Diana followed. The six horses drawing the coach were standing, heads drooping, looking almost asleep. The coachman and groom were down studying them.

"What is it?" the marquess asked, but Diana saw that he was glancing around.

The French? All senses snapping to the alert, she too studied the countryside. A fallow field to the right, with a church spire in the distance. A coppice to their left which could conceal any number of enemies. The wide road stretched ahead some distance, empty. Behind, however, it curved, and she could not see very far. Apart from singing birds and raucous crows, and the occasional low of cattle, there was no sound.

They were pushing on to London after the delay and so were a little late on the road. They could not expect a lot of traffic to pass by. However, the baggage coach should be right behind.

She turned back again.

Where was it?

She started to go to one of the outriders to question him, then changed her mind and leaned back into the coach to extract her pistol case from her valise. She'd felt strange about bringing her pistols with her, loaded, on this well-guarded journey, but now she gave thanks. She slipped them into her two pockets, then took the larger ones from the holsters by the door. The custom-made ones he'd used in their contest. Once sure they were loaded and primed she approached the outrider.

He had his own pistols out.

"What happened to the servants' coach?" she asked.

"Don't know, milady," he said, only glancing at her before returning to his vigilant surveillance of the area. "They dropped back a bit over the past mile."

The same problem with the horses? She went to where the marquess was talking to the coachman. "Yew?" she asked.

He turned to her, taking the pistols she offered without comment. "Quite likely. The symptoms fit."

It warmed her that he only glanced at the guns, that he trusted her to have checked them, but this situation was chilling.

Yew was a leaf that horses found tasty, but which put them into a deadly stupor. No inn would have yew near its stableyard.

"The outriders' horses seem fine," she said, taking one pistol out of her pocket to have it ready.

"They didn't change in Ware." He glanced at her. "You think we should ride them?"

"It is a thought. But it isolates us."

"Yet I don't relish sitting here waiting for darkness to fall."

Indeed, in the past minutes the sun had sunk lower, turning the whole sky a burning red and lengthening the shadows of the nearby trees. The groom and coachman were hurriedly freeing the swaying horses from their harnesses, but one was already down on its knees. "Poor creatures," Diana said.

"It's a peaceful death, all in all. Warner," he said to the nearest outrider, "ride to the next inn for transport. All speed."

The man spurred off at a gallop and the marquess turned to her. "Get into the coach, Diana."

She looked up at him. "That's the first time you've used my name."

He was scanning the countryside now. "It seemed a shame not to."

"I'm only getting in the coach if you come with me."

He glanced down. "You just want your wicked way with me."

"True, but at the moment I want you safe."

"I prefer to be out here."

She stepped right up against him. "Then I am a limpet."

"Don't be foolish. Do you suppose they would hesitate to kill you if you give them no choice?"

He took danger so coolly, so she matched his tone. "It might make them pause."

When he frowned and put out a hand on her arm, she said, "You will find it hard to remove me by force, and harder still to keep me away. So, what do I call you?"

"Master?" he asked shortly, but then added, "If you wish, you may call me Bey."

"I wish."

With a smile that seemed ridiculous in the situation, she returned to looking out at the eerily peaceful evening countryside. It wasn't eerie except in being completely unthreatening. Insects buzzed among the long grass and wildflowers by the road, and everywhere birds chirped and sang.

She heard a distant cowbell, and the warning bark of a dog. Noisy crows swooped about their nests in the coppice, and somewhere nearby a skylark sang with startling purity.

She thought of the invisible village that must cluster around that church spire. People there were doubtless going about their ordinary lives, unaware of drama close at hand. A movement caught her alert eye, but it was only a rabbit hopping up onto the road ahead and scampering over.

Everything was tranquil, even the dying horses. The horses, however, could not have eaten yew by accident.

She slid around so she stood back to back with him, she looking ahead, he behind. The groom and coachman were still attending to the poor horses, but the remaining outrider sat still and watchful, pistols in hand.

Pressing against his back—Bey's back—she regretted days of doubt and restraint. What if they died here? What a waste it would be.

Then she heard it. Hooves.

Wheels.

From the way they'd come.

She was facing the wrong way and shifted to look, flexing her fingers around the pistol.

It could just be the servants.

"It is, isn't it?" she whispered, relaxing a little as the coach appeared around the bend, coming at a normal brisk trot.

"It would appear so. Delayed, but not suffering our problem." He kept his pistol in hand, however, but down, against his body. Tensing again, she put hers in the concealment of her wide skirts.

"Miller," the marquess said to the outrider, "who comes?"

Heart pounding, dry mouthed, Diana watched the slowing vehicle. She couldn't see who sat inside, and had no way of recognizing the two men on the coach. The outrider would.

"The second coach, milord." Then he raised his pistol. "But—"

Two flames, then explosions of sound.

The outrider cried out, fell back, tumbled off—

Diana tumbled to the earth beneath the marquess's hand as she heard something smash into the coach behind them. Another *crack* and a third pistol ball ricocheted off the ground in front of them spraying dirt so they both flinched.

She had her pistol pointing forward by then and cocked. She sighted without elegance, firing at the open window of the coach. Almost simultaneously, the marquess did the same.

Someone cried out.

A moment to take breath, to haul out the other pistol, to glance around. Their coachman and groom hiding behind horses. Outrider on the ground. Dead?

The marquess fired into the coach and another cry said someone had been hit. How many were there? And how many guns? He'd fired his two. She had one shot left.

She stared at the coach window, ready to kill.

Then a movement to the side swung her attention away.

The coach's horses were panicked, and the coachman there was having to work full out to hold them in, to try to keep the coach in place. The groom, however, half hidden by his bulk, was carefully aiming a long musket at the marquess.

At Bey.

The coachman pretty well blocked all sight of the man with the musket. Elbows on the ground, Diana sighted anyway, making herself take a precious second to steady, to find that place that Carr always directed her to. She had only one shot between now and a terrible loss.

It was a moment of eerie silence except for the thrashing harness of the frantic horses. The assailants in the coach were either dead or wary and she couldn't afford to think of them. She aimed for the mouth of that musket because it was the center of her target. Surely she'd have to hit some part of the gunman.

No more time. She squeezed the trigger, felt the kick—

The explosion deafened her. Her pistol had never made that much noise before. Then she heard screams.

She stared up at the writhing, bloody men on the coachman's box, the coachman swaying sideways, head a mass of blood . . .

Then the driverless horses took off, coach racketing down the road, leaving a trail of gore in its wake.

Her ears still rang.

In the sudden, resettling silence, the marquess rolled onto his side, head propped on hand. "You are a most delightfully bloodthirsty wench," he said. But then his expression changed, and he gathered her into his arms, there in the dirt of the road. "Ah, Diana, weep. It hurts to kill."

She shuddered, but tears would not come. "I didn't expect . . . I just wanted to stop him. I didn't mean—"

He rocked her. "You must have put your ball down the muzzle. Then he pulled the trigger only a fraction after you."

"It exploded."

"Indeed."

Though her ears had stopped ringing, Diana thought she'd hear that explosion for the rest of her life.

Were they dead by now, those two shattered men? Darkness gathered . . .

Oh no. She'd fainted last time she'd killed. Not again.

She pulled free, scrambled to her feet, and despite swimming head, started brushing at her ruined dress. "Clara. And your manservant. We must find them."

"We can't do that just yet." He leaned in the coach and produced a flask of brandy and a small glass. He filled it and passed it to her. "Drink."

The quick fire of the spirit made her shudder again, but seemed to clear her head. "I don't regret," she said fiercely.

"Nor do I." He passed the brandy to his coachman with permission for him and the groom to drink, then he knelt by the fallen outrider.

She followed. The poor man was badly wounded in the chest, but not dead. "Do you have bandages in the coach?" she asked.

"I don't think so. An oversight." He was letting the grimacing man clutch his hand, and now he stroked the sweaty, livid brow. "I'll take care of everything, Miller. Don't worry. You did well. Everyone is safe and the villains have gone. Quite likely they are all dead . . ."

Diana went to her knees on the man's other side, praying, but it would need a miracle. Miller must be in terrible pain, and blood was pooling under him. His eyes were glazing, but he seemed to take comfort from his master's calm voice. Then, with a strangled, rattling cry, he went limp.

Diana covered her mouth with her hand. She'd never thought he'd live with a chest wound like that, but for a moment, under Bey's calm, she'd hoped.

He rested his hand on the man's face for a moment, almost like a caress, but then he rose and seemingly unmoved, wiped blood from his hands with his handkerchief.

She rose too, not knowing what to do or say.

In the end she decided to be practical, and gathered the outrider's two fallen pistols. He'd fired one, but the other by a miracle, hadn't gone off when dropped. "I do hope they're all dead," she said bitterly.

"So do I. And painfully." He took the spent pistol and the man's powder and shot and set about reloading all three guns.

Diana stood there, absorbing the fact that the attack had taken only seconds, and that the whole incident, including the outrider's death, had lasted only a minute or two. The plan had surely been expected to take even less time.

One shot for the outrider, one for the marquess, and then speed off. Miller's quick action had changed things, or perhaps it had been her insistence on standing close that had caused a momentary hesitation. She hoped so.

But she was beginning to shake.

His arm came around her and pressed her against his chest.

"I'm not going to faint," she insisted.

"Of course not."

"Don't humor me!"

"Of course not."

"I fainted after I shot Edward Overton. I hated that."

"I'm sure you did."

"He screamed, too."

"People generally do. The distressing thought about someone trying to shoot me is that I might end up writhing and screaming."

She looked up. "Don't joke about it!"

"I was not particularly joking." His eyes were gentle however, and she suddenly realized what had happened. Things had changed again.

They were Bey and Diana now. Comrades in arms.

Much more dangerous.

But wildly wonderful.

He stepped away, breaking the connection. "Do you wish me to reload your pistols?"

"Of course not."

Without protest, he continued to do the larger ones, and she took the balls, wadding, and powder flask from her pistol case. When she tried to pour the right amount of powder down the barrel, however, her hands started to shake. Strive as she might, she could not make them behave.

"Damn it all to Hades," she muttered and he turned.

He took pistols and powder from her. "Practice being the conventional lady, just for a little while. Sit in the carriage and swoon. I will endeavor to survive unguarded. In fact . . ."

He did something in the carriage. When he helped Diana up the steps, she found he'd created a bed, even producing a soft blanket from somewhere. A shelf stretched from the seats to the far wall, padded with the opposite seat cushions and back. She climbed onto it and stretched out. He placed the blanket over her, then leaned forward to kiss her temple.

"Peace be with you."

Diana wanted to ask him to lie with her.

She wanted something more. Wanted it more intensely than ever.

"I know," he said, brushing a finger over her lips. "It happens after violence."

But then he left, and she heard him speaking to the two remaining servants. She absorbed the fact that she really would have tumbled with him here with the servants nearby, and thought modesty, dignity, and reputation of no concern at all.

She tried to keep her ears alert for more trouble, but she feared she'd done as much as she could in one day. Carr had told her she needed to learn how to use her skills under stress, and he was right. If another attack came, she might not be able to cope, and that was intolerable.

It was full dark by the time they arrived at the White Goose Inn in Bay Green. The first outrider had returned with two ostlers and four horses to pull the coach the mile to the inn. He hadn't been totally shocked by the mayhem since they'd come across the other coach overturned, driverless horses tangled in the traces, and three corpses—two tumbled off the box and one inside.

"Had to shoot two of the horses, milord," the man had reported with a degree of stoicism which made Diana wonder how many such adventures Bey's men enjoyed.

They'd gathered a small audience in the road by then anyway, since three men had come over from a nearby farmhouse to check out the explosion, and the York Fly had halted to help. They'd certainly provided unusual entertainment for the weary passengers.

"Shocking!"

"What is the world coming to?"

"Is that really the Marquess of Rothgar?"

"So they say. There's certainly a crest on the carriage door . . ."

Diana stayed lying down, hoping she was invisible.

The Fly had no spare room and a timetable to keep, so it had rumbled off with promises to alert the authorities. She suspected Bey would rather have avoided that, but it was impossible.

The men from the farm had gone to find ropes to drag off the torpid horses when they finally died. The dead outrider—Thomas Miller—was wrapped in sheets and blankets and put into the coach beside her for the short journey. She didn't mind. She'd asked and found out that he had a wife and young children, and had grown up on Bey's estate, son of a tenant farmer there.

One of his own. She knew how that must hurt.

She wasn't sure how Bey traveled the short distance, but it wasn't with her.

The White Goose was too small and too close to Ware to be a major inn, but their bedraggled party received the best of care both because of rank and because of the furor of their story. The local magistrate—a Sir Eresby Motte—had already been summoned.

"Time for me to practice being a very conventional lady, I think," she said to Bey in the low-ceilinged inn parlor.

"And you, of course, would not know how to fire a pistol. To have created such carnage single-handed can only enhance my reputation."

Tempted to fall into wild laughter at that, she let the innkeeper's flustered wife lead her to a small but comfortable bedchamber and ply her with sweet tea. When Clara staggered in, however, disheveled but whole, Diana hugged her and surrendered to tears.

The story there was simple. No yew for the horses, but a frayed piece of harness that required a halt to fix. As the groom had worked on it, they'd been surrounded by four masked men and forced away from the coach behind some bushes. There, they'd been tied up, and the villains had made off with the coach to prosecute their murderous attack.

Four. She'd thought so, and yet there had only been three corpses. The fourth murderer was on the loose?

Diana shivered. It had been planned with such cold-blooded efficiency. No one could guard themselves day after day, everywhere they went. She longed to go to Bey now, to be with him, to guard him, but she knew that giving in to that would be another consuming fire. No matter what happened, soon they must part—he to his life, she to hers.

He would have to live or die without her.

She wasn't sure she could bear it, but she must.

Once Clara was calm again, Diana sent her to find a fresh gown. The maid soon returned. "I'm sorry, milady, but all your boxes were in the second coach. No one seems to know where they are, or what condition they're in."

Diana looked down at her muddy gown, but couldn't stir emotion over it. "Why wasn't something put in the boot of the main coach?"

"Well, milady, apparently there's a machine traveling in there, all bundled up in blankets and quilts."

Diana laughed at that. Of course the automaton would travel in style. She opened the small valise she carried with her, but a change of garments hadn't magically appeared inside. Some books, her writing case, creams and lotions with which to refresh herself, and her pistols. This might be the total of her possessions until she met up with the rest of her belongings in London.

Ah well, no need of vanity here, and she was far too weary to care. She and Clara ate the hearty soup sent up, then climbed into bed. Clara only had the one nightgown with her, so Diana made do with her shift.

Despite exhaustion, however, sleep would not come.

Soon Clara was snuffling softly beside her, but Diana lay awake, mind staggering through fear and around danger, and on to danger of another kind. That kiss. Then rushing forward again through fear and danger and bloody death, and all the changes it had brought.

To Bey.

The Marquess of Rothgar.

The *éminence noire* of England.

Her comrade in arms, embracing her in the dirt after death.

Holding the hand of a dying man, making death as tolerable as possible with a calm voice and steady eyes.

Glimpsed in a revealing moment later, as they waited for help to arrive, face stark with that death of one of his own.

Who was comforting the comforter now?

That, in the end, was her excuse for slipping out of bed, for pulling the pink cotton coverlet around herself, and venturing out into the corridor of the night-quiet inn. The innkeeper's wife had said there were only four good rooms here and no other guests, so it shouldn't matter if she picked the wrong one.

She hesitated for a moment, wondering what his reaction would be, but it didn't stop her. She quietly opened the door next to hers and found the room unused. She went to the two doors opposite and listened at each.

Nothing.

Did his manservant sleep with him? That would be awkward. Lord Rothgar, however, seemed a very private person. If there were enough rooms, she felt certain he would sleep alone. She carefully opened one door and peeped inside.

Regular soft snores.

With a suppressed laugh, she decided that must be Fettler. Surely the *éminence noire*'s throat would not dare to snore!

Closing the door again with only the quietest *click*, she turned to the next one—

And found the marquess in open-necked shirt and breeches, watching her. His dark eyes were completely unreadable.

Clutching the coverlet more closely, she whispered, "I wondered if you were all right."

For a moment he did nothing, but then he moved away from the door and gestured her inside.

Heart racing, she walked into his bedroom.

Chapter 15

It was a similar room to hers, not large, with space only for the bed, two chairs bracketing a small table, and a washstand. Simple quarters for such as they, but not unpleasing. It was clean and neat, and a bowl of fresh flowers stood on a table by the dark gable window. The pastel-shaded petals glowed softly in the light of the single, flickering candle. Sweet peas. When she sat on one of the wooden chairs, the heady perfume wove around her.

"Are you all right?" she asked.

He stayed standing. "Most people think me made of cold steel."

"Perhaps you encourage them to."

"Would it do any good to encourage you to?"

"I don't think so. I couldn't sleep."

"Hardly surprising." After a moment, he gestured to a glass and half-full decanter on the table. "Port. Indifferent quality, I'm afraid. My own is doubtless spilled on the road somewhere. But would you like some?"

She nodded, and he refilled the glass and passed it to her. Then he sat in the opposite chair. "We are safe here. There's no need to be afraid."

She took a mouthful of the port, which as he said was not of the finest quality, but welcome. "I'm not afraid. Our attackers died. It will surely take longer than a few hours to regroup."

His eyes rested on hers. "Did you recognize either of the men in the coach?"

"There was no time to—" She stared. "You noticed."

"Am I not omniscient? Four men with the coach . . ."

"And three corpses. But surely the survivor will flee."

"I'd rather catch him. Lady Arradale," he said, "were you perhaps trying to protect me from worrying knowledge?"

She smiled ruefully. " 'Tis my nature to protect."

"We are likely to trip over each other then. So, did you recognize anyone in the coach?"

"Truly, there wasn't time—for a mere mortal, at least." But then she realized. "De Couriac?"

"Not so mere a mortal after all."

"A deduction, that's all. Who else could it be? What if he pursues you here?"

"I am awake." When she glanced at the decanter, he added, "And no longer on guard. I sent immediately to London for reinforcements and they arrived a little while ago. This place is now guarded by my men. It truly is safe."

The knot of scarce-acknowledged fear untangled, and she took a deep drink of the port. "Why are they doing this? What can you do to harm the French?"

"I can oppose their principal objectives. They want to rebuild their fleet, and preserve their fortifications at Dunkirk, since that is their base for invasion. I want to see it torn down immediately."

"Invasion! England hasn't been invaded by a foreign power since the conquest."

"But has frequently been invaded by contestants for the throne. It will be the Stuarts again, of course."

Wine and weariness seemed to be making it hard to think. She put the glass down. "Then why hasn't Dunkirk already been destroyed? It was part of the peace treaty."

"It was part of three previous peace treaties and still stands." He took the half-full glass from her loose hold and drank from it. "The French are very fond of Dunkirk, and the acting French ambassador is working hard to preserve it. He has just come up with the delightful notion that the artificial canal there should not be demolished, but renamed the Canal Saint-George in honor of the English."

"You jest!"

"Alas no." He drained the glass, then with a steady hand,

refilled it and put it down between them. "The king is quite touched by the idea, especially as the first name suggested was the Canal Saint-Louis."

Diana had watched him drink, and now awareness of his lips almost blinded her to anything else.

Our kiss.

Trying not to suck in breaths, she picked up the glass and deliberately sipped from the place still moist from his mouth. "The king is so easily duped?"

"Perish the thought. And I mean that seriously," he said, though astonishingly vaguely. Even she could see that her words had been foolish, almost treasonous, yet he did not say more. His eyes darkened, and only then did she realize that she had just licked some port from her lips.

He looked away, to touch the petals of the flowers. "The acting French ambassador—a Monsieur D'Eon—is a very clever and charming man."

"And lethal?"

He drew a blush-pink blossom from the bowl and looked back at her. "Possibly."

A much more subtle blossom than the scarlet field poppy, and yet she was spinning back to that flirtation. She had no stiff bodice tonight down which a flower stem could be tucked. She was, in fact, shockingly under-dressed. Less than half her mind now on the conversation, she was still aware that he was talking to her as an equal, and even trusting her with things he must surely share with few men.

He leaned back, the blossom resting against his lips. She thought she saw him inhale. She took a large mouthful of port and let it travel slowly down her throat.

"D'Eon served well as a captain of dragoons in the war," he said, eyes on her, "and in other more secret roles. He once traveled days with a broken leg to deliver a dispatch. He is not a man to be taken lightly. He is also proud and ambitious."

He leaned forward and took the glass from her hand. Their fingers touched. Then he turned it and drank from the same place as before.

Suppressing a shiver with two causes, Diana asked, "What is he ambitious for?"

"The ambassadorship."

"Isn't there an ambassador en route?"

"But for some, hope springs eternal."

He offered the blossom.

She took it, drawing it close to her nose to inhale the sweet, spicy scent.

"I have reason to believe," he said, "that Monsieur D'Eon thinks that if he is brilliantly successful in his current role, the Comte de Guerchy will be told to stay home, and he will be given the full role and powers. And income. Which would be particularly pleasant, as he has spent some of the ambassador's funds already."

She caught the slight twinkle in his eye. "With encouragement from you, perhaps?"

"Would he believe anything I said? He has received authorization directly from his king."

She laid down the flower. "Forgery! My lord—"

"Don't disappoint me, Diana." His eyes still smiled. "These matters are rarely clean or tidy. I do what I must to confine France and prevent invasion. They have tried to invade twice this century through Scotland. That route is closed to them now the Highland clans are broken or tamed, but Ireland stands ripe for use, and the south coast is temptingly close. I doubt the French will ever give up their hunger to invade England. It will not be allowed," he added, and she recognized a personal resolution.

No wonder the French wanted him dead. He stood firmly in their way, and was not an easy man to move. He would not be distracted by personal ambitions, or flattered out of his purpose. He certainly could not be bribed.

"Don't frown," he said, picking up the flower and stroking it against her lips.

The perfume seemed suddenly stronger, and her lips trembled under the butterfly assault.

"But they are trying to kill you!"

"I'm safer now, I think," he said, still teasing her lips, her chin, her cheeks, with petals. "In Ferry Bridge it should have been an unfortunate duel. Today, a mysterious shooting. Now it's scandal and mayhem, with four corpses attached, three of them probably French. My suspicious death in the near future would raise altogether too many questions."

She gripped his wrist to still the flower. "Your unsuspicious death?"

"What could that be?" Unresisting, he said, "I'm a healthy man, and I intend to avoid obviously risky activities for the next little while."

Still, he could not guard against every possible "accident." She put both hands around his, and carried it to her cheek. "Today," she said, "in the middle of chaos. I thought . . ."

She wanted to retreat then, but she had already gone too far. Looking down at their hands, at a flower, she finished. "I thought what a waste our restraint might have been."

He did not pull away. Instead, after a moment, he drew their clasped hands toward himself. At the brush of lips against her knuckles, she looked up.

"And yet," he said, "the dangers have not changed."

"Isn't there a time for danger?" she whispered. "For risk? For casting caution on the flames?"

Mouth still brushing over her fingers, he let the flower fall. "Toss caution on the flames of passion? A common folly. Burns are remarkably painful, you know." But his lips still played fire against her skin. "You are speaking under the effect of danger and death, Diana."

"And you are not . . . Bey?" It felt so strange, so wonderfully strange, to use his name.

"Why are you still here? Why am I touching you?"

"Touch me more."

He pressed the palm of her hand to his open mouth, so her skin felt the hot moisture there. As he had done, so briefly, so naughtily, at the ball last year.

If you ever change your mind . . .

"More," she whispered.

Against her skin he asked, "How much more?"

She longed to cry, Everything! But the cost, the cost was

still too high. "I want . . . I want to touch you, and kiss you. Is that possible?"

"Of course." He moved their linked hands toward her lips, and she kissed his hand. The first time her lips had tasted his skin.

It wasn't enough.

"I want to lie with you. Skin," she breathed, scarcely daring to speak the words, "to skin."

His eyes were steady and unshocked on hers. "That too you can have."

"I mean . . . I mean without . . . more."

He smiled, creases deepening. "You can have anything you want as you want it, my dear. I am not a callow youth."

"But you?"

"Will feast on skin, touch, and kiss."

She tightened her twined fingers with his and rested her head on them. "Why does it feel like starvation then?"

He gently drew their hands back to his mouth. "Perhaps we can feast. When did you last have your courses?"

Idiotically, her color flared at that subject. "Weeks ago. They are almost due again. Why? Oh." She stared at him, remembering Elf's pamphlet. "There's always risk."

"Did you not want to cast caution on the flames?"

Air became scarce. She had come here hungry for this, yet feeling safe behind the fact that it was impossible. That it posed too great a risk to her carefully planned life, and his.

"There is no need," he said against her knuckles. "You can have just what you want. You wanted to see me, I believe?"

He let go of her hand and stood to begin unfastening the cuffs of his shirt.

Diana gaped. He was going to take her literally, and strip? She hadn't meant that. She hadn't really thought how they would get from current state to nakedness. As he pulled his shirt out of his breeches, however, she couldn't bear to stop him.

But it was the first step.

To where? To what?

Could she finally satisfy all her burning curiosity?

Here.

With him?

If it were only curiosity, however, she would not feel this breathless sense of peril. They really shouldn't. They were playing with truly perilous flames.

Her heart raced so unsteadily she feared she would faint, so she picked up the glass and took a deep drink. Too deep, so she choked. When she had her breath back, he was laughing, the sort of gentle, warm laughter that friends share. It melted her, turning her soft as the fat tears of wax sliding down the side of the uneven candle.

Honesty and friendship. Honest embarrassment. Friendly humor. With this man she could permit herself to be exactly what she was. Even uncertain.

Trust. Astonishing trust. She'd never realized how little she allowed herself to trust.

And he, who must live as guarded as she in many ways, was trusting her.

He pulled the shirt up over his head and dropped it. Then he tugged the ribbon off his hair so it fell loose around his face to his naked shoulders.

His broad shoulders.

Did all men look stronger out of their clothes, she wondered, studying him as he paused to allow her to. Paused, perhaps, to allow her to retreat, to run back to her room.

Oh no. She welcomed this fire, even though it could burn her to a crisp.

Dressed, his movements spoke of strength, but here strength was clear in long elegant muscles flaring up to those broad shoulders, and in a subtle ridging of muscle beneath the fine line of dark hair down his chest.

She looked up into his watchful eyes. "You're beautiful."

Perhaps there was the tiniest blush as he smiled. "A delusion, but I'm grateful for it. Shall we go on?"

She picked up the abandoned blossom and took strength from the perfume. "Yes, please."

He sat on the bed to take off his shoes and stockings, then unbuttoned the bands at the bottom of his breeches. He stood and slowly undid the fastenings at the waist, watching her.

When she made no objection—in truth her mouth was so dry she wasn't sure she could speak!—he removed both his lower garments in one.

She knew how men were made. She knew about penises soft and hard. She even had colored pictures in some of her books. There was nothing to surprise her here, and yet she turned dizzy at the simple beauty of a naked man in the flesh. So real. So close. She almost felt able to sense the heat of his body, to inhale the scent of his skin.

A perfect, naked man, partially aroused, and waiting. For her pleasure. "It's rather unfair," she said as steadily as she could. "As a standard for your gender, I mean."

"I assure you, there are many finer made than I."

"I'm not sure I could bear it."

When he laughed softly, she put the blossom carefully back into the bowl and stood. "My turn, I suppose."

"I can give you all you want and more as you are, Diana."

"Skin to skin," she reminded him. "Anyway, I want to. It's a challenge, and I thrive on challenges. You must know that. I just wish I had more layers to play with."

Standing there unconcernedly naked, he made one of his beautiful gestures, ruby ring flaring by candlelight, inviting her to compete.

With a deep breath, she loosened the coverlet as slowly as she could, letting it slide down her arms to the floor. Unfortunately, that left her only one garment, her silk shift. It was a pretty piece covering her to elbow and calf, of fine weave, and delicately embroidered, but she couldn't think how to draw out its removal.

"If you move a little to the left," he said, "you will have the candle behind you."

A glance showed her what he meant, and she moved then spread her arms. "Yes?"

His look was definitely more intense. "Yes."

She turned, therefore, slowly, raising her hands above her head. When she faced him again, he was intriguingly more erect.

"How revealing men are," she teased, but when she

thought how she might not let him complete the act, it seemed cruel.

"There are ways of dealing with that, without . . ." She couldn't say it, damn it. "I mean, I could . . ." Perdition! Anyway, what an idiot she was. He knew. Of course he knew.

At his raised brow, she muttered, "I have a great many books."

"I should have guessed. Rid yourself of that garment, wench, and come to bed." He slid under the covers, then lay there propped on one elbow, revelations concealed.

Come to bed. For some reason she'd not thought of being in bed with him like . . . like a married couple. She realized that her books never showed couples in a bed. On it sometimes, in chairs, on the ground, on cushions, on a swing, in a tree, even on a rocking horse. But not under the covers of a conventional bed.

There wouldn't be much to see under the covers of a conventional bed and that was doubtless the reason, but this unexpected twist almost killed her courage. There was so much more to it . . .

Get on with it.

She grasped the hem of her shift to pull it up over her head.

"Take it off downward," he said softly. "Show me your breasts first."

She straightened and looked down. The low neckline had a drawstring. She began to tug it loose, then with a wicked smile, she took three blossoms from the bowl and tucked them there, between her breasts.

Cold water trickled down her belly as she turned back to him, carefully unfastening the tie. She moved the silk down, letting the blossoms slide lower until they nestled between her naked breasts, which were pushed up by the neckline running tight beneath them. The darkness of his eyes and the warm perfume made her sway.

"I like this," she said, meaning the look in his eyes.

"So do I. Come here. Just like that."

Chapter 16

She knew she would feel less wanton naked, but she obeyed, enjoying feeling wanton with him. When she was close enough, he grasped the fullness of the front of her shift and drew her closer, eyes fixed on the flowers between her breasts.

The still desire in his face, the strong pull of his hand, started the tingle inside that she knew was desire. Desire she could finally satisfy tonight.

If she found the courage.

According to Elf's pamphlet, this close to her courses she was unlikely to become pregnant. But it wasn't certain. Nothing was certain. It would be an extreme, unnecessary risk to him and to her.

His lips brushed breasts and blossoms, and she heard him inhale slowly. Her hands rose of themselves to cradle his head there, her rings sparkling among his dark hair. His tongue stroked across to her right nipple, and she inhaled. Their eyes met, and it was as if he read her wonder. He smiled, then licked, then gently sucked.

She gasped, and he tumbled her onto the bed. His mouth played against her breasts again, teasing and sucking one then the other until her head was swimming and her muscles went limp.

"This isn't fair," she gasped.

His mouth stilled against her skin. "You want me to stop?"

"Never. That's why it isn't fair."

"A potent weapon in the male arsenal. Something a woman can't do for herself."

She knew she was red again, but she wouldn't deny that she gave herself pleasure. "There are things a man cannot do for himself," she pointed out.

He smiled. "I love a well-read woman. But not tonight. Tonight is for you, Diana." He took one of the scattering flowers and stroked her with it, around her breasts, up her throat, across her lips, perfume dizzying her, then back down, to tease her nipples . . .

But then he stopped.

When she looked at him, he said, "You have to tell me now, whether you want to take risks or not."

"Or you won't be able to stop?"

"I will stop. But you can't decide this in passion, when you are beyond reason."

"I'm already beyond reason," she whispered, feeling her body's aching need, and a burning hunger simply for him. To be as close to him as humanly possible. She closed her eyes and savored the heat and hardness of his body against hers, the special smell of him, and her, and perfumed blossoms. "I've never felt like this before. Never."

"I'm glad. But you must choose, now."

She opened her eyes to look at him. "I can't."

"Then we take the safe path."

Inside, her body wailed, but she agreed. "The risks are too great."

"Yes, they are."

He silenced unborn protests with his lips. No handclasp of a kiss this time. A burning, branding kiss that arched her and set the world afire. She hooked a leg over him, feeling his erection hard between her thighs.

Oh, how she ached to surrender. But she could not. They could not. No matter how she burned.

She thrust her hands into his hair, and protested when he broke the kiss. But not when he slid down to put his mouth again to her breast. Silk and flowers in his hand slid up to rub against her other nipple and she released a choked moan of pleasure, burning with desire.

She'd been wrong. The risk was slight . . .

No!

He'd been right before.

She'd been right before.

Tangled in fear and desire, she felt his erection stir, and tensed, breaking the wonders that had been gathering.

He raised his head to look at her, the edge of his hand-some features and the wave of his loose, dark hair, both gilded by the guttering candle. Lucifer. But Lucifer before the Fall.

"Trust me," he said. "For this brief while, my brave warrior maid, lay aside your burdens of power, dismiss your guards, and surrender in trust to me."

Caution clamored, instinctive and well rooted, but she smothered it. This was not just any man. "I'm yours," she said, and closed her eyes.

She kept them closed, living by her other senses. Touch, touch above all. Those hands, firm and gentle upon her as she'd dreamed they would be, sensitive fingers seeming to know just what would pleasure her best. His mouth soft, hard, dry, wet, hot—but then blowing, cold.

Hearing. The rustle of sheets as they moved together, breath close to her ear, the thick, deep pounding of her blood. His voice, sometimes soothing, sometimes teasing, sometimes merely humming pleasure as she hummed back.

Smell. Breeze-fresh sheets, crushed flowers, and him. His smell beneath a trace of the soap with which he'd washed. Her own soft perfume turning wicked. A mounting, spicy scent from both of them.

Taste. His skin against her questing lips, against her tongue, against her open mouth which seemed to hunger for him. His mouth, powerful against hers stirring . . .

She shuddered, clutching closer. Knowing. She'd given herself the release often, but this was different. Their coiled bodies made it different, engaging every part of her so she felt whirled into fire, spiraling up and out . . .

Rothgar watched her melt by candlelight, her lovely body glowing and sinuous with newfound pleasure and desire. It called him almost to will-break, assailing him with slick satiny flesh, soft murmuring sounds, and perfume of flowers and Diana.

Controlling every instinct, he gave her, as perfectly as he knew how, what she longed for. And only what she had agreed to.

She could be his. She would not resist now, he knew, likely would not object later, and it would be as safe as humankind could make it—

He blocked such thoughts, and slid his fingers between her legs again, into hot, moist readiness . . .

That could be his—

No.

Shifting, he pushed his fingers deep inside, blocking how it would feel if his erection was easing into her tight, hot vagina. Shuddering, he sweated with that need, but gloried in her responses.

She was lost in the senses now. She arched and he drank her soft cry in a kiss, moving inside her and against her. He returned to her lovely breasts to drive himself mad driving her to delirium.

Her arms locked tight around him as her body went taut. He drowned in the sounds of a woman's frantic pleasure, and murmured as she convulsed with it—encouraging words, soothing words, loving words.

Loving words he hoped she would never remember.

Loving words he hoped he could forget.

He gave her his lips when she quested for them, surrendering himself to a brief moment of deepest agonized desire.

Diana came to herself again in the kiss, and broke free to look up at him. "I was wrong. I want it all. Now."

He shook his head and moved away, but she snared arms and legs around to hold him. "I am not beyond reason. This is only now, isn't it? No tomorrows. Because of what it is. This. Ours. Like our kiss."

She felt the tremor running through him like fine music, and saw in the guttering candlelight the sheen of sweat on his flesh. "No tomorrows," he agreed. "This is impossible short of eternity."

"And we cannot have eternity." She wanted to weep, to

fight, but she wasn't sure he was wrong. All they could be certain of was now.

"Make love to me, Bey," she said, doing her best to pull him back down skin to skin. "Completely. Now. I could not live with the regrets. Now. *Please*."

He gave way suddenly, as if something had snapped like the drummer boy's arm. He moved between her legs, supporting himself on one arm, as he guided himself carefully into her.

She closed her eyes to feel, only feel, as the fierce hardness of him filled her.

Yes. Oh yes.

Like a warm wave, perfection swept over her. A perfection of the moment that said that this was meant to be. Two halves joined. The perfect key in the perfect lock.

She flexed her hips to make the union complete, braced for pain, ready to accept it without complaint, but then he was deep inside, filling her to satisfaction. Her eyes flew open to see his, dark and smiling.

"All that riding, I suspect," he said.

"You don't mind?" She herself felt slightly appalled.

"Would I want to give you pain at a moment like this? Don't disappoint me by being conventional, Diana. Come, let us die together." He pulled almost all the way out, then thrust in again.

La petite mort.

Oh yes. She, who'd never been romantic, wanted to die with him, die with him in truth if they could not be together.

She closed her eyes and caught the rhythm, wondering briefly if the bed was banging against the wall and telling the whole world what they were doing. She didn't care. She didn't care at all. The world could go hang.

The inner fire burst into flame again, and as she stiffened with pleasure she sensed him surrender, too.

She prayed it was as wonderful.

Or better. With such magnificence, it was easy to be generous. Her pleasure was not as intense this time but it ran deeper and seared her mind for delicious moments, leaving her blank, limp, and infinitely, perfectly satisfied.

As he moved off her, she murmured, hoping it sounded as appreciative as she felt. Then she opened her eyes to see him collapsed back on his pillow. Her smile widened. "You look gorgeously sweaty and rumpled."

He laughed, quietly but fully. "Even I cannot make love with chilly hauteur."

"With a Malloren, are not all things possible?" She'd learned it was his family's unofficial motto. His unofficial motto.

He laughed again, rolling his head to look at her. Truly a few days ago she never could have imagined him so relaxed. "I suppose I could have sex with chilly hauteur if I had to," he said, "but it would not be making love." He pulled her to him for a kiss. "And therefore, it could never be with you."

Love?

She caught it to her like a precious treasure, but she wouldn't ask if he truly meant it. She didn't know if it would be a blessing or a curse.

She knew, whichever it was, it dwelt in her. She loved him, as much for his virtues and their conversation as for the passion. But the passion had completed the magic circle.

She drew back to study his dark beauty, brushing damp hair off his high brow. *I love you, Bey Malloren.* Impossible words, for they would shatter the agreement they had here tonight.

No tomorrows.

But they had made love. Indeed they had. Fully and completely. The love they had made here tonight had to exist somewhere in the world. It would linger in her, and in him, changing everything.

But pray God, not as a child.

He echoed her action, brushing hair off her cheek, then kissing her again, lingeringly.

On impulse, she slid the large ring off her first finger—it happened to be a sapphire and valuable, but that was not the point. She took his left hand and it fit onto his ring finger.

With this ring, she thought, but did not say it.

He looked down at the blue stone, then kissed her one naked finger, looking at her with troubled eyes. In one sense, she knew, she shouldn't have done that, but in all other senses it was completely right.

Then he rolled out of bed, dampened a cloth on the washstand, and returned to wash her belly. She looked down, suddenly understanding.

"I wish you hadn't."

"Far safer."

He was right. To spill his seed on her instead of inside was an extra level of safety. But she wished he hadn't.

"Not in chilly hauteur," she said, "but mind still in control."

He returned to the bed, and pulled her into his arms. "Stop complaining. It wasn't what I wanted, either."

She snuggled up against him. "If I wasn't so . . . fulfilled at this moment, I could scream at fate."

His hand played in the hair at her nape. "Surrender to the moment, love. Tomorrow is soon enough for screaming."

That word "love" again, but he was resolved, even so. That this would be all. She couldn't complain, for it had always been clear, but she had hoped. Just a little.

They couldn't marry, but they could be lovers if they were very careful. No. She knew it would be impossible to avoid a child forever . . .

Rothgar held her, watching sleep creep over her. She looked like a weary child, her curls tangled, her lips parted a little, her lashes soft on her rounded cheeks. It had been a long, arduous day full of tension and danger, and now at last she could rest.

He had given her that.

Pray God he had not given her more.

They should be safe.

Once he was sure she was deeply asleep, he eased her out of his arms and onto her pillow, but rested there, studying her. At the different angle she still looked young, but now he could see her firm chin. The body he'd tangled with had not been childish at all, but that of an active, strong woman.

A truly remarkable woman.

He'd respected her for a year now, but she had led a pampered life and retained a streak of childish willfulness that was undesirable. He'd wondered how she'd behave when truly tested.

Today he'd found out.

Magnificently.

She'd faced danger coolly at his side. She'd killed for him. She hadn't foolishly made a fuss over it.

Last year she'd stirred his interest with her bold challenge to him, and even more with her victory, but he was not a man to be pulled into folly by an intriguing young woman. In the past few days, however, she'd shown she was his match in every area. She'd amused and alarmed him with her quick wit and understanding, her boldness and courage, her problems and needs.

Then she'd teased that dangerous kiss. *Their* kiss. Still, he'd remained in control. Not seriously threatened. Until tonight.

Unique.

Shattering.

Forbidden.

He looked at the multifaceted blue stone on his finger. Part of her gaudy armor against the world. It was a pledge ring, he knew, not just of affection but of protection. A bond of mutual loyalty and trust.

Putting the ring to his mouth, he looked at her, recognizing that here, unexpected and unwanted, lay his mate.

No, not unwanted, but impossible.

Sappho had said he was incomplete, that now his family was cared for, he had a void. No. She'd said that the void had always been there, covered by other demands. Other passions.

It had seemed nonsense, but now he saw that as usual, she was right. Unsuspected, he hungered for closeness, love, and intimacy. His siblings had not been a duty, but a necessity, and their needs had allowed him to resist marriage.

But now he faced temptation unprotected.

He had called her "love." Twice. He hoped she hadn't noticed.

Too late he saw how much wiser it would have been to have avoided this. He should have sent her back to her room.

He could even have brought her in, plied her with port, soothed her agitated nerves, and sent her back to bed.

Instead he had given in to the hungers burning inside himself, hungers he'd lived with for days now, thinking they were safe. That he would be, as always, in control of the machine.

Hubris, with predictable results.

A need as raw, as painful, as skinless flesh.

For protection, he left the bed and pulled on his clothes again, trying to re-create barriers, to cloak the pain. At the same time, he struggled to rebuild the guards around his mind.

This was all a result of peril and proximity. It would fade when he was back in normal days. Tomorrow they would arrive in London, and Diana would attend the Queen's Drawing Room. From there, she would move into the Queen's House. He would see her only briefly and in company.

They'd be late arriving in town, though. An excuse to put off her presentation for a few days—

Folly. The sooner she was within court circles the better. If all went well, she would return north within weeks, and they need never meet again. He would regret not being able to visit Brand at Wenscote, but it was necessary.

What if Diana returned to London for pleasure one day?

Then he would travel elsewhere. Paris was open to him again. Or he could go north when she came south. He laughed to himself at the folly of such a silly dance, but it would be the only way.

He closed his eyes for a moment, not trying to deny the pain. For him, and for her. Pain, however, was part of life. Fear of it did not govern an honorable man.

And in time, even the worst hurt faded and became bearable.

In shirt and breeches, he climbed onto his side of the bed but lay beneath only the coverlet, separated from her by sheet and blanket. He was unable to resist turning toward her, however.

As if sensing him, she rolled to face him, still asleep, and her arm reached out beneath the covers. Finding nothing, it stilled and she sank back into deep sleep.

He resisted the urge to kiss those parted lips, but lay watching her until, at last, the candle drowned in wax, and darkness brought him rest.

Chapter 17

Diana awoke in a state of peace and pleasure that turned to momentary confusion. Because someone had just kissed her.

She blinked up.

The marquess.

Bey.

She smiled and tried to untangle her arms to reach for him, but he stepped back. "It's nearly dawn. We must get you back to your room."

Instantly she recognized that the guards were fully in place. Wiser so, but horrible.

Groping around, she struggled to straighten her shift beneath the covers even though he had stepped away to look out of the small window. The pearl-gray sky was just beginning to brighten with yellow, orange, and pink.

He was completely dressed, even to his cravat and coat, and she felt slovenly as she slipped out of bed in the one creased, stained garment. She wrapped the pink checked coverlet closely around herself before saying, "Ready."

He turned and came to her as if they were a proper lady and gentleman about to leave for a stroll. She noticed then that the sapphire ring was not on his hand. Of course not. No tomorrows. But she knew he would keep it safe.

There were a thousand things to say, and yet none. She had pushed for that dangerous voyage with the implicit promise that they would return to shore today, would create no lasting, entrapping bonds.

She would keep that promise if it killed her.

He opened the door and glanced out, then turned back. "All safe."

She walked toward him, past him, but she couldn't resist a pause, a look. A plea.

All lightness gone, he put his hands to her cheeks and brushed his lips against hers. "We left the safe path. If against all odds there is a child, you must tell me."

She shook her head. "You know you cannot marry, and we cannot openly acknowledge a bastard. If I conceive, it will be my concern alone."

"That isn't true."

"But we must make it so. Don't fight me on this, Bey."

"Don't give me orders, Diana." But it was said without rancor, and, devastatingly, he put his arms around her and held her close, resting his head against hers for a moment.

When he straightened, there was no trace of weakness in his face. "*Adieu*, Diana."

"*Adieu*, Bey."

She did not look back as she hurried across the corridor and into her room. Clara still slept, so Diana quietly opened her jewel box and chose a ring at random to replace the one she'd given him. Then she slipped into bed beside the maid to lie staring up at the dark beamed ceiling, reliving, remembering . . .

Relinquishing.

Dressed in her stained gown, Diana joined Bey at breakfast. They were, thank heavens, not forced to make small talk, as Sir Eresby appeared again with reports and questions. Apparently he'd sent someone to make inquiries at Ware, and discovered that the assailants had been seen there, and were French. What's more, they had been with a Frenchman called de Couriac.

Bey made no difficulty over telling Sir Eresby that they had dined with Monsieur de Couriac and his wife in Ferry Bridge, that Monsieur de Couriac had been taken ill, and that the couple had left in the night.

The stocky, serious magistrate clearly did not approve of any of it. "Could he have held a grudge, Lord Rothgar?"

Bey raised his brows, entirely returned to aristocratic hauteur. "Over his illness? The food was provided by the inn, sir, not me. And who would plan murder over that?"

"What else could be cause for such a cold-blooded plan, my lord?"

"I have no idea, Sir Eresby. However," he said, rising, and extending his hand to Diana, "we must be on our way. Lady Arradale is expected at the Queen's Drawing Room today."

Diana gave him her hand, resisting the urge to curl her fingers around his, pitying the poor baronet so dauntingly put in his place.

Sir Eresby rose and bowed. "Of course, my lord. My lady." He didn't completely buckle however. "I will send to London if there are further questions."

Good for you, thought Diana as she let herself be led out of the dining room and to their coach. The scarred panel, however, shocked her back to yesterday.

"Are you all right?" Bey asked quietly.

"Yes, of course. I had forgotten."

They shared a glance about what had wiped horror from memory.

Then she looked away. "I'll be glad when our baggage catches up with us. Clara has done her best with this gown, but some of the dirt simply will not come out."

A metaphor for her life, that, she thought as she climbed into the wounded carriage. Not dirt, but changes that could not be reversed. Nor would she want them to be, even with the peril they brought.

Clara and Fettler were already sitting opposite her. Bey took his seat, and in moments they were on their way to London.

They did not talk, did not even pretend to read. Did not look at one another. As for that, he could be staring fixedly at her all the way, for she refused to look at him. It was not just the pleasure of the night which had left her adrift, it was the closeness, the intimacy such as she had never experienced before.

Rosa had warned that women had a tendency to fall in love with the men they made love to, but there was more to it than that. Quite by chance, Rosa and Brand had found each other, like two parts of a broken whole. A fit so perfect that all other matches instantly became impossibly flawed.

You or no other.

Bey was her lost half?

He and no other?

She recognized it to be true. He was the lost part of herself suddenly found, rashly fitted for brief moments against raw edges, which now bled afresh.

Why not? her rebellious side suddenly demanded. Why could they not have the completion, the wholeness, that was every person's right?

Was it not worth striving for?

Determined now, she analyzed the practical problems.

Her independence. That was nothing. She knew he would respect that.

But what of her appearance of independent power? Heaven above, the Marquess of Rothgar could overshadow anyone, and in a way that would work to her advantage. She would gain from having him as mate, as equal half. He would certainly feel no need to inflate himself by lording over her.

So what of geography?

That was both their enemy and their friend. They would have to find ways to divide their time between north and south, between his responsibilities and hers. It would mean separations, but being alone on her estates would help her to retain authority there. A lesser, ever present husband would be a much greater threat.

Truly, though she hadn't thought of it before, a great husband would serve her better than a lowly one.

It *was*, perhaps, possible after all.

She slid a glance sideways, borne on fledgling wings of hope. And collided with despair.

Her problems might have melted away, but his had not. His reasons for not marrying were as strong as ever.

She looked out of the window again, at the increasingly busy road and more frequent villages and inns that told her they were close to London.

Close to parting.

He was resolved not to carry tainted blood into his ancient line. He had not contradicted her when she'd said he could not marry her if she was with child, and she knew how agonizingly difficult that would be for him.

He accepted all his responsibilities—even a rebellious countess who was only a distant connection by marriage. His love for his family ran deep, and he was wonderful with children. The thought of rejecting his own child must be impossibly painful, and yet he was prepared to do it to keep to his firm resolve.

She prayed with deep sincerity that she not conceive. It would be terrible for her, but intolerable for him. No wonder he'd been so emphatic that they could not make love again.

She decided at that moment that if she did conceive a child, he would never know. She would find a way to hide the pregnancy and then foster the child out to someone on her estates. She would be able to keep an eye on it, though it would break her heart not to be able to claim it, love it, as her own. For his sake, however, she would do it.

Tears stung, and she fought them down, but they welled again. Wealth, power, love, and two strong wills, and what did it bring them? Two lives lived in separate, bleak landscapes, when a garden of sunlight and laughter lay in sight, almost in reach.

She thought of the automaton, traveling swaddled like a babe only inches behind her. For a mad moment it seemed that their unborn—pray God never to be born—son lay in the boot of the coach, crying for release.

Her fighting spirit rebelled. There had to be a way!

What, though? A marriage without children? Though the idea pained her, she would do it. However, Elf's helpful leaflet on preventing pregnancy made it clear that there was no way to be completely safe, even if he always spilled his seed outside her. The aim was only to space out children to make life easier for the woman and her family.

Lud, but if medicine offered a way for her to be rendered infertile, she'd accept the knife as the price, even though she'd weep for the children—their children—who would not be born.

She risked another quick glance at his somber, classical features. Of all the precious parts he might bring to a child, only one tiny part was suspect.

As if touched, he turned to her, asking silent questions. *What distresses you? Can I help?*

Muted by the servants, she replied with a slight shake of the head, and turned again to the safety of the window. Market gardens now, worked over like worker bees by people gathering vegetables for the crowded city. Their coach had slowed because of the crush of traffic moving into London, coaches, carts, and people on foot.

If only they could stop, freeze here, where at least they were together.

In London they must part, and a king awaited to be pacified, to be escaped unwed. For she knew now she could not marry another, even to escape an insane asylum.

You or no other.

The busy road slowed them, even though vehicles made way for the crested carriage. People in the street turned to watch the grand coach and outriders pass by, and her attention was caught by one couple.

A small child stood between them, hands in theirs like a link in a chain. The little girl pulled her hands free and obviously demanded to be picked up. The father did so, smiling. Her arm went confidently around his neck as she pointed to the coach, chattering.

They were close now, and Diana couldn't help but smile and wave at the little girl. She saw her own handful of rings flash in the sunlight, and the child's eyes and smile widen with delight as she waved back.

The coach moved on, leaving the family behind. Doubtless they thought they'd just seen the most fortunate of people, those who lived blessed and golden lives, when instead she felt like a beggar at their table.

Hard to imagine herself and Bey strolling down a street as a family like ordinary people, but easy to imagine him carrying a cherished child. As with little Arthur, he would be loving with his own children. As with his brothers and sisters, he would be a rock around which they could build fulfilling lives.

Being a rock must be so cold and hard.

The sudden shift was like the cracking of a dark wall, letting in the light. This was wrong. It was all wrong, and there must be a way to set it right, not just for her own sake, but for his. Especially for his. He deserved more of life, this magnificently generous man, than the cold land to which he had exiled himself.

He needed, in fact, to be rescued.

As simple streets became fashionable, she hunted for a way. She failed, but did not give up. They were two wealthy, clever, and powerful people. There had to be a way.

Fashionable streets and fashionable people intruded however, and she had to break the silence. "My lord, surely I cannot go to court like this." She touched her stained gown.

"Of course not," he said, but as if he truly hadn't thought of it until then. A victory of sorts, she supposed, to have distracted that controlled and logical mind.

"The baggage carts should have arrived," he said. "If not . . . Elf has left some clothes at Malloren House."

Diana had to fight a giggle. She and Elf were of a different build and height.

A rueful reflection of her humor warmed his eyes, but instantly, they cooled. "If your baggage has not arrived, we will send your excuses to the queen."

Excuses meant more time. More time with him. More time to discover the way. Perhaps, despite promises and willpower, another night.

"We're entering Marlborough Square," he said as the coach turned between rows of modern houses and into an open space.

She looked out at tall brick houses with dark railings in front, and lines of trees. There was even a pretty garden in the center, complete with duck pond. "It's lovely. I didn't expect so much greenery."

"There are many parks in London, too."

What banal conversation, and yet it was the best they could manage.

"This is Malloren House," he said as the coach turned into a courtyard in front of a mansion set apart from the terraces to either side.

She took refuge in teasing. "Only to be expected that you would have the largest house in the square, my lord."

"But of course. I own it all. No credit to me, however. My grandfather took a dislike to living in the crowded older parts of London and bought the land. As he planned his country estate, the fashion for these squares started and he decided to build it. My father completed the work."

The coach halted in front of the handsome portico and servants poured out to assist them.

"Why not Malloren Square, then?" she asked.

"My grandfather was a friend and admirer of the Duke of Marlborough." He stepped down from the coach and turned to assist her.

Journey over. And what a journey it had been.

As they entered the house it became clear that a message had been sent ahead to tell of the delay and the cause. Of course it had. They had been expected last night. Clearly, despite the attack and the death of his servant, Bey had dealt with a great deal of business before settling down with that decanter of port.

She still didn't really grasp the man he was, and so she looked around at his London home, wondering what it could tell her.

The entrance hall was oak paneled, and more in the style of the country house his grandfather had planned than the modern town house it had become. The oak was not yet painted in the modern fashion, but the room was saved from gloom by four long windows at the top of the sweeping staircase.

Pictures, furniture, and ornaments were all around, and all of finest quality, but unlike most fashionable houses, the effect was not of careful display, just the accumulation of the years. This great house managed to feel like a home, and she couldn't help thinking how wonderful it would be to be arriving as his bride.

It had to be possible! Two lives could not be wasted in this way. No family was free of physical and mental taint, and even people who seemed unflawed could have children with problems. She turned to speak to him, but he was giving crisp orders to various servants, organizing the machine again.

With a sigh, she strolled closer to one large painting. Bey in his robes and coronet looking haughtily down on lesser mortals. He looked remarkably chilly and intimidating. Just as she'd imagined him once.

She sensed him come to stand beside her and gave him a quizzical glance.

His lips twitched. "I deliberately chose an artist who was terrified of me. Don't you think it sets the right tone?"

"If you wish everyone to quake in their shoes."

"But of course."

She rejoiced that some trace of lightness remained between them. "You must give me the artist's name. I need a similar portrait just inside the door."

"You wouldn't terrify him. Which means he's a fool." He turned to speak to someone, then said, "The baggage carts arrived safely last night, and your boxes await you upstairs."

He looked unaffected by the news, but Diana could easily have screamed. She masked disappointment as best she could and allowed herself to be taken away to prepare for court.

As she climbed the stairs she became aware of another painting on the landing at the top. This one was of a couple in the fashion of a generation ago. Bey's parents, she assumed. The resemblance between him and the man was clear. Even though the painted features were a little softer, the dark hair and dark eyes were the same. He looked to be a much gentler man than his eldest son, however, though a little sad.

Then she realized that the russet-haired woman must be his second wife—the resemblance to the "red Mallorens" was clear. So, she thought, pausing beneath the portrait, that tragedy explained the haunted sadness.

The marquess in the painting was quite young. People tended to think of parents as middle aged or older, but a portrait such as this reminded that even parents at one time were in their twenties, and possibly as confused and uncertain as oneself.

Despite the waiting servants, she studied the second wife. Golden russet hair and a mouth generous with smiles and kindness. Beauty, too, which she'd passed on particularly to her oldest son, Bryght, melded with the father's dark coloring. It was the warmth and kindness, however, that shone through most.

A woman bitterly missed by all. Perhaps, having lost her, her husband had not fought very hard to live.

You or no other. She sensed it here, too.

Two halves which when divided left bleeding wounds, or at best, terrible scars.

There had to be a way!

She allowed herself to be directed on, to a suite of rooms in which the woodwork had been painted white, and Chinese wallpaper set in the panels. The furnishings were all of the latest style, too, delicately carved and inlaid with decorative woods.

"Lady Elf's rooms, milady," said the housekeeper. "Lady Walgrave now, of course, and with her husband's house to live in."

Long curtains at long windows. Birdsong from nearby trees, and quite close by, children playing. A poignant reminder of the life so many people took for granted.

Warmth, love, marriage, and children.

"We haven't unpacked your boxes, milady," the housekeeper continued, "since you are to move to the Queen's House, but if you would be so kind as to say what you require for the Drawing Room, I will have it prepared."

Diana put aside longings and focused on her coming challenge. If she failed with the king, Bey would feel obliged to keep his promise and marry her. She wanted it desperately, but only a full marriage. One in name only would be worse than none at all.

Therefore, she must create the correct first impression before the king and queen, and play her conventional role to perfection. One of the things he'd told her during her training for this was that the king and queen wished to support English trade. Fortunate, then, that her court dress was made from Spitalfields silk.

She turned to the housekeeper. "Clara knows where my court dress is packed. In the meantime, I would like a bath."

"Of course, milady. And tea as you wait?"

"Perfect."

Alone for a brief moment, Diana removed her small hat and rubbed her aching head. It wasn't really aching. It was tense. Even the bones felt tense.

Where was he now? Doubtless he too was preparing for court. Was he already naked under Fettler's unappreciative eye . . . ?

Rothgar made sure that everything was in order, and then started up the stairs. He paused, however, seeing Diana studying the portrait of his father and stepmother.

What did she see?

Nothing he could offer her.

To avoid overtaking her, he turned back to go along a corridor to a room at the back of the house. There he supervised the unbundling of the drummer boy and checked for new damage. Thank heavens he'd ordered it carried in the boot of the main coach. It seemed to have survived the adventurous journey safely. He sent a message to John Joseph Merlin to examine it at his earliest convenience, and to make an appointment to speak to him about the repairs.

The servants bowed out of the room, and he stood alone with the still and silent figure, strangely tempted to wind it and switch it on. To bring the boy to life. He hunkered down so they were eye to eye.

"You are likely to torment me, you know. Evidence of what might have been. Warning of what might be if the gods are unkind."

The eerily realistic glass eyes, fringed by long lashes, gazed back at him. They seemed to say, "*Do you truly not want me to be real?*"

He rose sharply and left the room, locking the door behind him.

Nothing had changed. The logic upon which he had based his life was still sound. This unsteadiness he suffered now was weakness, nothing more.

He was infinitely practiced at resisting weakness.

Chapter 18

Diana distracted herself by exploring the charming boudoir, but found little of interest. The paintings were insignificant, and the few books in a glass-fronted set of shelves unlikely to be Elf's choices. Elf had moved on to her husband's house, and these rooms held only ghostly whispers of her.

A side door opened into a bedchamber, and beyond, Diana found the dressing room. Clara and another servant were carefully extracting her formal court dress along with its awkward panniers, while others filled a huge tub lined with thick linen cloths. A fire already burned in the grate to warm the room for bathing.

It was not a newly laid fire. This had clearly been thought of ahead of time, too, and this evidence of planning chipped at her hopes. Most of the time, Bey ran his affairs with efficient perfection. Nothing was neglected or done on impulse.

Clockwork precision, not easily changed.

That clicked her thoughts to the automaton. Presumably it had been unloaded by now and placed tenderly somewhere in this house. The drummer boy looked as she had as a child. What had Bey looked like at five or six? Was there a picture of him as an even younger child, before his mother's cruel act? Did later ones show the change, even in childhood features?

When the housekeeper returned, followed by a footman bearing the tea tray, Diana asked, "Is there a portrait gallery here?"

"A small one in the corridor outside the ballroom, milady. Most of the family portraits are at the Abbey, of course."

"I would like to see the portraits that hang here."

The woman was clearly startled, for the tea awaited and the bath would soon be ready, but she curtsied. "Of course, milady. Be so kind as to follow me."

She was led past the stairs to the other half of the house where a wider corridor was indeed lined with portraits. Diana thanked the housekeeper and dismissed her, then turned to stroll by the pictures.

The first were ancient paintings, one small miniature going back perhaps to the early Tudor period. Farther along she found two large portraits of a man and a woman in the opulent dress of the Restoration. Probably Bey's grandparents, and again she saw a resemblance in the woman's sculpted lids and the man's classic bones.

Nothing here of his parents, however. She wondered if any portraits survived of his mother, and if so, in what secluded corner they hung.

The end of the corridor contained one moderately sized portrait surrounded by miniatures, rather like the sun and the planets. With a smile, she wondered if he thought of the arrangement that way, too.

The central portrait had to be Bey as a young man, a youth almost. It was probably the usual one painted in Italy when on the Grand Tour for he leaned against a stone pillar, book in hand, and revealed a glimpse of some Italian town behind him. She understood that many Italian artists kept a stock of canvasses already painted with background and pillar, so that the English milord could choose the one that suited his fancy, and have his figure painted in. This looked of that sort, but the artist had been skilled in capturing his subject as in life.

Bey had probably been about seventeen, and showed no sign of childhood shadows. A tribute, that, to his father and stepmother. He looked what he had been then—a young man with the world in his hands, enjoying life to the full. With his brilliant mind, she was sure he had enjoyed his Grand Tour as it was meant to be enjoyed—for learning and exploration of the classical world. The smile and wicked eyes told her he was already enjoying other aspects of foreign travel.

My, but the Italian ladies must have been mad over him. Devastatingly handsome, with the well-shaped bones already clear but softened by the lingering blush of youth. Those mysterious, guarded eyes were larger, brighter, and full of the joys of life.

He was handsome now, grown into himself perfectly, but there was something toothsome about such youthful beauty accompanied by lordly confidence.

She dragged her eyes away to look at the smaller paintings, but they were all of his half-brothers and sisters, also in their teen years. No baby pictures at all, which wasn't surprising. They were usually kept in less public areas and often done with the mother. Any pictures of Bey with his mother were likely hidden away, or even destroyed.

What was it like to have a parent whom everyone wanted to forget? No wonder it hovered over him like a shadow.

She looked back at the central portrait, but it gave no answers except to tell her that the shadows he lived with had not all come from his mother's dreadful act. The death of his father and stepmother had played a part. Rosa had said they'd died of a fever he'd brought back to his home.

She knew they would not want him to suffer for it, but he must know that too. At heart, it was his mother who chained him. She turned and walked briskly back to her room, resolved to find a way to break those chains.

She paused at the head of the stairs for another look at the previous marquess and marchioness who must want happiness for all their family. All now had it, at least in part because of Bey's loving care. Only he was left alone.

Help me, she mouthed silently. Then she hurried on her way.

Two hours later, Diana surveyed herself in her mirror and declared herself satisfied. Formal court events required wide panniers instead of the narrow ones or hoops of everyday. The panniers, however, served to spread the fabric of the skirt and show off precious materials, encouraging a blatant declaration of wealth.

Her cream silk did that perfectly, rioting with embroidered spring flowers and leaves. The same material formed the ruched border around the skirt and up the parted front to her waist, trimmed down the middle with glittering gold braid. Her petticoat was figured cream silk, and she wore shoes to match. The rich stomacher was formed of silk ribbon and gold lace, and a small bunch of the silk flowers nestled in the lace by her breasts.

Breath caught as she thought of last night.

Would the flowers remind him?

She hoped so.

She knew he would be working hard now to avoid, to block, to rebuild defenses, but she would do everything she could to break them down.

Then she recalled that her purpose at the moment was not to break Bey's will, but to convince the king that she was a safe, conventional lady.

She looked the part. She would be expected to be grand as suited her station, and court fashion required face paint which allowed her to pretend a delicate pallor. She protected her complexion so it was honestly pale, but now the healthy glow in her cheeks was hidden as well. She'd not darkened her brows and lashes, and that too made her seem more faded, less strong, especially with powdered hair.

Her eyes traveled to the flowers again, and she realized that her bodice was very low. Not unsuitable for court, but here was a chance to seem particularly modest.

"My fichu," she ordered. "The embroidered muslin one."

After a flurried return to the boxes, it was found and draped around her neck, the ends tucked between her breasts behind the flowers.

Better. Sickeningly demure.

With that in mind, she chose simple jewelry. She had left off her rings after the bath, even though they were her armor. They were too much of an idiosyncrasy to wear for this performance. Now she chose one small ruby and a modest

pearl. Around her neck and in her ears she wore a seed pearl
and ruby set she'd been given when sixteen. Paltry stuff.

She took a last look and nodded. Rich but slightly mousy.
No challenge to anyone.

Would Bey approve? She took up her ivory fan and went
to find out, foolish heart already trembling at the thought of
seeing him again.

After *such* a long time apart.

A footman was stationed in the corridor to escort her. To
her surprise, he took her downstairs and toward the back of
the house which would usually be the household offices.
With a tap on the door, he opened it and announced her.

Diana went in and found herself in a very businesslike
study. Most of the walls were covered with bookshelves and
drawers. A map drawer stood open with a map on display.
The huge desk in the center of the room was a masterpiece
of marquetry and gilding, but it was still a desk, and Bey had
been sitting there dealing with large amounts of paperwork
before rising as she came in.

He worked too hard, trying to hold the world together.

All the same, she smiled at his beauty in rich red silk and
elegant powder.

Then she saw the picture on the wall to one side of him.

A young woman with coiled dark hair, in a loose gown of
flaming red, sat apparently at her ease, but with an arrogant
or perhaps challenging turn to her body. At first glance she
seemed strong, her smile confident and sure, her eyes direct,
but almost immediately Diana sensed fear.

Would she have even thought it if she hadn't known what
was to come? For this surely must be Bey's mother. His
father's dark hair and eyes suggested a degree of likeness
that wasn't there. Bey had his mother's exact features in
stronger form—the high brow, the classic bones, the square
chin, the straight, sculptured nose with flaring nostrils.

Was that why he felt so threatened by her mental instabil-
ity?

Was that why he kept this picture here to remind him?

Diana knew that he had brought her here to see this. He
had even dressed in red to make the likeness clear.

Undeclared, the war was on, and this was his defensive attack. The picture was to remind her of the facts, and to convince her that he had sound reasons to walk away from what they could have and be.

Commanding her racing heart to calm, Diana moved closer to the picture, her stiff silks rustling in the quiet room. "She looks frightened. Did she not want to marry your father?"

He stared, as if surprised. "She made no objection that I've heard, but it was somewhat of an arranged affair, yes. Arranged by loving parents on both sides. Her mother—my grandmother—is still alive, and still convinced that my father drove her daughter mad."

This was the discussion she'd wanted, but not now when they had so little time. She was pressingly aware that clocks had chimed the half hour as she came downstairs. Deliberate. She knew it was deliberate, so they could speak of this, but only briefly.

Damn him.

She was at war with an expert, ruthless strategist, and must not forget that.

"You were a young child when she died," she said, meeting his eyes. "Perhaps your grandmother is right and your father was not kind to her."

"My father was very like Brand. Can you imagine Brand distressing any woman into madness? And besides, what unkindness, what cruelty even, could drive a sane woman to strangle her own newborn child?"

Diana gasped. "*Strangle.*"

"Would some other manner of murder be more to your liking?"

It was the Dark Marquess speaking, the one she had feared when they first met. She recognized, however, that this again was defense, frighteningly similar to his mother's angled head and fierce smile.

"That was a silly reaction," she agreed calmly. "And no, nothing external can explain her actions. But madness can come from many causes, some of which die with the suf-

ferer." She looked back at the picture. "Was it done before
or after the wedding?"

"Just before."

"Then her mother doubtless sought an explanation to her
liking, for the seeds were already there."

"In the blood."

She winced, realizing her words had reinforced his thinking instead of fighting it. How to fight the evidence of this
picture, however? His mother had not been entirely normal.

"It was in her at a young age," she argued. "There were
warnings. It didn't appear like a shooting star." She looked
at him again, looked him in the eye. "Have you ever de-
tected a trace of it in yourself?"

"Perhaps not," he said calmly, "but her blood runs in me,
and through me. A child of mine could look like that."

She felt frozen. How to fight that?

The clock chimed the quarter, and his eyes traveled over
her. "Ah, I see the pallor is not a result of my sordid family
affairs. You will do very well. You look suitably overturned
by your experiences. We must leave."

With one last, frustrated glance at the portrait, she flicked
open her fan and sank into a deep court curtsy. "As you will,
my lord."

He held out his hand to raise her, but she rose smoothly
by herself.

Instead of applause, he said, "Don't do that at court. Let
me assist you."

"Devil take it." Then she grimaced. "I know. Don't do
that, either."

"Precisely." He took her hand and kissed it, eyes dark on
hers. "For both our sakes, Diana, make no mistakes."

He was telling her what she already knew—that a marriage of rescue would be worse than no marriage at all.

She cast one last look at the dreadful portrait, then allowed him to lead her out to the waiting coach. A light town
vehicle, painted and gilded, with liveried footmen up behind.

A small crowd had gathered and some pressed forward.

Immediately she tensed, remembering that de Couriac was loose, and longing for her pistols.

She steadied herself. One did not show fear, or even concern, in public. These were the petitioners one would expect at a great man's door in London. Such people would know when he would emerge to attend a levee or Drawing Room.

All the same, it would be too easy for an assassin to lurk among them, and she searched the crowd for de Couriac. She didn't see him, but he could appear later, tomorrow, the next day, and she would not always be here to guard.

Oh yes, Bey had his armed servants around him, but she wanted to be there too, an extra pair of eyes, and an extra pair of pistols.

Damn the king. Damn the court.

He was accepting petitions, showing no sign of caution, so she threw him a warning. "I do hope these people are all well-intentioned, my lord. I am going to be extremely annoyed if I end up in the dirt in this outfit."

A smile tugged at his lips, but he said, "None of us can live under glass, my lady, like wax flowers."

He passed a handful of petitions to a servant behind, and moved on to a woman who fell to her knees before him, begging for help. Diana wanted to listen to her story now, and help her now. There was no time, however, and Bey only raised her to her feet, took her paper and passed it on, promising to read it as soon as possible.

Even from that, the woman looked eased a little, and dabbed at her tears. A child or husband in prison, perhaps? Now the woman had faith that the great marquess would help her, but he had another burden on his shoulders, another demand on his exhausted time.

She received petitions herself, but rarely in person, and never like this. And this, she suspected, happened every time he left his house for a formal occasion.

She suddenly wanted to shoo them all away, to protect him, but knew he'd be offended at the thought. This was part of the duties of his rank, and duty came before all.

As with his duty to keep his line free of taint.

She counted twelve petitions taken before they were clear

to walk toward the coach. Twelve souls depending upon him for something dear to them.

This, surely, hadn't been planned as part of their war, but it reminded her of who he was. Merely by rank he was one of the great, a source of hope for the desperate. As *l'éminence noire* he was known to have the ear of the king.

Most of England stood in awe of him.

Could she really break this man's will?

She glanced at him again, and again their eyes spoke, and she knew, because of what he was, especially because of the chilly eminence upon which he lived, that she had to try.

More than that. She had to win.

Then they both looked forward and walked toward the coach, the Countess of Arradale and the Marquess of Rothgar, on stage.

Chapter 19

As they approached St. James's Palace, the press of vehicles and avidity of the watching crowds broke Diana out in a sweat. These fashionable parades and the unfashionable pointing mob weren't her challenge. The king was. All the same, she had to work hard not to flinch from a thousand eyes.

And she'd thought her life confined and under scrutiny in Yorkshire!

"Drawing Rooms are popular with the people," he remarked in a bored tone she knew was designed to steady her.

"So I see. Do they gather for the levees as well?"

"Not to so great an extent. Ladies are generally more decoratively entertaining than gentlemen."

She glanced at his finery. "It is not apparent. And anyway, in the animal world the male has the gorgeous plumage."

"And if we follow Monsieur Rousseau, we must, above all, be natural." As the coach drew to a halt, he said, "I will suggest that the king command all ladies to attend in sackcloth and drab."

A footman swung open the door, and Bey climbed down, turning to offer her a beautiful, jeweled hand in plumage of lace and brocade.

"You do like to stir enemies," she commented as she descended and smoothed her glorious skirts.

"Alas, without enemies life might become dull. Speaking of which, let me present you to the Chevalier D'Eon."

Snapping to the alert, Diana went with him toward a slight man in rich brown with the striking red ribbon of an order across his chest, the medallion glittering. Bey himself wore the Order of the Bath on a red sash, and an imaginative mind might see the two red slashes as a bloody challenge.

The Frenchman saw them and stepped forward with the quick elegance of a good fencer despite his high heels. "*Monsieur le marquis*," he said in rapid French. "I am distressed, outraged—" Then he seemed to catch himself, and bowed, addressing Diana in English. "My lady, I beg your pardon for speaking in French. And here I am again," he added, with a rather arch flutter of embarrassment, "speaking to you without introduction—"

"Lady Arradale," said Bey, sounding amused, "may I present the Chevalier D'Eon, the most honorable *Ministre Plénipotentiare de France*."

Diana held out her hand and greeted the Frenchman in English. Bey's meaningful look had not been necessary. She could see that being thought unable to understand the language might be an advantage one day.

Of course, de Couriac knew differently . . .

Monsieur D'Eon bowed over her hand with exquisite grace, pursing his lips a delicate distance above her skin. "London is made glorious by your beauty, Lady Arradale," he said, but then his expression turned tragic. "And I am devastated that you have apparently been distressed upon your journey by some rascally compatriots of mine."

"It certainly was terrifying, monsieur. But," she added, sliding her hand free of his ardent grasp, "any country can produce rogues. We escaped with our property and lives intact." She turned adoringly to Bey. "All due to Lord Rothgar's formidable courage and skill."

His eyes flashed a humorous warning before he said to D'Eon, "It happened too fast for skill. I regret the deaths of your countrymen, however."

"As do I, my lord. I would like to have the questioning of them."

"Quite."

It was like a slither of blades.

"They were apparently associates of a Monsieur de

Couriac," Bey remarked, "whom we encountered in Ferry
Bridge. Do you know him, Chevalier?"

"De Couriac?" D'Eon said vaguely as they all turned to
join the people flowing into the palace. "He presented papers to me some weeks ago upon arrival. I know nothing
more. *Petite noblesse* from Normandy, if I remember."

"Ah, then perhaps the Comte de Broglie may know the
family. He resides in Normandy, does he not?"

One sharp glance from D'Eon told Diana that Bey had
scored a hit.

"I doubt it, my lord," D'Eon said. "Monsieur de Broglie
lives very quietly now he is out of power." He turned to
Diana. "Be assured, my lady, that I will attempt to get to the
bottom of this terrible affair."

He bowed and left to greet someone else. Escaped, one
might say.

"Who is de Broglie?" Diana murmured as they filed up
the stairs.

"D'Eon's secret superior," Bey said in a voice so muted
she could scarcely hear it, and with a look that told her not
to pursue it here.

Lud! What tangle was hinted at in that? D'Eon's only
master should be the King of France. Is it wise, she wanted
to ask, to tell him that you know?

With a flash of irritation, she recognized that Bey had just
thrown down a challenge to the Frenchman. She could understand that constantly waiting for these sneaky attacks
would test the patience of a marble statue, but she wished he
hadn't. Especially now when she was going to have to leave
him unguarded.

Especially when he had probably done it to ensure she
was not caught in any further attacks.

Ah, but she was going to hate being put in this gilded
cage.

As they made their way through the crowded corridors,
Diana could at least be grateful that the king refused to live
here in St. James's Palace. These dark and ancient passageways had seen their share of wretches heading for disaster,
torture, and execution, and the memories seemed to linger in

the walls. Some of the victims had been His Majesty's ancestors. Some of them had been hers.

Her pulse started a nervous beat again as she approached
the drawing room—as if a headsman might appear, ax in
hand.

She could see ahead now to where the king and queen sat
in magnificent garments and jewels, ladies- and gentlemen-
in-waiting standing behind. Most of those attending the
Drawing Room merely approached to curtsy or bow and exchange a word or two, but those being presented were given
a little more time.

After greeting Their Majesties, people moved around the
room chatting, taking care never to turn their backs to the
royal couple, though some seemed to leave quite quickly.
She wished she had that option.

When their turn came, Bey led her forward, and she sank
into her curtsy, head bowed. The queen gestured for her to
rise and Diana remembered to allow Bey to assist her. It was
clearly an excellent point. The royal couple looked as if they
were searching for monstrous aspects.

"We welcome you to London, Lady Arradale," said the
very pregnant queen with a strong German accent. She was
as plain as reported, with a rather monkeyish face and bul-
bous eyes.

"You are most kind to have invited me, Your Majesty."

Diana had forgotten how young the queen was. Only
nineteen. Not that age counted here. The king was a year
younger than herself, but that did not lessen the dangers.

The queen frowned. "I understand you have inherited
your father's property and title, Lady Arradale. I find that a
very strange thing."

"It is unusual in England too, Your Majesty."

"A cruel burden to put upon a woman's shoulders."

Diana looked down. "Indeed, Your Majesty."

"Strange, then, that you have not married."

Straight to the attack! Diana hoped she had the right expression as she met the queen's eyes. "Alas, Your Majesty,
but I have delayed in search of a man I could truly love."

Queen Charlotte's eyes did warm slightly. "*Das ist gut.*

But you must not delay too long, my lady, or you will lose your bloom. We will talk of this later. You will stay with me as one of my ladies for a while."

This had been arranged, but now was given the royal affirmation.

"You do me great honor, Your Majesty." Diana curtsied again to king and queen, and could move to one side. First engagement over.

However the king rose and stepped aside with them. "What is this I hear, Lord Rothgar? Brigands on our highway? What? In daylight? *French* brigands? What?"

"An unfortunate incident, sire."

"Unfortunate!" The king's fresh face reddened. "Intolerable. I have dispatched Colonel Allenby to look into the matter. I will not have such things, especially within ten miles of London! You are unharmed?"

"Completely, sire."

"And Lady Arradale?" The king looked at her, but Diana judged that she was not expected to actually speak for herself.

"Unharmed also, Your Majesty, though distressed, of course."

Diana blessed her pale powder and tried to look distressed.

"It would be unwomanly not to be," the king stated. "But three brigands dead, my lord? What? I know you to be a formidable man, but how did that come about?" Then he gave an irritated shake of the head. "Not now. You must return to the Queen's House and relate the whole story."

Bey bowed. "With pleasure, sire. If you wish, I could convey Lady Arradale there in my coach."

The king nodded and returned to his duties.

Diana looked up at Bey. More time together? Irresistible, but it only extended the pain. Had he perhaps just given in to a moment of weak temptation?

There was no way to tell from his manner. He led her around the room introducing her to ladies and gentlemen who seemed grateful to see a new face. Especially, she soon realized, a face attached to such an unusual creature as a peeress in her own right and a very wealthy woman. Everyone seemed to have a perfectly wonderful son, brother, or nephew.

This sort of heiress hunting was the least of their problems, however. She didn't like the queen's plan to find her a husband, but otherwise she thought it had gone well.

Perhaps Their Majesties had expected her to clump in here in breeches, brandishing a weapon. That was another unfair aspect of the way the world regarded women. It was assumed that they could not be strong without attempting to dress and act like men. That a woman who liked pretty clothes and jewels, and cared about her complexion must be a simpering ninny.

It was the sort of thing she would love to discuss with Bey, but certainly not here. When next would they have a chance to talk in private? That precious cup, their conversation, had only been sipped, and she thirsted for more.

The company thinned out, but they, of necessity, lingered on. Literally "in waiting." Diana sighed. This was likely to be her life for the next few weeks.

"Tired?" he asked.

There were no chairs, of course. She'd been trained for this, too—to stand, poised and still for as long as necessary, and even to suppress a sneeze if one crept up—but they were not skills she practiced much. He doubtless had it perfected, for he seemed completely at ease and inexhaustible.

"Impatient," she admitted.

"Yet patience is the best remedy for every trouble."

"Plautus." She rolled her eyes. "I had to write that out, in Latin, a hundred times once."

His lips twitched. "And I am falling into the role of teacher again. It seems safer. You are young."

She looked into his eyes. "I am *not* too young. That, at least, does not stand between us."

He nodded. "No, it does not."

She actually thought of pursuing the matter here, which showed how foolish this all was making her. Instead, she looked idly around, fanning herself. "This life will be hard."

"I fear there is nothing I can say in response to that which will not sound like a lecture."

She flicked him a glance and saw a smile in his eyes. "Then I will lecture myself. Marcus Aurelius: Think not this is misfortune, but that it is good fortune to be given the opportunity to bear it well."

His lips twitched. "Something else your tutor set you to writing as a penance?"

"Indeed. In English and the original Greek. In response, as I remember, to my anger at being confined to the house for a week in summer. Something to do with Mistress Hucken's chickens . . . I was fortunate, though. He never guessed how much more I would have hated having to sew words into samplers."

"Alas, the queen likes her ladies' hands to be occupied with useful work. In particular, needlework."

Diana groaned, then realized they were smiling at each other. Doubtless in a most revealing manner.

A quick glance assured her that no one seemed to be observing them, but she hastily moved over to study a picture on the wall. It was an eminently safe picture of a country house in a tidy, geometric garden. Not a lot of scope for discussion there, but they managed until the king and queen were finally ready to take their leave.

Soon now, soon, the parting.

She had forgotten that she was to travel with him. A reprieve, but one of perhaps only a quarter of an hour. Still, she thought as they settled into the coach, she would not waste it. No time to discuss the complex issues that separated them, but time to satisfy her curiosity.

"Now," she said as they rolled off, "tell me more about the Comte de Broglie."

"Ah. I hoped you had forgotten." He turned toward her. "I doubt the information would be of use to you."

"No? I am going to be very bored in the next weeks. A little skillful observation would pass the time. I noticed that you did not want Monsieur D'Eon to know that I speak excellent French. I might hear something useful to you?"

"Diana, being a spy within the royal household is a dangerous thing."

She blinked at him. "I hadn't thought of it quite like that." After a moment she grinned. "Consider me a gossip, then. I'm sure conventional ladies are expected to gossip."

He covered his face with his hand in mock despair.

"And," she added brightly, loving this moment for its sparkling self, "it would be much more to the point to be a well-informed gossip than one with no idea of what is going on."

"You are irrepressible, Lady Arradale."

"I do hope so, Lord Rothgar."

Smile faded into something much more dangerous. His hand lowered and moved as if he would touch her, but was controlled.

"Very well," he said, cool once more. "But bear in mind that what I am about to tell you is known to very few, and the French do not know we know. It must stay so."

They were already passing out of the narrow streets around Saint James's and into the greenery of the parks. Perhaps ten minutes left. "I can be discreet."

"If I didn't think so, I would tell you nothing. King Louis of France is, in effect, running two separate governments, especially with regard to foreign affairs. The open, official one, and a secret one known only to the few."

This was startling enough to distract her from other matters. "Why?"

"Because kings are surprisingly hemmed in. By traditions, by favorites, by formality. King George often uses me as his private intelligence. King Louis is constrained by the much more rigid world of Versailles. He finds it particularly difficult to escape his ministers or La Pompadour."

"I thought she was old and retired."

"But still has her influence, and anyway this all dates back to the years of her prime. Don't interrupt. We don't have much time."

Indeed, they were completely surrounded by parkland now.

"Years ago, Louis set up a secret chain of command running parallel to his official government. It was to pursue his own aims and policies when they conflicted with official ones. It also feeds him independent information, something all monarchs need. The Comte de Broglie is officially out of favor, but he is the head of this alternate government, and the Chevalier D'Eon is a key player. He has direct contact with the king."

"And the new ambassador who is awaited?" Diana asked.

"Guerchy. The choice of official circles."

She frowned over it. "If D'Eon is King Louis' man, why isn't he ambassador? Surely the king could appoint whomever he wished."

"D'Eon's come far, but he's an adventurer. He doesn't have the rank or fortune for such a position. More importantly, a suggestion of such unusual royal favor would raise suspicions. A secret agent must stay in the shadows."

"You don't."

"I'm not a secret agent. I employ some, however. They are decidedly shadowy."

Diana blew out a little breath. "How extraordinary. And exciting. I begin to see the appeal of a life close to the center of the world. So, if King Louis' secret ministry differs from the official one, what do they plan?"

"What we spoke of last night. Revenge. The French government wishes to lick its wounds, but Louis wants to go to war again as soon as he thinks he can win. Above all, he wishes to invade us."

For a moment, she was tempted to take the conversation back to last night, but she knew there was nothing more to be said on that just now, and she needed this information to be useful to him. "Does the king not know about Monsieur D'Eon? I mean, King George?"

"He knows none of this."

"Can't you enlighten him?"

"Not yet. The king lost his father at a young age and is inclined to seek another. He will grow out of it, but at the moment he would like to think 'dear cousin Louis' a worthy mentor."

"The king of an enemy nation?"

"We are at peace, and Louis has been king for many years. He has experience. With D'Eon as blushing handmaiden, Louis is making great efforts to be everything George could wish."

"I still think you should tell him. You must have evidence."

"Shadowy evidence. Ambiguous phrases and coded messages. If I made any impression at all, he would confront D'Eon with it. That would reveal that we know. One of the perils," he said with a meaningful look, "of dealing with youth."

"I would never do anything so foolish."

His eyes rested on her. "I don't suppose you would. Young women are often a great deal wiser than young men. Why do you think wise men marry younger women? It is in the faint hope of an equal match."

"Ah!" she said, but then suppressed the rest of her thought.

"As I said," he murmured, "very wise."

Wise? To push away this gift they were offered? She'd thought she knew the treasure within grasp, but these few minutes in the coach, talking as equals, as friends for the first time, had increased it tenfold. She wanted this as she wanted sunlight and breath.

She looked away for a moment to gather strength. Strength not to beg. Begging would only hurt him. He knew how precious it was as much as she did, and he had excellent reasons for sacrifice. Before her blurring eyes, railings passed. They must be at the Queen's House already!

Mere minutes left.

"Pay attention, Diana," he said as if he did not guess her emotions.

Blinking to clear her eyes, she turned back.

"Proof of Louis' secret government is sketchy," he said, looking away, as if judging the time left before they arrived at the brick house. She knew he was deliberately not looking at her moist eyes.

"Everything I have"—he carried on—"appears harmless unless one believes the code, and I cannot risk giving the code to the king. Having it will cease to be useful if the French find out."

"My," said Diana, putting all the calm and control into her voice that she could muster, "wheels, within wheels, within wheels. You act alone?"

"There are people in our government aware of my work."

"Rather shadowy after all."

"Only from certain angles." He turned to look at her, shadowy indeed, but from other causes, she knew.

"So," she asked. "What can I do?"

"Observe and listen, especially if D'Eon is with the queen, and gossip to me later. But be very, very careful."

"So I will see you?"

He became very still. "Did you think I would abandon you?"

"No, but . . . daily?"

"Most days. I have the entrée here. A mild interest in your progress will not be unseemly."

The coach was turning in front of the house. Almost the end! "Will we be able to speak privately?"

"Probably not."

They halted. But, she saw, they were not yet at the doors, for the king's coach preceded theirs. "How will I give you reports then?"

After a thoughtful moment, he said, "A code. The queen can be Rosa, and the king Brand."

"Clever. What of D'Eon, then? I know," she said with a smile, "he can be Samuel, Rosa's prize ram."

And he laughed. Fully, looking years younger. "Scurrilous wench, and in D'Eon's case, probably inappropriate."

"Why?" she asked, smile wide enough to be painful.

"That's another long story," he said, laughter simmering to smile, but still smiling. "Who will be the French King?"

As the coach jerked forward again, she said, "Dirk, her Flemish stallion. Believe me, to describe Rosa in avid conversation about horse and sheep breeding is not at all contrived."

His lips twitched, but he was recovering control. "Very well. But be careful."

As the coach moved in front of the doors she clutched the plan to herself. It was a thread linking them, and perhaps that was why he had created it.

And he had laughed.

"Is that all I can do?" she asked. "No stealing letters? No breaking codes?"

He gripped her hand, down on the seat, where the approaching footman would not see. "This is not a game, Diana. Be wise."

She looked ahead, trying to appear uninvolved, but trembling at his touch. "It is not easy to be wise."

His hand surrendered to tenderness. "No. But it is possible."

Rebellion flaring, she looked him in the eye. "With a Malloren, all things are possible?" she queried.

"Exactly."

A footman opened the door.

Their hands slid apart.

He stepped down and turned to help her.

As she descended the steps, she said softly, "Then prove it so, Bey."

His hand tightened on hers, and he looked almost shocked.

She'd shocked herself. She'd never thought to challenge him directly like that, but, by Jupiter, that *was* his motto, and a life together must be possible. The moon would weep at the waste of them living apart.

"Despite that motto," he said when she was by his side, "I am not God. Some things are beyond me."

"Which things?"

"I cannot fly, for one," he said shortly.

This was not how she wanted them to part, but she must persist. He had laughed. She could give him that. She could give him laughter and life.

It had to be possible.

She fussed with her skirts to steal a moment more. "Perhaps you accept false limits. Daedalus flew on waxen wings, and I have heard you described as Daedalian."

"In connection with his skill in building clever labyrinths, not faulty wings." He cut the moment short by taking her hand and leading her toward the door through which the king and queen were already disappearing. "I seem to have constructed a damnable labyrinth for us."

"This is *not* all your doing," she stated, eyes forward. "And Daedalus did fly."

"And persuaded his beloved son to fly. Then Icarus flew too close to the sun, so his wings melted and he fell to his death."

She halted, forcing him to stop and face her. "They both flew to escape an intolerable prison. Perhaps Icarus thought it worthwhile, even as he fell."

He seemed suddenly the man she had first met, the Dark Marquess. "You are going to fight me on this?"

She raised her chin and met his eyes. "Hasn't it always been clear that a duel lay between us?"

After a silent moment, he turned once more toward the door. "Pray not to the death."

She let him lead her into her gilded prison, quivering, but not in nervousness at this confinement. What had she done? What wild flight had she started, on fragile waxen wings? She would be Daedalus, however, to his Icarus, and she would somehow construct wings with which they could escape. Not her confinement at court, but the dark tower in which he had walled himself for life.

Not now, however. Now she must act her part, here within these elegant, conventional walls.

The Queen's House had been built by the Duke of Buckingham, and only recently sold to the king for his new queen. It was grand, but more of a noble's house than a royal palace. She suspected that this house's appeal for the young couple was its simplicity. That and the fact that it was modern and set in parkland.

It was less daunting than she'd feared, and less infused with dark history than St. James's Palace. All the same, she didn't expect to enjoy living here, especially when her time with Bey was likely to be brief and closely chaperoned.

The royal party were waiting at the base of the stairs. The

king said, "My lord, attend me," and stalked off toward an open, waiting door.

With only a brief farewell, Bey followed him.

Thus, abruptly, he was gone. Though it felt like tearing flesh, Diana made herself not stare after him. Instead, she looked as placidly as possible at the queen and her attendants.

"Come," the queen ordered, turning toward the stairs. "Attend me as I change, Lady Arradale."

Chapter 20

Diana would have liked to change out of her awkward costume herself, but she was virtually a servant now and followed meekly upstairs to the queen's suite of rooms. Charlotte's two German keepers of the robes fussed and clucked her out of her stiff garments, and indeed, she looked tired.

"I am glad you are not averse to a husband, Lady Arradale," the queen said. "It will please His Majesty. And you are sensible to want to marry a man with whom you can live in accord. A bad marriage can be a miserable thing. You think a suitable man hard to find?"

"Yorkshire does not present a great selection of my age and station, Your Majesty."

The queen nodded. "London has many such men. The king and I live quietly, but we hold small parties now and then. We will invite suitable men, and soon you will find one to your taste."

It sounded ominously like a command, but Diana dropped a curtsy. "It would be a blessing, Your Majesty." It was the truth, for there was only one man to her taste.

"And if not," the queen said, sliding her arms into the sleeves of a light robe, "we will choose for you. His Majesty and I did not meet before our wedding, but the choice was carefully made by others, and is to our delight."

Diana swallowed alarm, but she drew on Bey's grueling practice and merely said, "You are very kind, Your Majesty."

The queen nodded approval, and walked into another

room, lively with crimson hangings, paintings, and bowls of flowers. She sat with a weary sigh, resting swollen ankles on a velvet footstool.

Diana followed, trying to assess this arrogant purpose about her marriage, and decide how to deal with it. But then she was hit by the heavy scent of a large arrangement of sweet peas.

"You like flowers, Lady Arradale?" the queen asked.

"Very much, ma'am," said Diana, wondering if she was blushing. Last night. Only last night . . .

"Good, good. We have pleasant gardens here, and you are free to enjoy them. You will not find your duties difficult, I think. You will read to me sometimes, and let me practice my English with you. Do you play an instrument?"

"The harpsichord, ma'am, and the flute."

"There is a harpsichord in the next room. Play for us."

As the queen began to chatter to her attendants in German, Diana obeyed the command, even managing the tricky business of backing out of the royal presence without tripping over her skirts.

She seethed with resentment at being ordered to entertain, but she reminded herself that she must be the perfect, conventional lady. It wasn't as if this was a burden of her sex. If she'd been the Earl of Arradale ordered to amuse the queen, she would be bound by duty to oblige, as the Marquess of Rothgar obeyed the king's commands.

Where was he now?

When would she see him again?

She pushed such thoughts aside. She'd end up mad herself if she sank into that kind of thing.

Grateful to at least be out of sight, she sat to play a piece by memory. This was an excellent opportunity to assess the new twists in her situation.

The queen sounded a great deal more determined on marriage than she'd expected, and she was clearly spokeswoman for the king. Diana could end up fighting two challenges rather than one. A battle with the king and queen to avoid their choice, and a battle with Bey to convince him that marriage was a risk worth taking despite uncertainty.

Lud! She still couldn't believe she'd thrown that gauntlet down. She meant it, however. It was her whole life and his. She would not let it slip away. Life was uncertain. Not to accept that was to freeze like a stone statue.

She let her fingers wander by themselves through the simple piece, and wondered again when next they'd meet. After all, it was central to her purpose. She could hardly change his mind if he avoided her completely.

He'd promised to see her frequently, however, and she knew he would keep that promise, through duty if nothing else.

Again today, though?

Or would she have to wait until tomorrow?

When tomorrow?

She suppressed a rueful laugh. This was insanity, but it was the common insanity called love. She didn't mind if they fought or kissed, so long as they met.

Well, she did mind, but she'd take any meeting over none. Even simply being in the same room would be some solace.

She realized her fingers had stopped. She pulled out of her wistful thoughts and changed to a lively and demanding tune. She would somehow find a way to change Bey's mind. In the meantime, she must also charm the queen and avoid attempts to force her into marriage. She'd heard that the queen was very fond of music and an excellent performer herself. This might be one way to mellow her.

In a little while one of the German attendants came to inform her she could leave to change out of court dress. She found her room small but adequate, and at least it was private. Clara was just finishing putting things away, bubbling with excitement to be in a royal household and greatly impressed by the servants she had already met.

Diana was pleased someone was happy here. She stripped out of court dress, and changed into a more comfortable gown. When she checked her appearance in the mirror, she realized it was the pale yellow and cream which she'd worn to welcome the Dark Marquess to Arradale.

A different world. A world where she had, as he'd pointed out, been playing games.

How could the world change so utterly in a few short days?

With a sigh, she sat at the elegant desk to write to her mother and Rosa. She had to give some account of the attack on the road before word reached them, and assure them she was well.

The letter to her mother was easy, but the second troubled her. Rosa had been her confidante for most of her life, her dearest friend, her companion in mischief, and guardian of secrets. Rosa had a different personality, too, and her practical opinions had often been useful. She longed to relate everything and hope for wisdom in return, but she wouldn't put it past the king and queen to read her letters.

She imagined what she would say if Rosa was here. "I'm determined to marry Bey, to make it possible for him to marry me."

"How?"

Trust Rosa to move straight to the point. "I don't know. That's for later. For now, I have to prevent the king and queen trying to arrange my marriage. What should I do if they pick a husband for me?"

"Refuse?"

"It's not that easy, Rosa. It would give great offense. And there is the threat of the madhouse. I'd have to accept Bey's rescue, then."

"Marry him? In name only? I don't think you can do that, Diana."

"I know, I know. But if it came to that point, what else could I do? Marry some oaf picked out by the king? I think not, and Bey would never allow it. Anyway, would it be so terrible? We'd at least have each other's company."

"You'd live the rest of your life like a starving woman at a forbidden feast!"

"There would be many dishes I could taste. His company, his conversation, our shared interests. Oh, Rosa. I know what you meant about Brand, now. I thought you demented to put such weight on the fact that you could talk about farming with him, but it is wonderful to have shared interests. To really talk. The time in the coach was magical and we hardly touched."

"But the forbidden would be always there, desperately desirable but never to be tasted. It would drive you mad."

"You say that because you have the feast in full. Without him I will starve. Starve to death."

"Too extreme, Diana."

"I feel extreme. I rage against the barriers that stand between us!"

"And what are those barriers?"

Diana sighed. "His will. His purpose," she admitted.

"You want to break his will? Turn him from his well-considered purpose?"

Yes, thought Diana, unable to put that confession into even imaginary words. It was a terrible thing to contemplate.

To the imaginary Rosa, she argued, "It is the only way."

"It could destroy you both."

Diana looked down and realized that while running that imaginary conversation through her head, she'd dipped her pen and written "Bey," a half dozen times, then ornamented the cluster of words with ruffled sweet peas.

Love. She'd always thought of love as hearts and flowers, as spring blossoms and blushing smiles. Not this spiny, starving hunger, this feeling of being stranded in rags on a bleak winter moor, and being willing to do anything, *anything*, to return to the sun.

She dipped the pen and scribbled all over her betraying marks. She was clear in her purpose now at least—to shatter the iron will of the man she loved.

May God have mercy on them both.

Rothgar accompanied the king to his rooms, almost stunned by Diana's last comments. He had faced seemingly impossible tasks before and proved his motto correct. He'd even taken the notorious Chastity Ware and restored her virtue so she could be received at court and marry Cyn without problem. There was always a way.

But here he faced no external barrier, only his own resolve. To alter that with honor was as impossible as flight, ancient Daedalus be damned. Such flight was impossible, anyway. He'd witnessed an attempt to recreate Daedalus's achievement, and it had been clear that no man had the strength to flap wings large enough to carry him.

Some things were impossible despite all human effort.

As the king was disrobed by his attendants, Rothgar tried to find his familiar cool mind, but awareness of Diana's needs and pain rocked him. He could starve himself, but he had not prepared for the agony of starving her—

"My lord."

Rothgar found the king staring at him. "So lost in thought, my lord?" George said as a valet assisted him into a loose robe. "Thoughts of mortality, what?"

"Your pardon, sire?"

"The bloodthirsty attack."

Rothgar suppressed the words, *Oh that*, which would make him seem ready for Bedlam. Had it really been less than a day ago?

The king indicated a chair, and they both sat.

"Now," the king said, "give me the entire story."

He obliged, downplaying any outstanding bravery except that of his dead outrider.

"Brave man, brave man," said the king, his youthful face earnest. "Does he leave a family? What?"

"A wife and three young children, sire. Of course they will be well taken care of."

The king nodded, but said, "I will send them a letter of thanks."

"You are most generous, sire." Nothing, he knew, would soften Ella Miller's loss just now, but perhaps in the future she and her children would value the king's special mark of respect.

But then the king wished to speculate. He had clearly sent for and read Sir Eresby's report.

"This de Couriac. You suspect him of contriving the attack?"

"I can't say, sire. I believe I recognized him there."

"But why would he do such a thing?"

Since it did not suit him to point to official French involvement, Rothgar mentioned the unfortunate events in
Ferry Bridge.

The king shook his head. "Mad indeed! And one innocent
life lost because of it, what? I commanded Monsieur D'Eon
here as soon as I heard."

"The chevalier seems quite overset. May I ask what explanation he had for you, Your Majesty?"

"He too speculates that it might be a crime of passion. Apparently the wife was of that type." He frowned. "A mistake
to dally there, my lord. What?"

Rothgar's unruly mind tried to wander to memories of
Diana coming to rescue him. Of rubbing her feet. Of wanting—

No.

"I did not dally at all, sire. I merely assisted the lady when
her husband was taken ill. Lady Arradale was present most
of the time."

"Ah yes. The countess. Not what we expected. What do
you make of her?"

Rothgar wondered if he was actually blushing. "Your
Majesty will have assessed her for yourself by now."

The king nodded. "A pretty woman, and she seems to
think as she ought. Will she resist marriage?"

"Quite the contrary, sire," Rothgar said dryly. "In fact, she
could be said to be set on it."

"Capital, capital! The queen and I have talked of this.
Lord Randolph Somerton, what? Second son. Needs a good
property. Charming. Sound. What?"

Rothgar was startled by this firm choice, and what a
choice! An arrogant popinjay with wastrel ways and a demanding father in the Duke of Carlyle. "Would that not concentrate a great deal of northern power in one family?" he
suggested carefully.

The king frowned. "But she must marry in the north,
mustn't she? So her lands will not be neglected?"

"The roads are much improved, sire. Lady Arradale and I
would have spent only two nights on our journey if not for
the unfortunate incident."

The king pursed his lips. "Sir Harry Crumleigh then? His estate is in Derbyshire. Capital fellow. Or Lord Scrope, since she's the quiet type. Shropshire, and he's looking for a second wife."

Thought of Diana as "the quiet type" almost caused a laugh, but the list of candidates was not at all amusing. Sir Harry was a favorite of the king's because he was an inexhaustible rider, but if he'd ever read a book, he'd done it in secret. Lord Scrope was so amiably inoffensive he'd bore Diana to tears in days, and he was still mourning his first wife. Where the devil had all this purposeful planning come from?

"If I might suggest patience, sire? The countess has only just arrived in London, and suffered a terrifying incident en route. It would be kind to give her opportunity to rest and settle before presenting her with suitors."

After a frowning moment the king nodded. "Very well, but I'll see her married before she returns north, my lord. Now," he added in a change of tone, "this will interest you! The King of France has sent me an automaton as a peace gift."

"Indeed, sire?" Rothgar said, mind still caught on the king's unexpected resolve.

"Chevalier D'Eon is to present and demonstrate it to us tomorrow evening. You will attend?"

D'Eon? "With pleasure, Your Majesty."

"We will, of course, also show the one you gave us last year."

"I am honored it finds favor still."

"It does," the king said, standing. "You serve us well, Lord Rothgar, in all things, and we thank you. We wish you well in all things in return."

"Your Majesty is generous, as always," Rothgar said and took his leave.

He walked down the corridor, resisting the temptation to seek Diana out, to make sure that she was safe. He knew no harm could have come to her, but in view of the gathering host of suitors, he felt an absurd romantic urge to race to her rescue, like a knight errant saving his lady from a dragon.

It could not be. That interlude in the coach had been unwise, and had led to that challenge. And anyway, he had
other responsibilities. Ella Miller should hear of her husband's death from him, so he must ride to the Abbey today
before the news reached her.

Where the corridor and stairs met, he made himself take
the stairs that would lead him out of the house, away from
her.

Still, their parting had been abrupt, and she was under his
care and protection. On unconquerable impulse, he entered
a reception room and wrote a short note.

> *My dear Lady Arradale,*
> *I trust you are now comfortable in the queen's care, and*
> *that all your possessions have arrived safely. If I can be of*
> *any further assistance to you, I will do all that is possible.*
> *Consider me always,*
> *Your most humble servant,*
> *Rothgar.*

A suitable note in correct phrases, but with underlying
meanings. She would note, he hoped, the reference to what
was possible. He folded it and sealed it with his ruby signet,
then left it in the hands of the footman. As he climbed into
his coach and commanded all speed home, he made himself
turn his mind from the impossible to think about matters that
could be more neatly managed.

The choice of an automaton as the French king's gift was
not extraordinary, especially as some of the masters of the
craft were French and King George's pleasure in such things
was known. It was equally well known, however, that automata were an interest of his own. He had given the king
his first one—the Chinese pagoda which had unfortunately
been used in an attempted assassination.

Rothgar was pleased that the villain who'd caused its destruction had been killed, for it had been an exquisite work
of art. Last Christmas he had replaced it with a simpler
piece—a shepherd and shepherdess which the king and
queen enjoyed.

Now a similar gift had arrived from the King of France.

Considering the duel with Curry and the strange machinations of Monsieur de Couriac, it did seem as though D'Eon was subtly attacking him on many sides.

Why?

And, he suddenly wondered, was D'Eon responsible for the king's determination about Diana's marriage? Someone must have been stoking the fire beneath that pot to bring it to such a boil, and D'Eon had the ear of the king and queen.

Yet, what concern could Diana's marriage be to the French?

None.

To D'Eon personally?

He would certainly love to marry a fortune, but he must know that the king would never permit her marriage to a Frenchman. Besides, as he'd hinted to Diana, D'Eon's sexuality was a matter for conjecture. He flirted, but he'd never been known to take a mistress.

What's more, in his adventures, he'd spent time at the Court of Russia impersonating a woman and living as one of the late tsarina's ladies. Many doubted the story, but Rothgar knew it to be true. D'Eon had been spying for his king, but had been extremely convincing from all accounts.

Male, female, or hermaphrodite, D'Eon was ambitious. But not, surely, for marriage to a great English heiress. However . . .

As Rothgar left the coach and entered his house, he thought he'd found the pattern. He'd have seen it days ago if his brain hadn't been tangled by an alarmingly attractive woman.

As he'd told Diana, D'Eon needed a coup to be made ambassador. The obvious coup would be persuading King George to rescind the order to destroy Dunkirk, and D'Eon had openly been working hard at that.

Why hadn't he seen that D'Eon would think himself his greatest barrier? The king sought his advice, and he had been firmly in favor of weakening France and preventing another war. Above all, he had argued for the destruction of the military installations at Dunkirk.

So, he thought, as he entered his office, perhaps D'Eon had become desperate and decided to remove the obstacle in his way.

First the duel with Curry. When that failed, another attempt, doubtless with a more skillful swordsman—de Couriac.

The attack on the road, though? It seemed too crude, too hastily planned, for D'Eon. Possibly de Couriac had lost his head and acted without instructions. Perhaps the reward offered had been too great to lose, or perhaps he feared the consequences of failure.

And de Couriac was still at large. Diana had been right in warning of the danger of crowds, but as he'd said, he could not live like a wax flower under glass.

It was an interesting pattern, however, and needed to be considered. If D'Eon had recognized that Diana was under his protection, and was meddling in her affairs to distract him, what else might he try? Intolerable to have innocents dragged into this.

She was safe for the moment, however, so he put that aside and picked up the petitions. His other work could wait, but sometimes these matters were urgent.

As he unfolded the letter from the distraught woman, however, he couldn't help but smile at D'Eon's genuine fury over de Couriac's attack on the road.

His death in a duel with an Englishman posed no risk to the French. Even a duel with a Frenchman over an unfaithful wife could be unsuspicious. An open attack on the king's highway by four Frenchmen was another matter entirely. D'Eon was hobbled now, and must know it. He couldn't afford any more attacks that could be traced back to the French.

It would be a few days at least before D'Eon could come with some new device.

He read the scrawled and tearstained letter.

Mistress Tulliver's only son and chief support had certainly been unwise, and was condemned to transportation, but his offense was only the theft of some gentleman's clothing in an attempt to cut a fine figure. She claimed it was his first crime. He could at least look into that and perhaps find a way to seek mercy for him.

He made a note and looked through the other petitions. A few were requests for small amounts of money, and he approved all but one. The others required more thought, so he put them aside. It was nearly three and he had a long ride ahead of him.

All the same, he could not leave without taking some steps to control D'Eon. The man was blocked from direct attack on him, but that might lead him to meddle even more in Diana's affairs.

As official representative of France, he was untouchable, but there were other ways.

He sent for Joseph Grainger.

Grainger, a young and serious man, was both his lawyer and steward of his business affairs. He was also manager of his more secret activities. He gave the man a string of orders.

". . . and get a list of D'Eon's debts and creditors," he concluded.

"Yes, my lord."

Rothgar took pity on the impassive, but surely curious, man. "His finances must be a mess. He's living in state as a full ambassador without the ambassador's emoluments or any private income. I have indications he's already dipped into the money waiting for Guerchy, but he must be borrowing, too."

"You will buy up his debts, my lord?"

"Precisely." Rothgar rose. "Have the word spread that he's not a good risk."

Grainger closed his notebook, frowning. "Is he a bad risk?"

"A terrible one. Yes, I'm likely to end up with a bunch of bad debts and that offends your tidy soul. Consider it an extravagant expense."

"Yes, my lord," Grainger replied, still with a subtle tone of disapproval. Rothgar didn't mind. It was Grainger's job to disapprove of financial losses.

"And double the watch on him. I want to know everything

he does, everyone he speaks to, in and out of the embassy.
That's all for now, but send Rowcup to wait for me here."

Twenty minutes later, in plain riding clothes, he returned
to his study and found his resident forger waiting for him.

Rowcup was a fat little man who pleasantly combined
passion and skill in his illegal calling with total loyalty.
Rothgar had saved him from hanging for his crimes because
it was clear that forgery for Rowcup was not a means of
making a living, but a gift he could not put aside.

He employed him openly to make exact copies of manu-
scripts and records that threatened to disintegrate, but sometimes he used him for more dangerous matters.

Today they constructed a letter in the style of the secret
ones D'Eon received from the King of France. In it, Louis
praised D'Eon's work, and encouraged his illusion of un-
touchability. Finally, the king hinted that he understood the
need to put forward a glorious presence in London, and that
even if he was forced to let Guerchy take up his post as ambassador, all D'Eon's expenses would be covered.

As Rowcup completed his work with a perfect seal, he
shone like an angel with pride. The letter was sent to be
woven into the secret communication stream between
France and England, and Rothgar quickly reviewed the steps
taken.

That was enough for now. With the supply of borrowed
money tightened, D'Eon should have less time for thinking
up trouble for others. With luck, he'd start dipping deeper
into the ambassador's moneys, which would really put his
head on the chopping block.

He was about to leave when Carruthers appeared with a
folded paper. "Mr. Merlin's report on the automaton, my
lord."

Rothgar glanced quickly through it and saw immediately
that the machine could not be completely repaired in time
for tomorrow, so he put aside the thought of eclipsing the
French automaton. He sent orders for the work to be started
immediately anyway. If there was to be a war of automata,
he might need his little drummer boy.

He headed for the door, but turned at the last minute to

look at the portrait of his mother. What had Diana seen? Madness, apparently, in the intense eyes and tense body, but madness there before the birth of children.

He had no memory of his mother other than the dreadful one, and had never asked. But he had often wondered. Had she ever held him tenderly? Sang songs to him, played games to make him laugh? All the things he had seen his stepmother do with his half-brothers and -sisters.

Had she loved him? Or had she felt the same hatred she'd felt for little Edith?

The main question, however, had always been, how like her was he?

He left, closing the door, but thoughts would not be shut away.

For years he'd convinced himself that he was cold, as perhaps she had been cold. He'd thought he lacked the ability to bond closely and warmly, and had no need of it. It seemed strange now, but he'd seen himself as taking care of his family out of logic and duty.

Cyn's sickness had shattered that illusion.

Walking briskly toward the front of the house, he felt again that shocking pain, remembered the furious rebellion against fate. He'd fought death—with a Malloren all things were possible—and against all odds, he'd won. He, doctors, nurses, and Cyn's robust constitution, had defeated death.

Never after, however, had he thought he was of a cold, unloving nature.

He'd felt some of the same rage last year when he'd found Brand unconscious, when he'd feared a brain fever or some other fatal condition. On realizing the truth, that rage had turned to the people who had drugged him.

Rosa and Diana.

He felt anger at neither now, but his longing for Diana burned as fiercely. Death, however, was an easier opponent than honor. Despite Diana's challenge, her battle was already lost, defeated by the madness in his mother's fierce eyes. No trick of fate had turned her mad. She had been born that way. Honor said that blood must end with him, despite Diana's grief.

He took his hat, gloves, and crop from Fettler, waiting by the door. He must not think of her as Diana. Opponents in a duel, after all, should never be on first-name terms.

Lady Arradale. To be protected, but never to be loved.

He strode briskly out of the house, mounted his horse, and attended by two armed grooms, rode out of London.

Chapter 21

Diana sat in contemplation of the simple letter from Bey. Idiotic to feel touched almost to tears by it, but it was the first personal letter between them, and it was something tangible of his. She was only just realizing that though she had given him a ring, he had given her no keepsake, no symbol of connection.

It was doubtless deliberate. A symbol, in fact, of his intent to keep them apart. She smiled therefore at the note, which must be a sign that he was vulnerable after all.

And he had laughed in the coach, laughed in free amusement he must rarely allow himself.

It was tempting to hide the note away as a secret treasure, but it was carefully unrevealing, so she left it, folded, on the small escritoire in her room. There, she could see it at a glance whenever she pleased.

It was precious, but it also contained that guarded remark about the possible. He'd intended it as a warning that their marriage was not possible, but it made a useful reminder of her purpose. With her also, she resolved, all things were possible. She just had to find the way.

One thing she must do was investigate the matter of madness in his family. If his mother's family was full of the odd and the lunatic, then she might have to give up her purpose. She had a duty to her own line, after all, and introducing insanity into it would be wicked. Her opportunities for investigation were limited at the moment, but there must be libraries here. Once she understood the ways of court, she would find a way to spend some time in them.

For the moment, however, she must be completely conventional and definitely not clever, so she picked up one of the light books she had brought with her. One of the ones hardly glanced at on the journey because of Bey's presence beside her.

She sighed at that, thinking back to her state of mind at the beginning of the journey, when she'd merely been attracted and curious. How strange to have been blind to the powerful fire that burned between them.

He, apparently, had recognized it sooner—

Oh, enough! She must not let herself think about him night and day. She settled to reading Pope, trying not to let eyes and mind keep slipping away to the folded paper and all it represented.

The *Rape of the Lock* was engaging, and did distract her with its sharp commentary on London and courtly ways. She smiled at one passage about life at court, for though it was a description of the court of Queen Anne fifty years ago, she suspected the same was true today.

> *Hither the heroes and the nymphs resort,*
> *To taste awhile the pleasures of a court;*
> *In various talk th'instructive hours they past,*
> *Who gave the ball, or paid the visit last;*
> *One speaks the glory of the British Queen,*
> *And one describes a charming Indian screen;*
> *A third interprets motions, looks, and eyes;*
> *At every word a reputation dies.*

She paused, a finger in the page. That was a warning, if she needed it, that she must pursue her aims under a hundred eyes, many of them willing to harm her—and Bey—for amusement.

She was suddenly assailed by longing for the north. People there were not always kind, and sometimes there were enemies, but at least there was a rough kind of honesty.

And here she was, in love with a southerner. Even if she managed to break his will, how were they to manage their vast responsibilities? What would happen to the inheritance? She did not want her title swallowed up in his.

Her mind bounced fruitlessly around her problems, so she was quite relieved when a page came to tell her she was commanded to the queen's drawing room. No mention of the purpose, but she sensed that she faced a battle of some sort.

She touched up her pallor with extra powder, and reminded herself of her chief purpose. She must convince the king and queen of her safe, conventional nature, and avoid any attempt to coerce her into marriage.

She entered the drawing room to find that the king was sitting beside the queen. She'd been right. Her inquisition was to begin. She took a steadying breath and went forward to curtsy.

"Are you comfortable here, Lady Arradale?" the king asked.

"Perfectly, Your Majesty," Diana lied.

"Good, good. Your situation is one of unusual privilege," he stated, "but it does not alter the fact that you are, and always will be, a woman. What?"

"Yes, sire," Diana said, perilously tempted to say "no" and see what he made of that.

"A woman's mind is different," he continued. "It cannot understand the subjects and subtleties which engage the minds of men."

After a stunned pause, Diana hastily said, "Indeed, sire."

She was not to be questioned, but *lectured*. Then he pulled some papers out of his pocket and consulted them. By the stars, he'd brought notes!

He looked up at her, earnest and young. "It is well known that women cannot learn Latin or Greek, Lady Arradale, and if they try it damages their brains. Those subjects, however, shape the logical mind. Therefore, women cannot decide great matters, for they would act on emotion not logic. For that reason, it is against God's law for women to speak on matters of importance. Consider Corinthians: 'It is a shocking thing that a woman should address the congregation.' What?"

Diana fought a temptation to spout excellent Greek and
tried to look pious. "I see, sire."

He nodded. "So you also see, I am sure, that your notion
of attending Parliament like a man was folly."

"Yes, sire," she said, for indeed it had been. Bey had been
correct in seeing it as a childish thing. She couldn't help
thinking that without it, however, she would not have come
south, would not have spent that journey with him, would
not have been there to protect him, would not—

She hastily pulled her attention back, for the king was
continuing. *Remember your purpose here, Diana.*

". . . women are blessed with the natural kindness and
gentleness suited to their role as wife and mother," he said.
"This, however, deprives them of the harshness, resolution,
and physical strength necessary for their safety, meaning
that they must be under the protection of men. Did not the
great doctor Hippocrates write: 'Women by nature are less
courageous and weaker than men'?"

Diana almost fell into the surely unintentional trap of saying that indeed he did—of showing that she knew classical
literature. She impulsively decided that a minor argument
might make her meekness more believable. "If you will permit, Your Majesty," she said demurely, "women are generally physically weak, but I would argue that they can be
courageous when defending their children."

It worked. He nodded sharply with approval. "You show
a true womanly wisdom, Countess. Care of her offspring
must be a woman's first concern. But this is part of the
whole, what? If a woman is too physically active, if she
seeks to develop manly strength, she will die in childbed, or
bear monsters. What? What?"

Diana longed to ask: *How is it then that peasant women
labor in the fields, carry huge loads, and work dawn till
dusk, and still bear children as well or perhaps better than
languishing ladies?*

She kept her eyes down, and the words inside.

At least her meekness was having the desired effect. From
abrasive, the king's tone became positively mellow as he
continued, "If a woman has concerns outside the home,

clearly she must neglect her proper duties to her family.
Xenophon wrote: 'The gods created woman for the domestic
functions, the man for all others.' You see, Lady Arradale,"
he said, looking at her with well-meaning earnestness, "these
truths were established even in ancient times, never to be
altered."

She suddenly burned to make a passionate declaration of
women's rights and abilities—in four languages besides English! Or to demand a pistol and show just how helpless she
was. She could even point out that these were *pagan* beliefs,
not Christian, but she remembered her lessons and said, "It
does seem so, Your Majesty."

He beamed. "Good, good. Women are happiest in their
natural setting—enjoying the gentle and domestic arts, min-
istering to their husband, and caring for their children. As
my dear queen does." He patted the beaming queen's hand.
"We wish only to see you so blessed, Lady Arradale."

"I thank you, sire."

And thank heavens for the rigorous training Bey had
given her in the coach. It had not quite covered this, for he
too must have expected an inquisition rather than a lecture,
but it made it possible for her to mouth the correct inanities.

And had ended with that kiss.

With that night . . .

". . . you will soon be a wife, and happier for it, Lady Arradale, what?"

With a jerk, Diana tried to capture what she'd missed.
Still thinking of that night at the White Goose, she said, "I
pray for it most earnestly, Your Majesty."

He stared a little at her fervor, but then nodded. "Excellent, excellent! We are most pleased that you will submit to
our choice."

Her heart thumped, then galloped. She'd just agreed to
that?

"Now," he continued, all smiles, "I understand that you
play well. A lady who excels at such a suitable talent is
clearly not the unnatural creature we thought. Will you
oblige us with more music?"

Diana escaped to the keyboard, close to fainting with

panic. Stupid, stupid, *stupid*, to have slid into distraction! Sentimental mushy-mindedness when she'd needed to be all cool reason.

And now, disaster! She'd failed them both.

She was tempted to pour out her fury at herself on the poor keyboard, but she played instead a very calm, conventional piece, seeking calm and clear thought.

How to get out of this?

Having agreed to accept the king's choice, it would be even harder to escape without giving grave offense.

Perhaps she could claim to have changed her mind.

No, that would never work.

Perhaps she could appear to be truly seeking a man to love. Delay at least.

She grimaced as she played. She was going to have to tell Bey about this, and he'd be justifiably disappointed in her.

Plague take it all. She'd keep her wits about her from now on, but she feared that she'd made a serious mistake, and at first test. He'd been correct in thinking that she wasn't equipped to face this world, though she knew it would have been a great deal easier if she'd been as indifferent to him as she'd once pretended to be.

When would she have to tell him? Though she hated that thought, she longed to see him again.

Where was he? Was he thinking of her as much as she was thinking of him? Or were his defenses so strong he could block all awareness of what they had?

Hard riding could keep a mind focused and off impossible treasures. After three hours, and three changes of horses, Rothgar arrived at his estate. He went first to break the news to Ella Miller's mother and sister, then took them with him when he went to tell Ella of her husband's death. Then he went on to give the news to Miller's parents and return with them to the widow.

Eventually he could leave the grieving family comforted a little by the fact that Thomas had died bravely and quickly. They also knew that Ella and her children would always

have the cottage and a comfortable income. Not much sub-
stitute for a man, but all a mortal could give.

Proof if he needed it, that he was not God, and not in control of the machine. With a Malloren, all things were not
possible, or Miller would be with his wife and family now.

He rode his horse around to the stables, then walked up
past the kitchen gardens and into the formal grounds, suddenly aware of the emptiness of the huge, magnificent building before him.

What was he to do with himself here for the rest of his
life? Collect Anglo-Saxon fragments and sort through petitions? Live mostly in London, trying to improve and correct
the chaotic political machine, every effort subject to the
whim of a young monarch?

Looking at the ranks of windows, glinting gold and empty
in the sun, he knew what he wanted. He wanted to spend
most of his time here, and fill this house again with a family, a happy family.

No.

This yearning would pass, and the chaotic political machine would keep him very busy.

His unexpected arrival at the Abbey caused a flurry, and
as always there were matters to be taken care of. Doctor
Marshall, curator of the Anglo-Saxon artifacts, wanted to
discuss new acquisitions. His land steward wished to review
matters previously dealt with in letters. His house steward
tried to present designs for a slightly different livery. Rothgar sent the latter off with a sharp comment and briefly regretted it, but only briefly. Petty timewasting. Elf had
managed such things and he was feeling the loss of her more
and more.

The truth was, he thought wryly, he needed a wife. Since
he would not marry, he needed someone to act as his chate-
laine and hostess. On sudden impulse he wrote a brief list of
the spinsters and widows among his relatives, women who
might be pleased to take the position. It was the practical solution and affirmed his course.

Despite will, however, it brought Lady Arradale back to
his mind, along with thought of the king's determination to

marry her off. Logic told him she wouldn't be being dragged to the altar at this very moment, but it was suddenly intolerable not to be close at hand.

He had planned to spend the night here, but now he glanced out of the window. The sun was already kissing the treetops, and the idea of more hours in the saddle made him groan, but it was possible.

He ordered fresh horses and a light meal, produced quickly, but recognized a wavering of his will. She was in no danger. He just wanted to breathe the same air . . .

He rose abruptly and went upstairs. He did not go to his suite of rooms, but up another flight to the children's floor. Ten years now since these rooms had gone to sleep, when Cyn and Elf had moved to the lower floor to take their places in the adult world.

He walked into the nursery, unused for even longer, waiting like a dormant plant for the next generation of babies. A generation that would not come. Bryght's children would be born and raised at Candleford, and unless he himself was careless enough to die too soon, come here only as adults.

He set one ornate cradle rocking, the crunch of the rockers eerie in the deserted room. In fact, Brand's Jenny had slept in it a month or so ago. This floor had blossomed briefly to life then, with Bryght's Francis, and Hilda's children.

He set the other cradle rocking—an extra one had been made when the twins were born—remembering how much larger everything had seemed when he'd been a three-year-old, hovering fascinated over his new baby sister. She'd been tiny and wondrous, with delicate fingers and those huge, intent eyes which had seemed to look at him and recognize him.

Brother.
Mine.

People had always said he couldn't remember, but he remembered enough.

He remembered his mother, coming up from her bed that day instead of having the baby brought to her, still in her scarlet bedgown, her dark hair loose down her back. Dismissing the servants, but letting him stay. He'd always wondered why. But then, he didn't think she'd planned to do what she did. He'd give a great deal to know what she had planned when she came upstairs.

She'd picked up little Edith and walked with her, murmuring words he hadn't been able to hear. They hadn't sounded comforting. Not like the nurse's soothing, loving murmurs.

He remembered being worried.

Perhaps the baby had felt that way too, or perhaps his mother had held her too tightly. Edith had begun to cry, and it had rapidly built into the wavering squawk of the angry, frightened newborn. Ever since, that uniquely desperate sound had struck panic into him—a desperate need to act, to do something.

His mother had sat with the screaming, red-faced baby and quite calmly—he'd never forget the calm—closed her hand around little Edith's throat. The silence had been shocking.

He'd run over, crying, "No!" He'd tried to drag his mother's hand away. She'd looked at him blankly and buffeted him across the room with the full strength of her free hand.

He'd crawled to the door, blindly terrified, quiet as a mouse, then run screaming, hurtling past gawking servants, with only one thought. To get to his father, who could surely put all this right.

If he'd stopped, if he'd been in control of himself and explained to the nearby servants exactly what was going on, would they have acted sooner? Would they have been in time . . . ?

He came back to the present with a shudder, sweat cold down his back. The cradle still moved slightly from the rocking he'd started.

If he'd done the right thing, Edith would be a grown woman now, with husband and children of her own. Perhaps with a special smile for her brother. And he might be a different person. One able to—

Enough.

He looked around the room one last time, then left, closing the door. It had been a pilgrimage of sorts, and had served its purpose. There was no possibility of marriage for him. Ever. He must extricate the Countess of Arradale from her predicament, and despite her challenge, send her safely home.

Already he felt the pain of it. More than that, he knew her pain would be as great.

That was almost more than he could bear, but not quite.

He must never risk putting children in those empty cradles.

"It is a miracle to have a child, Lady Arradale," the queen said. "You do not want to miss it."

They were in the queen's gardens, the little one-year-old prince the center of attention for all the ladies. In sunshine, and helping the prince to make a daisy chain—making it for him, really—Diana was almost enjoying herself.

"I would like to have children, Your Majesty," she agreed, silently adding, but only Bey's.

"Lord Rothgar distresses my husband by his refusal to marry and sire children."

Diana looked up sharply, wondering if she'd spoken her thought out loud, but then she knew she had not. The connection was completely in the queen's mind. Was it possible that the king and queen would choose *Bey* for her?

Though she wanted nothing more, that had to stop. A forced marriage would be torture.

"I understand his mother was . . . afflicted, Your Majesty."

"She murdered her second babe," said the queen bluntly. "A terrible thing which has surely sent her to hell. It need not concern him, however."

A parent in hell might concern anyone, Diana thought, but said, "Perhaps he fears to carry the problem in his blood, ma'am."

"He has not spoken of it to you?"

Under the queen's scrutiny, Diana worked to appear cool and rather bored by the topic. "We know each other very little, ma'am. A few days last year, a few days this, and the journey."

"Oh." The queen shifted, to smile down at her son. "Come show me your pretty daisy chain, *herzlieb.*"

Diana gave him a hand so he could toddle over and present the flowers, relieved that the queen's attention had shifted.

When the queen had praised the flowers and picked him up, however, she said, "Many women would envy you that journey, Lady Arradale. They might feel you had wasted a golden opportunity."

"To flirt with the marquess, ma'am?" Diana asked, as if the notion had never crossed her mind.

The queen's mouth tightened, and she turned her attention back to her babbling son. With a sigh of relief, Diana began to edge backward, but the royal eyes fixed her again. "So, Countess, would the idea of the marquess as husband be an equal surprise?"

"A complete one, ma'am," Diana said, sure she was showing all the appropriate shock, but it was shock at having it stated so bluntly. What was she to do now?

"Put your mind to the matter, and perhaps it will cease to be so startling. My husband the king thinks it would be an excellent idea."

"But the madness, ma'am!"

"Doubtless a brain fever or such. In all other respects he is a desirable husband, yes? You cannot claim that he is unpleasing to women, or has any lack in manly parts."

"No, but—"

The queen cut her off with a gesture and waved her away, and Diana escaped before she said something disastrous. As she backed into the next section of the garden, however, panic made her want to clamber over the iron railings and flee.

She'd come here to persuade the king that she was no danger to his country. Then she'd thought she had to escape numerous unnamed suitors. She'd never expected to have to fight a determined attempt to push her into the arms of the man she loved.

Despite hating having to tell Bey what a mess she was making, she desperately needed to see him and hear his advice. She needed to warn him, too.

She thought briefly of sending him a message, but it was impossible to say anything to the point even in code without creating a connection between them that must be avoided.

Even when he came to court, she thought with a hiss of annoyance, they would have no time in private. She would have to use the code. Pretend she'd received a letter from Rosa . . .

Coming up with the best innocent phrases, she stroked a lovely, full-blown rose.

At her touch, it disintegrated.

She stared in shock at the carpet of creamy pink, remnants of beauty destroyed by her touch.

Nothing—not even a Malloren—could put that rose back together again. She gathered some of the fallen petals as if she might find some way to stick them back on the stem, then held them to her nose, inhaling the sweet perfume. Warm from the sun, they were like soft skin.

Like his skin, which in places was smooth and soft.

And in places hard.

Swept back to the White Goose, she knew their consummation had been as foolish as it had been wonderful. Despite their efforts, it would leave her in anxiety until her courses came. Even if she escaped that disaster, she would be left in bitter longings all her life unless she could find a way to change his mind.

To change a noble purpose fixed years ago and for good reason.

She opened her hands and let the petals float back to the ground. Her intent was *not* destructive. She would not think that. It offered hope of true happiness.

This plan of the king and queen's did not, however, even though she saw that it came out of good intentions. He could not be forced.

She returned to planning the right words to warn him.

Chapter 22

Rothgar was finishing the hasty meal and being merciful by looking at Ingram's designs for new liveries—which seemed to him little different than the ones in use now—when Sir George Ufton was announced. The stocky man hurried in, looking strangely pale. "My lord, thank the heavens you are here!"

"Sir George. What has happened?"

"Georgie! My son George. He's been taken up as a horse thief!"

Rothgar guided the man to a chair and poured brandy for him. "Now, Sir George, tell me exactly what has happened."

Uncharacteristically disordered in the telling, the story was quite simple. Young George had been passing the time at market day in Dingham by gaming at an inn—something his father would have words with him about. He'd lost to a horse trader, and agreed to pay part of his debt by delivering a horse to the next village.

The horse trader had then cried thief, and the local magistrate, Sir Hadley Commons—no great friend to the Uftons—was planning to hear the case within the hour.

As Sir George mopped his head, and drank his brandy, Rothgar considered the extraordinary situation. He was certain the young man was innocent, so this must be mischief. With what purpose? He couldn't imagine Sir George having cunning enemies . . .

But he had.

The Uftons had been in London recently, had been presented by him. That made a connection . . .

D'Eon again. It had to be. Another attempt to draw him away from court. Another intolerable use of his innocent connections.

But this time, he thought with sudden interest, he was on the spot and might be able to catch D'Eon's minion with red hands. It would be very useful to have someone in the enemy camp.

He rose. "I will go with you, Sir George, and help you sort this out. It cannot hold water."

Sir George stood and wrung his hand, tears glimmering in his eyes. "Thank you, thank you, my lord. Thank heaven you were here today!"

"A blessing, indeed," said Rothgar, guiding the anxious man out to the horses.

His horse and his two mounted grooms stood ready to take him on the first stage back to London. He hesitated for a moment. This mission killed all chance of that, unless he wanted to ride across Hownslow in the dark, which would be folly.

Return to London today had been folly anyway, and if matters were as he suspected, he could best serve Lady Arradale here.

They entered Dingham against a stream of people, carts, and animals. Market day was winding down and people were heading home.

The small town still bustled, however, for a fair number of people were topping off the day in the inns and taverns. Market day always ended that way, and with the magistrates tidying up the day's misbehavior at the Anchor.

After leaving their horses with the grooms, they entered the inn past a woman receiving a summary whipping for thievery, watched by a cheering crowd. A glum-looking man stood under guard nearby, waiting his turn. Sir Hadley liked to keep the peace very firmly.

People made way immediately for the Marquess of Rothgar, and a whisper ran around the crowded room. Sir Hadley looked up sharply from where he sat in the middle of his bench of magistrates and frowned. But then he ignored them and went on with the questioning of an elderly man. The three magistrates conferred, then Commons pounded his gavel. "Guilty of giving short measure. Fine of three shillings or twenty lashes."

Grumbling, the old man pulled some coins out of a purse, paid his fine, and hurried away.

George Ufton was called next. "You will see, Sir George," said Sir Hadley, "that I held back your son's case until your return, as requested."

Though it was not said pleasantly, Sir George nodded. "Obliged, Commons."

The magistrate inclined his head to Rothgar. "My lord marquess. You have an interest in this case?"

"I always have an interest in justice, Sir Hadley. Proceed."

Rothgar knew ways to take command of a place, and he used them now, though he stayed to one side of the room, observing. The accuser, the horse trader, was the most likely villain, but D'Eon was subtle, and whoever had set this up must have been lingering in the area waiting for a chance. It could be a local man. Whoever it was, he would have him soon.

For my lady, he thought, wryly amused at his inability to keep his mind from drifting to her. This was the evening of her first day at court. He wondered how she was surviving, and whether the king had questioned her yet . . .

He realized that young George had been brought out, and shook his head. *You will be no use to your lady,* he told his foolish half, *if you cannot observe, plan, and be logical.*

The young man looked rumpled and frightened, though he was making an admirable attempt to be dignified. His hair ribbon had gone so his hair tangled loose, and somewhere he'd fought, for his nose had been bloodied and his lip split. When he saw his father a touching mix of shame and relief shone in him.

Seventeen, and despite his predicament, a son to be proud of.

Sons. Sons like the drummer boy, with Diana's clear eyes and stubborn chin. Daughters with lopsided ribbons—

He pushed such thoughts away and paid attention. The accusation had been stated, and the accuser was explaining his complaint. Stringle, the horse trader.

Rothgar assessed the man. Not local but not obviously suspicious, either. A good, solid Englishman, but then D'Eon would hardly use a Frenchman for this.

Middling height, middling build, square face, and wearing decent but well-worn clothes. He told his story simply, and with a suitable sorrow at being caught up in such events.

If he was the villain, he was good. Very good.

Three other men stepped forward to attest to the truth about the card game—that young Georgie Ufton had played, and lost. These were local men, and not happy to be telling their incriminating tale, though two of them he judged to be lazy troublemakers. Could one of them be a hired liar? And yet they all told the same tale.

Georgie and his father had turned pale, for this hung together well, and horse stealing was a hanging matter. Rothgar had no doubt that in the end he could save the young man from the worst of his folly, if even only by force of rank. He wanted more, however. He wanted one of D'Eon's men wriggling on a hook.

When the magistrates had questioned the witnesses, Georgie was given the chance to speak.

"I didn't do it, good sirs," he protested. "I lost the money, yes, which was stupid, but I didn't steal the horse. This Stringle asked me to take the horse to Cobcott as part of the debt."

Sir Hadley addressed the room. "Did anyone else hear about this?"

Silence.

"We were in the stables, sir," Georgie said.

"In the stables? But Mr. Grigson said that you begged for time to pay, and Mr. Stringle refused on the basis that he must travel on to the next town. You then left, promising to return soon with the money. Mr. Stringle was never in the stables."

"Yes, he was," Georgie protested.

The magistrate turned to the group of men who'd testified, but they all agreed that Stringle had remained at the table.

Rothgar watched the interplay, and made up his mind. It had to be Stringle, and it was time to take a hand. "With your permission, Sir Hadley."

"Honored, my lord!" said the magistrate, looking smugly certain of the case.

Rothgar looked at Stringle, and saw the little shift in the eyes when the man recognized possible danger. Rothgar almost smiled. It was pleasant to have his suspicions confirmed. Now to hook the man.

He turned to Georgie. "Mr. Ufton, when you went to the stables, was your horse ready?"

Georgie frowned at that. "How could it be, my lord? I hadn't ordered it."

"So you saddled it yourself?"

"Yes, my lord. There was no one there just then."

"That wouldn't have taken long, though."

"No, my lord, though someone had moved the blanket and tossed it with some others, so I had to find it."

"And how ready were you when Mr. Stringle found you?"

"I was just about to mount, my lord."

Rothgar nodded and turned to the honest witnesses.

"Gentlemen, if you would be so kind, perhaps we can go over the last part of the incident again. You were all playing at cards?"

One of the younger men said nervously, "Nat and me were, milord." He indicated the man by his side. "The others were just watching."

"And how much did you lose?"

"A few shillings, milord. The play ran pretty even. Or I wouldn't have stayed in. I know my limit."

Rothgar asked the other man and received a similar answer. "Play didn't seem even for young Mr. Ufton, did it?" he observed. "Was he wild in his play?"

"A little, milord," said the first man. "But just sunk in bad luck."

Rothgar turned to gaze at Stringle. "Very persistent bad luck."

A murmur went through the room at the implication that the play hadn't been entirely fair. He saw Stringle's eyes shift. He was the stranger here, and it wouldn't go well with him if he was thought to be a cheat. The first prick of the hook.

Rothgar turned back to the witnesses. "Now, when Mr. Ufton left the table, Mr. Stringle stayed behind, yes?"

They chorused agreement.

"For how long?"

That brought an attack of puzzlement, and the five men looked at each other.

"He stayed a while," said one.

"Still there later when my daughter came to find me. Waiting for Mr. Ufton."

"Didn't move, milord."

"What was he drinking?" Rothgar asked.

"Ale, milord."

"How many pints, would you say?"

Again they looked at each other as if shared wisdom might be better, but then one of the men who'd watched the game said, "At least three pints, milord. And I see where you're heading. Stap me, if he didn't go to take a leak now and then."

"Did he do so after Mr. Ufton left?"

"I think he did, milord. Just for a moment."

Slowly, the other men nodded and agreed.

"And he went out of sight."

"Oh aye, milord," said one of the card players. "Mistress Wilkins don't have pissing in the tavern."

Rothgar turned back to Stringle, suppressing a contented smile. "Do you dispute this, sir?"

"No, milord," the man said stoically. He was good. "I went outside to relieve myself a time or two, but not to the stables."

"But out of sight."

"I'm a decent man, milord," Stringle said, meeting his eyes.

Rothgar quirked a brow at him, and turned to the magistrates. "I submit to you, sirs, that it was possible for Mr. Stringle to have spoken to Mr. Ufton in the stables."

"But Georgie Ufton made off with the horse, my lord," Sir Hadley protested.

"Thinking that was what Mr. Stringle wanted. After all, when stopped, he hadn't sold it."

Sir Hadley leaned back, looking sour. "If Georgie Ufton is honest, then Stringle is a perjurer, and I'll see him hang for it!"

"I've told nothing but the truth," stated Stringle, but when Rothgar turned to him he saw both anger and fear. On the hook. Now, would he come smoothly to the net?

"Perhaps," he offered, "it was a simple misunderstanding, Mr. Stringle. Perhaps you might have said something to make Mr. Ufton think you wanted him to deliver that horse?"

"I don't recollect it, my lord." But then the man added, "It's possible, I suppose. Those three pints of ale weren't the only ones."

Sir Hadley glared. "Then I'll have you whipped for a drunken reprobate!"

Rothgar turned the full power of his authority on the man. "Wiser, perhaps, to let it pass, Sir Hadley, don't you think?"

After a frustrated moment, Sir Hadley pounded his gavel. "Not guilty. Next!"

Rothgar let Sir George wring his hand, then left him to deal with his son. He turned to see the accuser struggling away through a hostile crowd.

He caught up. "Mr. Stringle."

The man turned. "You've got your young friend off, my lord. Are you after me now?"

Rothgar took his arm. "I merely mean to see you safe to your horses." Though scowling, the crowd fell back, leaving a path clear to the door.

Stringle's arm was stiff in his grasp, but he walked to the door and through it. "What now, my lord?" he asked, hard-eyed.

Rothgar let him go. "I just saved your neck."

The man stayed silent.

"I know the man you work for—rather unpatriotic, wouldn't you say?—and I suspect that this plot was aimed largely at me."

Stringle flinched, but didn't admit guilt. Yes, he was good. Rothgar wouldn't mind employing him if the man knew who was master.

"You could be of use to me, Mr. Stringle. There is a lady in London, living at the queen's court. The Countess of Arradale. I am particularly concerned that nothing happens to distress or inconvenience her."

The man looked genuinely startled. "What would I have to do with a lady of the queen's court, my lord?"

"Perhaps nothing. If you were to go to London, however, and put yourself at the disposal of the gentleman who hired you, you might be surprised."

"I'm a country horse trader, my lord. What would I do in London?"

"Oblige me."

The man paled at the tone. "I could just disappear."

"You would find it very hard to go beyond my reach."

The man's eyes met his resentfully. "I go to London and hang around a certain man's house, and let you know if anything turns up about the lady. Then what? When am I free? My trade is horses, my lord, and I'd rather stick to it."

"Wiser to have done so all along, wouldn't you say? When Lady Arradale returns to her lands in the north, you may leave London. In the meantime, if you hear anything about her, or any plans concerning her, send a message to me at Malloren House. I am also very interested in the activities of a Frenchman called de Couriac. You will be well paid, and I will do you no harm if you serve me well." He left the alternative unspoken but clear.

After a moment, the man nodded. "I'll do your will, my lord."

"I thought you might," said Rothgar, and watched as he strode off.

Chapter 23

Rothgar arrived back in London the next day with only enough time for the tedious preparations for court. After the levee the king summoned him as usual to review recent events, and to debate again the fate of Dunkirk. It became dismayingly hard not to snap at him.

He escaped at four. Since the king was returning for dinner with the queen, it was out of the question to visit the Queen's House. Besides, he told himself firmly as he returned home, he would have the opportunity this evening to make sure Lady Arradale was well and safe. That was soon enough.

Once out of court clothes he went to his office to methodically work through the stacks of work awaiting him. His mind tried to wander, but he kept it to the tasks before him. All these documents represented people and issues needing his attention.

Most were administrative papers to do with his estates and business affairs. He knew Grainger, Carruthers, and other employees would have gone through them carefully, but he read each one as was his practice before signing it.

There were also letters and reports connected to the many charitable matters he supported, and the usual solicitations from artists and publishers. An agent reported the finding of some jewels perhaps belonging to King Alfred, and another a portrait of an ancestor he'd been trying to add to the family collection.

He was tempted to put aside a dauntingly thick report on some land he had acquired in the colonies, but he knew where his weak-willed mind wished to go so he pinned it to trade.

Eventually, however, all was done and he looked at his empty desk with some grievance. Hard work had provided the closest thing to peace he'd experienced in days. He looked ironically at the sketch of himself on the study wall, the one done in preparation for his stern portrait.

Where was that confident, invulnerable man?

He rose abruptly and sought distraction elsewhere—in the room where Jean Joseph Merlin and an assistant were working on the drummer boy.

"When will it be mended?" he asked, wincing to see the figure stripped of clothes, with many of its pieces spread around on white cloths.

The young man looked up, but with a hint of impatience. "Within days, my lord," he said with an accent. He was Flemish by birth. "As you said, the damage is not great, but it has stood idle so long that I wish to check all the parts. There was rust," he added, with the hint of a shudder.

"No other breakage?"

"No, my lord." Merlin relented and walked over to the heart of the machine. "It is a masterpiece. Vaucanson, for sure, and of a complexity I've rarely seen. The subtlety of movement—"

"You operated it?" Rothgar asked sharply.

"Of course not, my lord. I can read cogs and levers as Mr. Haydn reads music."

"My apologies." Rothgar couldn't help but touch the lad's lifelike head, stroking the subtly colored skin.

"Wax," Merlin said. "Again, a masterpiece. One could think he would breathe. In fact . . . it could be done with the addition of bellows. I have heard of one that actually plays a flute."

"No." The notion of this child taking its first breath was appalling. "Leave that to God."

"As you wish, my lord."

"Is there any way I can help?"

"If you are willing to clean and polish, my lord."

It was a familiar arrangement when Merlin was here, and

Rothgar could steal the time. There were any number of other things he should be doing, but he sat at a table and began to clean the complex pieces of metal. Almost immediately, his tension eased.

Perhaps it was a flaw to find clockwork mechanisms so soothing, but if so, it was one he permitted himself. If he gave up court he might study the subject further, and perhaps become able to read cogs and levers like music.

He smiled at the thought of himself as an eccentric, living in comfortable robes, and shuffling around Rothgar Abbey fiddling with clocks.

Alone.

It was not particularly amusing, after all.

"Now the war is over," he said after a while, "perhaps you would like to visit Monsieur Vaucanson in France."

Merlin looked up, eyes bright. "I would indeed, my lord."

"I will arrange it. He has also done a great deal of work on industrial machinery."

Merlin grinned. "Never fear, my lord. Any machine enthralls me, and I will report back on everything."

Rothgar smiled and returned to his task.

As he polished a piece with fine grit, he glanced at the child's head. He rose and carefully moved the head so it was looking directly at him, then sat again to his work. Merlin and his assistant glanced over, but without particular curiosity.

The head was astonishingly realistic, and on top of the rods of the mechanism, it looked disturbingly like the victim of an execution exposed on a pike.

Alas, poor Yorick, Rothgar mused, thinking of Hamlet with the skull. This was no skull, however, or rotting head. This was a clever child with a hint of willfulness and mischief in the curving lips and large, adventurous eyes.

This was the young Diana.

Rescued and about to be made whole again.

Life, however, was not a machine to be cleaned of rust and fixed so it ran to order once more.

The adult Diana could be rescued from an unwanted marriage, but he doubted she could be made whole again. If she returned home unwed, she would be shackled by awareness of the king's suspicious watchfulness.

Then there was the other thing. Their foolhardy night at the White Goose. In bringing her to life in that bed he had created a break in her, and not in her nonexistent hymen. By any normal standard, after taking a lady's virginity a gentleman was honor bound to marry her, but it was even more unfair to introduce a virgin to pleasure and abandon her.

Would Diana live in chastity for the rest of her life? Or would she marry out of desperation? Or, even worse, would she become the sort of woman who took lovers carelessly whenever she felt the need?

Of course she'd challenged his resolve not to marry. She needed marriage now to be whole.

So tempting to save her. To follow the path of conventional honor to the place he longed to be. Had that lurked in his mind in the White Goose, leading to that weak folly?

Intolerable if true.

He gathered willpower and pushed aside temptation again. What he wanted, what she wanted, must not, should not, be.

The child's clear eyes challenged him as hers had challenged him yesterday. *With a Malloren, are not all things possible?*

"No."

When the two men looked at him, he realized he had spoken aloud. Talking to himself? Wasn't that a true sign of madness?

As the men returned to work, Rothgar looked back at the child, quirking a brow as if they shared a secret. It almost seemed as if the child's smile deepened. Ah, to have a son like this, to share innocent secrets with.

I am your son. If you have courage to find me.

He looked away then, down, to the complex curve of metal in his oil-stained fingers. Not Diana, but a child of theirs, and now it too challenged him for its very existence.

Was his denial courage?

Or despicable weakness?

Folly again, but it was as if the child were lost, wandering the same bleak road that he wandered through life, crying for someone to find him and care for him, someone to take him home.

He could not bear to leave a child crying—

A knock on the door broke him out of these Gothick thoughts. Carruthers came in. "Your pardon, my lord, but some messages came which you might think important."

Rothgar rose, both relieved to escape, and reluctant to abandon the child here in the hands of strangers.

He made a sudden resolution, and put it into silent words, looking into the drummer boy's eyes. *I promise you this, at least. If Diana is with child, I will marry her. No child of mine will ever cry alone.*

He picked up a spare cloth and wrapped it around the exposed mechanism beneath the child's head, like a blanket.

"Dust," he said blandly to Merlin and the others, and left the room.

The messages were indeed important, especially the copy of the one from D'Eon to Paris complaining that de Couriac was mad and uncontrollable. D'Eon asked urgently that the man be recalled to France before he created more mayhem.

As he'd thought, de Couriac was D'Eon's man, but one known to the official powers in Paris, not to the secret ones run by de Broglie. It was also clear that the attack on the road had not been D'Eon's plan.

This all made de Couriac dangerous, but also useful if he could be found.

It was intriguingly unclear whether D'Eon knew where the man was now or not. If de Couriac was serving the official French powers, he might have sought refuge in the embassy, and D'Eon might not feel able to dispose of him himself.

Stringle might turn out to be very useful indeed.

He dressed in finery again, for this afternoon was the day for his own levee, when all gentlemen who wished could come to his house to speak to him. He chose black to suit his mood, but richly decorated with jewel-like flowers. In powdered wig and glittered orders, he entered his reception room and indicated that the doors of the house be set open.

Because he'd been out of town the previous Friday, the levee was heavily attended, though most of the men who passed through his reception room were merely paying respects. A few had more serious matters to discuss with him, however. As always, they wanted the king's ear. He used that privilege sparingly, as he explained to them. There were written petitions here too, which he passed to the attentive Carruthers.

It passed the time and occupied his mind, and when it was over, a number of the men had been invited to dine. They would all go on to the Queen's House afterward for the presentation of the French automaton.

Where he would see Lady Arradale at last.

It only occurred to him then that the clothes he wore were the ones he'd worn to the ball at Arradale over a year ago. She had worn magnificent red silk, and it had been like a very interesting clash of blades.

Once weakly opened, the door could not be shut. His mind slid to memories of their dance then, when he'd been probing to see if she was the sort of woman to drug a man and then demand sex from him.

He'd soon decided she was not. Oh, she played the game well, but was far too skittish over any serious move toward seduction.

He remembered her retreat, but he also remembered the look in her eyes when she'd asked, *"What would have happened, my lord, if I had not objected to . . ."*

Ah, that had been a warning of all that had followed. He hadn't heeded it, however, because unconsciously he'd already been intrigued and attracted.

"To my kissing your palm? Why, we would have indulged in dalliance, my lady."

"Dalliance?" she'd asked.

"One step beyond flirtation, but one step below seduction."

"I know nothing of dalliance then."

"Would you care to learn?"

Thinking back, he wasn't sure exactly what he'd intended then, what he would have done if she'd taken him up on the

cynical offer. It had been the unrecognized beginning, however, and he had eventually taught her. At Bay Green.

Catching a surprised look from Walpole, he knew he'd
missed something.

"I was merely pondering one of life's mysteries," he remarked. "That momentous developments sometimes start
with careless impulses."

"Like the war of Jenkin's ear, my lord," said Walpole.

"Precisely." Rothgar followed that line into war and in-
ternational relations, which was what he should be con-
centrating on anyway. Paying attention to the conversation
this time, he inserted delicate warnings about France, and
about the Chevalier D'Eon's finances and motives. Some
of the men present were ministers of the crown, so they
were fertile ground.

All the men were wealthy, so he also managed some personal business and gained their support for Elf's latest charity for the support of war widows and orphans.

However, despite politics and benevolence, he was aware
that the passing hours were just that—time to pass before he
could travel to the Queen's House for the evening.

Fred Stringle left his horse at the stable attached to the
French embassy, and walked up to the back door to knock.
He gave his name, and asked to speak to Monsieur D'Eon.

"Why should he speak to the likes of you?" asked the
tired maid. "Anyway, he's off to court at any moment."

Stringle pushed in past her. "Just send the message, luv."

In minutes he was being led to a room on the ground
floor. A simple reception room, but on the right side of the
house, the gentlemen's side.

The little Frenchman came in, stepping crisply, frowning,
all a-glitter with satin, lace, jewels and fancy orders. "What
are you doing here? What has happened?"

"Trouble, sir. That's what's happened."

"Trouble? What trouble? You have not entangled young
Ufton in something?"

"Oh, aye, I entangled him all right. Horse thievery. A
hanging matter if it really stuck."

The man's eyes fixed on him. "So? What trouble?"

"All would have been well if a bloody marquess hadn't thrown his weight around."

The little man sucked in a breath. "Rothgar? But he is in London."

"Yesterday, he was in Dingham Magna rescuing young Georgie Ufton from his fate."

The sharp eyes narrowed. "And you came here? Why? You are nothing to do with me, nothing."

"I wasn't followed, sir, if that's what you're worried about." It amused him to add, "No one knows I'm here except those who already know. But things got a bit hot in Dingham, you see. Perjury and the like. I thought it'd be wise to disappear for a while, and where else but here?"

This was the tricky part, because he wouldn't put it past this fire-eating little Frog to stab him where he stood.

But D'Eon only hissed between his teeth. "Very well. In fact, you could be useful to me. Developments have made it difficult for me to use my countrymen at the moment." He looked at Stringle. "The marquess is a very astute man. He must have realized you were causing difficulties."

Another tricky spot. "Aye, and he tried to find out who set me up to it, but I slipped away."

The Frenchman smiled. "He will guess, I think. It is no bad thing to know that we are at war."

Stringle would rather have the damned marquess ignorant of his very existence, but he risked a question. He thought of himself as a man without allegiance, but the marquess's comment about patriotism had stung. He'd entangle a naive lad for money, but he didn't like the thought of serving the king's enemies. "War over what, sir?" he asked.

"Over power, of course. What else is war ever about?" With an airy gesture, the Frenchman said, "Find yourself a room here and keep out of the way. I will tell you when I think you can be useful."

Stringle left, glad now to be working for the marquess to thwart the enemy.

*   *   *.

The Chevalier D'Eon left the room disappointed, but only mildly so. He had set a number of traps to make distracting trouble for the Marquess of Rothgar, and hadn't expected all to succeed. He could sigh for Stringle's plan, however. A young neighbor in danger of hanging would have taken Rothgar away for days, now, adding to the void created by his sentimental absence in the north. To leave the center of power for a mere wedding! D'Eon felt close, so close, to his goal, to persuading the English king to countermand the order to destroy Dunkirk.

The plan with de Couriac would have been even better if the fool hadn't bungled it. The thought of the marquess bedridden with a wound, perhaps for weeks, far away in the north, was enough to make him weep.

All would then have been easy, he thought as he headed for the front of the house. He would become ambassador, doubtless with a title to go with it. His life would be as smooth and glorious as the reflection pools at Versailles . . .

It still would be. He had served his king faithfully for over ten years, refusing nothing, putting his life on the line again and again. This was his, this place, this position, and everything that came with it.

He would—

A man stepped in front of him.

He leaped back, hand flying to his sword, then halting. "De Couriac?"

The man, a bloodstained bandage around his head, bowed but without great respect. "Monsieur D'Eon."

D'Eon seized his arm and dragged him into the nearest room, his office. "What are you doing here? All England seeks you!"

"Then where else could I come?"

"You could take ship back to France."

"You don't think the ports will be watched?"

The man's tone was disrespectful, perhaps even hostile. D'Eon considered his next words.

After the debacle with Curry, he'd sent to Paris for an expert swordsman who could do what Curry had failed to do— put the Marquess of Rothgar out of play with a serious but not fatal wound. De Couriac had appeared to fit the part perfectly, and it had seemed simple enough to set up.

Lord Rothgar was going north with his family, but returning south alone. He had rooms engaged at Ferry Bridge. Simple to have de Couriac wait there to intercept him with the tempting bait of an actress from the King's Theater as his wife.

How it had gone wrong, he did not yet know, but the next step had told him that de Couriac had other plans.

That attack on the road had not been planned to wound. It had been planned to kill. Doubtless under orders from Paris that he had not been aware of. Dangerous, very dangerous.

"How did matters go awry in Ferry Bridge?" he asked.

"Interference. By a certain Countess of Arradale, the arrogant bitch."

D'Eon twitched at such crudeness, but ignored it for now. "Ah. And what of the disaster on the road? What were you thinking!"

"Death. How does it matter how he dies so long as he dies?"

"But I did not order his death."

"The king did."

D'Eon stilled. Was it possible that the king had sent an order not through him? Did the king no longer trust and support him? There had been indications, warnings even from friends in Paris, and from de Broglie.

But then there were the private letters he received . . .

No choice but to appear the master. "How dare you outrun your orders like that? How dare you recruit other French agents to your ridiculous plan?"

De Couriac reddened with anger. "I have the authority. Direct from Paris. Direct from Versailles."

"You think you outrank me?" D'Eon said softly. "Perhaps you even think you can defeat me with the sword?" He let his hand rest on the beribboned hilt.

The other man stiffened, his own hand grasping his sword. D'Eon knew de Couriac must think himself almost unbeatable. But the almost was important, and his own reputation was equally formidable.

After a long moment, de Couriac took his hand away. "Of course not, monsieur. I apologize if I have offended you."

D'Eon let some extra seconds run before nodding and taking his hand from his own sword. "So," he said, "what orders do you have from Paris?"

"To remove the marquess."

"From play, not from life."

"That was not specified."

"It is, now, by me. And it must be subtle. You understand?"

After a moment, de Couriac nodded.

"Very well. I am for court and cannot dally. Let me make it clear that we cannot afford any more incidents connected to this embassy! I have another plan stirring, and two possible English tools. You encountered Lady Arradale, you said?"

"Oh yes." The man's lip curled. "I have a score to settle with her." He put his hand to his bloody head. "She spoiled the plan, then gave me this."

"She hit you?" The pale and simpering Countess of Arradale? "With what? Her fan?"

"With a pistol ball, down in the dirt, steady as you please. She probably fired the last shot that killed Roger and Guy."

Though he was having to reevaluate many things, D'Eon waved that aside. "Do not let personal concerns get in the way. The countess is now at the queen's court, and cannot easily be touched. However, there is also a stupid Englishman who has hopes of Lady Arradale's body and her wealth. He can be used. I will work on a plan. We are in accord?"

"As long as I can have my revenge on Milord Rothgar and the countess. They caused the death of Susette."

"The actress?" D'Eon queried. "How did she become involved in violence?"

"She was a violent woman," de Couriac said rather blankly. "She stabbed me."

A laugh escaped D'Eon.

"And of course I had to kill her," de Couriac continued. "She knew too much by then. But we were old friends, and they must pay for it."

D'Eon lost all impulse to laugh. The man was deranged. He thought for a moment of killing him here and now, but it would not be easy and he was already late for the soirée. It was also possible that King Louis might disapprove.

What would the madman do next, however? He must be given something to do.

"You may stay here," he said. "If you can disguise yourself, try to strike up an acquaintance with a young man called Lord Randolph Somerton. He likes to gamble, and is often found in a hell called Lucifer's. But do nothing without my approval. Nothing."

"I am a master of disguise. I have even worked in the theater now and then."

"Excellent. We are in accord, then."

"Completely, monsieur," said de Couriac, with all the sincerity of a snake.

D'Eon hurried away, already planning another letter to Paris demanding that de Couriac be recalled, and devising a few possible ways to dispose of the man without suspicion.

He was beginning to feel entangled in mysterious coils, however. His debts were alarming, and for some reason he sensed that his favorite moneylenders were drawing back from him. He had access to the ambassador's funds here, but that was risky.

He entered his coach and ordered all speed. He could not possibly be losing King Louis's favor, but the prospect sent a chill through him. Then he remembered that he had just received another reassuring letter, and leaned back against the satin squabs.

All would be well. De Couriac was mad, or bluffing, or both. Or he could be a tool of his enemies in France. That mattered nothing as long as his king smiled on him.

But he still had to sway the English king, which meant he must at least distract the Marquess of Rothgar.

To that, he sensed, Lady Arradale might be key.

Lady Arradale, who apparently was not at all as she appeared.

Chapter 24

When Rothgar arrived at the Queen's House, he found the event surprisingly crowded. The king and queen rarely held large parties in what they considered their private home. Part of the crowd was in honor of the gift, no doubt, but he realized the invitation list had been expanded to provide Lady Arradale with suitors. Among other eligible men, he saw Somerton, Crumleigh, and Scrope.

Over my dead body, he said to them, then summoned every scrap of devilish cool and moved forward to play his part.

He went first to pay his respects to the king and queen in the grand salon, where a shrouded shape sat on a central table. On a table to one side, the shepherd and shepherdess he'd given to Their Majesties last year was unconcealed.

D'Eon would have seen that piece, and Rothgar had no doubt that the French king's gift would be more spectacular. He wished the Chinese pagoda still existed, for it would eclipse most other machines. Or that the drummer boy was ready for display.

Ridiculous to be staging a war by automata, but that's how it seemed to be. His mind played whimsically with the idea of two swordsmen—one French designed, one English—and an actual duel.

Collecting his wits, he greeted the royal couple. The queen obligingly pointed out Lady Arradale, standing to one side with a chatting group. There was no need. He had seen her as soon as he entered the room—or perhaps sensed her was more accurate.

Without looking again, he knew she wore moss green and gold. That she had been smiling, but looked pale. That, however, could just be her clever paint. He needed to find out, but not yet.

"We are very pleased with Lady Arradale," the king said. "A charming young woman. Quite as she ought to be. Make some man an excellent wife, what?"

"Yes, sire," Rothgar said, thinking that she must be playing her part extremely well. Truth was, she'd make an impossible wife for most men.

"Excellent company for the queen," the king went on. "Fond of children. A fine looking woman, what? We'll be dancing at her wedding in weeks."

He bowed and expressed delight at the thought.

The king shot him a look, and he abruptly realized that something else was going on.

Then the king said, "Lady Arradale has agreed that if she cannot make up her mind, we will choose her husband."

It took all his skill not to react to that. Why, short of torture?

"Better for her to make her own choice, though, what?" the king was saying. "Difficult here, with the queen and I living quietly. The lady should have the chance to meet many gentlemen, what? Get to know them. Dance, that sort of thing."

"I think so, sire." Rothgar was still trying to assess the extent of this problem.

"A grand entertainment, what?"

Rothgar actually echoed him. "What? An entertainment here, sire?"

"No, no. Not with the queen so near her time. Anything you could do, my lord?"

He suddenly understood.

Arrange her courtship ball? It was as good as a command, however, and he was known for unusual and magnificent balls and masquerades. "A masqued ball perhaps, sire? Such things are romantic."

The king nodded, a gleam in his eye, and Rothgar knew

he'd attend in disguise. "Capital, capital! How soon can it be done?"

"Perhaps two weeks, sire?" If the fates were kind, the queen would take to her bed early, and he could extricate Lady Arradale then.

But the king frowned. "Two weeks, my lord? No, no. Sooner than that. And anyway, in two weeks there will be no moon. Monday is the full moon. Why not then?"

Rothgar raised his brows. "That is very soon, sire."

"It cannot be done? You have worked such miracles before, my lord." The king's sly look warned of what was to come. "Don't you say, 'With a Malloren all things are possible,' what?"

There was no escape. "It can be done, sire, if you will accept the use of features you have seen before."

"Of course, of course. It will all be novel for the lady. And give a chance for one of her admirers to win her heart, what?"

Other guests awaited, so Rothgar stepped back from the royal couple wishing he knew exactly what the king had in mind. He wished to go immediately to Lady Arradale, but that would be too revealing. Instead, he strolled casually into the anteroom where the musicians played.

There he found Mr. Bach, the queen's latest protégé. Rothgar had commissioned some music from him, and also arranged the copying of his collection of keyboard music written by his father. That music had great elegance and clarity, and he asked Bach to play a piece of it during the evening.

He was in great need of clarity.

"Of course, my lord," Bach said, continuing to conduct the small orchestra. "The queen is graciously appreciative of my father's music, too."

"How does the Diana piece progress?" Rothgar asked, an idea stirring. Before going north, he had commissioned Bach to write music for the Rousseau cantata. "I am holding a masqued ball on Monday, and have it in mind to make it into a true one in the old style."

"To stage a masque, my lord?"

"Exactly."

The man's eyes brightened with interest. "The music is done, my lord, and performers could be found at the King's Theater."

Rothgar settled the details then moved on, wondering if he'd regret that impulse. Ordering music for the Diana cantata had been a whim, intended only as a teasing gift to an intriguing lady. Now it would make her the focus of his ball.

She would be the focus anyway, with the court knowing she was available for marriage. A reminder of the powers and folly of love seemed in order. For both her and himself.

When he judged the moment right, he allowed himself to follow the pull he'd resisted, the pull toward the countess. Her chestnut hair glinted in the candlelight and even beneath her powder, her skin glowed like a pearl. Despite corset and hoops he could see the curve of her lovely body and painfully, he longed to gather her into his arms.

Just that. To hold her.

What a strange path they had followed to be so intimate without ever enjoying simple embraces.

He forced such thoughts away and approached, noting Lord Randolph Somerton hovering beside her.

Like a vulture over a juicy meal.

An ill-dressed vulture. Somerton should not wear violet.

Devil take it. It would be the final idiocy to descend to petty, spiteful jealousy.

Somerton was blond and handsome in a broad-shouldered, strong-boned way, and popular with ladies. Any number of young hopefuls had tried to catch his eye, but it was well known that he needed an heiress. As a duke's son, he should be able to find one, but he'd not seemed to apply himself until now.

Diana's wealth and power must be too tempting to let slip away, particularly as rumor said his father was tired of his gaming debts. At the moment, however, no one would guess that he was an idle wastrel.

D'Eon was also of the group, but with his lively hands and wide smile, he seemed as harmless as a lovebird.

Masques indeed, with everyone playing a part.

The countess did not pretend to be unaware of him, wise woman, and turned as he approached, with a nicely judged cool smile. "Lord Rothgar, how lovely to see you again so soon."

He kissed her hand, assessing, seeing no sign of desperation. "London being London, dear lady, we are likely to intercept quite often." He greeted the others and was immediately asked by one young lady about the attack on the road.

"Do satisfy Miss Hestrop's curiosity, my lord," Diana said, fluttering her gold lace fan as if nervous. "I have done my best, but alas, I was too overset to notice anything except the awful noise."

"You admirably refrained from shrieking or clutching my pistol arm, Lady Arradale. I am sure I owe you my life."

Half-hidden by her fan, she gave him a brief, scathing look, and he abandoned unwise teasing to tell the story yet again.

"How terrifying, Lord Rothgar!" exclaimed the young lady. "I fear to travel at all!"

"I'm sure it was an isolated incident, Miss Hestrop."

"And you fought the villains off single-handed? How brave."

"Hardly that—"

"*Mon dieu*, my lord!" exclaimed D'Eon. "You are too modest. Three enemies slain, and you with only two pistols. Come now, you must tell us how you achieved this magic."

"Luck," Rothgar said, but detecting a suspicious edge to D'Eon's comments. "Which might amount to the same thing as magic."

"Luck is delightful in all aspects of life, my lord. But please, explain this good fortune."

"My outrider fired once, and alas, died himself as a result. My first shot took the other assailant inside the coach. My second accounted for the other two by a freak, but in far too gruesome a manner to describe before the ladies."

Did D'Eon's sharp eyes look disbelieving?

Miss Hestrop, however, was protesting, and demanding the full story.

The countess raised her hand—a strangely naked hand without her extravagance of baubles. "My lord, please do not speak of it!" she said in a rather overdramatic tone. "My head still rings with the explosion. And the screams . . ." She swayed toward him. "Oh dear."

He put his arm around her, and for a brief moment let himself hold her close. But then he had to lead her toward a sofa.

It was but a moment in his arms, but Diana felt as if those raw edges joined, then ripped apart again as he settled her on the seat and moved away. Leaning back, eyes closed, she gave thanks for her pretense of upset, because it allowed her a moment to recover from shocking pain.

Why hadn't she known how immediate and physical her response would be?

And for him? She slowly opened her eyes and glanced into his concerned eyes.

"My dear countess, a million pardons for distressing you."

It carried layers of meaning, and she said, "This is not your fault, my lord. Please don't distress yourself."

"But I must." He turned away then, however, to command wine for her.

She wanted to argue, but they were not alone. The group she'd been with had flocked with her and hovered, hungry for more details of bloodshed and violence. Hungry too, she was sure, for any morsel of scandal.

> *"A third interprets motions, looks, and eyes;*
> *At every word a reputation dies."*

She shuddered, desperate to order them away. She tried not to stare at Bey as her hope of survival, but even so, when he turned back, glass in hand, she felt as if she could take her first real breath.

But then an equerry came over with the king's inquiries about the incident, and about Lady Arradale's welfare. She summoned control, sipped the wine, then rose to assure the man that she was perfectly well now.

Some around her tried to revive the subject of the attack, but in moments, the king commanded attention for the display of the new automaton. When D'Eon stepped forward to make a pretty speech about peace, harmony, and eternal brotherhood, Diana took a relieved breath. She'd never imagined what it would be like to have to be with Bey under a hundred avid eyes.

Since all attention seemed to be on D'Eon, she risked a glance at Bey. His eyes moved to hers, and she saw all his deep concern.

She smiled slightly and answered an unspoken question. *I am all right.* With subtle use of the language of the fan, she added her message. *I love you.*

He turned sharply away to look at the shrouded machine and D'Eon still orating. Diana wafted her fan. She would protect him from the king's scheme. She would try not to burden him with her own pain. But she would never deny the truth of what they had.

D'Eon ended his speech, and with a grand flourish, uncovered the gift. "The dove of peace!"

Candlelight danced on mother-of-pearl feathers edged with silver and marcasite, and flashed from tiny diamonds at the end of each feather tip. Gasps of admiration ran through the room, but Diana shot a quizzical look at Bey, and it was returned. They both saw that the automaton's action must be quite simple to require such an excess of glittering ostentation.

D'Eon moved the lever and the whir of machinery began.

Rothgar concentrated on the machine, warning himself not to look at the countess again. These speaking looks only increased pain, and could betray them.

The shimmering bird turned its head this way and that, flexing its neck a little—mechanically, very simple—then it lowered its head and seized an olive branch off the ground. With a very audible click the branch notched into some connection, so that when the bird straightened its head the twig was in its beak. Then it spread its wings to reveal words picked out in gold underneath.

Peace. *Paix.*

Everyone applauded again and gathered around. In control of himself now, Rothgar held out his hand to the countess. "Would you care to inspect the toy, my lady?"

She smiled slightly at the word *toy*, and put her hand in his—a brush of soft fingers that spoke of other matters entirely.

"I would rather see the other machine operate now, my lord. I understand you commissioned it for Their Majesties."

"A romantic trifle." He listened to himself to be sure his voice spoke only of polite interest. "But if you are curious, my lady, it must certainly be played."

He turned toward the king, but she said, "A moment, my lord."

Wary, he asked, "Yes?"

Wafting her fan, she said, "I thought you would wish to know that I received news of Brand and Rosa."

Their code. He assessed who could hear, and decided it was safe. She should have thought, however, that some people here would know exactly what letters and messages she received.

"They are well?" he asked.

"It appears so, but I'm surprised by how much time Rosa is spending with Samuel, her best ram." She smiled and nodded to a passing couple. "She seems to find him fascinating."

He found himself struggling not to laugh at the image, though the real message, that D'Eon was frequently with the queen, was not humorous.

"More fascinating than her husband?" he asked.

"Brand is so very busy, you see. I cannot think it wise, even though Rosa doubtless tells him all about matters among the sheep. It all seems somewhat dangerous. To me."

"Male animals can be dangerous," he answered, catching the deliberate ambiguity of the last phrase. She felt threatened by this? Perhaps that was why she had slipped up.

"You are nervous around rams, Lady Arradale?" he asked.

"It is not that—"

But Somerton joined them then, with a rather proprietal air and Miss Hestrop ignored on his arm.

Rothgar noted the countess's lips tighten, but she immediately smiled again and continued, "Rosa takes great interest in my marriage, my lord." As an aside to the other couple, she said, "I speak of my dear cousin. She is concerned for my happiness, she and her husband."

"Only natural for them to care about your choice, my lady," Somerton said. "Doubtless they'd be pleased if you married a man of the north."

She gazed up at him like a perfect ninny. "You might think so, my lord, but their recommendations are so strange. One is a shallow popinjay, and another an eastern potentate. Is that not absurd?"

"Ridiculous," declared Somerton, looking justifiably puzzled, and completely unaware that he'd just been called a popinjay. Lord save him, Rothgar thought, but the woman would have him in open laughter soon.

Again, however, the message was startling. The king and queen were pushing her into marriage with himself? Foolish not to have anticipated that, but he'd thought that he'd convinced the king long since that he would never marry.

"Why do they take such an interest in the matter?" he asked to give an opening for more information.

"Alas," she said, "I might, in a distracted moment, have given Brand the impression that I want them to make the choice."

Confirmation of the king's words. It disappointed, but this clever use of their code made him want to smile.

"Then you must correct that, Lady Arradale," Somerton said sharply. "It must be your decision alone."

She smiled at him. "Oh, thank you, my lord. I do think so."

"I think an eastern potentate sounds exciting," said Miss Hestrop with a giggle. "Silks, jewels, and elephants."

"In Yorkshire?" the countess asked with a blank look.

Miss Hestrop gave a pitying look, and Rothgar intervened. "Silks would certainly be chilly in the northern winter, and the elephants would catch cold. But jewels are welcome anywhere, especially large, glittering ones. Would you not agree, Countess?"

She eyed him over her fan, eyes wide and guileless. "Such as sapphires, my lord? An eastern potentate offering large glittering jewels would be very welcome, yes. Very welcome indeed."

"Over an honest Englishman of good heart?" demanded Somerton, face reddening with outrage.

"It would be a hard choice, Lord Randolph," she said. "These decisions are so very difficult . . ." She placed her hand on Somerton's arm. "Do let's stop thinking about it and ask the king to demonstrate Lord Rothgar's automaton."

Rothgar offered his arm to the expectant Miss Hestrop, full of admiration for the countess's performance, though she might perhaps be in danger of overplaying her part.

She was doing so well, however, that he wondered what had distracted her into giving the king the final choice. It had been a serious mistake. Whatever it was, he couldn't entirely fault her, having suffered moments of unusual distraction himself.

The king was even being cunning. The approved list of suitors was designed to be unsatisfactory. He had wondered why, and now he knew. It was intended to push him into saving the countess by offering marriage himself.

The king doubtless meant well. He sincerely believed that marriage and fatherhood was the happiest possible state. How far would he go, however, in pursuing his aim?

As the king went to switch on the other automaton, Rothgar saw him cast an annoyed look at Lady Arradale on Somerton's arm, and an even more annoyed look at himself.

Lord save him from newly-fledged family men!

Diana found herself in the best position to view the machine, and as soon as the king had switched it on, he moved to her side to comment admiringly on its many fine features. Unfortunately, she also had Somerton on her other side, inclined to stand too close, and to touch her quite unnecessarily.

Also unfortunately, the king also commented admiringly on the many fine features of the gift-giver. Subtlety had clearly ceased to play a part, and she genuinely feared what

the king would do next. What would happen if in the end she
had to give a blunt refusal?

It was a most excellent machine, however, richly ornamented, but this time in perfect taste. Against a silver tree
with bright enameled leaves, a lifelike shepherd and shepherdess sat cheek to cheek. Every branch held tiny feathered
birds, and others poked heads out of nests.

The quiet turning of the mechanism had been instantly
drowned by birdsong pouring from open beaks. The birds
moved in other ways, too. Some just turned a head or
opened a beak, but a few rose to stretch and spread their
wings as if they would fly.

Now the shepherd and shepherdess, dressed in real
clothes like her drummer boy, came to life. Both heads
turned to look at each other with longing, and his porcelain
hand rose to rest on her shoulder. Then, slowly, they swayed
together so lips gently touched lips.

Then the action reversed, and they drew apart, eyes
locked, until they finally looked away and settled to their
original positions. Almost unnoticed the birdsong trailed
away so that stillness and silence came together.

She applauded with everyone else, but tears ached. Poor
shepherd. Poor shepherdess. One kiss was all they were allowed.

For eternity.

"It is only a machine, Lady Arradale," Bey said quietly,
joining her.

"But a magnificent one, what?" declared the king.

Diana made herself turn to the king and smile. "It is a
marvel, sire." Seeing D'Eon nearby, she diplomatically
added, "They both are."

"And so, which do you prefer?" the king asked.

It was like a dousing with cold water. This had clearly
been a contest of sorts, and one with implications. She was
supposed to judge?

Thanking heavens for her supposed conventionality and
limited intellect, she hid behind her fluttering fan, looking
around as if for advice. In reality she was thinking, hard.

The chevalier smiled at her.

Bey raised a brow.

"Your Majesty," she declared at last, "they are both *perfect*!" She allowed herself to flutter, both her fan and her manner. "I know little of such machines, I must confess. But—I admire the dove for its sentiment, sire, but the shepherd and shepherdess for its romantic design."

"Well said, well said!" declared the king. "And both machines please us in the same way. Chevalier, my thanks to my cousin of France. And my Lord Rothgar, my thanks again to you."

As the machines were set to work again, this time in unison, Diana couldn't help think that her automaton surpassed either. In any contest, it would win because of its haunting realism.

She'd been thinking about the drummer boy over the past day. She had given it to Bey because she'd no longer wanted it in her house to trouble her mother, and because he had the expertise to see it well cared for. Now she knew it might be an uncomfortable possession for him, too.

It was, in a way, herself as a child. She'd also begun to think of it as one of the children she longed to have with him. Maybe he would never think of it that way, but if he did she might have given him an intolerable burden.

"You look pale again, Lady Arradale." Lord Randolph put his arm around her, trying to guide her back to the sofa.

She resisted for a moment, almost looking back at Bey for help, but then she remembered her purpose. She must not give the king and queen any encouragement for their hopes. That meant she must not spend too much time with him, or appear interested in him.

She'd probably already been unwise this evening, but with luck no one had noticed. She caught one subtle glance of concern from him before he turned back to the automata and the king. She deliberately leaned against Lord Randolph.

"Some wine, Lady Arradale," he suggested with tender concern.

"How kind."

How cruel, she thought sadly. She was raising the idiot's hopes simply to disguise her feelings for Bey.

Lord Randolph had reason to think himself a candidate, after all. He was high born, handsome, and courteous, though he seemed a little too aware of his qualities. His conversation was all of himself, but that was common enough with men. Even if he were perfect, however, she wouldn't want to marry him, and in normal circumstances she would give him no encouragement.

Now, she had to throw up a diversion, and Lord Randolph was her victim. Though sorry for it, she flirted with him, lightly, but sufficiently to encourage him. Sufficiently to be noted by the king and queen, she was sure.

Of course, since they planned to choose her husband if necessary, favoring any one man was dangerous. Perhaps if she seemed to be flitting between a few, it would delay any choice.

Therefore, when Lord Scrope came over to inquire about her welfare, she smiled warmly at him. The viscount was a genuinely kind man, who enjoyed speaking of his children. He also spoke a great deal of his dead wife. Commendable, but Diana felt that his new bride would have a ghost in the bed.

As Bey's bride would lie with the ghosts of his dead mother and sister? She stopped her eyes from seeking him out, and told herself that it would not be so, because he would take no bride as long as those ghosts lingered.

Unless he had to rescue her . . .

She caught the king's eye on her, and he did not look pleased. Good. She laughed at Lord Randolph's latest foolish sally, and patted Lord Scrope's hand sympathetically. Sir Harry Crumleigh came over and started talking about horses, which was at least an interest she could honestly share.

All three returned her interest warmly, and she ached for it.

She wanted no more broken hearts in the world.

Weakly, she let her eyes slip once again to where Bey chatted with a lively group. He'd clearly said something witty, and Cynthia Hestrop clung to his arm, laughing up at him in a deliberately enticing way. He caught Diana's eye, returned her gaze coolly, then smiled at his wanton admirer.

She made her eyes move on—and saw the king watching her. Had he caught that exchange?

Plague take them all.

Feeling like an animal in a cage, with every movement observed and scrutinized, she turned back to charming and encouraging her wretched suitors.

Chapter 25

The next day, Diana awoke with one pressing question—when would she see Bey again? Ridiculous to feel that he was the watch spring of her life, but a day without the sight of him, without a moment of conversation, seemed worthless.

Then she remembered that she had to continue to pretend that other men were of greater interest. She flopped back on her pillow with a moan. It had become clear last night that they were all taking her encouragement seriously, and beginning to compete.

There was also the matter of the masquerade that Bey was to host only three nights from now. When word of that had spread, the court had bubbled with excitement, and Diana had understood that his grand spectacles were eagerly anticipated. She'd heard of Grecian and Chinese themes, and one at the Abbey which had included medieval jousting.

It all sounded like great fun, except that the king had made it clear that she was to use the occasion to get to know her suitors better, and make up her mind.

Why the devil was he in such a hurry!

With a sigh, she rolled out of bed and took her breakfast while Clara prepared another modest outfit for the day. Perhaps she could put everyone off by looking sickly. She painted her face more densely than before, seriously wondering whether she could construct some of the ugly, pustulant pimples she'd worn last year. Too dangerous, however, for they could smear if touched, and this was not a game.

Thinking that she'd first met the marquess in that guise,

she knew it hadn't been a game then, either, but she hadn't realized it. No, though cloaked in silk and smiles, this was a duel between herself and the world, with possibly fatal consequences. She checked her appearance one more time, then went to join the queen in the garden.

Because she was an addition to the queen's circle, there was little for her to do, and many to be jealous of their duties. She sat quietly, therefore, occasionally joining in the conversation, but free most of the time to look for ways to change Bey's mind about marriage.

She definitely had to gain access to the libraries here, but was afraid to damage her image as a rather silly woman. She doubted she would ever find conclusive proof that he could never father a deranged child, though. Such a thing was surely unprovable. So, she had to convince him in some way that the risk was tolerable.

She suppressed a sigh, sure that in his mind, no such risk was tolerable when by self-denial all risk could be avoided.

She could plead her own pain. Another suppressed sigh. He knew. Complaining to him would be to twist the blade in the wound.

The arrival of Lady Durham with her two-week-old baby was a welcome escape from these thoughts. The queen had apparently demanded the visit, for she loved babies, and she immediately insisted on holding the tiny creature, cooing to it in German.

Diana hovered with the other ladies, as charmed and enchanted as anyone. She rarely saw such new babies, and this was very tiny. Six pounds, the mother said, but healthy.

The baby girl was sleeping when she arrived, but soon obligingly opened huge dark blue eyes, and didn't cry to see a strange face hovering. Diana was surprised by an intense longing to hold the child, but not surprised to instantly think how magical it would be to hold Bey's child, him her loving husband close by.

A shadow fell over her shoulder.

"Lady Arradale," said a man behind her.

Though disappointed, she turned to greet Lord Randolph.

She would rather stay to watch the baby, but the queen urged her to step apart with him.

He carried her hand to his chest with embarrassing ardor. "Lady Arradale. A perfect bloom in a perfect garden. I vow, my lady, you have stolen the blush from the roses!"

Diana kept her smile in place and thanked heavens for a man who would never spout such nonsense. She had no choice, however, but to permit Lord Randolph to court her in his absurd fashion, so she tried to balance mild encouragement with suppression of his smug confidence.

It was a relief of sorts when the baby began to cry, but less of one when the crying wouldn't stop. Diana turned to see the queen trying to sooth the babe while Lady Durham and her nursemaid hovered, clearly wanting to take the child but not willing to snatch it from royal arms.

"The dear thing is cold," declared the queen. "Bring a blanket!"

The dear thing was now red-faced and warbling newborn outrage.

Very unwisely, a lady picked up a blanket that belonged to the prince. He shrieked and turned red-faced too, creating far more volume than the tiny baby.

"*Herzleib, nein!*" cried the queen, finally passing the baby to the anxious mother. "Bring my darling to me. Lord Randolph, run instantly for another blanket!"

Diana thought for a moment that Lord Randolph would refuse this menial task, but he bowed and did take off at a run. The prince's nursemaid brought him over to the queen, but he squirmed and shrieked in a thorough tantrum, probably because his mother had been holding another child so long.

"Lord Rothgar!" The queen suddenly spoke in the tones of one who has seen the Second Coming. Diana whirled, and indeed, he was there, at the edge of the garden.

"Come," cried the queen. "You will know what to do for my poor child!"

For some reason, the prince chose that moment to turn silent, staring at the still man. Thus, the frantic baby's squawks were the only sound.

Bey turned and walked away.

The queen gaped, and for a moment everyone stared after the man who had just broken every courtly rule. Snapping out of shock, Diana cast reason and caution aside, picked up her skirts, and raced after him.

She had to pursue around the house, out of sunlight into shadows, before she found him, standing completely still.

She halted beside him, slightly out of breath. "What is it?" she asked, even though she guessed.

He breathed, and if it were not impossible, she'd think it was the first breath he'd taken in minutes. Still looking ahead, he said, "I cannot endure distressed babies. A weakness . . ."

His sister. His mother. "It's just hungry."

He turned to her, looking almost normal, but pale. "I know."

"You have offended the queen."

His lips twitched a little. "I believe I understand the ways of royalty."

Diana took a deep breath herself. "Well then, at least this will put you far back in the competition for my hand."

She was rewarded by the ghost of a true smile. "An unintentional bonus. You are well?"

"Well enough." She suddenly realized that they were alone here, so close to the house that they could not even be overlooked by a window. Could she go into his arms, particularly when he needed comfort?

Too dangerous. Too dangerous by far.

"What will you do?" she asked.

"Return to the queen and apologize. Once the crying stops."

She realized that he had halted where he still could faintly hear the noise, and that it had just stopped. She realized something else. Bey had a powerful urge to cherish and protect. Walking away from distress must wound like a blade, and it spoke clearly of how terrible such things were to him.

All newborns cried.

Did he have another reason for not having children, one that even love might not be able to overcome?

He held out a hand. "Time to return, my lady," he said, superficially the perfect courtier again.

She placed her hand in his and he led her back toward the queen's garden. "What of your situation after racing after me?" he asked.

"I'll say I thought the queen commanded it."

This was their first private moment since the coach, and now they were approaching the corner of the building. When they passed it they would once more be in sunshine, and in view.

Will breaking, Diana halted and pushed him against the brick wall. There, one hand behind his head, she kissed him, not long, but deeply, and rested for a moment afterward inclined against his body.

She took, he did not give. Yet because he did not resist, she knew he took, too, took contact and comfort. He did not break free either, so they stayed together for perilous minutes, until she found the strength to step back from him, to take his hand and restore the way they had been before.

He stopped her then, merely by a pressure on her fingers, and they stood looking into one another's eyes.

"I'm sorry," he said.

"This is not another burden for your soul," she stated. "I refuse to accept that role, Bey. We are as we are. I will not deny it. We will also survive, no matter what."

He raised her hand and pressed a kiss to it. "Your courage shames me. I will endeavor to do better."

"You are perfect."

"Clearly not."

Moments later, apparent images of propriety, they stepped into sunlight and view. Both children were gone.

"Lord Rothgar!" the queen screeched. "Present yourself!"

He dropped Diana's hand to go forward and bow, but the queen snapped, "And you too, Lady Arradale!"

Diana sank into a deep curtsy, and let him raise her.

"Lady Arradale," the queen demanded, "we did not give

you permission to leave our presence. And you turned your back!"

"I beg your pardon, Your Majesty. I thought you commanded me to bring Lord Rothgar back."

"Would I send you rather than my guard?"

"Yet she succeeded in the task, Your Majesty," Rothgar said, drawing the queen's fire, as he surely intended.

The queen's eyes narrowed. "By what means, I wonder?"

"Sweet reason, ma'am." He bowed again. "Forgive me. I was overset by the children's distress. Your Majesty, in your wisdom, will know why."

The queen's glower softened slightly, but she said, "Then perhaps you should not have children, my lord."

"My thought entirely, ma'am."

Diana could have laughed at the queen's look of annoyance, except that this was all so heartbreaking.

"Why are you here, my lord?" the queen snapped. "Disliking children as you do."

He didn't protest that unfair statement. "On a mission of charity, ma'am. Lady Arradale prepared to come south at a moment's notice, and might need to visit the shops and merchants here to supplement her wardrobe. If she wishes it, I could arrange for my secretary to carry out any commissions she might have."

"Lady Arradale?" The queen turned to her, still frosty.

"There are some items, yes, Your Majesty." Despite logic, Diana's heart began to dance with anticipation. To Hades with his secretary. If she went shopping, surely Bey could escort her.

"Why make do with a servant?" the queen asked, as if picking up her thought.

At that moment, Lord Randolph hurried up with a white blanket and didn't quite manage to hide irritation that the children had been taken away.

The queen smiled at him anyway. "Lord Randolph will escort you, Lady Arradale, along with Mistress Haggerdorn and a footman." She turned the smile, now almost triumphant, on Bey. "Thank you, my lord, for the suggestion."

He seemed completely unmoved as he bowed and took

his leave, and perhaps he was. Diana would like to think that his plan to spend some time with her had been scuttled by his offense to the queen. It was more likely, strong-willed as he was, that he had always intended his secretary as her escort.

His walls were still intact.

Or were they? He had come to see her at least. And she had stolen—seized—that kiss! If he were truly beyond hope, he would never have permitted that.

Fragile hope stirred, but for now, she must leave with the smug Lord Randolph. London was rivaled only by Paris for its merchants, but Diana was in no mood for shopping. She wanted to consider her minor victory, and plot new strategies.

Above all, she wished she were with Bey.

As they entered a coach for the short drive to Bond Street, Diana couldn't help wondering what sort of shopping companion Bey would be. Strange to think of him in that role, but it was a fashionable diversion for a lady, even a married lady, to take male admirers with her on such expeditions. He must engage in it sometimes. His taste was excellent, and she was sure he knew all the special and unusual emporiums.

With Lord Randolph, alas, they promenaded along the obvious route, and Bond Street was horribly crowded. Diana decided to make the best of it, however. There were some items she needed, and she could perhaps use this to reduce Lord Randolph's enthusiasm for marriage to her.

She became a very slow and indecisive shopper.

When that failed to wilt his good humor, she turned to wild extravagance. It only slowly occurred to her that this was a terrible mistake. The evidence of her wealth had him virtually licking his lips.

Oh, perdition. She must keep her wits about her instead of letting her mind drift all the time as to whether this material, that lace, or that hair ornament would most please Bey. Her head was spinning anyway from the press of people and the constant racket of wheels and din of street-sellers' cries. York or Harrogate were never like this.

When she was jostled and someone stepped on her foot, she couldn't help thinking that Bey would miraculously accomplish a shopping expedition in more comfort! When she saw the brass plate by a door, she dashed gratefully into the relative calm of a mantua maker's house. The place was busy, but it seemed like heavenly peace.

As soon as her name was known, the proprietor herself swept out, to usher her into a private room, ply her with wine and cakes, and take her order. Fashion magazines and dolls were produced, and Mistress Mannerly began to make quick skillful sketches of ideas. Since both she and Diana knew what was wanted and were in accord, the designs were worked out efficiently, with Lord Randolph lounging nearby, knocking back the wine, mind obviously vacant.

A vacant-minded husband might seem better than a clever one—Bey excepting—but Diana thought it would drive her mad. An hour in Lord Randolph's company had shown that he had no thought that wasn't self-centered and selfish. It wasn't that he was stupid, but that he was mentally lazy. No one had ever given him reason to try to think, and it had never occurred to him to do so on his own. He was doubtless pursuing her fortune so keenly because it would mean that he need never think again other than what to spend it on.

With a sigh, she reviewed the orders and approved them. A new light traveling gown to replace the one ruined in the adventure, and another grand gown for evening affairs, though she hoped to be gone before it was ready. She couldn't resist ordering a delicious powder gown in fine layers of pale green silk. That was definitely not for her role at court, however, but for after her escape.

She suddenly realized that she was planning to wear it for Bey, but stopped herself from canceling the order. She was still determined to change his mind, and it would be wonderful on a wedding night—

"Anything else, milady?"

Diana snapped herself out of dreams, and recalled a picture in the fashion magazine. She flipped back through pages.

"The Grecian costume, my lady?" said Mistress Mannerly, alert to a new commission. "Classical draperies are in vogue for masquerades."

Diana considered the picture of the willowy woman in artlessly draped cloth that resembled a Greek peplos. "It could be Diana, could it not?"

"Indeed, my lady. A pretty conceit."

She had brought her usual masquerade costume, that of Good Queen Bess, but now the idea of being the Virgin Queen had completely lost its appeal, and not because she was no longer a virgin. Now she could imagine only too well the lonely years of the great queen, whose position had made it perilous to have a man by her side. Diana had always liked to think that Elizabeth had at least enjoyed one lover—perhaps Courtenay, or Leicester—but now that didn't seem consolation so much as torture.

If she went to the masquerade, she would rather be someone else, and why not Diana the Huntress?

"The masquerade is two nights from now," she told the mantua maker. "Can this be made in time?"

"Of course, my lady. Though it is not as simple as it appears"—*don't expect this to come cheaply*, Diana interpreted. "White silk, my lady? Or fine linen for authenticity?"

"By all means let us be authentic," Diana said, rising. "And accessories. Mask, slippers, jewelry—though that can be paste. Bow and arrow, painted silver."

The lady curtsied. "It shall be exactly as you wish, my lady."

Diana left the establishment, spirits a little lighter at the thought of attending the masquerade as Diana, for Bey would surely take the point. In fact, her view of the masquerade brightened. The point of such affairs was to allow a little secret intimacy. Surely she and Bey could steal some time together.

"You are enchanting when you are happy, Lady Arradale."

Diana started, having completely forgotten her companion.

"Oh," she said airily, still trying to give him a dislike of her, "shopping is my chief delight."

"Then be assured, dear lady, that as your husband I would never restrict your merchant voyages, and never quibble at the bills."

Diana only just stopped herself from snapping that her bills were no concern of a husband's anyway. "As your wife," she couldn't resist saying, "I would not interfere with your purchases, either, my lord."

He looked more puzzled than outraged. "How could you, indeed?"

She longed to jab him with something sharp, but back into her part, she fluttered her lashes at him. "Are you saying that my wishes would carry no weight with you, my lord?"

"Ah, I see." He carried her hand to his lips. "In that way, my dear lady, you would rule me entirely."

Still fluttering, she said, "Oh, I do hope so."

He kept hold of her hand, there in the street by their waiting coach. "Are we agreed so easily, my lady?"

"Agreed?"

"That we are to be wed? Their Majesties will be pleased."

"No," Diana said, pulling her hand free. "We were speaking hypothetically, Lord Randolph."

"Come, come. It is not becoming to play hot and cold, dear lady. You know you have made your choice, so let's be done with it."

Diana hastily climbed into the coach, cursing again the fact that she was letting other matters tangle her wits again. As soon as he sat opposite her, she said, "You took me amiss, my lord. I need time to decide."

"You are playing games, my lady. I will inform the king as soon as we return."

"Then I will deny it!"

With a patronizing sigh, he turned to Mistress Haggerdorn, sitting beside her. "Lady Arradale was quite clear, was she not?"

The German woman said, "It did sound so, Lady Arradale."

"Then at the least," said Diana, "a lady has the right to change her mind."

"Ah, so you do admit that your mind settled briefly on the intention to marry me, dear lady?"

With an inner groan, Diana realized she'd been right in thinking that he wasn't stupid. He was clever enough to almost trap her.

She retreated into silliness. "Oh lud, my lord, you tangle me up so! Yes in truth, I am considering you as a husband. I like you very well. But we have known each other only days. I cannot make my mind up so soon. Please don't speak to the king just yet. My mind is quite spinning with the excitement of it all."

He took her hand and patted it. "Your mind will stop spinning once it is settled. Be guided by me, Lady Arradale. Only say the word and you will be able to put aside all cares except for the adornment of your beauty."

She made herself gaze at him as if this idea was a blessing. "If only I could, my lord. But my dear father instructed me never to make an important decision in a hurry. For his sake, I must take at least a week."

His look was all quick, sharp speculation, and she realized that he'd been playing a part as much as she had. Not that he was any less selfish and self-centered, but that he was more so, and shrewd and ruthless with it.

Then the look passed, and he was smiling again. "A week then. But if you decide sooner, my love, I will be waiting anxiously. Every day."

My love. How could two pleasant words sound so slimy?

Diana returned to the Queen's House regarding it more as a refuge than a prison. She knew Lord Randolph couldn't trick or force her into marriage, but having him stalking her with smiling, predatory intent made her skin crawl. What was worse, she'd have to behave warmly toward him until she broke down Bey's dark walls.

At least she didn't have to speak to any of her suitors again that day. The queen demanded a complete description

of Diana's purchases, and a viewing of those she had
brought back. Later, after dinner, some members of the
King's Theater came to give the royal household a private
recital. In Diana's honor, it was to consist of selections from
Mr. Bach's popular opera, *Orione*, which featured the goddess Diana.

Diana tried to use the time to think of ways to escape one
man and capture another, and within the week, but the
lovely music swept away clear thought. She could welcome
the release from worry, but it also carried away her defenses.

Since she spoke Italian, she could easily understand the
story. Orion wanted to marry the sweet maid, Candiope, but
the goddess wanted him for herself. It was based on a classical myth, and in that myth the goddess Diana eventually
killed the man she desired.

For the first time, she wondered if her battle of wills with
Bey could lead to such disaster. Listening to the singers,
however, she saw herself and Bey more in Orion and his
beloved Candiope, with the king and queen as the angry
god.

But then, the king *wanted* her to marry Bey, and was
likely to wreak havoc if she didn't! Lord Randolph was the
jealous, grasping lover, but he had no godlike properties at
all.

As usual in this mad time of her life, no one was playing
their correct role.

Then Candiope sang: *"We must obey the will of the gods
and never see each other again. But alas! without thee my
days must be spent in sorrow."*

Orion replied: *"Cruel parting that tears from me all I
treasure, yet does not put an end to a wretched existence!"*

The words cut too close to reality, and coupled with the
swell of lovely music, they brought tears to Diana's eyes.
The end of Orion's aria on lost love, found her swallowing
in a desperate attempt to hide them.

"Now, now, Lady Arradale," said the king, coming over
to her afterward, and even offering his own handkerchief,
"we cannot have you unhappy, what?"

She blew her nose. "The music was just so lovely, sire."

"Very fine, is it not? But I think your tears come from your unsettled situation, what? Like all women, you find it hard to make up your mind, and you are making yourself miserable over it. Time to make your choice, what?"

Cloaking panic, Diana gazed up at the king. "It is such a hard choice, sire. So many kind men, all with their virtues."

"And thus all suitable, what? Come, come, we can't have you falling into a melancholy, and the uncertainty is distressing to the queen. You must make up your mind."

"In a few weeks, sire . . ."

"No, no! You are overset. I could swear you have grown paler since you came here. A person could sicken, even go mad, under this indecision . . ."

Diana stared at him, sure that that mention of madness had not been accidental. "But, sire," she said desperately, "you said I should have the masquerade to help me decide!"

"After the masquerade, then," the king said firmly, patting her hand. "Your suitors may have that final opportunity to win your heart. But if you still cannot decide, we will settle your mind."

There was nothing to say but, "Thank you, sire."

He retired with the queen then, and Diana could flee to her room. Oh, but she needed to speak to Bey. Had there been any way to avoid this latest twist? If so, she couldn't see it. The king was determined, and his choice would be Bey.

This left her with only two days, however. Two days to change Bey's mind, one of them Sunday, when the court was quiet. The prospect of disaster hovered.

No, with a descendant of Ironhand, too, all things were possible. She would find a way.

Lord Randolph was at Lucifer's losing at hazard when the Frenchman joined the table. A Monsieur Dionne, with an old-fashioned beard and no particular distinction as far as he could see, but a gentleman with money to lose.

However, it was himself who continued to lose. Damned

dice. He had no idea what his tally was, but his father would cut up stiff about it again.

No he wouldn't, he thought with a private smile, because any day now flighty Lady Arradale would make up her mind, and she'd as good as said he was her choice.

Idiot woman with her chatter of eastern potentates. That was no problem, however. He'd keep her at home and pregnant, and she'd be no trouble. If she was, she'd soon learn better.

All that lovely money. Shame he couldn't have the title, too . . .

"My lord?" It was the Frenchman offering him the box.

He shook, and missed the mark again, devil take it.

"Luck is a wanton bitch, is she not, my lord?" said Dionne, offering his snuff box.

Lord Randolph took a pinch and found it excellent quality. Perhaps Dionne, despite appearances, was good for a temporary loan.

The man smiled at him. "Not that you need to worry about these minor losses. All London says you are likely to win the hand of a wealthy lady."

"It is as good as settled," he agreed, preening.

"My felicitations, my lord." Dionne turned to watch the play. "Though I have heard some speculation that the lady will go to the great marquess."

Lord Randolph felt a chill on his neck. "Rothgar? Nonsense. Everyone knows he will not marry. His mother was a raving lunatic."

The Frenchman shrugged. "Men change their minds. I understand Lady Arradale is a very rich woman, and a beauty besides."

"Dammit—" But Lord Randolph collected himself. "Mere gossip," he said coolly, rolling the dice again, losing again. "And if he harbors hopes, he is bound to be disappointed. The lady as good as promised me her hand this very day. It is to be announced on Tuesday."

Dionne seemed genuinely delighted for him. "That is excellent news, my lord." He raised his glass of wine. "I toast your good fortune."

Lord Randolph returned the toast and the congratulations of the men around the table, but inside he was pricked by doubt.

Rothgar? The woman didn't even like him. She'd commented on how chilly he'd been during the journey south, how he'd spent all his time on papers, hardly even speaking to her.

All the same, he was a man of power. What would happen if he decided to have her anyway?

An hour later, de Couriac slipped back into the French embassy, the warm glow of the perfect plan burning inside. Never mind D'Eon. He would have it all.

He had come to London with orders from the foreign minister to achieve two things—the death of the Marquess of Rothgar, and the disgrace of the Chevalier D'Eon. His plan would achieve both, and also avenge his poor Susette.

Yes, suffering for the countess, and then death for the marquess. He would need some help. He began to consider who in the embassy would be most useful, and most willing to keep their mouths shut.

Chapter 26

As Diana had expected, Sunday provided no opportunity for intimate conversations. She went to chapel with the royal household, and attended the less formal Drawing Room that followed. Bey was there but it was impossible to do more than exchange a few commonplace remarks. Lord Randolph was inclined to hover possessively, but she deliberately behaved coolly to him.

She did manage to slip in something to Bey about Brand being impatient for a decision, and that by the morning after the masquerade, everything would have changed. At that, however, others around began to demand details of the theme and decorations for the event, which he teasingly refused to give.

It became clear that he was involved in the planning, which surprised her. But then, perhaps not. He was Daedalus, and enjoyed automata and machines. A complex entertainment could be like a machine, manipulating those who attended.

How on earth, though, did he find time? Did he sleep at all?

Had he slept at all that night in Bay Green?

Was it her imagination that he looked tired?

If she had the care of him, he would sleep. Long hours of peaceful sleep within the compass of her care.

Diana returned to the Queen's House even more determined. Time was short, and she must cease flitting around the emotional edges and attack the primary enemy—his mother's madness. Thus, she needed the library, no matter how poorly it fit with her persona.

She bluntly asked for permission to find something new to read, and it was given without question.

When she entered the big room, many books tempted her, but she searched only for the ones that might tell her about Bey's mother's family. Soon she had established that the family appeared to be normal, with only the usual number of untimely deaths.

To check, she consulted different volumes in search of obituaries of his two uncles and an aunt who hadn't lived to a great age. All three obituaries were brief, showing no sign of the brilliance that burned in Bey, but they indicated normal lives and natural deaths. His aunt, mother of six children, had died of smallpox; one uncle of some internal rupture and infection; and the other after eating bad shellfish.

An investigation of two previous generations threw up Mad Randolph Prease, but further research showed that he'd been a hero on the king's side during the civil war, known for his death-defying feats of bravery.

She replaced the last book, sure in her mind that there was no particular hazard in Bey having children, but also knowing she hadn't changed anything. Bey must know his family history. He would have carried out this investigation himself, perhaps more than once. His character, his course in life, was to strive for absolutes. For perfection. Why risk children at all when there was the slightest chance of passing on insanity?

Sitting quietly at a library table, Diana wondered how that could be changed. She had to persuade him to accept fallibility, to accept risk of imperfection. Somehow he had to let go of his belief that the world would falter and fall if he missed one tiny step.

Could any person change that much?

She almost despaired, but then she remembered the kiss. The kiss she'd stolen from him in the shadows the day before. A week ago, he would have stopped her and escaped, but yesterday he had submitted and accepted.

At the White Goose, he had not intended their joining, but it had happened, the first break in his control. That had been *in extremis*, however. The kiss had not. Though troubled, he'd had his wits and strength, and still he had accepted it. In the end, she had been the one to step apart. The thought gave her blessed hope. Perhaps he could allow himself the gift of human fallibility.

She rose and looked around at the walls filled with books, containing the wisdom of the ages. Ironic that in the end it came down to human will and action, imperfect though it was.

She was determined, however. At the masquerade she would be Diana. Pray God her hunt did not end in tragedy.

To account for her time in the library she picked two books, one of poetry and one of travels in Virginia. When she returned to the queen she was commanded to read from the latter, and it proved to be entertaining, passing the time.

When she eventually retired for the evening, Diana planned a focused analysis of her situation, and the drawing up of a strategy for the masquerade. However, she found that the Diana costume had arrived, and had to try it on. She stripped down to her shift then put it on top.

"No stays, milady?" Clara asked, scandalized.

"They would be ridiculous under this." All the same, Diana was a little taken aback by the revealing nature of the gown.

The fine linen was opaque and the artless folds were constructed over a sturdy lining. All the same, it left one shoulder naked, and seemed to cling to her figure. Her hips and bottom, normally hidden beneath hoops and skirt, were clear beneath the drape of cloth. Her breasts, normally confined and kept still, protruded and . . . moved! She took a few dancing steps, and they definitely *moved*. What was worse, in moments, her nipples pushed forward at the fabric.

"Stays," said Clara firmly. "Or at least a binding, milady."

It was tempting, but it would ruin the effect. This gown was supposed to be worn like this. And anyway, she remembered Bey's reaction to her breasts, the way he'd looked at them, touched them, tasted them . . .

Her nipples poked forward shamelessly, and she knew her cheeks were turning red. Oh, she couldn't—

When her whole life lay in the balance?

Of course she could. She'd seduce him at the ball if she judged it would achieve her purpose.

"Nonsense," she said, shrugging to try to rearrange the folds at the front. "It's a masquerade, not a formal ball. Give me the accessories."

Dour-faced, Clara helped put on a silver belt and arm-band, then a headband that was part of the mask. The mask itself was a marvel in silver and pearl, covering both eyes but curving down the left side of her face above and below to make a crescent moon. The goddess Diana's symbol was actually the full moon, but the design was too clever and beautiful to quibble at.

With a smile of excitement, Diana slipped into silver Grecian slippers, and slung the quiver of silver arrows across her back. Then she picked up the white bow.

"Gemini!" Diana exclaimed. "It's real!"

"What is, milady?"

"The bow. When I said I wanted things to be authentic, Mrs. Mannerly took me literally."

Diana had amused herself with archery now and then, and she knew the feel of a good bow. Carefully, she drew this one, and it flexed perfectly. She took out an arrow and found it real, too, painted silver. She nocked it, aiming at a rather sorrowful hermit in a painting on the wall.

"My lady!" Clara screeched.

"Hush! You'll have the household in on us."

"Well, don't you be firing that thing—"

Twang! Diana released the arrow, and it thudded right into the spot she'd aimed for, a branch near the hermit's head. "A very good bow, even though twelve feet is not much of a challenge." She nocked another one, and turned toward the open window. "Perhaps I should fire into the garden to see how far it can shoot."

"My lady!" Clara protested.

Teasing, Diana walked to the window and took aim at the

railings, but when Clara pursued, hissing protests, she lowered her weapon.

"Oh, but that was fun," she said. "Like stepping back into comfortable shoes. I tell you, Clara, the shoes are beginning to pinch unendurably."

"Which shoes, milady?" asked the unimaginative maid, snatching bow and arrow from her. "The yellow ones?"

Diana laughed. "Not real shoes. I'm being metaphorical. Ignore me."

As Clara put the weapon in a drawer, the cloudy sky shifted, and the full moon sailed out. Diana looked up at her true symbol, ruling the dark sky, washing the world with pure, pale light. The moon was the place where all things wasted on earth were stored. Misspent time, and squandered wealth. Broken vows, and missed opportunities. Above all, wasted, lost, and squandered love.

No wonder it glowed so brightly tonight, and swelled so huge.

As the clock in the hall of Malloren House struck a quarter to ten, Bryght Malloren sent Portia, carrying the sleeping Francis, up to a hastily prepared bed. He cast a glance at Rothgar, who had greeted their unannounced arrival with mild surprise and complete imperturbability.

"Elf insisted that we make our explorations of the north brief and hurtle back here," Bryght said, indicating to the servants which items needed to go up to their rooms immediately. He looked again at his brother. "Is she right? Is something amiss?"

"Nothing at all," Rothgar said. "I am holding a masquerade tomorrow, however, so your presence is welcome. I assume Elf and Fort went on to Walgrave House."

"He managed to persuade her not to come here at this time of night, but she'll be over first thing in the morning to ferret out your secrets."

"I have no secrets," Rothgar said blandly.

Bryght gave him a look. "Then she'll be delighted to run an entertainment for you again."

"It is already run, but if it amuses her . . ." Rothgar indicated the corridor that led to his study. "Would you care for a nightcap?"

Bryght organized the last of the luggage and accepted the offer. His brother seemed calm, but that didn't mean a damn thing. He'd be calm if he'd just drunk poison. As soon as the door was shut and he had the wine in hand, he probed with a direct question, "How is Lady Arradale managing at court?"

"Ah," said Rothgar, seeming amused, "I wondered if that was Elf's concern. I believe the court will survive the experience."

Bryght laughed, but said, "She's avoided marriage?"

"Thus far. It has only been four days."

Bryght sipped from his glass and decided to be blunt. "Elf's right. The hair on the back of my neck is stirring. What's going on, Bey?"

His brother didn't so much as twitch. "At present Lady Arradale appears to favor Lord Randolph Somerton, Carlyle's second."

"I don't know him. Will they suit?"

"A charming young man whose father would dearly like to see him provided for."

"Sounds like a slimy wastrel. She can do better than that."

Rothgar, however, had turned, sipping wine, to look out of the window.

After a moment, Bryght said, "Bey?"

His brother turned from the window, through which the full moon glowed. " 'Some thought it mounted on the lunar sphere/Since all things lost on earth are treasured there.' Pope. Our weaknesses and follies stored on the moon, beyond reach of mortal man. Or even of Daedalus and his waxen wings." He smiled at Bryght. "However, what you have lost on earth is likely a fine for traveling on Sunday. Don't expect me to fly to the moon to find the money for you." He drained his glass and put it down. "I have other matters to take care of. Good night."

Bryght stared at the door clicking firmly shut behind his brother. 'Struth, Elf had been right. This was all damned peculiar, but also hopeful. They'd speculated that Lady

Arradale might have cracked their brother's resolution, and something was certainly cracked!

He went to the window and toasted the huge, pearly moon. "All hail, Diana!" he said softly. "May you triumph over the forces of darkness. I'll certainly help in any way I can."

Diana took off the costume, and Clara laid it carefully in the armoire, then tidied away the box and wrappings. "There's a paper here, milady."

Diana turned, pulling on a loose wrap. "The bill?"

"It's sealed, milady."

Diana took it and studied the seal. It was just a lump of wax without imprint so she snapped it open to read the contents.

Not a bill. A message.

Lady Arradale, we must speak of private matters. You will understand. If you can, contrive to meet me by the gazebo in the queen's garden tonight at ten. A small door at the beginning of the east wing will provide an exit. R

She stared at it, excitement and panic beginning to beat. A clandestine meeting! An appalling risk to her and especially to him. If they were caught, the king and queen would insist on immediate marriage, and there would be no rational objection.

Clearly there must be a powerful reason. Bey was not so weakened as to ask for this meeting out of need.

Or, she thought, stilling, it could be a trick.

She hurried to her writing case and took out the note he had sent before. She compared again and again, but it was definitely his writing. Gemini! She'd have to go, but she suddenly shivered. She didn't like to think herself a coward, but creeping around deserted gardens at night did not appeal. She looked out at the full moon. It would light the way, but the garden would still be an eerie place. And what if she were caught?

At the best, it would be horribly embarrassing.

Still, she must go, and the clock said ten to the hour. "Clara, no questions. Find my dark brown traveling dress."

"What—"

"No questions!"

"Stays, my lady?" the maid ventured.

"No, no. The dress, and quickly."

The wide-eyed maid began to dig through the lowest drawer in the armoire, and Diana sat to load one of her pistols.

Just one.

Not the out-and-out panic of two, but the caution of one.

Chapter 27

The ground floor of the east wing seemed to be storage rooms, and deserted, and Diana found the unlocked door without trouble. It opened with well-oiled ease, and she suspected that servants used it frequently to slip out in the evenings. There were guards at the official gates, but there must be other ways out of the grounds. If needs be, the railings were climbable.

A path led toward the gardens at the rear, and she followed it, making herself walk calmly along rather than creeping like a thief. If she encountered anyone, she would just say she wanted some fresh summer air. In a while, pretense became reality, and her fears eased. No one was out here to harm her, and it truly was a beautiful summer night, drifting with subtle perfumes from rose, stock, and mignonette. To add cream to the dish, she was about to have a clandestine meeting with Bey.

Whatever his purpose, this surely was a golden moment for hers.

She came to an arch through the tall hedge around the queen's garden and paused, listening for any sound. She was no longer afraid, but she wished Bey would show himself. The silence was eerie. She told herself that she was early, and made her way across the lawn and around bushes toward the gazebo near the wall.

When it came in sight, shining pale in the moonlight, she could see no one inside.

"Hello?" she called softly, caution creeping up her neck. She slipped her hand into her pocket to the reassurance of the pistol as she stepped cautiously through another arch in a hedge.

A hand grabbed her arm. Before she thought to scream, another covered her mouth. She tried to pull her pistol free, but a second man passed some sort of bond around her, cinching her arms to her body. She kicked and her hard shoe connected with the man's kneecap.

"*Sapristi!*" he hissed, and slapped her head so she saw stars.

"None of that," said the man still covering her mouth. "Get her legs tied and she'll be helpless."

Still cursing, the Frenchman wound something else around and around her legs, then he stood and growled in French, "Not a sound, milady, or any more tricks or I'll knock you out. Understand?"

De Couriac!

Despite a small beard, she'd swear it was him, and who else here knew she spoke French?

Fool! she berated herself. *Fool!* She should have guessed. If Bey could produce convincing forgeries, so could anyone else! But what was the purpose of this? What did the French want with her?

De Couriac thrust his face close to hers. "*Comprenez vous?*"

It was him, and fear poured through her. She nodded, trying desperately to decide whether it would be worth screaming anyway as soon as she could.

The Englishman took his hand away from her mouth, saying, "Don't make any trouble, milady, and you'll be all right." He sounded uncomfortable with what he was doing, and even as if he was promising safety.

Before she could decide what to do, de Couriac picked her up and hurried toward the wall at the back of the grounds. The Englishman climbed to sit astride the top, then she was hoisted up and lowered helpless into other arms.

She gaped when she saw who it was. Lord Randolph Somerton!

"What are you doing?" she said in a furious whisper. "The king will see you hang for this!"

"Not a bit of it, my dear," he said with a smug smile that made her long to have her pistol free and shoot him.

He carried her to a waiting coach and deposited her quite carefully onto the seat. Then, with a lordly air, he dismissed her captors.

"Are you sure you can manage?" asked de Couriac. "She's a hellcat."

"Respect your betters," Lord Randolph snapped. "Begone!"

"Frogs," he muttered, then moved out of Diana's sight to give some directions to the man on the box. She cursed the fact that she couldn't hear them, though what use they'd be, she couldn't imagine. She was wrapped tight as a swaddled baby and could find no way to escape.

She noted that these bindings were unlikely to hurt her, and hoped that meant that Lord Randolph was up to mischief not wickedness.

He climbed in to sit opposite her.

"What is all this about?" she asked as calmly as she could.

"Isn't it obvious? We are eloping."

"You're mad!"

"Still thinking I'll hang, my lady?" He produced an enameled snuff box and took a pinch. "Put your anxieties to rest. The king will not be offended. Quite the opposite, in fact. He is to reward me handsomely. With an earldom, in fact.

"Yes," he added, as she sat there, dumbfounded, "I'm to be not just your husband, but full earl, with all the privileges, powers, and properties attached."

"The king would never support an abduction!"

"You think not?"

His glossy confidence made her waver. Would the king endorse this, perhaps to get rid of the blight on his kingdom she represented?

But surely the king wanted her to marry *Bey*.

Or, she suddenly wondered, had his behavior in the queen's garden turned the royal couple completely against him? She tried desperately to remember any sour nuances earlier at the Drawing Room. She didn't think there'd been any . . .

"The king *told* you this?" she asked.

"Of course."

"In person?"

He looked down his nose at her. "The king has many demands on his time, Lady Arradale. I received his instructions by letter."

Lud! She'd been tricked by an excellent forgery, so she couldn't look down on him for suffering the same fate. But why? The French . . .

Time for that later, now she must convince him to return her before any of this came out.

"But Lord Randolph," she said, trying to keep to her foolish persona while making her point, "how can you be sure that the letter you received from the king wasn't a forgery?"

"A forgery? You little widgeon"—oh, how she hated that smug, superior smile—"the letter carried the king's seal."

She opened her mouth to point out how easy that was, then shut it, appalled. Forgery of the king's seal was *treason*!

"I see you understand at last," he said. "Don't be afraid. I'll be as good a husband as you allow me to be. Give me no trouble, and I'll be kind."

Diana suppressed a growl, and strove for silliness. "But what if your letter *was* a forgery? I don't want to be married to a man in the Tower for treason."

A flicker of uncertainty did cross his face, but then smoothed away. "Don't be foolish. Of course the king wants you and your property in a man's hands, and who else but mine?" He leaned forward and tapped her nose. "I have to thank you, my pet. Without your little games I'd have had to make do with being a countess's consort. Now I'll have it all. What's more, until my father dies, I'll outrank my damned elder brother."

"What games?" she asked, wishing she'd dared bite that finger.

"Why, your will-she, won't-she at the shops yesterday, and your making sheep's eyes at Lord Rothgar at the Drawing Room today, just to make me jealous."

"I did not!" she protested, truly offended by the description.

" 'Methinks the lady doth protest too much.' " he said with a chuckle. "After all, you ran out eagerly enough in response to a letter from me, didn't you?"

R for Randolph? She almost let out that she'd thought the R was for Rothgar. In fact, her mind was scurrying around the fact that the letter had been in Bey's handwriting. A forgery to deceive them both! Clearly Lord Randolph was someone's dupe.

And de Couriac had been part of it.

This was a French attack on Bey.

Oh Hades, she was bait! He was to come after her, and be killed somewhere in the secret dark where it could be blamed on footpads.

"It was that which alarmed the king, you know," the fool was saying, lounging at his ease. "You showing interest in Rothgar. Running after him in the garden was just too much, my dear. The last thing the king wants is more power in that man's hands."

What should she do?

What could she do?

She had to get the dolt to untie her.

"The marquess will not marry," she said. "Everyone knows that. I was just having a little fun with him." She wriggled. "Please, Lord Randolph, won't you untie me? I'm getting pins and needles."

He glanced out of the window. "Not long now. Then I'll untie you, my pretty, never fear."

At the look in his eyes, she went cold. "You're not to do anything until we're married!"

"Am I not?" All humor left him, and he seized her chin. "Let us start as we mean to go on, Diana. I tell you what to do. You do not tell me."

Striving to hide pure rage, Diana forced a weak smile. "I'm sorry, my lord. But please. It wouldn't be right. Why can't we be married properly with a big wedding? I've always wanted a big wedding."

"Too late, my dear. But when we return from Scotland,

you can have a grand wedding if you wish. I will allow you anything within reason as long as you're a good, dutiful wife."

He sat back again, confident lord of his world.

Diana had never before been aware of swelling with rage. It made the bindings constrict around her, and her head pound. She closed her eyes, hoping to hide it. Oh, she'd kill him. He couldn't keep her tied up forever, and as soon as she was free, she'd kill him.

Even though he was a stupid, arrogant dupe, and the Chevalier D'Eon was the true villain.

The coach slowed and turned and her eyes flew open.

They'd arrived somewhere and Lord Randolph intended to *rape* her. If there was any hope of rescue, it would come from Bey, and he'd be riding to his death. She fought down panic. She'd have her chance as soon as he untied her, and then he'd see about dutiful wives!

The moon showed a country lane between hedges. Someone must have the job of telling Bey where to come, for this spot would not be easily found. Would he be wary?

What about Clara? Would she have raised the alarm? Though it would all be horribly embarrassing, she'd welcome the king rousing the army to find her.

No, plague take it. She'd trained the maid too well not to kick up a fuss over her occasional adventures, and now she reaped the bitter harvest. It might be morning before anyone at the Queen's House knew she was missing.

The coach stopped in front of a simple cottage where faint candlelight gleamed behind two windows. There were no other buildings nearby.

An ideal spot for murder.

An ideal spot for rape.

Panic started to dance inside. She tested her bonds again. No slack at all. She tried to tell herself that she wasn't helpless. She couldn't be! But she felt it.

Lord Randolph opened the door, stepped out and spoke briefly to the man on the box, then he reached in to gather her into his arms. She stiffened, trying to keep from touch-

ing him, but then made herself relax. The more compliant
she seemed, the more likely she was to have a chance.

In fact, she relaxed inside. He couldn't rape her tied up
like this, so her chance would come.

Soon.

The carriage rolled off, carrying on down the lane, and he
carried her through the door into an unused kitchen. This
was clearly a two-room cottage, with perhaps a loft over-
head. Was she alone with him here?

She shivered, but really, one against one was better odds.

He kicked the front door shut, then carried her into the
second room. A bedroom with one large, simple bed.

She couldn't help noticing that he showed no strain. She
forced back fear. So, he was strong. She had a pistol.

Untie me, she willed at him.

Instead, he laid her on the bed, and stood back to look her
over with smug, greedy satisfaction.

"You're a cozy armful, Lady Arradale, and I'm a lucky
man." He sat and put a hand on her left breast. She couldn't
help but try to fight, and achieved nothing more than a
twitch.

"No stays?" he asked, and grinned. "Didn't want any in-
conveniences in our way, eh?" But then his fingers tightened. "I do hope you're not in the habit of playing these
games—"

"No! You're hurting me! I was already out of my stays
when I found your note."

He slowly gentled his fingers, then stroked her, but his
eyes stayed cool. "I'm going to be angry, my dear wife, if I
find you already broached. I like deflowering virgins. So,
why did you come to such a scandalous assignation?"

She tried to look coy. "I was bored. And your message
promised entertainment, my lord."

He chuckled. "I suppose you were bored. Dull as plain
water, the court of King George III. Well," he said, standing
to strip off his coat, "I don't suppose you're bored any
longer, and I will be delighted to entertain you."

She was still tied, but if he touched her again she was
going to throw up. "Please don't do this now! Not here!"

He shook his head, taking off his waistcoat. "Gads, you virgins. Always kick up a fuss. What the devil difference does it make when or where?"

"I want to be married!" she wailed, writhing desperately against her bonds. "I want to be in a better bed than this. I want rose petals!"

He burst out laughing, and she could see that in other circumstances he'd be handsome, even seductive. The dense idiot couldn't imagine that any woman might feel sick at the thought of him forcing sex on her.

He walked out of the room and she sagged, though her heart still thundered. Had she made him stop? Was he rethinking? She tested the bonds again, but they were lengths of cloth, well knotted, and nothing was going to break them.

He walked back in and tossed a handful of rose petals over her. "There, my dear. Don't say I don't humor your whims." Then he pulled off his cravat, and took off his shirt to reveal a broad, furry chest.

The petals were not sweet pea, thank heavens, but even so, her mind flew back to the White Goose, to Bey stripping for her pleasure. This corrupt reenactment brought tears to her eyes, and desperation to her soul.

Dear God, let Bey find me!

But then she remembered it could bring him to his death. *No! Keep him away. I can bear this, even rape, rather than his death.*

Lord Randolph sat on the bed and pulled off riding boots and stockings. In moments he stood in just his bulging breeches, and shook his head at her as if she were a silly ninny. "Don't be frightened, my rose. We're to be married, so it's no sin, and it'll only hurt the once. I'm a clever lover. You'll soon come to enjoy it."

If he'd growled or said terrible things, Diana could bear it better. This confidence, this smug belief that this was normal, was going to drive her mad. As was the fact that she was still completely helpless. Until now, she hadn't really believed that this could happen to her, that there'd be no way out, no magical rescue.

She began to shake, and hated the weakness of it.

He leaned down and smoothed a hand over her brow. "Hush, now. Don't get in a state. See, I'm going to untie you."

Diana stilled. At last. At last. Just a moment with her pistol. Just one moment. She gazed up at him. "Oh, thank you, Lord Randolph."

He produced a knife and placed it by the knot in the cloths around her legs. "Call me husband, my dear."

Diana looked away as if bashful. "Husband."

The knife snicked through the cloth, and she almost tried to kick free. *No. Patience,* she told herself. *Wait until he releases your arms.*

But then he straddled one leg and knotted the cloth around her other ankle.

"Why are you doing that?" she cried, trying too late to kick him.

He wrapped the cloth a few times around the rough post at one corner of the bed end and knotted it firmly. "I'm sorry, my dear, but you might try to fight. You'd likely hurt yourself, and we can't have that."

Realizing her peril, she really tried to fight then, but there was nothing she could do to stop him tethering the other ankle to the other corner.

Chapter 28

He stood to look at her. "You're damned strong for a lady, my dear. But I'm stronger. Never forget that. I'm going to do your hands now. With your legs tied, you can't get away, and you don't want to make me angry, do you?"

Any chance of convincing him she was weak and willing had gone, so she said, "You can rape me ten times a day, Lord Randolph, and I won't marry you. In fact, I'll see you hang for it."

He just laughed. "You'll change your tune."

When he cut the cloth around her arms, she was ready to go for her pistol, but he captured both wrists and tied them to the bar that ran across the top of the bed.

Stretched out, Diana knew total helplessness for the first time in her life. Blinding, numbing fear welled over her, but she fought it.

Ironhand, she chanted silently.

She came from a line of northern warriors who had died in battle, and in dungeons, and under torture. She'd not disgrace them here. And she'd meant what she'd said. Nothing he could do could make her say her vows to him, and sooner or later she'd see him dead for it.

If he raped her, so be it. It would be nothing next to the rack, or being hanged, drawn, and quartered.

He eyed her, and she remembered thinking that he wasn't as stupid as he seemed. "You're quite a surprise, Lady Arradale, but don't get overconfident. As you see, you can't fight a determined man, and if you don't behave, I'll find ways to make you."

"Whips, now. What a bully you are."

Anger flickered, but he picked up a rose petal and stroked it up and down her neck. She'd rather he hit her. "If necessary. But there are other ways. Everyone cares for something, and what you care for, you'll lose unless you are a completely dutiful wife. Words, however, are feeble women's weapons. You can berate me if you insist."

"Oh good. You're a slimy turd from a very sick animal."

He stared at her in shock, then slapped her. Not hard. A sting, no more, and she had to admire his restraint for he was clearly outraged.

"More language like that and you'll be black and blue. You're clearly not the lady you appear to be, but by God, as my wife you will be."

He picked up his knife and cut open her bodice, calmly and carefully peeling it back until her breasts were completely exposed. She couldn't help but try to twist her hands free, but she could do nothing, nothing!

"Very nice," he murmured, tossing the knife aside and gathering both breasts in his hands. "Wealth, power, and a luscious body. I do appreciate my good fortune, wife. Never doubt that. Now, let me show you how nice this all can be."

He began to roll one nipple between his fingers, quite gently, and with a part of her shocked and horrified mind Diana sensed her body's automatic reaction.

She closed her eyes and tried to block out the feel of his intrusive hands and the irritating tendency of her body to respond like a mindless thing. Tried to concentrate instead on the searing satisfaction of killing him at the earliest opportunity.

Taking out her pistol and shooting him. She could imagine the shocked disbelief the moment before he died . . .

He was suckling her and her damnable rogue body twitched.

Shooting would be too quick. Too indirect.

Picking up his knife and plunging it deep, again, and again—

Sharp sting on her cheek again.

Her eyes flew open.

"No, you don't," he said, still smiling. "Keep your eyes open. It's not wrong for me to touch you like this. Not as your husband."

"You're not my husband."

"Yet. I'd kiss you, but I fear you'd try to bite. Think what you're missing."

Then he moved lower down the bed and used both hands to push up her skirts to her waist. She tensed, thinking he'd have to feel the pistol, but her pockets were stiff, and he was far more intent on her.

"Very nice," he said, pushing her knees apart to expose her further. "Stay like that." He moved back to unfasten his breeches.

No. Though she was powerless, she would not submit. She closed her legs as much as she could, took a deep breath and screamed. It felt so good, she screamed again, louder. Again, and again, and again!

"Damn you, shut up!" He clapped his hand over her mouth. Gleeful to finally be fighting, she tried to bite. He grabbed his shirt one-handed and shoved it into her mouth, more and more until she was choking.

"Now will you shut up?" he snarled, straightening, his hair wild, and his eyes more so. "By God, if you didn't own a large part of the north I'd cut your throat and leave you to rot."

Panicked by the cloth against her throat, Diana made herself calm and breathe through her nose.

He glared at her, then smiled again, extremely unpleasantly. "I think you need a lesson, wife. You can stay like that for a while."

He took something out of his pocket—a flask—and went to sit on a settle beside the fireplace. As he tilted it and drank, he watched her with sickening satisfaction.

It might be wiser to close her eyes, but she felt she had to keep watching him, as if sight might help in some way. She struggled for every breath, struggled not to choke, struggled not to show fear.

"Remarkable," he said after a while. "I'm going to have to break you, of course, like a rogue horse. Or I could just clap you in a madhouse. Ah, a reaction. I gather the king's holding that threat over your head. A husband is in a much better position, and I suspect I could goad you into public insanity quite easily. So sad. Your unnatural position is to blame, of course."

He rose, came slowly over to the bed, and pulled the shirt out of her mouth a bit. "Going to behave now?"

Though she could hardly bear the thought of the cloth back deep in her mouth, she just looked at him. With a smile, he tied it in place, but not stuffed deep.

"See, you are completely at my mercy. I can do with you as I please. Even be kind." He picked up a rose petal again, and stroked it around and around her breasts. "Doesn't that feel sweet?" He put it close to her nose, where she couldn't help but breathe in the perfume. "Doesn't it smell sweet?"

Then he suddenly squeezed her nose shut, cutting off all air.

"Or I can be very unkind."

Though a cry escaped, she fought not to breathe in through her mouth, not to suck the cloth back down.

He laughed and let her go, then ungagged her entirely. "Your choice, my arrogant lady. Kind, or unkind." He unfastened his bulging breeches.

She sucked in deep breaths, but would not give him the satisfaction of a reply. She closed her eyes, and resolved to keep them closed. That was the only power she had left.

"Think you can resist, don't you?" he said in an unnerving sneer. "But bodies are funny things, *wife*. You'll doubtless not enjoy the first time, but we have the rest of the night, and I intend to use every minute of it." He thrust her legs apart again. "I'll make you explode with pleasure sooner or later, and then you'll change your tune. Remember that."

"As final words, they have a certain memorability."

Diana's eyes flew open. "Bey," she whispered, wondering if her mind had escaped into fantasy.

Lord Randolph, a step away now, red with fury.

Lord Bryght, a pistol aimed at him.

Bey here, with her, pulling her skirts down, and cutting her bonds with three quick slashes of a knife. Like a reflex, she jerked into a protective huddle, knees to exposed chest. He gathered her, still locked like that, into his arms.

"Hush, hush," he murmured, and she realized she was weeping.

She didn't want to weep!

But weak tears poured like a river in flood, conquering any will to stop them. His arms tightened and he rocked her, still murmuring words she couldn't hear as she wept till she ached, wept till she burned, wept till she could weep no more.

"Hush now," he said, words making sense at last. "Poor Lord Randolph is awaiting your pleasure."

That snapped her sore eyes open, and saw her would-be rapist, arrogant despite his still-open breeches. As she'd thought, Lord Bryght had him under control of his pistol. Bey seemed almost calm, but Lord Bryght emanated cold fury.

Diana realized she'd unlocked herself from that protective knot at some point, and now she moved out of Bey's arms, clutching around herself the coat she hadn't been aware of before. Bey's coat. He was in shirt sleeves, watching her with deep, dark care.

Silently, he pulled a long cravat pin from the lace at his throat, and gently loosened her clutching hands from his coat. Deftly, he pulled her bodice together and wove the pin through the cut edges so she was decent again.

Still shivering slightly, she dragged her pistol out of her pocket at last, and cocked it. "I vowed to kill him."

"He is yours."

"You can't do that," Lord Randolph said, suddenly pale. "For God's sake, Lord Rothgar, take that off her before she has an accident."

Diana growled. "I *need* to kill him."

"He is yours," Bey said again. "Somerton, she could put a pistol ball between your eyes at thirty paces, so wherever she hits you, it will not be an accident. I recommend between the legs, Lady Arradale."

Lord Randolph went white, and covered himself with his hands. "By God! Lady Arradale, remember the king!"

"You stupid man, do you really think the king would have ordered this?"

"I have his letter!"

Bey put his hand on her pistol. "Perhaps he should live a little longer. What letter?"

"He claims to have a letter from the king proposing this plan to prevent the union of our two estates. But Bey, de Couriac was part of this. It's the French. I think it's aimed at you—"

"Hush," he said. "I know. This place is well guarded now." He looked at Lord Randolph. "The king will be outraged by this abduction, and he wants a marriage between myself and Lady Arradale."

"You lie. I have the letter in my coat!"

Bey rose and went through the pockets of Lord Randolph's abandoned jacket.

"You'll see I'm speaking the truth," the man said. "Let me fasten my breeches."

"No. You were keen enough to unfasten them, I assume." Bey stood with a folded sheet. He studied the seal in the light of the one candle, then opened the piece of paper.

"See?" said Lord Randolph, folding his arms again.

He wasn't a stupid man, Diana thought, but one blinkered by arrogance and self-importance. He truly thought the king's favor was real, and would save him.

"Indeed I see. An excellent forgery. The king will be even more outraged."

"A forgery!" Lord Randolph stepped forward and snatched the letter. "It has the king's own seal."

"Fabricating a seal is even easier than copying handwriting."

"Someone sent me a letter in your handwriting," Diana said. "That was cleverly done, too."

"I apologize. I should have thought to set up some code to verify such things."

Diana gathered his coat closer around herself. "If you try to take the blame for this, I'll shoot *you*. Despite illusions on the subject, you are not God."

He laughed briefly, but Lord Randolph exclaimed, "*His* writing? You thought the note from me."

"No," she said, "I didn't."

"You strumpet!"

Bey backhanded him so he staggered back into the wall.

"You are a fool, Somerton, and the world would be better off without fools. You deserve to die for what you did here, but that is in Lady Arradale's hands. But if you say one word more that is less than respectful, you will meet my sword."

"Perhaps I would win," the man blustered, hand to his face.

"You must be extremely good then, because not only am I skilled, I hunger to drive a blade through your heart."

At the calm but chilling words, Lord Randolph's face turned a bizarre mottling of terror and rage. "I won't meet you! You can't make me!"

"Then I would kill you where you stand. Now, tell me how you received the message from the king."

"It was slipped to me. I don't know how! I thought it was real!" He was shaking now, eyes darting between Bey, Bryght, and Diana. Weak though he was, she almost felt sorry for him.

"And you wrote a letter inviting Lady Arradale to the tryst? And sent it where?"

"As instructed. To Mistress Mannerly's. You will see in the letter that it says so!"

Bey looked at the letter again, and read it completely. "You are indeed a fool, Somerton, to believe His Majesty would go to these lengths."

"I didn't know."

"So, what of de Couriac?"

"Who? I don't know a de Couriac!"

"The Frenchman who helped you."

"Dionne. He's called Dionne. I met him at Lucifer's. He turned up at my rooms just after I received the note . . . I suppose I must have spoken of it. He offered to help. For a little money. I took him up on it though. I'm short of cash at the moment. It was a false name?"

"Very similar to D'Eon," Diana remarked.

Bey folded the note and put it in his pocket, then gently drew Diana to her feet. "Come here, Lord Randolph, and lie upon the bed."

The man went white. "By God, what do you intend?"

"That you do as you are told. If you live, you have many lessons to learn, and obedience can be the first."

"Go piss yourself."

Diana glanced at Bey wondering what he planned, and how he was going to enforce his will. He simply looked at the younger man, and after a time of silence that seemed almost unendurable, Lord Randolph staggered toward the bed. "What are you going to do?" he asked, but in a broken whine.

Bey pushed him quite gently on the shoulder so he sat, then again so he was lying. "I have no designs on your beautiful body," he said, picking up a strip of cloth. "Stay still." He began to tie Lord Randolph's wrists to the bed. "Diana, if you wish, you may do his feet."

Diana put down her pistol, appalled by this calm application of terror. It didn't stop her fierce satisfaction at tethering her tormentor's trembling feet to the bed so he ended up as helpless as she had been, his floppy private parts exposed by his open breeches.

"What are you going to do?" he asked again, white-edged eyes darting around the room. "For God's sake, Rothgar, Malloren . . ."

Bey looked down at him. "I am going to do nothing. We men are going to leave you at Lady Arradale's mercies. If you survive, I will send people at dawn to cut you free and put you on a boat for the Americas. Your father has property there, I believe. Do not return."

"No! Look, I never meant her any harm. We were to be married! You know what women are like . . . !"

The door shut behind the two men, and Lord Randolph stared up at her. He tried a weak smile, fighting his bonds. "You don't want to hurt me. I didn't really hurt you."

She leaned forward and slapped him, just hard enough to sting.

He grinned a bit. "There, see. You feel better now, don't you? Hit me again if it helps."

She thought of fondling him, but whether he'd like it or hate it, she couldn't bear to touch him there. She remembered her need to kill him, but now he was a broken, pathetic thing, her loathing had shrunk to a nugget. He wasn't worth it.

She picked up the knife still lying on the floor, and laid it against his flaccid penis.

"No," he choked. "Don't. Don't . . ."

"Just remember," she said, looking into his terrified eyes, "for the rest of your life, remember that any woman you meet might be like me. We're clever at hiding our strengths, we women, so you'll never really know. And no man can guard himself day and night forever, especially not from a lover or a wife."

She stroked the tip of the blade up and down him. "If you'd completed what you planned, I would have killed you at the first opportunity. But before I killed you, I would have gelded you. Remember that. Remember me, and treat all women with the fearful respect we deserve." She pressed the blade into his flesh, then, just enough to cause blood to run.

He cried out and twisted up to look at himself, then collapsed back again, weeping. Probably with relief.

She dropped the knife on the floor. "Goodbye, Lord Randolph."

With that, she left the room.

Bey was waiting and she went straight into his arms.

"How is he?" he asked, as if it was of little concern.

"Intact. Are you disappointed?"

"Not unless you were merciful out of weakness."

"I don't think so. I don't want anything about him to linger on me, not even his death. Can we go now?"

"Of course." He made a gesture and a man rode forward and dismounted to offer his horse.

She saw that as he'd said, there were men around on guard.

Even so, she said, "I think I was bait. I think de Couriac's out here, trying to kill you."

"I suspect not, or not yet. I was supposed to be here much later. But we should leave. Can you ride?"

"Of course."

Bey helped her mount, adjusting the stirrups and arranging her skirts as decently as possible, then he mounted his own horse.

"Slow or fast?" he asked.

"Fast. Fast riding makes a poor target, and it's what I need."

Chapter 29

She kicked her horse hard and it took off, thundering down the lane, the wind whipping through her hair. Dangerous in the dark in unknown territory, but she wanted this, needed this. In moments he was by her side, guarding, but not controlling.

She grinned for him and watched ahead, blessing the moonlight. They'd been on a road before turning into this lane, so there must be a turning soon. A signpost helped, and she swung the horse around the bend, hardly slackening at all. Then she headed flat out for London, the dome of St. Paul's a dark silhouette in the distance against the paler sky.

Illegally, she jumped the toll gates, not allowing anything to get in her way. She wanted to fly, and she wanted to carry him beyond danger.

He stayed with her, but a glance back showed their escort falling behind. Not wise, perhaps, but speed was better. And she needed the blood rushing through her body and the power of the horse between her thighs, the wind against her skin, and the target growing closer and closer.

She almost went down twice on the rough road, but she held the horse up and he was strong and gallant. As fields became town, the road improved, and as the way became easier her madness eased. She slowed to a canter, and then down to a walk, patting her horse and murmuring praise, so he arched his steaming neck with pride.

Bey slowed beside her, and side by side, they walked the horses along streets silent except for the drumming hooves of the escort trying to catch up.

If de Couriac had been around, he could not be here now.

"Was that ride wisdom or folly?" she asked.

"Who can tell? We seem to have survived. If I had been more careful, it would not have been necessary at all."

"I believe I commented on this illusion that you're God."

He didn't smile. "There were a number of things I could have done to prevent this."

"Bey, if you take any injury to me as a wound on your soul, I cannot bear it!"

"A dilemma, is it not?"

He was in a damnably strange mood, and she couldn't deal with it now. "Should we let Lord Randolph live, even abroad? He might hurt others."

"We are not God," he said dryly. "And it was your choice."

She glanced over at him, white shirtsleeves and skin cool and pale in the moonlight.

"I could not kill him," she confessed, "and now I don't know whether it was strength or weakness. I'm even weak enough to feel a bit sorry for him, tied up there. What if someone comes across him. Or rats . . . ?"

He did laugh then. "A tender heart after all. The man whose horse you ride stayed behind to make sure he doesn't get badly nibbled. Bryght's gone to organize his escort to a ship."

"Have you arranged my return to the Queen's House so efficiently?"

"Don't sound disgruntled. I may not be omnipotent, but I can at least be efficient."

The pounding hooves grew louder, and then his men were there, ranking on either side, horses steaming in the night air.

"I'm inclined to believe the omnipotence," she said. "How did you come to rescue me in time, and with armed guards?"

He said something to the nearest man, and soon he and another were riding ahead, scouting as if this was the wilderness rather than a quiet London street.

"I took five minutes to gather them," he said flatly. "It could have been five minutes too long."

"No, you were right! Madness to ride off alone."

"And I am definitely not mad, yes?"

Damn him and his mood, and the fact that even with moonlight she couldn't really read his features.

"You said you were supposed to arrive later?" she asked. Too late, she thought, shuddering at the malicious planning that lay behind this. Who hated her enough for this?

D'Eon? She would never have imagined it.

"One of the men who captured you was in my pay," he said. "He had no notice, or he would have warned me. It was what he was there for. As it was, he had to go through with it."

"The Englishman. The one who didn't want me hurt."

His head turned. "You were hurt?"

She wished she'd held her tongue, but she said, "De Couriac. He hit me."

He made no comment, but continued, "It was sheer luck that Stringle was given the job of telling me where to find you." Sheer luck, it was clear, was intolerable. He hadn't changed. He was still stuck in bleak perfection. "He was to get the message to me at midnight. Instead, of course, he found me immediately."

At that moment, a nearby clock began to strike midnight, with others near and far picking it up. Diana shuddered at the thought of being in Lord Randolph's hands until now.

Then she realized that if she'd not screamed, if Lord Randolph had not gagged her and enjoyed watching her struggle for breath, Bey would have been far too late. Dear heaven, but it would have destroyed him.

"You hired this Stringle," she offered. "Your watchfulness did save me after all."

"There was too much luck involved, and even with luck, we were almost too late. And I wasted that five minutes."

She didn't know what to say, for now she realized how he felt. It was offensive that his sanity had been preserved by chance. Delayed shock and the night air set her shivering, despite his coat.

They were into fashionable streets now, but it was Sunday and quiet, though one coach did rattle past, a pale face peering out nervously at them.

What did that traveler think of the strange group? What would they think if they knew who it was?

Midnight, she thought. "Will de Couriac be there now, do you think?"

"I hope so. I left two men in addition to the one watching Somerton. They're to take him alive if possible."

The chill was setting in, and she suddenly desperately wanted to be home. Though she didn't know where home was. "You didn't tell me how you were getting me back into the Queen's House with no one the wiser."

He glanced across at her. "A wave of my sorcerer's wand. . . . In fact, we're going to Malloren House."

"Why?"

"Because of the difficulties of returning you to the Queen's House."

"But . . . Clara won't have raised the alarm."

"Will she not?" He sighed. She heard it. "I can't let you out of my sight, Diana. Not yet."

She inhaled in surprise, and then again to savor it, like perfume. Some of the chill in her melted to warmth. He was in a strange state, but this might also be the first step to capitulation. To a chance for them.

When he said nothing more, she asked, "What will we tell the king?"

"The truth, of course, but that's for later."

They were entering a wider street lined with grand houses. They must be close to Marlborough Square.

"What was the plan?" she asked. "Is the Chevalier D'Eon truly involved in such a sordid affair?"

He turned to look at her. "That, I intend to find out."

Fear stole her breath. "Don't fight him."

"Don't give me orders. Unless, that is, you reciprocate, and let me order your every step for my comfort."

"Damn you."

He turned to look forward again. "Hell and I are old familiars."

That didn't sound like capitulation.

"Won't taking me to Malloren House make it difficult for us to stay unwed?" she asked, hearing a touch of bitterness she could not suppress.

"Portia's there. She and Bryght turned up not long ago, pushed to racing back south by Elf's instincts."

"Instincts about tonight? That's impossible."

"Instincts about you and me." He glanced at her. "She warned me off at Arradale."

"Damn her."

"You want the whole Malloren family consigned to hell?"

"At times, yes."

"She was right. I should never have let you close when I knew I could not give you all you deserve." Voice cold as moonlight, he added, "It's true, is it not, that now you will have no other?"

"When we first met, I was determined to have no one at all. Wanting no other is progress of sorts. What of you? Have you made any progress?"

"Three steps closer to hell," he said, and turned into a lane. The lane must run behind Marlborough Square. Weariness sank over her. How could she fight him if fighting pushed him closer to hell?

Soon they were in a mews, and grooms hurried out. "All's well, milord?" asked the one taking Bey's horse. He didn't seem surprised to see his master in shirtsleeves, or Diana riding beside him in Bey's coat.

"Yes, thank you, Bibb." Bey slid off and helped Diana down. She half expected him to move away from her once she was on the ground, but he put an arm around her as if it were the most natural thing in the world.

Gratefully, she moved close to his warmth, and to hope that would not be suppressed.

Was she to return to court? Suddenly, all those days locked in unnatural restraints, constantly observed, apart from him, became intolerable. Come what may, she would not return.

Why should she and Bey let themselves be tormented this way anyway? For what?

For duty, and honor, and responsibility . . .

She sighed, and slid an arm around him, feeling spine, and muscles, and strength. Duty, honor, and responsibility could not be shrugged off like a garment that had become uncomfortable. They ruled still. Ruled both of them.

Perhaps he heard the sigh. His arm tightened as he took a lantern and led her down a path toward the back of the house. She half expected servants up and waiting as in the stables, but he used a key to open a small side door, and inside, though a candle waited, the house lay silent.

If Portia was chaperon, she wasn't present to perform her duties. The one flickering flame created an intimacy in the dark, even when they went through a door into the glory of the owner's side of the house.

Her heart began to speed and she shivered in a different way. Up till now, safety had been enough. His presence had been enough. Now, however, his strong, warm body against her stirred other needs.

True needs. She needed him to wipe away everything that had happened. To promise it would never happen again.

She'd have to fight him, though, to get what she longed for, and she wasn't sure she could do that anymore.

Would it be another step toward hell?

She let him lead her upstairs and into a room, a grand bedroom where he lit two branches of candles. Thick carpet and rich rose-pink hangings. He moved away, and to her shame, she clung. It could cause scandal and make matters cruelly worse, but suddenly she couldn't bear the thought of being alone.

"It's all right," he said, gently untangling her fingers from his shirt, and sitting her on the big bed. "Wait there. I'll be back in a moment."

She began to shake. Fighting a weakness and dependence she despised she shed his coat, but a prick startled her. It was his pin, still holding together the cut edges of her bodice.

Abruptly, she hurried to the washstand, pulling out the pin.

Water in the jug.

Lukewarm, but that didn't matter.

She splashed it into the bowl, lathered the cloth, and washed her breasts. Washed them over and over, trying to scrub away even the memory of Lord Randolph's hands there. His eyes on her—

Suddenly aware, she turned, clutching her bodice back together, and found Bey watching her.

He came over, a white garment in his hand. He worked it over her head so it covered her, arms and all, with soft cotton fresh with the scent of washing and blowing in the wind.

She relaxed her grip on the bodice. "I'm sorry. I don't know why—"

"Hush." He turned her, and beneath the cloth, undid the fastenings down the back of her gown. He stepped away then, and she stripped it off herself. Did he think she didn't want him to touch her?

With an inward shudder, she realized that in a way, he was right. Her skin felt all awry, and she didn't know what she wanted.

"Do you want a bath?" he said.

In a way she did, but she didn't want servants. She didn't want to be looked at yet.

"No." She untied her petticoat and let it fall. Then she shed the last soiled and ruined layer, the shift, and put her hands into the sleeves rolling up the cuffs.

Only then did she turn to him.

"Better?" he asked, standing a surely precisely judged distance from her.

It was one of his shirts, and it hung to her knees protectively. "I'm being silly, I know—"

"No. Except in saying that. Allow yourself to be weak, Diana."

I wish you would.

Aloud, she said, "I can't. I mustn't be weak. That gives him a victory of sorts. That washing was a victory for him. A bath would be a victory for him. If I act like that, I'm admitting he dirtied me. That he changed me in ways that will linger." She raised her chin. "I'm braver and stronger than that."

"Ironhand. But you leave me adrift. What can I do for you?"

"Bey, don't! Don't ask me to be weak for you."

He closed his eyes for a moment. "Do I need people to be weak?" he asked, as if truly adrift. "I didn't think so."

His distress burned away hers. He was deeply shaken, far more deeply than she'd guessed. He needed to care for her as much as he'd needed to kill Somerton, but it was something else he would sacrifice for her if she needed it.

Oh God, she felt as if she held crystal in her hands, impossibly thin and fragile crystal that could be shattered by the slightest thing.

Wise or not, she stepped forward and took his hands. "Take me to bed, Bey. I need you to hold me."

After a moment, he swept her into his arms and carried her to the bed.

He couldn't know, even he could not know, that Lord Randolph had carried her to that awful bed, but it was like the beginning of a perfect realignment. "I do need this," she whispered.

"You shall have everything you need," he promised. "And no more."

At the bed he paused, holding her to him for a heart-stopping moment, then he laid her down carefully as if she were the fragile crystal, and filled to the brim with water.

"What do you need now?" he asked.

And she suddenly knew, though she wasn't sure she should ask. "I want you to tie me to the bed."

"What?"

His shocked pallor made her say, "No. That's silly. I don't need—"

"You want to reenact it? Why?"

All she could give was honesty. "The worst thing was being helpless. Completely helpless. I'd rather have been fighting even if he hurt me, even if he hurt me badly. I want to relive that fear and conquer it. But I see it's too much. I shouldn't have asked."

He sat on the bed and looked at her. "You'll be the death of me," he said, but a hint of humor, a touch of color, told her that perhaps this was all right. She'd given him something to do, something difficult, and that was what he needed.

"You're sure?" he asked.

"Yes."

"Don't run away," he said dryly, and went into the next room.

She heard tearing sounds, and he returned with four strips of embroidered black velvet.

"What are they from?" she asked, wide-eyed, but she thought she recognized the exquisite black velvet coat he'd worn to the Queen's House two nights before. Which he'd worn to the ball in Arradale an eon ago.

"If we are to do this," he said, "let us do it with a degree of elegance." As he tied one strip loosely around her right ankle, he said, "Will it spoil the experiment if I promise to stop whenever you ask me to?"

Diana had to think about that. "Yes, I think it would. It wouldn't be at all frightening then."

He tied the other end of the cloth to a bedpost. "I don't want this to be frightening."

"Nor do I, but it has to be." With one leg tethered, her nerves flinched as if they held a memory of earlier terrors.

He tied the other ankle, face set and cool.

"I don't want to hurt you, Bey," she said helplessly. "You asked what you could do."

"I think I had in mind a foot massage." But a little lightness stirred as he looked at her. "It's all right. I'm just nervous about what you might want me to do once you're fixed in place." He looked at the bed head. "I'll have to tie your hands to the corner posts. There's nowhere in the middle."

She stretched her arms out. "I'm supposed to feel like the victim, not you." But then she twisted to look up to where he was tying her right hand. "I'm forcing you, aren't I? Isn't that a bit like rape?"

"Don't overdramatize this. However, I am not making love to you like this. That would be rape, and of me, not you."

She followed him with her eyes and he walked around to

tie her other hand. "I won't. I wouldn't. I just need to feel this, and deal with it."

He tied the last knot and sat on the bed again. "What are you feeling?"

"Panic," she said, looking up at the satin canopy, where before there'd been cobwebby beams. "It's silly because I know you won't hurt me, but it's beating there like a drum." She turned her eyes to him. "I'm even afraid that you'll go away and leave me like this."

"Diana, this is pointless. You aren't fighting an unreasonable fear. You *are* helpless. If I was a villain, you'd be right to be afraid."

"But not to show it. Would you show fear in this situation?"

"No," he said and placed a hand on her abdomen.

She jerked, instinctively trying to reach down to control his hand. "Don't."

"I believe you set the rules," he said, circling his hand there over the soft, fine cotton.

She wanted to cry stop. She knew that if she really demanded it, he would, but she worked instead at controlling panic, and at not showing fear.

He slid his hand up, between her breasts, to rest at the side of her throat. "Your pulse still races."

"No one can control their pulse."

"It is possible, but very hard. Control your breathing instead. That, anyone can do."

He put his hand back on her abdomen. "Push my hand up and down with your breaths."

She focused on that, and slowly the panic eased.

Her whole body relaxed into his hand, comfortingly warm and strong against her.

"I'm rather comfortable now," she murmured, and still breathing against his hand she let her eyes drift shut so she could sink into a peaceful warmth that was completely new to her.

Then his hand left her. She opened heavy eyes to see him cutting her velvet tethers. As she brought her arms down to her side, she explored a sense of wholeness and completion that was inextricably connected to him, to her feelings for him, and his for her.

It was if they created something between them which was impossible apart. If she'd fought before, it had been with half her heart. Now she felt invincible.

She had to be.

"That foot massage?" she murmured.

His eyes met hers, smiling slightly. "We are in harmony at last."

He left, but returned with a small vial, and sat on the bed by her feet. He poured oil onto his hands, and the rich scent of sandalwood crept over her. She was floating even before he took one of her feet and began the magic.

No stockings this time, just his strong, skilled hands on her.

"It's wonderful. It seems to relax my whole body."

He smiled slightly, but didn't speak.

"I want to be able to do this for you. Is it possible?" she asked, deliberately asking about more than the moment.

"My will is shattered," he said, beginning on the other foot with a touch that told her that she could ask anything of him now and he was powerless to refuse.

It wasn't right though. It was because of what had happened tonight. Because of her danger, and his failure to protect. Perhaps it was also because he had sacrificed the healing power of bloodshed.

For her.

She couldn't accept an offering of guilt.

"That isn't good enough," she said.

"I know."

She lay silent as he worked magic on her feet, wondering where they went from here. His lids guarded his eyes but she knew he was, as he had said, shattered. She could do anything with him now, demand anything.

The last thing he needed, however, was more guilt.

What she wanted was his acceptance of his right to love.

"It is possible," she said, but she knew words weren't enough, not for him. He was a man who had to be engaged mind, body, emotions, and soul. And the mind—the brilliant analytical mind—still held firm.

He made no response, just put more oil on his hands, and continued to manipulate her feet.

She watched him, wondering at the journey that had brought them here, fretting at the controlled calm of his classic features. He needed her, she knew, but she wasn't sure what the need was, or how she should fulfill it.

She knew what she needed.

When his hands began to slide away she sat up and captured them. "It's still safe."

"It's never completely safe." His lids rose, and she saw dark, guarded eyes, but she saw the shattering too.

Dear Lord, what should she do?

"It's as safe as before," she said, moving closer. "Stay in me this time."

He wasn't resisting, but his hands were passive in hers. "I am yours to command in all things."

If she claimed to need his love to wipe out Lord Randolph, he would comply. But he did not want it. She thought for a moment of demanding it anyway, because he'd come to like it—

Hades. She sounded just like Lord Randolph!

She let go of him. "I simply hunger, Bey. Tell me it's right for us to go through eternity alone."

He moved back and stood. "You are a devilishly ruthless woman."

"Ironhand." With a prayer to her ancestors, she straightened and took off the shirt. "You mustn't do anything you don't want to," she said, eyes on his. "Remember that."

Then she slid off the bed and undressed him.

She unfastened the long line of buttons down his silk waistcoat, and pushed it off. Then she undid his cravat, unfastened his collar and cuffs, pulled his shirt out of his breeches, then up over his head. His simple acceptance of what she was doing might have daunted her if she'd allowed herself to be daunted. He could stop her with a word, she reminded herself. Surely it wasn't wrong to do what he wanted, but couldn't quite bring himself to do.

When his chest was bare she gave it one quick kiss, then pushed him to sit on the bed. She knelt to remove his shoes and stockings. Scruples won then, however, and she looked up at him with exasperation. "Are you just going to sit there?"

"I don't know."

"It's as if I'm raping you!"

"Perhaps you are."

She stood. "Don't say that."

"If we have not honesty, we have nothing." He stood, however, and removed his remaining garments, revealing physical interest, at least.

"Is it just the body?" she asked. "The most horrible thing about Lord Randolph was that my body responded. I wanted him to be a vile rapist, but he was damnably clever." Tears suddenly stung, and she glared up at him. "You are not to be swayed by my tears. Never. You understand!"

"Of course not," he said dryly, and brushed a tear off her cheek. "It's not the same, Diana. My body and heart want you. Only my cursed will reminds me of other things. You understand, don't you?"

She rested against his chest, his erection hard between them. "Yes, I understand. This has to be complete, body, heart, and mind or it will destroy us both. But tomorrow we face the king, and the consequence of this mess. Can we not at least have now, imperfect as it is?"

"It would be another burden on the moon." He took her hand and led her to the bed. When he'd pulled down the covers, he climbed in and said, "Join me."

She did, and he drew her into his arms, and for her, at least, it was as if the bleeding halves joined, taking away all pain and sorrow. They lay like that for long blessed moments, then kissed, their kiss, and the world was lost.

There was skill in his careful touch, but she didn't want care or skill. She rolled on top of him, straddling his thighs. "This is my time. The time of the full moon."

Eyes on his, she seized the vial of oil from the table by the bed. "Flee, Hecate, queen of the dark," she said, pouring a thin stream onto his chest, "and surrender this poor mortal to Diana, and the light."

She put the vial aside and massaged him, praying for courage to follow lessons from her books. Praying the lessons were right and would drive him out of his controlling mind.

She massaged the oil into his chest, watching his lids flutter shut, either in relaxed surrender, or in a desperate attempt to hide his reactions. Then she worked lower and lower, dizzying herself with the feel of warm skin over powerful contours of muscle.

Excitement and nervousness built, and part of her wanted to retreat, to accept whatever he was willing to expertly give. She made herself follow her plan, however, and slid her hands at last around his hot, hard erection.

A shudder ran through him, sending a sense of power into her.

"I love you," she said, and slid one hand up, then the other, loving the hard and soft feel of him, but only too aware that she didn't really know what she was doing.

"You can play teacher, if you want," she whispered. "I've never done this before."

"Heaven save me if you learn more." His chest moved as he sucked in deep breaths and between her thighs, his legs tensed.

"No Socratic method?" she teased, and with a prayer to goddesses everywhere, she lowered her head to touch her tongue to the tip, to swirl around it.

He choked out a sound, and it didn't seem to be pain.

"You will come inside me?" she asked.

"Or?" His voice was hoarse.

"Or I will do my best to drive you mad."

She looked down, and suddenly any trace of reluctance fled. She longed to taste him, and put her mouth over and sucked.

"Behold a lunatic!" He surged up and seized her, and she was flat on her back, him deep inside before she caught breath.

With a happy laugh, she wrapped her legs tight around

him as he drove in and out. She did nothing more but surrender and let him purge the last tawdry remnant of Lord
Randolph's pathetic assault.

She had to think, when she could think again, to decide
whether he was still inside. When she realized he was, she
hugged him and said, "Thank you."

He still lay over her, heavy but welcome, and she ran her
fingers through his hair.

"I will never let you go," she said, rubbing her cheek
against his head, "so you might as well surrender to the lunatic moon. Or I'll just have to seduce you every full moon
for the rest of our lives."

"The full moon," he said almost sleepily, "is tomorrow."

"Is that an invitation?"

He didn't reply, and she realized he was asleep. Despite
his weight pinning her, she smiled through tears of love and
joy.

Surrender at last.

Chapter 30

She woke as if from a dream to bright sunshine shafting through a slit in drawn curtains.

Alone.

Bolting upright, she saw nothing to suggest the night. No oil, certainly no lover. Even the pillow he would have used was smooth.

Had she dreamed it? No. Traces of oil remained on the sheets, in stains and sensual perfume. He'd been here. He, the essence of him, had come within touch of her questing fingertips.

More than that. For a short time he had been hers, mind, body, and soul.

But now he was gone, and his careful obliteration of his presence filled her with despair. The final battle had not been won because it wasn't a matter of will, after all. That could be changed by a stronger will.

For him, it was a matter of the soul.

What, save God, could help with that?

Muddled last night, she'd assumed she was in his bedroom, but of course she wasn't. This room, though grand, held no personal items. Anyway, he wouldn't take her there and risk her reputation. Not the omnipotent, omniscient, infinitely controlled Marquess of Rothgar. She beat her hands on the bed. Damn him. Damn him. Damn him!

Then she sank her head in her hands. She had to face the day as well. The king. Society. Him.

Oh God, oh God. They could end this day forced into marriage to save her reputation. If he'd retreated behind the walls again they'd be in a worse state than when they'd begun.

She struggled out of bed and splashed her face with the cold water in the bowl. What was known? What would be said? What would the king's reaction be to this scandal?

Would the king see her as the innocent victim, or as a cause of trouble? She knew Bey would have come up with some clever explanation of the rescue, and for bringing her back here, but what could explain her slipping out of the house in response to a note from a man?

Turning back to the bed, she saw a bloodstain, and burst into wild laughter. At last her courses had begun, but now it might make people think she'd lost her virginity here!

A knock on the door. Diana spun to face it, but only Clara came in, wide eyed and bearing a jug of hot water. "Oh, milady, I'm so glad you're all right! I didn't know what to do, and that's the truth. I kept quiet, but I was so worried!"

The big jug tilted, and Diana rescued it. "It's all right, Clara. You did the right thing." So, Clara hadn't raised the alarm. That might help. "What happened?"

"I couldn't sleep a wink, of course. And then at first light that Madam Swellenborg came to say you'd been kidnapped, and rescued by the marquess, and I was to pack up your things to move here." She'd begun to stare at Diana, however. "Is . . . is that a *shirt*, milady?"

Diana looked down and felt her face burn. "My dress was ruined," she said, adding as coolly as possible, "I have my clothes here, then?"

Had she been tossed out of the Queen's House in disgrace?

Clara's mouth snapped shut. "Yes, milady. What gown do you want to wear, milady?"

Sackcloth and ashes? "Oh, I don't care." Diana turned toward a mirror, reluctant to see what she looked like.

Lud, thank heavens only Clara had seen her like this. The rumpled shirt hung half off one shoulder, the long sleeves rolled roughly up. Her hair was tousled, her eyes, heavy, and she simply looked like a shameless wanton.

"Choose something sober for me." She tore off the garment, but then held it to herself for a moment, breathing in the blended aromas of sandalwood and sex. Then she tossed it on the bed and called, "Bring my pads, too, Clara. My bleeding's started."

No child, she suddenly thought. She didn't want one from this, but an ache shuddered deep inside because she could not be sure of the future. She ached for the children that might never be, for the father he might never be.

No. She had come close to victory, and would not let it slip away. Even if she did have to seduce him every full moon for the rest of their lives!

She washed herself then put on the things Clara brought her—the long pad of cloth, and the belt and binder that held it in place. At least she didn't suffer at this time as some women did. She needed all her energy and strength to deal with the coming day.

Clara brought a pale blue dress and all that was needed with it. "Will there still be the masquerade, milady, what with all this?"

The masquerade! Tonight.

It seemed an age since she'd tried on her Diana costume. Would the ball still take place? She didn't know what she wanted.

As she took the shift the maid passed to her and put it on, Diana asked, "What's going on in the house? When did you get here?"

"Not long after sunrise, milady," Clara said, putting the stays over Diana's head and beginning to lace them up down the back. Rather tightly. Clearly an attempt to restore propriety. "Don't know if you know, milady, but you're in the marchioness's rooms. Not used for ages, of course."

There was dark meaning in Clara's words.

"Only fair," Diana said lightly. "If you remember, Lord Rothgar slept in the countess's rooms at Arradale."

"But they're not exactly short of rooms here, milady," said Clara with a particularly fierce tug on the stay laces.

Oh heavens. The last thing she needed was Clara deciding to play watchdog.

As she stepped into the petticoat and tied the waist, Diana looked around the bedroom of the Marchioness of Rothgar. Likely, it had last been used by Bey's stepmother, the smiling woman who'd put a broken family together again, but perhaps failed to completely heal a broken child. She'd probably conceived Lord Bryght early in the marriage and been naturally absorbed with her own children. It was, however, a shame.

Numerous pictures hung on the walls, but she went closer to one. A young child still in skirts sat on a chair in the sprawled way of the toddler, while a boy of about five leaned on the back. Both were dark haired, but while the younger one was chubby and dimpled, the older was slender and sober, and could be said to be hovering protectively.

Bey and Bryght, she was sure of it. She'd never thought how it must have been for him when his first half-brother was born. Had he perhaps hovered, guarding? Or had he avoided?

She looked at that serious child, and he looked back at her, very different to the drummer boy which was a representation of herself at a similar age. As she looked, however, the face seemed to come alive for her, and she saw the hint of a smile and the steady, fierce intelligence, already observing, assessing, remembering.

She wondered if he'd intimidated this portrait painter as much as he'd done the later one. She wished she'd known him then, but that was nonsense. She'd not even been born.

She dragged herself away and stood in front of the mirror to put on the open blue skirt, and the striped bodice. "A good choice, Clara. Becoming, but not frivolous."

"Thank you, milady." The maid fastened the hooks down the front, but then looked up anxiously. "Are you ruined, milady?"

Clara was asking a specific question, but Diana said, "I hope not. However, it's probably time to face the music. Do you know where the marquess is?"

"I believe he's gone to the king, milady. Lady Walgrave's here, milady, and hoping to take breakfast with you if you will."

Elf. A bit of the tension lifted. "Tidy my hair, then bring breakfast and tell Lady Walgrave I will be pleased to see her."

Perhaps Elf would have some notion how to break through her brother's final barrier.

And what dangers lurked in doing so.

Rothgar was ushered into the king's presence where George was working at a desk, reading and signing documents. Apart from a brief nod to acknowledge his arrival, the king ignored him until all the papers were dealt with. It was not a snub. George was thorough about these matters, and took his duties seriously. At last he waved his secretary away and stood. "Shocking matters, my lord."

"Deeply so, sire."

"Is Lady Arradale all right?"

"Distressed, sire, but recovering."

"Your note was not very informative, my lord. I'll have the complete story, if you please, including why Lady Arradale was not returned here immediately."

Rothgar had expected displeasure. "The latter is simplest to relate, sire. The countess was distressed and in disorder, and I thought the queen should not be disturbed. Lord and Lady Bryght arrived at my house last night, so she was chaperoned."

"Is she harmed?"

"We were in time."

"Thank God, thank God. Damnable business. Damnable. Lord Randolph must be mad!"

"As for that, sire, he was to some extent incited into folly." Rothgar produced the letter. "He received this."

The king frowned at the seal, then opened the letter. He turned puce. "By Jupiter, who dared to do such a thing? My signature. My seal. The royal seal. On *this*!"

"Indeed, sire." Rothgar rescued the letter from the royal fist. "And the letter that persuaded Lady Arradale out into the night was equally skillful. Somerton doesn't know where the letter came from, but he was assisted by a Frenchman whom the countess recognized as Monsieur de

Couriac. The same de Couriac we encountered in Ferry Bridge."

The king stared. "What? Why? Even if that maniac is after you, why help Somerton abduct the countess? What? What?"

Rothgar shrugged. "It is known that the countess is to some extent under my protection, so I would be bound to take action at her injury. I suspect the entire plan was a trap for me. Though it is possible," he suggested, "the French seek any and all ways to stir discord."

"We are at peace, my lord."

"Yet some of your subjects still resent the peace, sire. It is possible some of the French do too."

"But what is the point?" the king demanded. "Am I likely to go to war over a woman's abduction?"

It was time, unfortunately, to be blunt. "I believe the point, sire, is to remove me. Clearly some in the French government do not believe that you are firm against French expansion and aggression. They must think that my advice is crucial to your policies. An error, of course. They could be misinformed—by the Chevalier D'Eon, perhaps?"

The king had been pacing, but now he stopped. Rothgar wished he knew what the king was thinking, but his supernatural powers stopped short of that.

The king suddenly turned to glare at the letter in Rothgar's hand. "What am I to do about that? My hand and my seal, and the content is vile!"

"If we find the forger, we could punish him, sire, but we would have to reveal the nature of it. I have hopes we can keep Lady Arradale's misadventure from public knowledge."

"Indeed, indeed. But I want de Couriac hanged. Somerton too!"

"That, too, risks stirring scurrilous talk, sire."

The king glared. "I am to do *nothing* about such an affront? I will not see Somerton at court again. Even if he was a dupe of the French, he is a blackguard."

"I believe the Duke of Carlyle would be happy to see him

tied to his properties in Virginia. I could arrange that, if Your Majesty would speak to the duke about it."

"Good riddance," the king muttered. "But what of the true villains?"

"I would be honored if you would leave that to me, sire. I will arrange their punishment."

After a moment the king nodded. "Inform me when it is done, my lord." But then he added, "And what of poor Lady Arradale? She has lost a suitor."

"Indeed, sire. Perhaps it would be wisest to put aside this matter of her marriage for some time. It can only distress her."

The king's eyes narrowed, and there was a suspicion of a pout, but he said, "Very well. Very well. You may tell her she may return north if she wishes, but I hope she will attend your masquerade before she leaves. It would be a shame to miss it, especially living in the house."

"I think so, sire. But with that event in mind, I must return."

The king nodded, but when Rothgar was at the door he said, "I hope you came here well guarded, my lord."

Rothgar smiled ruefully. "In a coach with armed outriders, sire. A folly that seemed wise."

"Good, good. We would not want to lose you."

Chapter 31

Bryght Malloren was looking for his brother. After checking the obvious places, he tapped on the door of his mother's old boudoir. Inside, however, he found only Elf and the countess, and no useful information.

"You are concerned about him, Lord Bryght?" the countess asked, looking somewhat anxious. He wished he could ask her directly what had happened here last night.

"Yes."

"Why, Bryght?" asked Elf. "Did something go amiss with the king?"

"I don't know since he's gone into hiding."

"Hiding?" Elf echoed. "Bey?"

The countess didn't scoff. She half rose, but then sat again. A woman of intelligence and self-control. "Might he be involved in the final details of the masquerade?" she asked.

"No one has seen him, and there are some details still to be settled."

"Oh dear." Elf did rise at that. "I must go and see if I can help. This is very strange. Diana, do you wish to come with me?"

The countess disappeared into thought, then said, "No. I must stay here." To Bryght, she said, "I believe there is an automaton here, my lord. Your brother might be attending to it."

Bryght stared at her. "Of course. He finds them soothing. Any idea, Lady Arradale, why he might need to be soothed?"

Her gaze was steady, strong, and clear. "He has devils to fight. And angels. The angels are doubtless the most difficult."

Bryght nodded, and left the room with Elf. As soon as the door was shut, Elf whispered, "Will he? At last?"

"With God's help and ours. I wish to hell Brand were here, but as it is, I'll have to play second in the unholy battle with the angels."

He left her and went swiftly along the corridor, down stairs, to the small room at the back. Beyond the plain door, he heard birdsong and a drum. He entered without knocking, not knowing what he'd find, just as song and drumming stopped.

Rothgar, still in court dress, was sitting at the workbench. He wasn't using the tools there, however, merely gazing at an automaton. It was the figure of a boy in a blue suit with a drum hung around his neck and drumsticks in his hands. Rothgar's eyes flicked immediately to Bryght. "Is something wrong?"

"You're hiding."

"Is that so wicked?"

"It worries those of us who are unused to it. But we'll learn to survive."

"Then why are you here?"

"Where else would I be when you are fighting angels?"

"Fighting angels?" Bey asked quizzically.

Bryght sat in a simple chair near the automaton, feeling as if he was indeed going into battle. "That's how Lady Arradale described it. You should marry her."

Bey's eyes moved to the automaton. "Behold Lady Arradale as a child, transmuted to male. A loving gift turned unconsciously into a weapon aimed straight at the heart of a man's wife and beloved daughter."

Bryght looked at the child's winsome face and saw a hint of the countess's stubborn chin and clear gaze. He could see immediately what Bey meant, but was floundering in the other layers. Dammit, he loved the complexity of numbers, but had no gift for these human labyrinths.

He kept it simple. "After last night, I can see a hundred

reasons for you to marry Lady Arradale. Give me one why you shouldn't. And forget the madness in your blood."

Bey's eyes moved back to his. "Convenient if possible."

"That's your angel, Bey. You think it's a holy angel, but it's Lucifer in all his proud glory."

His brother leaned back. "Or you are. 'And the devil taketh him up into an exceedingly high mountain, and sheweth him all the kingdoms of the world, and the glory of them, and saith unto him, All these things will I give thee . . . ' Wanting is no excuse for taking, Bryght."

"She loves you. Have you thought what this does to her?"

"Constantly."

"Have you made love to her?" Rothgar didn't answer, of course, but that was answer in a way. "Then you cannot walk away from her."

"We have an understanding about these things."

"Understanding doesn't heal a broken heart." God help him, he didn't have words to penetrate his brother's damnably guarded and complex mind. He leaped to his feet.

"You are not a machine, dammit! Nor are other people. Nor is the world." He leaned forward on the workbench across from Bey's startled eyes. "Infallibility is not possible. Security is not possible. Life is risk. I died a thousand deaths when Portia was having the baby. Hours and hours, and sometimes I heard her cry out. I promised there'd be no more. She laughed."

He turned away, but went on with what he had to say. "I held out for a while, doing my best not to get her with child, but she said what I'm saying to you. Life is risk."

He turned back, but his brother was looking down now, trying to escape. Was he having some effect?

"In fact, the risk isn't too great for her. Despite her size, she gave birth easily with no damage. It wasn't even a long travail, though it seemed days to me. The horror was in my mind. And the arrogance, thinking I could play God and avoid life. She wants more children. I want more children, and more than that, I want to give her what she wants."

Bey suddenly covered his face with his hands, but Bryght went on. "Yes, your mother went mad, but would you feel

this way if she'd gone quietly mad and sat in a secluded
room talking to the walls?" He leaned forward over the
workbench and gripped one of his brother's rigid wrists.
"You're still running from the murder, Bey. Trying to make
it not be true."

He didn't know if that was complete nonsense. It had
come from somewhere deep inside without thought at all.

Bey's knuckles went white as he clutched at his head.
"You are offering me what I want." He relaxed his hands
and looked up. "What you want, in fact."

"You won't get out of it that way. Yes, I want you to marry
and have children. But I want life for you. Because, Bey, I
love you." It was something he'd never said before, and he
sat suddenly on the chair on his side of the bench.

"We all know what you've done for us," he said, "and
what it's cost you at times. We all want life for you now."

Suddenly other strange words popped into his head and
he threw them down before he lost the nerve. "We want you
to have your just reward. All your life you've paid the debt
to little Edith, but she joins us in wanting you to be happy.
In knowing you deserve happiness."

He felt himself blushing under his brother's astonished
gaze. What a load of sentimental blabber!

But Bey stood and turned away. "I need to think, Bryght."

"You do too much thinking!"

When his brother made no response, he knew he'd gone
as far as he could. With one last worried look, he left the
room. He closed the door, and stood there, wondering if
there was more he could say or do, whether he should go
back.

Then a bird began to sing, and a drum began to beat.

He was playing with the damned automaton again.

By evening, Diana had still not seen Bey, but she wasn't
alone in that. Elf hadn't either, and she complained—imper-
fectly hiding concern—of all the last-minute details she'd
had to settle for the masquerade.

She'd arrived in Diana's room, already in a delightful
wasp costume. "There's even a troop from the King's The-

ater who are to perform a masque under Mr. Bach. They seem to know what they are supposed to do, so I left them to rehearse." She looked at the costume laid across the bed. "Diana? How perfect."

"Where *is* he?" Diana asked. At the moment she was only in her shift. If he wasn't going to attend the masquerade, neither was she. "Does he often do this?"

"Never," admitted Elf with a shrug. "But that's hopeful. If he was his usual impervious self I wouldn't be at all sanguine."

Diana had broken down and told Elf all, which was a huge relief, even though Elf hadn't been able to assure her that Bey would see reason. She twisted her hands together. "He wouldn't . . . wouldn't kill himself, would he?"

"No!" exclaimed Elf, though she turned pale. "No, truly, he wouldn't. It would go against all he believes."

"So would marrying me, apparently. I received a note from him. The king gives me permission to return north tomorrow, unwed."

"Oh no!" Elf took Diana's hand and dragged her to the sofa, then poured her wine. "Port?" Elf queried, but she passed it over.

"It's a particular favorite of mine," said Diana feeling tears ache around her eyes. "Sent specially by Bey. I hoped . . ."

Elf eyed the crystal decanter, then poured herself some and sipped it. "His special sort. Be honored. From the Quinta do Bom Retiro."

Diana recognized the name, and the butler had presented it with reverence, but she said, "He would hardly send me inferior wine."

"He had no need to send any," Elf pointed out, looking more cheery, "and believe me, he doesn't supply this to every guest."

"A sweet farewell, then. And ordered this morning, apparently. It means nothing."

Elf cocked her head. "You and Bey both like lemon water, too, you know."

"So?"

"So, you are extraordinarily well suited!"

"Many people like lemon water."

Elf waved it away as if Diana had missed the point. "And you knew where he'd be. In the workshop. Bryght talked to him there. I couldn't really follow what happened—I don't think Bryght told me everything—but he did seem to think something had happened."

"Good or bad? But you don't need to persuade me we are suited." Diana laughed. "What a weak word! He is the blood in my heart and the breath in my mouth. I know I am the same for him, but what if he holds to his resolve?"

At last, Diana told Elf the thing she'd held back, the feeling she'd had last night that Bey was desperately fragile.

"You want to break him, don't you?" Elf asked, but she looked worried, too.

"No," Diana said. "I've realized I don't. I want him freed of the shell that imprisons him. But I want *him* to be whole. What if I have broken him? What if that's why he's behaving so strangely?"

Elf bit her lip, but then said, "He'll be at the masquerade. His sense of duty would never let him abandon that. We'll find out then."

"I'd kill myself rather than destroy him."

"And he'd do the same for you. Let us pray, instead, for life."

Diana sighed, and took a deep drink of the magnificent port. Then she put the glass aside and stood. "Help me on with the costume then. It is time for Diana to hunt."

There was no formal dinner before the masquerade, since in theory everyone wanted their costumes to be kept secret. However, Diana found herself swept into a family dinner with Bryght, Portia, Elf, and her husband, and was soon on first-name terms with everyone. It was clear they all accepted her as Bey's bride, even though they had doubts that there would be a wedding. A strange state of affairs, but it made dismal sense. As if she were the affianced bride of a man who had died.

Bey apparently was in his rooms and alive, but no one had

spoken to him since Bryght, and when Elf had knocked, Fettler had politely denied her admission.

After a flurry of concern, the family had resolutely not spoken of it, and most of the conversation had been about their northern trip. Diana was struck again by the seriousness with which they took their business affairs. Portia shrugged and said that she had enough to do with a child to raise, but Bryght was deeply involved with the northern canal systems, and with plans for them farther south. Fort was in charge of some kind of partnership between himself and the Mallorens to do with wine and spirits. He was also clearly developing his own family's business affairs, with an eye especially to his younger brother Victor, soon to return from time in Italy.

Her own knowledge of northern industry, of lead mines and wool production, was absorbed greedily. By the time the meal drew to a close, she realized new wounds threatened. She genuinely liked the Malloren family and their spouses. They already felt like a family of her own, and losing Bey would also lose her this.

Fort was to her right, and he squeezed her hand. "I'm tempted to call him out for the pain he's causing you. But then he'd kill me. No," he corrected her wryly, "that's not true. He'd let me kill him to save Elf from pain, which of course would be stupid because Elf would enter a nunnery and weep forever more."

Elf, on his other side, swatted at him, but she didn't look amused. "He's doing the best he can, Fort."

"He's making life into a labyrinth, as usual. I know all your hearts are bleeding, but I have to confess to a degree of satisfaction to see Daedalus lost in his own maze."

It was an interestingly perceptive way to view it, and pointed to a truth. Daedalus was the only one who truly knew the way out.

Chapter 32

The masquerade came to life on its own, it seemed, designed by a master hand and executed by efficient servants. By the time the family emerged from their meal, the public areas of the house were mysteriously underlit, though at the top of the main stairs an artificial moon shone in welcome. In the entrance hall a solitary flautist played, a haunting, mysterious sound to greet the excited, whispering guests.

Elf took Diana's hand and led her to slip among the masked guests. "You want to experience this as it is designed to be experienced," she whispered.

"Why?" Diana asked, but Elf wouldn't say.

As they climbed the stairs, a Harlequin stepped up beside her. "Diana the huntress? You can hunt me, my lovely."

Not the man she was interested in. "Perhaps later, if you find me again, sir."

Would Bey be blending with his guests, or waiting in the ballroom as the master of this performance? She pinned her faith to Elf's belief that he would be here somewhere. He had to be.

Would she recognize him? She felt she must, but if the disguise was deep enough he might succeed in hiding from her. She began to scrutinize everyone.

Most people were not heavily disguised, and it was easy to tell they were not him. Some, however, were wearing the Venetian costume of encompassing cloak, hat, and mask which made it hard to recognize the person beneath.

She studied lips, hands, and voices.

No, he wasn't among those around her.

Aware of nervous cries ahead, she passed through a Grecian arch into the corridor outside the ballroom. No sight of the portraits tonight, for it had been turned into a sort of maze, with twisting passageways just wide enough for one person.

Daedalus, indeed.

The walls of the passageways were painted gray, and a gray cover hung over, only high enough to let a tall man pass. Some light filtered through the cloth from above, but it was still an eerily dark, enclosed, serpentine route. Though she knew where she was, and that she was in no danger, Diana still felt pressed in and threatened. She heard giddy female exclamations around her, and manly reassurances.

All part of the game.

Elf was just behind her, and whispered, "Just wait till you see this!"

They stepped out of the maze and into night.

Not black night. Starlit night, where more ethereal wind instruments played.

The whole room must have been hung with dense black, and against it, stars had somehow been devised. Larger lights made planets, including Saturn and its rings. In the center, however, hung another huge moon, realistic markings clear and perfect.

"How is it done?" she whispered to Elf as they moved into the room among gasping guests. She felt cloth beneath her feet, and realized the floor was covered in black, too.

"A sphere of white glass painted with the shadows of the moon, and with oil lamps inside. We used it at a midsummer night's ball a few years back, and the maze even longer ago. This is nearly all put together from old stock."

But, Diana thought, circling to take it all in, this was the work of a master hand, and he'd been supervising this even as he dealt with all the other matters.

She explored one of the small grottoes that had been made along the walls, where silver trees and branches glowed under concealed lights, and benches invited.

"We have those for all the masquerades," Elf said. "Just give them a new coat of paint."

Diana looked at her. "You don't want me to be impressed?"

Elf shrugged apologetically. "I don't want you to think he's superhuman."

"I don't. Where is he? Do you know what costume he's wearing?"

"No," said Elf. "Honestly."

"I'm going to find him."

Diana set off to circle the room, studying faces as best she could in the dim light, listening to voices, above all letting a secret sense hunt for him. In one corner she found a Grecian temple on a dais, unilluminated as yet, and wondered briefly what part that would play. She went on her way, hunting, hunting . . .

Pausing to look up again at the miraculous moon, she found that from this side, a ghostly face smiled down. The man in the moon looking amused at human folly.

"A shame to have to use an artificial one, when there's a real full moon sailing the skies outside."

A painful shiver of delight spiking down her spine, she turned slowly. He was all in black, and she couldn't tell any details except that his mask was a black mirror of her own, so that his paler skin made a crescent moon amid total darkness.

"How did you know about my mask?" she asked.

"Am I not the omniscient *éminence noire*?"

"Is that what you are? The costume?"

"Not precisely. I'm lord of the night. Literally and figuratively. I even have stars." He raised his hands, and with astonished delight she saw that he wore a large, glittering jewel on every finger.

She thought of her own naked hands with regret, but before she could comment, he said, "Come, let us play the part of gods, and start the celebration."

He sounded light in spirit, and there were those rings. Could she hope? She went with him, dizzy with anticipation, frustrated by uncertainty, then surprised when he turned behind a secret panel and ran lightly up some dark stairs to where musicians sat.

At his command, the winds ended their faerie music and an introduction to the minuet began. He drew her down the gallery away from the musicians and their candles, then parted a dark cloth so she could see the moon straight on, and the clever containers that gave the star effect. It didn't steal the magic. As long as he was by her side, the magic could never end.

She could also see the dancers, as he'd implied, from a godlike eminence.

"It pleases you?" he asked.

She turned to him. "It pleases me."

So tempting to say more, but he was still a mystery to her, and she would not throw away this moment. Instead, she dared to slide an arm around his waist then turned back to watch the merrymakers down below, him warm by her side, his arm around her now.

She'd never experienced this before, this comfortable twinning in the peaceful, private dark, unthreatened for the moment by urgent problems.

But then, as the first dance came to an end, she realized something, and had to speak. "Could de Couriac be here?"

"No. All the guests have had to unmask for a moment as they entered, and Stringle—the man who captured you—is there to check."

"Didn't people object?"

"They were told it was for the safety of the king. That's him, by the way, in the Roman armor with the gilded helmet. And for this event, all other entrances are guarded. You are safe."

It was his safety that worried her, but she did not say so. Instead, knowing him safe, she returned to happy thoughts. "I could stay up here forever, here with you."

Dangerous thoughts. She wondered how he would react.

He held her a little closer. "Sometimes the gods are kind. I apologize for avoiding you today. We could have spent the day—"

"Don't. Don't put yourself always at my service."

But did he mean it was the last day? That he'd let her leave tomorrow?

He turned to her. "I am always at your service. Are you not at mine?"

Breath caught. Where was that leading? "Of course. But sometimes I need to be alone. I would grant you that freedom, too."

He raised her hand and kissed it, and at the look in his eyes, her heart burst into speed.

Surely that meant—

A trumpet blew.

Diana jumped with surprise and looked down to see that the Grecian temple was illuminated now, and the grassy sward held an adult and children sprawled around in sleep. They all wore wings. Cupids?

"What's happening?" she asked.

He was laughing, perhaps a little wildly. "My special surprise for you," he said unsteadily, "but come too soon. I must have lost track of time here with you, love."

"Love?" she said, but he had taken her hand and was hurrying her to the stairs.

She pulled back. "Stop. What were you going to say?"

He pulled her close and kissed her quickly. "It will keep. Come. You will enjoy this."

With a helpless laugh, Diana let him take her downstairs, back into the crowded ballroom, but once there, they were stuck. Everyone was pressing toward the temple, seeking the best view. Short of rude violence, they could not get close.

"You see," he said, and she still heard laughter, "efficiency exploded to pieces. You were supposed to be in pride of place." He moved backward instead, and swung her onto a gilded bench in a grotto. Then he leaped up beside her, and they had a wonderful view.

His lightness in movement and expression, the look in his eyes just before they were interrupted, all made her tremble with hope, made her long to demand that he complete what he'd been about to say. Now.

But she could wait. And perhaps this was all part of it, for Cupid was the god of love . . .

From somewhere came the pure voice of a castrato.

> *"The sun was now descended to the main,*
> *When chaste Diana and her virgin train . . ."*

A woman dressed exactly as Diana herself was walked out, accompanied by four handmaidens in Grecian dress, all wearing classical full-face masks.

> *". . . Espied within the covers of a grove,*
> *The little cupids, and the god of love,*
> *All fast asleep, stretched on the mossy ground,"*

The actress Diana took up the song in a rich contralto.

> *"Fell tyrants of each tender breast,*
> *Sleep on, and let mankind have rest.*
> *For oh, soon as your eyes unclose,*
> *Adieu to all the world's repose."*

Her attendants joined in harmony as they plotted to break Cupid's bows and arrows, and carried out the deed. Then they joined hands and danced.

> *"Our victory's great,*
> *Our glory is compleat,*
> *No longer shall we be alarmed.*
> *Then sing and rejoice,*
> *With one heart and voice*
> *For Cupid at length is disarmed!"*

Cheers started up in various parts of the ballroom, and the clever actors repeated their piece until people knew it well enough to join in.

At the front of the stage, the actress playing Diana encouraged her impromptu choir by calling out the next words ahead of the singers.

> *"Ye nymphs and ye swains,*
> *Who dwell on these plains,*
> *And have by fond passions been harmed.*
> *Secure of your hearts,*
> *Now laugh at his darts,*
> *For Cupid at length is disarmed!"*

As the ballroom rocked with the noise, Bey was shaking with laughter so the bench rocked beneath Diana's feet. Laughing too, she grabbed a branch of an artificial tree, grateful to find it solid.

"Now what could anyone have against love?" he demanded. "But you'll see," he added with a brilliant glance at her, "love triumphs as it should."

Diana gripped the branch harder, but if Bey looked at her like that, she wasn't sure she'd ever be balanced again.

They were eye to eye, and moving toward a kiss when a male voice broke into the song. She looked and found that Cupid, perhaps feeling left out by the third repetition, had leaped to his feet. He, too, wore a full face mask, this time of a placid youth.

"Oh cruel goddess!" he sang, in a voice that was strong but not as skillful as the actress Diana's. *"But I scorn to moan. Revenge be mine!"* He shook his gilded bow.

"Lud," Diana remarked, "I think he'd play Mars better than Cupid, but then, this matter of love is a battle, I suppose."

She glanced teasingly at Bey, but he was now intent on the stage.

"Still one unbroken dart remains." Cupid seized it from the ground, and nocked it in his golden bow. *"I lance it through . . ."*—the unsettlingly blank mask scanned the audience—*"what heart?* Come then, my lords, my ladies," he continued in a speaking voice, "who wants to feel the bite of love, to have more love in their heart?"

Unease crept across Diana's shoulders, and suddenly Bey leaped down and moved forward. She tried to follow, but the crowd closed after him. In fact, everyone pushed forward trying to get closer to the god of love.

Some were cheering, some were jeering, but they all wanted to be part of this fun.

With a muttered curse she returned to the bench.

She saw Bey then, cutting ruthlessly toward the tall figure in the gilded Roman helmet, who stood directly in front of the dais. The king.

Trouble?

The whole room seemed to be inviting love or jeering at the thought, and the Cupid egged them on. The other actors stood back, letting him play the audience, his arrow of love still seeking a target.

Diana suddenly focused on the Cupid's shouting voice. Foreign. She'd assumed Italian, like most opera singers, but could it be French? And his voice was not well trained.

De Couriac?

Bey was near the king now and she wanted to scream a warning. But of course he knew. That's why he'd gone.

But de Couriac wanted to kill *him*.

She heard the king laughing and cheering with the rest. Heard him call, "Shoot me, god of love. I can't have too much love for my queen, what, what?"

As people cheered, the Cupid obediently turned the arrow in the king's direction.

Chapter 33

Diana instantly saw from the way it flexed, that the bow was real. That was when she remembered that she, too, had a real bow and arrow. Doubtless one of the few usable weapons in the room.

Bey had reached the king now. What would he do? Pull him to the ground and cover his body with his own?

Heart pounding fit to burst, she pulled off her bow and nocked one of her silver arrows, wishing she'd had some more training with it. Wishing she'd had more of Carr's lessons in firing under stress.

Her hands were shaking and sweating enough to slip.

Perdition! She wiped them on her linen gown.

The king stood there, inviting the shot, and Cupid drew the string a little farther back. There was a moment of quiet, as if perhaps people suddenly wondered . . .

Then Bey stepped in front of the king, arms spread, light dancing on his starlight rings. "Your pardon, sire, but I think I have the greater need of love."

A ripple of excited comment passed through the room, cut through with shock. Bey had his back firmly to the king.

"Though in fact," Bey said in apparent good humor, "you are supposed to shoot the goddess Diana, are you not?"

"But you invited me to shoot you, my lord," the Cupid said.

The mask altered sounds to some extent and Diana

found herself horribly uncertain. It would be terrible to make a mistake.

With a pistol she might try to knock the weapon from his hands, but she wasn't that good with a bow, and this was a scarcely tried weapon. She could hit a man somewhere with it, she was sure, but that was all.

It must be de Couriac, though. Why else would Bey be shielding the king?

Bey began to move forward, arms wide, inviting the shot, eclipsing the king even more. She silently berated him, but of course he could do nothing else. The king above all must be protected, and no innocent could be allowed to suffer.

By now, the whole room was quiet, as people sensed something strange, but were probably unsure whether it was part of the masque or not.

As Bey moved closer and closer to the dais, he spoke. "I think, perhaps, you are not the god of love, sir, but the god of destruction. Your arrow is intended for me, Monsieur de Couriac?"

The king exclaimed, and other people gasped and questioned. A panicked shift Diana dared not look at told her things were finally happening. But Cupid was drawing back the string of his bow the final few inches and Bey was so close he could not miss.

But not close enough to attack and stop the shot.

Now or never. After a second's terrified hesitation, Diana pulled all the way back, sighted, and with a prayer to heaven, loosed her arrow. It thunked deep into de Couriac's chest, and his arrow flew wildly to quiver in a wall. With a horrid cry, he crumpled upon the false grass beneath his feet.

The actress Diana fainted, and the little cupids ran away screaming, but then Bey was there, hiding the writhing body from the panicked guests. Diana, dazed, saw Bryght, Elf, Portia, and Fort trying to handle the shouting, swirling guests, but some illogically were rushing to escape the ballroom.

Someone was going to be hurt.

The king was behind a protective wall of men, but he suddenly pushed free, helmet and golden breastplate gleaming in the lights.

"See," he called loudly, "it was a solitary madman, and all over now. Calm, calm, my good people. All is safe."

And calm did settle, with everyone turning to face him.

"I am safe, as you see, thanks to Lord Rothgar's courage . . ." He seemed to falter then, and Diana knew he'd suddenly questioned where the fatal arrow had come from.

She hastily jumped down from her bench, but she knew some people had spotted her.

She heard Bey's voice. "Your Majesty, my deepest apologies for this incident. Supper is laid out below. Perhaps it would be best if everyone retired there now."

The crowd, soothed, shifted, but then someone called out, "Who fired the arrow?"

"The real god Cupid, jealous of being supplanted?" Bey said, clearly attempting to pass it off, but it would never work.

Diana said, "I fired the shot."

A way opened before her, but the guests exploded into chatter again. Enough gossip here to last a twelve-month.

She moved into the clear space near the king, and Bey immediately came to her side. The temple and the grass before it were empty once more, except for a bloodstain.

Blood she had spilled . . .

"You are skilled with a bow and arrow, Countess?" the king asked, seeming more startled than angry. Yet.

She gathered her composure. This time, she would not collapse. "It is an interest of mine, Your Majesty."

"Perhaps you hit him by luck?" the king offered.

It was an opportunity to escape, but she would not take it. With only a slight glance at Bey, she said, "No, sire. I am quite skilled with a bow, though more so with a pistol. As these skills have twice saved the man I love, I cannot regret them."

A new burst of exclamations from the crowd around.

Bey took her hand. "Lady Arradale and I have a debate ongoing about who should be protecting whom, sire, but I admit that I cannot regret it either. A strong, courageous wife, skilled in the defense of herself and others, is a pearl beyond price."

Diana's breath caught, in joy at the declaration, but in fear at the challenge he had just thrown down before the king. Few here would know that it went against the king's beliefs, but the king recognized it, and his expression froze.

After a moment, he said, "I see, I see. Well, let each man choose his own meat, I say, and," he said, turning his back, "let us all go and choose our meat from the marquess's feast, what? What?"

He led the way out of the ballroom, the company streaming after, buzzing now with speculation that the great marquess might be out of royal favor. For seeking to marry the peculiar countess?

In moments, Diana and Bey were alone beneath the full, glowing moon.

She waited for him to speak, but then plunged in herself.

"Wife?" she asked.

He suddenly took both her hands. "Do I assume too much? There is still risk—"

"Life is risk!"

He laughed softly. "I think someone else said that to me recently. And," he said, humor wiped away, "brought another dark thought to mind. You bearing my children."

"Dark?" she queried, a sick feeling growing. Could he still not accept that possibility?

"Your mother did not bear children well."

She sucked in a deep, relieved breath. "My mother bore me very well, apparently. She could not carry her other babes long enough, that is all."

"That must be heartbreaking of its own."

"So," she said, "I carry a risk too. I'm willing to trust the wings and fly."

He brought her hands slowly to his lips. "I am unaccustomed to allowing myself such wicked self-indulgence."

She brought their joined hands to her lips and kissed his,

holding them tightly. "I'm not. Surrender to Diana and the moon."

Was heaven almost in her hands?

His eyes were dark and steady. "I have been lectured on the beauties of imperfection. I am, all imperfection, yours, if you do not mind."

She stared at him in dazed disbelief. This was true? He was hers? If she did not *mind*!

"A full life," he said, "with risks as a full life must have. But if the gods are kind, with love, joy, and fruitful labors."

She wrapped her arms around and hugged him as tightly as she could. "Damn you, I'm going to cry."

She felt him laugh, then his lips on her unmasked cheek, kissing away tears. He pulled off his own mask, then hers, then kissed her, questing at first, then settling.

Their kiss, with all the magic it had brought them from the first.

Entwined, they kissed beneath the glowing moon, a kiss unhindered this time by other things. They explored the different textures and tastes, blending souls through heat and moisture, assuring themselves that yes, the maze was conquered, the battle won, the wondrous flight begun.

After, she leaned against his chest, within his arms.

"Was that yes?" he asked, but a deep warm contentment in his voice told her he knew.

"I want to be alone," she whispered. "Together, alone, for days. Weeks. Forever."

She felt his head rub against hers. "In time, for a little time. Now, alas, we must deal with the aftermath. But first," he added, "I have a star for you if you will take it, my lady."

He slid the ring off his little finger, and held out his hand.

Trembling, she placed her left hand in his. "I feel as if I could truly fly. Shall we go up to the roof and try?"

He laughed. "Reckless wench. Even with a Malloren, all things are not possible."

"Reckless," she said, savoring it. "Are you a little reckless now, Bey?"

"I am what I am, love, and somewhat raw with newness, but like a newborn I need you as I need breath. Can you bear it?"

"Can I bear anything else?"

"A miracle then," he said, sliding the ring onto her finger. "And thus impossible. Like a perpetual motion machine. Or flight."

She looked at an enormous multifaceted diamond, surely the largest, most sparkling gem he could find in a ring. She laughed with sudden, soaring delight. "You know what I love most about you, Bey?"

"Tell me." Though she'd seen him mellow a time or two, she'd never seen him glow like this.

"You like me as I am. You do, don't you?"

"I adore you as you are. I adored you from the moment you pressed a pistol into my back."

"A rough wooing. I want a promise."

"Anything."

"Don't try to change for me. I love you as you are, too."

He took her hand, thumb rubbing on the ring. "I thought you'd been fighting to change me."

"Do you feel changed?"

"Utterly."

"Then this is wrong."

"Diana," he protested.

"The essential you mustn't change," she said fiercely, praying she wasn't throwing away the moon and the stars. "I want you only to have changed as we all change, moving forward in life, in tune with our natures."

He stood in thought for a moment, thumb still rubbing gently on the ring he'd placed on her finger. "Yes, I see. You're quite correct. You'll have to put up with omniscience, omnipotence, protectiveness, and a devilishly strong will. Can you bear it?"

"I adore it," she said, and spotting a certain sapphire on his right hand, she moved it to his left, and kissed it there. She longed to drag him off to a bedroom and ravish him, but as he'd said, they had duties here.

And, now she thought of it, she had her courses.

She turned to leave the ballroom with him, hand in hand. "What are we going to do about the king?"

"If he chooses to be offended, so be it. My allegiance above all is to you." The smile he sent her was astonishing in its warmth. "I hope to have my own small world to cherish soon, so England can go hang."

She laughed and shook her head. "No one can change that much. I was thinking—you might appease him by giving him the drummer boy."

He raised their linked hands and kissed them. "We are in accord as always. You won't mind?"

She shook her head. "It's a lovely piece, but carries too much pain. Perhaps we'll make a little drummer boy of our own."

"Ah," he said lightly, leading her back through the entrance labyrinth, "but will it end up Lord Arradale or Lord Rothgar? Or both, poor mite? Our problems are never ending."

It was a practical concern, for she still wanted to preserve her earldom's independence, but she wouldn't let it shadow the moment. As they emerged into the brighter corridor, she said, "Our problems are nothing, as long as we're together. Together, we can rule the world."

"Don't say that in front of the king. Come on." He tugged her to run lightly down the stairs. "Let's face the lions. You're right, alas. I can't let England go hang just yet, at least not while it's at supper in my house."

They found excited masqueraders eating, drinking, and reliving the event of the year. Bey and Diana progressed through the four rooms generating even more excitement by formally announcing their betrothal.

More than one man said something like, "You'll not want to be getting on the wrong side of a wife like that, eh, Rothgar?"

Diana decided it was good to be reminded of the real world. Most of the men here would be frightened by her skills and powers, and would try to mute her in some way in case she eclipsed him. She had found one of the few men strong enough and fair enough to let her fly free.

As Bey had said, sometimes the gods were kind.

A frown from the king, however, reminded her that he was one of the traditional men. Abruptly, he beckoned her over, and a hint of fear flickered. He couldn't prevent their marriage, but if he'd turned against them, he could make things difficult.

A glance showed that Bey looked unalarmed, but that, she suspected, meant nothing at all. He led her to the king, formally, hand in hand. She curtsied, but Bey raised her immediately.

"Lady Arradale," the king said, in the suddenly quietening room, "you are a very unusual woman."

"I fear so, Your Majesty."

"I spoke to you once on the dangers of women seeking manly skills."

"You did, sire."

He frowned, and she began to wonder if he could indeed throw her in the Tower for some reason. Firing a weapon in the royal presence? It might be a crime.

"At that time," he said, "you remarked to me that a woman is to be admired for defending her children, and I agreed." After a moment, he said, "The same thing could be said of a woman defending her husband, what?"

She let out her held breath. A peace offering, and not easy for him. Diana curtsied again. "I think so, sire."

He nodded, but as she rose, he said, "I pray, madam, that you have *two* sons."

Bey spoke then. "You will permit us to keep the titles separate, sire? We thank you. But what if we have only one son?"

Diana tightened her hand on his. He was asking the king to agree to the possibility of another countess in her own right at Arradale, pushing the king's tolerance, here in public.

Eventually the king nodded, but coldly. "If it is God's will."

Bey bowed deeply. "You have our most sincere thanks, Your Majesty. May I repay you with a gift?"

"A gift?" said the king, brightening.

"Lady Arradale owned an automaton based on herself as a child, but it was broken, so she gave it into my care. Now, we would like to give it to you, sire, as a sign of our eternal devotion and loyalty. If you would be so kind as to step into the hall, it can be demonstrated there where all can see."

The king rose enthusiastically, and the word spread so everyone packed into the hall, up the staircase, and around the landings above.

The drummer boy was wheeled out. "'Pon my soul, Lord Rothgar," the king exclaimed, "this is a fine piece! Let's see it work, what?"

Bey switched it on, and the drummer boy went through his paces perfectly, charming the king and everyone there. After three windings and repeats, people still clamored for more, but the king ordered it taken on its way, promising a further display at the Queen's House soon.

Diana was pleased to see it go. Not only was it a re-minder of her family's hurts, but now to her it seemed trapped, like a child of her own forced to perform in a limited way, as she had been threatened by so many limitations.

That seemed morbid. Perhaps she was just tired. Bey left her to escort the king out of the house, and the other guests began to leave, clearly happy with the event even though it had been cut short.

She was tempted to seek her room—to explore her happiness and relive the dangers and death, but she longed for Bey too, so she waited, but out of the way, not wanting more avid speculation. Alas, after this she would probably always be an object of curiosity, but she could bear it.

With Bey at her side.

But one guest did approach her—a woman in a beautiful shell-pink gown who had made little effort to disguise herself, for she wore only a narrow black mask.

Before she could speak, Bey appeared and took Diana's hand. "You must have had a sorry evening, Monsieur D'Eon."

Chapter 34

Diana stared, fascinated by D'Eon's illusion of femininity. Paint and powder could achieve a great deal, but he had the mannerisms and gestures down perfectly. And above his low bodice, *breasts* swelled!

Perhaps he was just plump, she thought, as tension swept away idle thoughts. Here was the master hand behind the attacks.

D'Eon waved his lacy fan. "It would have been a sorrier one, my lord, had that madman achieved his end."

"You disown him?"

D'Eon shuddered. "Emphatically."

Bey's brows rose. "You expect me to believe you are innocent of the various attacks on my life?"

D'Eon was an astonishing image of outraged innocence. "I have never sought your life, Lord Rothgar. Never."

"What of Curry?"

The fan wafted again. "A wound, no more."

Diana almost spoke her opinion of that, but she decided to be a fascinated observer of this verbal fencing.

"De Couriac's orders in the north were the same," D'Eon said. "I did not realize he was so unbalanced."

"Or that he was under other orders, perhaps?" Bey said.

D'Eon's red lips tightened. "Or that, my lord."

"You expect me to accept these attempts to wound me without affront?"

"*C'est la guerre, monsieur le marquis.*"

"Then perhaps you are a prisoner of war, Chevalier."

The little man stiffened. "You cannot touch the ambassador of France."

"Acting ambassador," Bey gently reminded him. "Soon Monsieur de Guerchy will come, and your cloak of protection will be removed."

"Perhaps, perhaps not." D'Eon's eyes were steady. "Like you, my lord, I serve my king, and serve him well."

"Kings are not always faithful to their servants. In time, Chevalier, you will die for involving Lady Arradale."

D'Eon glanced at her, seeming genuinely puzzled. "My lord? An irritation, perhaps, but aimed to take you in the end precisely where you now so happily stand. You would risk all in a duel over that?"

"You have a very strange notion of what is irritating."

At the icy tone, D'Eon stared. "What has happened? All I have done is to encourage the king to seek to match you up. In view of your declared intention not to marry, it seemed likely to distract you from other matters. I admit, I hoped it might bring about a falling out for a while. But this is not of what you speak?"

Bey studied him for a moment.

D'Eon swore in French. "De Couriac! And the offense was great?" He looked at Diana. "You are all right, my lady?"

"I was rescued," Diana said, guessing that Bey did not want details revealed.

D'Eon stood a fraction straighter. "This was nothing to do with me, my lord. But I admit a fault. I did not kill de Couriac when I saw him for the rabid dog he was. He came with orders from Paris. It was difficult. I should have realized, however, when he claimed you were to blame for the death of the woman who played his wife."

"She was found strangled, but it was nothing to do with me."

"Oh no, he killed her. He said as much. A rabid dog, as I said. But a French dog. For the honor of France, *monsieur le marquis*, I will meet you."

No, thought Diana. *I will not allow this now! Not when I have everything my heart desires.*

But D'Eon said, "Do not interfere, Lady Arradale. Sometimes a man has a need to fight."

Despite that, Diana tried to find words, but he had already turned to Bey. "Not, I think, to the inconvenient, undiplomatic death, but to the blood? First blood. You will not find that easy."

Diana bit her lip. She'd remembered Bey's words about her ordering him to be safe. She was not to do that unless she was willing to be controlled that way by him.

Fear fluttered, though, and she began to think this night would be too much for her after all.

Where were Bryght or Elf who might be able to deflect this danger?

Bey said, "You are correct about my need to fight, monsieur. But I could hardly duel with you in skirts."

"I can arrange matters. It must be now, I think, that we cauterize this wound. Come, where do we do it? I will defend the honor of France!"

Bey looked at Diana, and she saw that he was thinking of her, and ready to step back to save her from concern. D'Eon had been right, however. Bey needed this.

She had no idea whether D'Eon was acting with good intent or ill, but against all instincts, she said, "To minor wounds only. Please."

D'Eon executed an elegant, flowery bow that wasn't ridiculous despite his feminine dress. "I will not kill him, Countess. Or even damage him badly enough to affect your pleasure. My word on it." He turned to smile at Bey. "I must tell you, my lord, that I have never been beaten."

Bey smiled back. "In a serious contest, neither have I. Come, let us return to the ballroom."

He led the way by back stairs, so any hope Diana had that they would bump into Bryght or Fort faded. As they went, however, instinct told her that this was right.

She still prayed. Accidents could happen, and though she thought D'Eon was honest in this, it was still possible that he intended death, and was coming at it in a subtle way.

They detoured to Bey's rooms for rapiers, then walked into the silent, deserted, black-shrouded ballroom. The moon and stars still glowed, giving a certain amount of light.

D'Eon stepped out of his heeled shoes, then discarded his overskirt and petticoat, showing that he wore satin breeches underneath. Peculiarly female on top and male below, he chose a sword and balanced it for a moment in his hands. Then he nodded and began making some passes with it.

Diana could tell immediately that he had not boasted about his skill.

Bey took off shoes and shed his robe, and he too was wearing breeches and shirt. He took off all his rings except the sapphire, and gave them to Diana.

"Is this wise?" she had to ask. "What if he does plan murder?"

"He still has to make the hit." He turned to D'Eon. "Monsieur, what of your corset? It must hamper you."

The Frenchman flexed his shoulders. "Not at all, my lord. I indulge in vanity, but not to that extent. You are ready?"

Bey bowed. "I am completely at your service."

He walked toward D'Eon, but Diana made a sudden resolve, and spoke. "Monsieur D'Eon," she said, and the man turned to face her, painted brows high. "I still have my bow, and a number of arrows. If there is any foul play here, I will kill you."

After a still moment he smiled, and blew her an extravagant kiss. "*Magnifique!* You are indeed worthy of the great marquess, and if de Couriac was not already dead, I would kill him for you."

"No you wouldn't," said Bey. "*En garde*, monsieur."

With shocking suddenness, the blades clicked together, and the two men became intent only on each other. It should have been a ridiculous mismatch simply because of height and reach, but Bey had never thought so, and he'd been right.

D'Eon was, quite simply, brilliant. His agility was astonishing, his balance perfect, and the blade, even though it was strange to him, seemed a smooth extension of his body.

It took a moment for Diana to realize that Bey was almost

as good, but only almost. It was the height and reach that leveled it, but it was level.

Too level? The blades seem to hiss close to flesh with every daring move.

The fight burned with energy, nothing at all like the bouts she had with Carr. Did Carr fight like this sometimes with skilled men, moving at fierce speed around a huge room, taking terrible chances with vicious speed and strength that could so easily kill?

They swirled close, and she had to quickly back out of the way to be sure of not distracting them. No chance of that. Neither had eyes for anyone or anything but each other.

Almost, she thought, like a deadly minuet.

As the fight went on, she could hardly believe that neither of those wicked, flashing blades had drawn blood. She found that she was sucking in air as they must be.

D'Eon's powdered wig had gone, and his hair straggled. Bey's hair had been loose to begin with, but now tangled with sweat.

"What the devil's happening?"

She started at the low murmur in her ear, and glanced once at Bryght who had appeared at her side, Fort nearby. She looked back quickly, however, feeling that her attention alone stood between this and disaster.

"A friendly fight, of sorts."

"Friendly . . ." Bryght muttered, but at that moment D'Eon moved quickly out of pattern, lowering his sword, and Bey checked a thrust.

It stopped.

The Frenchman sucked in deep breaths. "We will kill each other out of exhaustion, my lord . . . You are satisfied?"

Bey lowered his sword, too, and when he had his breath, said, "Perhaps. You were right. You are extremely good. A little better than I am."

D'Eon bowed, and did not dispute it. "So, the record is swept clean?"

Bey replaced his sword in the case. "You say you have no plans to kill me, monsieur, but what of your masters in France? Someone instructed de Couriac."

D'Eon shrugged. "I will try to convince them that it would be extremely impolitic now for a Frenchman to create more havoc in England. You will always have enemies there, however."

"I am glad of them. The passion of one's enemies should mark the stature of one's triumphs. But was there any true attempt to kill the king?"

"No, I am sure not. King Louis would have no wish for it. No king is happy with the idea of regicide. I think that was merely to draw you out for attack. Your protective instincts are very well known."

"How dismaying to be so predictable."

"So now?" asked D'Eon. "You have a beautiful lady as your bride, my lord, and happiness ahead of you. We can put this all behind us?"

Bey turned to face him. "Not quite, monsieur. You did, after all, attempt to wound me. I have arranged some discomforts for you in return." With a smile he added, "*C'est la guerre, non?*"

The Frenchman's eyes narrowed.

Bey continued. "However, I will offer a friendly warning. You have enemies in France, and have not perhaps always received accurate information. Take care."

D'Eon's features pinched, but he merely said, "We shall see, my lord." He passed over his sword and picked up his clothes. "Good night, my lady, my lords."

"What discomforts?" Bryght asked as the Frenchman left the room.

Bey pushed hair off his face, and replaced D'Eon's sword in the case. "His influence is already undermined with King Louis, along with his master's, de Broglie. Guerchy comes soon, only too keen to put him in his place. What's more, D'Eon has been encouraged to keep copies of all materials relating to his dealings with the king. Insurance of sorts, but a keg of gunpowder beneath him."

"King Louis will be frantic!" Diana exclaimed. "I'm never going to trust anything I read again."

Bey came over to her, and gently relieved her of the bow and arrow she was still clutching. He passed the weapons to

Bryght and put his arm around her. "I said we needed a code. Perhaps sweet and pea."

Disheveled and sweaty, he still glowed with the exertion of the fight. She saw that it had scoured away some last, lingering mark. "Very well. But add scarlet and poppy."

"So that's where it started?" he said. "With the poppy?"

She looked around and found they were alone. "No, it started, as I remember, with pimples."

"And pistols."

"And dalliance," she murmured, remembering, "which is one step above flirtation, and one below seduction."

"Ah. Would you care to dally a little, my lady?"

She turned to face him, hand on his chest. "That depends, my lord, on where it leads. My courses are on me."

He kissed her, but said, "Good. I'm saving myself for my wedding night."

She laughed, surprised to find herself perfectly content with this for the moment, with togetherness and conversation. She moved apart a little to look again around the ballroom, where the great moon still glowed and the stars still shone. "It's a shame this was all wasted."

He took her hand. "It's bits and scraps. We can put it together again some other time, and this will certainly be one of the most talked about entertainments of the decade."

"We," she echoed with a smile. "I love that. I am happy now, here, but how long till our wedding?"

"Are you asking me to name the day? In two weeks, then, when the moon is dark and your powers leashed."

"Do I frighten you?"

"To death," he said, but smiling. "I believe I will survive. I liked the sort of wedding Brand and Rosa had, with family and friends. Considering our stations, however, I think it should be on a grand scale."

"Having seen what you can do in days, I can't wait to see what you can achieve in weeks."

"Miracles and marvels. But we have those already. Will you marry me in the south? At Rothgar Abbey?"

"Gladly. It would be too soon after Rosa's wedding at my home, and I want to be part of your life here, too."

"Two weeks from now, then," he said, slowly drawing her into his arms. "At Rothgar Abbey. A country wedding, open to all."

"But suitably magnificent. Rosa and Brand must be there."

"Of course. I'll have to send riders to Scotland to find Steen, too. I'm sure Hilda will want to attend my final conquest."

She touched his face. "Do you feel conquered?"

He kissed her palm. "Completely. I'm delighted." Then he kissed her lips, sweeping her into magical night. They broke apart eventually and wandered the now silent house, talking, touching, kissing.

Eventually they arrived at her bedchamber, the marchioness's bedchamber. He entered with her, but moved on to the adjoining door to his rooms. He paused however, to say, "You must order any changes here you like."

"I think I like these rooms as they are. But you must put some thought to the redecorating of my spouse's bedchamber."

A smile crinkled his eyes. "Don't touch a thing. I long to be taken with violent passion upon that virginal bed."

Chapter 35

Two weeks later, the grounds of Rothgar Abbey were thrown open to the world, and the world came—to dance on the lawns, feast from the long tables, and drink from the bottomless bowls of ale, punch, and lemon water.

Six maypoles stood tall, wound with bright ribbons—so delightfully phallic, Bey had remarked.

A full medieval fair took up the deer meadow, with jugglers, fire-eaters, and those skilled at sleight of hand. There were contests in everything, from the greasy pig to butter churning, arranged so that as many country people as possible would take home a handsome prize. There were even contests for the children, so that soon little ones were running around to show off ribbons, toys, and bells.

Their vows were said in a simple ceremony attended only by close friends and family. Afterward, however, Bey and Diana, both dressed in magnificent white brocade, both with hands covered with glittering rings, strolled around so everyone could see them and wish them happiness.

It was all amazing, undiluted joy, but then Diana felt Bey go tense beside her. Seeking the problem, she saw him looking to where a frantic girl stood with a bundle in her arms, a bundle emitting the unmistakable staccato squawks of a very new, very unhappy baby. The girl jiggled the bundle, looking around, and calling, "Mam? Mam?"

Understanding the effect of this, Diana hesitated between pulling him away and trying to stop the noise. She hurried forward. "Where's its mother, my dear?" she asked, trying to think of some way to calm the baby before Bey ran away or did something else he'd hate.

Then he was there, taking the child before one of the gathering matrons could. Diana hoped it wasn't as obvious to anyone else that he was pale and sweating. The baby didn't magically calm, but over the angry, warbling squawks, he managed to say, "Go find your mother, child."

"Thank you, milord," the wide-eyed girl said and ran off.

One of the women came forward then. "Give it to me, milord. I'll feed it till the mother comes."

He handed the bundle over, and the woman loosened her bodice, murmuring soothingly, and put the child to the breast. After a moment or two, the cries stopped.

Peace returned.

Diana took his hand and led him back a little. "Are you all right?"

Though he still seemed pale, he smiled. "Yes. Amazingly so. I don't suppose anyone likes that sound, but I can cope with it. I've always worried that I might—"

"Strangle it? Bey!"

"Just try to stop the noise." He looked down at her. "I know now I can enjoy our children, even if they are so rude as to scream at me."

She hugged him, there in front of an interested, indulgent crowd, and then the errant mother ran up, puffing, to thank the impromptu wet nurse, and put the baby to her own breast.

Bey gave both mothers a golden guinea, and then he and Diana strolled on. Diana hadn't thought the day could be any more perfect, but she realized now that she'd suffered a small doubt. She'd never thought he'd hurt a child, but she had wondered whether he'd be able to enjoy their children fully.

Now she knew. It wouldn't be easy in the beginning, but it was possible. Especially with a Malloren. ·

She looked around at the festivities, which seemed set to continue until nightfall. "I don't wish to sound unappreciative of your wonderful entertainments, my lord, but when can we be private?"

He looked down at her. "Anytime you wish, my lady. The house is peaceful and ours."

They tried to slip away, but Rosa and Brand spotted them and set up a cry, so that in the end they had to run to the house through a storm of flowers.

Every one of the family insisted on an embrace as they went—Bryght, Brand, Hilda, and Elf who hugged them twice, once for herself, and once for Cyn. When they ended up in Bey's sunlit bedroom, the flowered carpet gained a hundred new petals.

Then catching another perfume, Diana turned to see a huge bowl of flowers by the bed—a mixture of sweet peas and poppies. She picked out one of each and, grinning, tucked them behind her low white bodice.

They undressed each other with slow delight, and slid beneath cool sheets to lie for a while simply in one another's arms.

"Skin to skin," she said. "This is almost enough."

"But not quite," he said, and kissed her. Their lovemaking was languorous and lovely, and led like a river flowing deep and smooth, to where they had so longed to be.

"And that," said Bey a very long time later, "is perfect enough even for me." He stroked a curl from her brow. "Truly, beloved, sometimes the gods are exceedingly kind."

AUTHOR'S NOTE

Ever since his first appearance in *My Lady Notorious*, I've been bombarded with reader requests for Rothgar's story. I hope this has lived up to everyone's expectation. Though I didn't plan it from the first, the Malloren series has turned out to be individual stories, but with the marquess's story running through them all. This love story stands alone, but if this is your first Malloren book you may want to find the others and see the complete journey.

They are:

My Lady Notorious (Cyn and Chastity)
Tempting Fortune (Bryght and Portia)
Something Wicked (Elf and Fort)
Secrets of the Night (Brand and Rosa)

The first two are currently out of print, though we hope to correct that, but the last two are available. You can order them through your favorite bookseller, or direct from this publisher. If you want to be kept up to date about reissues and new publications, please see the contact information at the end of this section.

As for this story—I came to realize that Rothgar needed a woman who was his equal, and thus, Diana was born, first appearing in *Secrets of the Night*. Yorkshire was an ideal setting for her because in the mid-eighteenth century that was still a long way from London and central control.

I also came to see that this story had to move into the

highest levels of the nation to truly show these characters as they should be—mighty aristocrats, living at the center of the eighteenth-century world. Paris, of course, would have argued about that, but the French system, strangled by the centralized power of Versailles, was already in decline. London was the seat of power, and would be for more than a hundred years.

The background to this story is true. Louis XV really did run separate governments, and the Chevalier D'Eon was one of his top men. D'Eon is one of the famous minor characters in European history because of confusion over his gender. He did spend time at the Russian court as one of the tzarina's ladies, and have a brief but brilliant military career. The strangest part is yet to come when this book ends, however, and I like to think that Rothgar's actions explain the unexplainable.

You can read about D'Eon in the biography *Royal Spy*, by Edna Nixon, and you'll find that no one has quite made sense of his diplomatic career in England. During his time as acting French ambassador he showed increasingly irrational confidence, as if he felt invulnerable. Friends in Paris, and de Broglie himself, were constantly urging caution. Of course, as we now know, he was also receiving Rothgar's forged letters from the French king, promising complete support!

Over the next couple of years he will indeed find that his situation stings as King Louis withdraws his protection, and he has to flee the embassy. He ends up for a time in a set of rooms in London, guarding the collection of documents which the king wants destroyed, knowing they alone keep him safe. He has the place booby-trapped with bombs, and employs a small army of his own to defend it.

In the end, perhaps because of real affection, George III agrees to give D'Eon protection in England, and Louis agrees to pay him a pension for his valuable service. But on one bizarre condition: D'Eon is to wear women's clothes for the rest of his life. (Perhaps Rothgar had a hand in that, too.) This he does, leading to the never-ending speculation as to whether he was male or female.

Is this the end of the Mallorens? Well, I'm certainly not going to disturb the happiness of Hilda and Steen to create a story there, but I hope to set other books in this world. Fort's brother Victor is soon to return from his grand tour. Perhaps he will be hero material. Or perhaps I will simply find new characters in the fashionable world of England in the 1760s, characters who will meet the Mallorens so we can all follow their, hopefully tranquil, lives.

I enjoy hearing from readers. You can contact me through Meg Ruley at the Jane Rotrosen Agency, 318 East 51st Street, New York, N.Y. 10022 (SASE appreciated) or by e-mail to jobev@poboxes.com.

You can ask to be on my e-mail list, which means you will receive a few messages a year about upcoming books and such.

There is also a mail-list group where readers of my books can talk about them. I try to visit most days. You can join by going to http://www.onelist.com/subscribe/jobeverley.

My web site contains a complete book list and many relevant links, especially to English history. It also has a few scenes of Rothgar and Diana that were cut from *Secrets of the Night*. The address is http://www.poboxes.com/jobev.

And finally, a wish for you:

May the gods be exceedingly kind.

Dear Reader:

Welcome to the exciting world of the Malloren family.

I've been fascinated by the Georgian period and Georgian men since I was a teenager. There's something so sexy about a dangerous man who dresses in silk and lace, isn't there? Especially when he's wielding a sword.

With the Mallorens, I've particularly enjoyed writing about a family, with the interesting bonds and conflicts that brings. Friends come and go, but family is forever, especially when there's someone like the Marquess of Rothgar determined to hold everyone together. He, of course, has a particular obsession about protecting his half siblings from harm, while they don't always appreciate his efforts. But that doesn't stop them loving one another in their own special ways.

You can read more about the Malloren family in: *My Lady Notorious, Tempting Fortune, Something Wicked, Secrets of the Night,* and, of course, *Devilish.* But there's more. *Winter Fire* features Rothgar's enemy and cousin, Lord Ashart, and *A Most Unsuitable Man* is about Ashart's penniless friend and the heiress he should have nothing to do with.

There will be more stories in the Malloren world. I won't abandon those delicious men. To learn more about the Mallorens and all my other books, please visit my Web site at www.jobev.com. From there you can easily subscribe to my monthly e-mail newsletter and be kept up-to-date about new and reissued books.

All best wishes,
Jo